T0095176

PERSEPHONE'S BLADE

JAMES T. PALMER

iUniverse, Inc.
Bloomington

Persephone's Blade

iUniverse books may be ordered through booksellers or by contacting:

iUniverse
1663 Liberty Drive
Bloomington, IN 47403
www.iuniverse.com
1-800-Authors (1-800-288-4677)

ISBN: 978-1-4502-7188-2 (pbk)
ISBN: 978-1-4502-7189-9 (ebk)

Printed in the United States of America

iUniverse rev. date: 12/6/2010

Turn back, O man, forswear thy foolish ways.
Old now is earth, and none may count her days.
Yet thou, her child, whose head is crowned with flame,
Still wilt not hear thine inner God proclaim,
"Turn back, O man, forswear thy foolish ways."

Earth might be fair and all men glad and wise.
Age after age their tragic empires rise,
Built while they dream, and in that dreaming weep:
Would man but wake from out his haunted sleep,
Earth might be fair and all men glad and wise.

Earth shall be fair, and all her people one:
Nor till that hour shall God's whole will be done.
Now, even now, once more from earth to sky,
Peals forth in joy man's old undaunted cry:
"Earth shall be fair and all her folk be one!"

Clifford Bax, 1919

Prologue

Professor Lynne Brady examined the tobacco plant's leaves, her eyes noting the fine striations and veins. In the artificial light it looked greener than the others she'd worked with, but that was to be expected, after all. She plucked one of the leaves from the plant's stem, raised it to her nostrils and sniffed at it. *To think of the number of people you've killed*, she thought. *Now it's time you did some good.* She crushed the leaf between her fingers and smelled the residue again. This time the faint odor of tobacco reached her olfactory receptors. She nodded and smiled to herself.

A tall woman with long, straight gray hair, Lynne was edging closer to what many would consider retirement, but at sixty she felt there were many good years left for her to complete her life's work. After all, she thought, the breakthroughs only come at twilight, never at dawn. It occurred to her that the longer she could string out the twilight, the more likely she would achieve the goals she'd set years ago. It had started out as an exploratory effort, supplemented by calculations and molecular biology. The idea had at last bloomed in the form of the plant whose leaf she had just destroyed. Her vision would be seen by all, after a quarter of a century of research.

But not quite yet. She knew it wasn't time. There was still so much to be done, so many variations to explore before the company she'd founded could publish its findings. There were trade secrets to convert into patent applications, conference presentations, and publications, to say nothing of the press releases that had to be well timed. Timed just right, of course, to achieve new funding to help commercialize the product.

Lynne knew that commercialization was a can of worms she was unwilling to open at this stage. On occasion she'd let her imagination run wild with thoughts of all the things she could do with the product, but it all came back to one fundamental question. How could this help people? There were many ways, of course, but what she didn't want to see was the question changing by a single word.

How could this kill people?

Her jaw set as she contemplated the question anew. Turning to face her office window, she looked out at the red dirt that stretched as far as her eyes could see. What a perfect place! God's own country, indeed. She closed her eyes and silently thanked her Maker for giving her the mission, brains, and resources to bring it so close to fruition. Then she asked for forgiveness for what she'd done, just in case it hadn't been in the plan as originally envisioned by the Lord. Lastly, she said a prayer for the two young women. *Those* two.

She snapped out of her reverie as someone called out her name behind her. "Hello, Lynne," a deep, American male voice said. Turning around, she stared in surprise at the tall figure, a man dressed in a dark suit, twenty years her junior, who held out his arms. "Can a former post-doc give his mentor a hello hug?"

"How – how did you know I was here?" she stammered. She walked towards the man and tentatively wrapped her arms about his neck. "I wish you'd called, we could have met –"

He cut her off. "Just happened to be in the neighborhood. Couldn't come all this way and not see my favorite biologist."

She let go of him and stared up into his face. He was clean shaven, his almost black hair cut short. Flashes of gray at the temples gave him a distinguished air. Years ago she'd thought him to be cute, although she'd stopped short of approaching him with any kind of romantic intent because he was one of her post-docs. Now he'd graduated to handsome, with intense blue eyes that looked deep into hers. And then he did something she'd never expected. He took her face in his hands and appeared to be about to kiss her, but instead placed his lips against her ear and whispered something.

Her face blanched, and then her eyes opened wide in horror as the needle pierced her neck. It only took a second for her to collapse. Her visitor caught her limp body before it fell to the ground. He laid her on her office couch, whipped out a two way radio from his pocket, and pressed the talk button.

"All done."

"Gotcha," came the reply. It was all he needed to hear. Help would be on its way in a few minutes.

Two years later, Demetek Corporation's chief executive officer, Donald K. Strathmore, greeted the assembled throng. His voice was clear and deep,. "For those of you new to the company, I'd like to say a few words about our mission and our management team. As to the former, I have no doubt that you are all excited about the prospect of changing our climate for the better. Despite the Luddite denials voiced by so many in our government and that of our so-called closest allies, the imbalance created by greenhouse gases and global warming will one day threaten to destroy our planet. This will happen, if not in our own lifetimes, then in those of our children and grandchildren. My kids are only in their early teens, but it won't be that long before they are young adults faced with an even more threatening horizon than we are. But we at Demetek can do something about it. We can change this alarming trend, together as a team."

He paused as his message sank in. "I'd like to introduce you to Dr. Etienne Goudreau, who is our Senior Vice President of Research. We recruited Steve, as he wishes to be called, from McGill University in Montreal, where he was one of the most highly respected researchers in the field of protein biochemistry. I'm sure you've seen his papers in Nature, Science, and Cell, among other prestigious journals. Steve got a little tired of the cold Quebec winter, not to mention the politics of academia. So we're very glad to have him on board on the other side of the world."

Goudreau smiled at his CEO. He was a slightly built, blond-but-balding, blue-eyed man wearing a poorly fitting suit. Strathmore returned the grin and continued. "Also joining the team as our head of legal affairs is Mr. L. Montgomery Dayne. Monty has a distinguished record in patent litigation as well as international contract law, and if you don't know how tricky it is when companies governed by different legal systems get into bed together, then just ask Monty. He'll be glad to paint you a picture." The thin-lipped attorney forced a grin beneath a bushy gray mustache.

"Finally, I'd like to mention our co-founder and chief scientific officer, Dr. Justin Hernandez. For those of you who don't know Justin, he hails from Austin, Texas. He was the driving force behind TXA Biochemicals, which you all know about because they are one of our major suppliers. We're very lucky he left the US to help launch this great company."

Hernandez waved at the dozens seated before him. His deep blue eyes seemed not to look at anyone in particular. Instead they appeared to glare right through everyone they regarded. His handsome face, while wearing a smile, showed no warmth.

"You've all been recruited here because of your unique skills, experience, and interests in building a better world for us all. Every one of you has his or her part to play in meeting our company goals, and a lot will be asked of you in the next few months. Our technology is second to none, our vision is grand, our goals are ambitious and you, our people, are equal to the task. It's going to be a tough road ahead, but when we do the hard yards, the rewards will be there. But remember, this is not about money. This is about helping the planet, about changing the world we live in. Our climate is in deep trouble, but there is no better place for us to show how it can be changed for the better than right here in the Australian outback." As he spoke, Strathmore waved his hands in an outward motion, as if to draw attention to the expanse outside. "Here in the Northern Territory, and at our Western Australia site, we have the ideal natural laboratory. This is one of the hottest and yet one of the least polluted places in the civilized world. Much of the terrain around us is desert, but we have the power to transform this land and others. We will be a beacon for the rest of the world to follow, an example of leadership that transcends politics and greed. You, our scientific leaders, will have the chance to light that beacon and let the whole world see the glow!"

A younger man in the back row – there were only three rows – let out a sigh. It was an affectation rather than an expression of boredom, but Strathmore didn't see it that way. "Matt," he said crisply. "Why don't you tell us a little about yourself, and why you came here." It was more of an order than a request.

Dr. Matthew Gilstrap had a freckled face, a two-day growth of beard, and short brown hair graying at the sides. His brown eyes appeared slightly glazed, but he did prefer not to spend time sitting in meetings hearing sales pitches and boilerplate corporate visions, missions, and goals. The laboratory was where he was most comfortable. He had recently completed a two year post-doctoral fellowship at the University of California in Berkeley, and the move from San Francisco to the Northern Territory was more than culture shock enough. The lab, at least, was a haven where he could feel more at home than anywhere else.

The salary was what had drawn him. Unusually for Australian companies, the compensation package was every bit as lucrative as the offers he'd received stateside. The few people he'd talked to before accepting the position in Alice Springs had warned him that he'd be making a lot less money than at some of the Bay Area biotechs, with fewer benefits to boot. However, his case turned out to be exceptional. A bit of online research revealed that the cost of living could be less Down Under. The potential of buying a house that wouldn't have him in hock up to his eyeballs for the rest of his life tipped the balance. He reasoned that in a few years he might actually own the house rather than just a few doors and a couple of toilets. On the flip side, Matt realized that his network of friends would be severed the moment he hopped on the Qantas plane to Sydney. Sure there was the internet, email, video calling and stuff, but it wasn't quite the same as going to the micro-brewpubs, hanging out on Telegraph Avenue in the coffee shops, heading across to the City for Saturday night partying. And they didn't have a fraction of the venomous creatures in San Francisco compared to the number in the outback.

"Yeah, right," Matt said. He gave a modest two sentence biography, starting with his North Carolina undergraduate education, but finished up with a bang. "I came here because my doctoral thesis work is why this company exists."

A few of the others in the room looked doubtful, even scornful at Matt's arrogance and immodesty. Strathmore himself raised an eyebrow; there was truth in his statement, but he hadn't expected it to be voiced as such.

Justin Hernandez bailed his CEO out. "Protein crystallography is an art form, as anyone who has ever obtained a crystal structure of such a complex system will tell you." He glanced sideways at Steve Goudreau, who nodded subtly. "Dr. Gilstrap developed a high throughput method that allows us to obtain protein crystal structures far faster than any other method developed up to now. Ten times faster, in fact. We don't call Matt "Ten-fold Gilstrap" for nothing."

Nobody laughed. Only Strathmore barely cracked a smile. *Typical*, thought Hernandez. *Biologists are all the same.* "We've all brought something unique to this party. We're all in this to deliver, and with the fantastic resources and facilities that we have at our disposal, we will deliver faster than was ever believed possible. We have a one year horizon, and by the end of that time I expect we will have a product ready to go. This is going to be hard work but it will be a lot of fun. More importantly, we will all have made history." Hernandez let his words sink in, and then sat down.

With that, the meeting adjourned. Small groups broke up and made their way towards offices, labs, and cubicles. While the facility was ultramodern on the inside, it showed only a small shell on the surface. Any observer, walking or driving by, would see a modest one-floor office building with a single door out front, and a delivery bay in the rear. Not that any would simply drive by – the entire facility had been sequestered nearly twenty kilometers west of Alice Springs' town center. Surrounding the building was a high-security fence, fully electrified but for one access gate that was guarded 24/7. Its circumference of five kilometers enclosed an area of the outback whose reptilian and arachnoid surface denizens had no idea what was going on in their own back yard. And they didn't care.

Pacifica, California
One month ago

The headaches were returning, she told him. Each time they came back, the symptoms were more intense, but the duration of physical torture was the same. What changed were the psychological aftereffects, the unspeakable depths of gloom, the sheer darkness of what was becoming. The worst part was the inevitable despair. While the pains would abate, an overwhelming blackness would follow, shrouding her in misery and helplessness. The hopes of success, love, family, and security were draining away, and there was nothing she could do to rekindle them.

She said they were probably a recurrence of hormonally-induced migraines that she'd suffered for several years from the age of twelve, almost until her eighteenth birthday. They'd then returned sporadically for the next few years, and then had stopped completely. They had come at the same time of her cycle, not every time, but five or six times a year in her teens, starting out like a needle in her right eye, forcing her to lie silently in a dark room until merciful sleep took over. Doctors had said the only thing she could do was to take painkillers and ride it out. After all, it was not that uncommon – but if only some of the migraine treatments now available had been on the market twenty, twenty-five years ago, at least she wouldn't have suffered as much.

Everything had changed after the trial. The darkness inside her vanished. The black wings of despair flew away forever, bringing her peace at last. She knew the price could not be tallied by any accounting, but as her life began anew, she did not care. She was free from her confinement. Her sentence had been commuted.

She looked up from the letter she was writing and looked in the mirror. Staring back at her was a diminutive, raven-haired, blue-eyed woman with flawless alabaster skin, whose mischievous smile always broadened into the most beautiful grin her husband had ever seen. But she was not smiling any more. Fear, maybe determination, had replaced the bright, cheerful expression she wore before the headaches began coming back. She remembered the first time, almost a year ago, but it felt different than when she was a young girl, growing into womanhood. It was less a migraine than a tightening band around the back of her skull. The aura that came with it gripped her like a vice. It lasted for an hour or so, and then the pain eased. When the agony abated that first time, she wept with relief. Her husband had come home to find her sobbing on the sofa, unable, or at least unwilling to explain what was wrong. She just shook her head silently and dabbed at her eyes with a tissue. He sat beside her quietly, rubbing her spine, and from time to time squeezed her hand gently. Then he made her a cup of chamomile tea, and stayed with her, not interrogating, badgering, or doing the typically male thing of trying to fix it all instantly.

It happened three more times before she made her decision to leave. The strain her illness placed on their marriage was worse than anything else they'd gone through. The children whom they'd lost were scars that could never quite heal, but this time her husband felt like he was losing her too. She was succumbing to an illness whose remission was inevitably drawing to a close. It was like an incurable, metastasizing cancer, he thought. Worse, he sensed she was drifting away from him, faster and faster, as she described the horrors of her pain, while he remained powerless to help.

The second time it happened, she'd told him, after the initial squeezing behind her head went away, dark thoughts entered her mind, violent, demonic images. They always came within half a day of the headaches. As a young teenager, she recalled, they could even appear as nightmares, screaming, murderous scenes where she was not so much the victim of terror but the deliverer thereof. If the images entered her mind when she was awake, she would suffer self-hatred, guilt, and inwardly directed rage. Yet, as she recovered from each episode, vestiges of the fundamental gentleness and sweet nature she'd cultivated allowed her to return to him, but it was becoming progressively harder each time.

The doctors had found nothing wrong with her. CAT scans and MRI's taken at two different sites all showed her to be a normal, healthy individual. Suggestions of psychological or psychiatric counseling were reasonable, but after a handful of attempts to "talk it out" she had tired of the therapists' incessant "How does that make you feel?" patter. They'd been trained that way, of course, to refuse to answer questions directly, but she simply couldn't tell them how she felt. They had been no help at all.

Now, it seemed as though there were very few avenues left to her, maybe only one. Her visitor had found her atop one of the hiking trails on the far west side of the California Bay Area peninsula. She'd poured it all out to him, every last detail. In return, he'd given her a flicker of hope. What he told her that afternoon was even more profound than the terrors she'd experienced as a girl, or as a young woman before the trial. So incredible, even, that she would not dare record it directly to paper. All she could do was hint at it in her final letter to her husband. If that was her last, maybe her only gift to the world, it would be worth giving.

She looked down from the mirror and continued to compose her final letter. She finished it a few minutes later, folded the two sheets, and placed them inside an envelope. She wrote her husband's name and their address on the outside, sealed it, and gave it to the man standing over her. "Don't mail it until the time is right." *As if there could be a right time.*

He took the envelope from her solemnly. "It'll be done. We've taken the necessary precautions. There won't be any mistakes. Devil's Slide in exactly two hours. The gas and incendiary will kick in. You'll see."

"What will you do then?" she asked, her mouth set in grim realization.

"We fix it. Just like Chicago." He removed his tweed jacket and draped it over the chair. Sweat was beginning to collect under his arms, staining the dark blue shirt.

She stood up and faced him. "God, what have I done?"

He placed the envelope on the table and encircled her in his arms. "If it helps any, I'm sorry."

She buried her face into his chest. There was something vaguely familiar about the scent, an old hall of learning perhaps. How ironic, she thought as the memories came back.

Chicago. Where it had all started.

"Me too," she said, looking up at him. "Thank you."

They stood like that for several minutes. At last, he let go of her and stood back. "You trust him, don't you?" he asked, a frown creeping over his forehead.

"With my life," she replied, steel in her eyes. "As I trust you with my death."

The man reached over the chair into the interior pocket of his jacket and withdrew a syringe. He removed the sturdy plastic cap protecting its needle and plunged the hypodermic into her arm. Within seconds she collapsed into his arms, unconscious.

He gently laid her on the couch. He then recapped the needle, put the syringe back into his jacket, and slipped the garment back on. Finally, he pulled out his mobile phone and made the call.

The reply was simple. "Yes?"

"She's ready."

BOOK 1
THE SUICIDE MACHINE

Chapter 1

Dr. Marcus Black stared at the note for the thousandth time. It was crumpled at the edges from all the handling, and starting to fray. It said, in Kay's familiar delicate cursive handwriting, "Hi Honey, I'm sworking late. Love you always, K, XOXOX." The S in front of the word "working" was crossed out. When Marcus had first seen the note, he'd wondered what it stood for. Still at work? No, that wouldn't make any sense. How could she have been still there and delivered the note for him to find on the kitchen table, underneath a bottle of his favorite dark ale? Seeing Wendy and Jack for drinks? No, they were away at a conference in San Diego, three hundred and fifty miles south of their Peninsula home. Shopping? Maybe that was it, he'd thought at the time, picking up an anniversary gift for him. That was what they'd found in the car. It had helped identify her.

No. It wasn't anything like that. She was about to write "I'm sorry." Then she was going to go away for ever, but at the last moment, she'd relented and given him some made-up excuse that she was still cranking things out at the office. *What a time to lie*, he'd thought. *What a stupid, goddamned time to lie.*

The knock had come at the door two hours and three bottles of ale after he'd first seen the note, right in the middle of the seventh inning. The A's were hosting the Royals that day, and were tearing them apart. Pro baseball didn't have a ten run rule, unlike the slow pitch softball Marcus used to play while obtaining his doctoral degree in biochemistry, and he didn't care. He loved to watch his beloved Oakland ballclub thrash the opposition, and for some reason enjoyed seeing the Kansas City team lose more than any other.

His visitor knocked three times, and then rang the bell twice more. Marcus ignored it, not wanting to open up to any kids peddling chocolates for school fund raising, but when the third ring came, he got up to answer it.

He wondered whether Kay had left her key behind, and if so, she wouldn't be very happy if he didn't let her in. Not that she'd been anywhere close to cheerful for the last few months. Perhaps the late evenings, long hours, business travel, and the demands of paying off a whopper mortgage in the expensive Bay Area were getting to her. Yet it wasn't just that. A darkness seemed to have settled over her of late. There had even been a few times in the past year when she'd suffered thrashing nightmares and terrors. He would throw off the covers, take her sweat-drenched body in his arms, and hold her until the sobbing stopped and the steady breathing of deep sleep returned. Then he would retrieve the sheet and duvet, carefully cover her up, and try to return to slumber himself, usually without success.

When he opened the door, he half expected to see his wife standing there wearing a sheepish grin of forgetfulness, but how he would have changed everything just for that! Instead, he saw a diminutive Filipino, late forties, early fifties perhaps, he couldn't tell. The man was wearing a brown jacket, a loosened tie around his neck, and a shield in his left hand.

"Mr. Black?"

"Yes."

"My name is Detective Sergeant Leo Sampang. I'm with the Pacifica Police. Might I come in?"

Marcus frowned. "Yeah," he said, slowly. "What's up?"

The noise from the television in the other room reached a crescendo as yet another Oakland batter treated a Royals pitcher disrespectfully. "Can we talk quietly?" the cop asked.

"Sure," Marcus replied, his pulse quickening. He led Sampang into the living room and motioned for him to sit down. He reached for the remote and hit the mute button, leaving only the visual on the large high-def screen.

"Mr. Black, perhaps we could talk without the game on?" the detective suggested.

Okay. Whatever you say. Marcus pressed another button on the remote, and the picture disappeared. "What can I do for you?"

"Sir, do you own a Lexus sedan with the license plate 4KRNMB?"

The answer was yes. He also owned a slightly larger one with the license plate 4MBNKR. Well, half owned, at least. He and Kay shared ownership of the vehicles but reversed the letters on the tags to mean "For Kay Rasmussen and Marcus Black" and vice versa. His friends kidded him about the vanity plates, but he didn't care. Most of them were still attached to their old Hondas and Toyotas. "Yes. That's my wife's car."

The next few minutes rushed by in a blur as Leo Sampang gently broke the news. Marcus replayed the scene time and again as the subsequent weeks dragged on. It became like a worn out videotape with some of the frames missing, as he tried to recall what Leo was saying. Every time he got to the part where the cop asked him to come to the morgue and identify the body, his mind went blank, as if someone had erased that part of the recording. The memory only started up again, hours later, when he was standing over the sheet on the gurney and someone asked him to identify the ring. The medical examiner warned him that he should only look at the hand and nothing else, and he had taken the M.E.'s advice. Even now he was grateful that he hadn't asked the pathologist to lift the sheet. He wanted to remember her the way she was, before the depression had started, before the violent burning death at the base of Devil's Slide.

Their first meeting was nearly ten years ago, right after he'd moved to the Bay Area to take a job at the recently built Foster City XUSA facility. His company had morphed over the years from an East Coast-based biopharmaceutical company into a strictly virtual organization relying on in-licensing and outsourcing activities for revenue. The business model was now common in the industry. XUSA, a private corporation headed by Lawrence "LC" Claypool, a multimillionaire with a conscience, was one of the most lucrative. LC had plucked Marcus from a major drug company whose Michigan labs were to be closed down. Marcus had jumped at the chance to move out to the Bay Area. Back then, he'd been an eager thirty-year-old single male who'd never been west of Chicago. It was an adventure, a chance to shine at what he did best.

He'd met Kay the second week after his arrival in San Francisco. One of his XUSA colleagues, a Royals diehard who would later become a close friend, suggested he attend a Bay Biotech get-together at a local Mexican restaurant one evening. A rival company's human resources manager had organized the event for those new to the area, sending invitations to over a dozen companies. Slightly shy, he had gone anyway, to discover a flock of like-minded scientists and technicians, some fresh out of school, some a generation older than he, all with very few local acquaintances.

His reluctance to come along caused him to arrive late, and when he arrived there were very few places left to sit. The HR manager had worked with the staff at the Mexican joint to arrange a long row of tables, but they were nearly all fully occupied. The only place left was at the end, and he found himself next to a young Chinese man who appeared more interested in his tortilla chips than making conversation. Opposite the Asian was a slender, beautiful young woman with shoulder-length black hair, a perfect complexion, the deepest blue eyes he had ever seen, and a sensual mouth that turned upwards ever so slightly at the corners.

He sat down at the table and looked at each of his companions.

The Chinese guy was the first to speak, between mouthfuls of nacho chips. "Hello, I'm Jie." He pronounced it "jay."

The young woman followed. "I'm Kay."

Marcus thought for a moment, and then said "I'm M."

The man called Jie dug his hand into the communal basket of corn chips and fished out another fistful.

"Em? Short for, let me guess, Emmitt?" Her voice was slightly raspy. He wondered if she smoked, but he didn't care. All he could think of was that he had just stumbled onto an amazing opportunity. If, of course, she was available.

"Ah, no." He sneaked a glance at her hands. Tiny, delicate hands, fingers perfectly tapered. Not a single ring or a tan line to signify temporary or recent removal thereof. "Marcus. I thought we were doing introductions by initial. Just thought I'd keep the pattern going. Maybe I should have said L. Wait, that wouldn't have worked. That's not what my last name begins with either. I'd have had to say B. Oh, crap. Sorry I skipped a letter."

She was looking at him with a look of utter amusement in her eyes. Then her mouth broadened, revealing an almost flawless set of teeth, with one lower incisor just out of alignment. She said nothing.

"I'm an idiot, aren't I?" Marcus said.

"Babbling, blithering idiot," she said. But her eyes danced. "It's really Kay." She offered her perfect little right hand.

Marcus reached across to shake it and promptly knocked Jie's beer all over the basket of corn chips. "Clumsy too," he admitted, leaping up and knocking the table with his knees. The entire end table went flying. Filled plastic mugs and assorted appetizers showered the next table of four. Well before any wait staff arrived with towels and mops, Dr. Marcus Black had managed to irritate a third of the newest members of the Bay Biotech contingent. It was probably the quickest he'd ever pissed off a group of scientists in his life.

The one exception was Kendall "Kay" Rasmussen. She thought the whole event was hilarious. They hit it off immediately, talked long into the evening, and even when every other person at the gathering had left, and the cleanup crew was piling chairs upside down on the tables, Marcus and Kay were still there. Memories of the spilled beverages and salsa remained only as permanent stains on their clothes.

Kay lived with a guy called Javier, she'd said. They weren't getting along too well, something about her long hours as a newly hired molecular biologist and his long hours as chief business officer at a Silicon Valley software firm. Marcus lived alone but said he was thinking of getting a ferret.

"Not in this state," Kay told him. "They're illegal."

"What about gerbils?"

"Them too."

"Why did I bother moving here, then?"

She took his hand in hers. "Marcus, I haven't a clue why you moved here. But I'm glad you did. You're just about the weirdest person I've ever met in my whole life."

"Because I like ferrets?" He squeezed gently. Her fingers were so delicate he felt he might break them.

"That's right. And gerbils. And showing up at Mexican restaurants wearing a T-shirt that says 'I'm Stupid. Just Like The Shirt She's Wearing Says.' And because you're a nerdy clumsy buffoon who introduces himself by his initial. Please tell me you're not a sociopath, please?"

"You're not a sociopath, please."

The tiniest hint of sadness flashed before him, but it went away as soon as it came, to be replaced by the smile, once again, this time explosively gorgeous. Good Lord, was she incredible or what, he thought.

"Will you marry me?" she asked, blowing his mind completely.

A month later, she told him she was planning to move out of Javier's Redwood City house. He asked her if she would share his one bedroom rental apartment. Three months after she moved in, it was his turn to propose, but this time for real. She accepted immediately.

Marcus twiddled the ring on his left hand. It felt warm to the touch, no, hot. Burning hot, like the flames that had consumed her body in a fiery death, taking his soul along with hers. He didn't think he could ever recover, and like so many times when he'd replayed the scene in his mind, he just wanted it all to end.

Kay's note fell to the coffee table, where it rested among month-old newspapers, unopened mail, and empty food containers. Marcus knew his house was a mess. Bills were unpaid, his bereavement leave was soon ending, and he would have to find a way to pick up and move on, but he still didn't care. He endured endless nights, bereft of sleep, nights without Kay by his side, her scent now replaced by the stale stuffiness of unwashed bedding. All he could do was think, regret, hope that somehow he could turn back the clock and help her.

His friends had rallied around. Some had offered simple platitudes. Others had been less sensitive, through no real fault of their own. They just didn't know how to talk to someone whose wife had driven off a cliff for no obvious reason. Only one or two could even look him in the eye and urge him to talk about how he was feeling, to share his pain. Even then, he couldn't bear to be around loving couples and families whose lives went on merrily enough in their own way. He was the one whose life was destroyed, and no amount of well-meant kindness and sympathy could even amount to understanding.

Detective Sergeant Sampang, of all people, had known more about how to help Marcus than anyone. At first Marcus thought it was because of his professional detachment, possibly because he knew more facts than anyone else. Ultimately it was because he told the truth, no matter how painful. There were no signs of foul play or vehicle tampering. While the wreckage was a blackened mass of twisted, molten metal, the forensics experts hadn't found any obvious incendiary or accelerant. The body was burned beyond recognition, but dental record analysis confirmed what Marcus had told the M.E. that fateful night. Dr. Kay Rasmussen, aged thirty-nine, perished in a car accident.

A month after the event, Marcus learned it wasn't just an accident. That was when the real free-fall began, and when it did, he almost wished he'd just left everything to rot. It started when his XUSA higher-ups welcomed him into the company's inner circle. It ended several weeks later, when he realized that everything he believed in was a means to an end more far-reaching than he could ever have envisioned.

Chapter 2

FOR THE LAST SEVEN years the scene had been identical, Jacques the waiter noted. His real name was Jack, and he'd been born and raised in St. Joseph, Missouri. Yet to the customers of Le Bleu, an exclusive French restaurant located just off San Francisco's Justin Herman Plaza, he was known by the Francophone alternative, and not unjustifiably, for his "Franglais" had three decades of refinement. It had been the only job Jacques had ever worked since migrating out west. His exquisite timing, delivery, and unobtrusive service had gained him better tips than most. In his private life he enjoyed a happy and fruitful marriage, with three children and six grandchildren. His entire brood lived in the Bay Area. The only manner in which he had strayed from Middle American normalcy was his five-nights-a-week acting job requiring a contrived accent.

The scene itself was a semi-private location away from the window and as far from internal people-watchers as possible. Jacques knew by now that it was the couple's anniversary, and had expected them to appear as they did every year at 7:30 pm on this day. Each time he began with the same patter: "What can I get for Monsieur this evening?"

The man had a rugged, expressive face. He was in his mid-forties, had short curly graying hair, blue eyes, and a nose with a healed but asymmetric break that he wore like a badge of honor. Every year he asked for the same item. "Your second-best filet mignon, s'il vous plait, Jacques. Bleu, of course."

The waiter smiled knowingly. "And for Madamoiselle, the best?"

The woman sighed, feigning annoyance. "You should know by now it's Madame! But thank you anyway, and yes, I would like the best." Which, given the locale, was likely to be magnificent. The second-best wouldn't be half bad either.

Jacques completed their orders, promised to return with the wine list shortly, and left the couple in peace. Bradford King took his companion's hand and squeezed it gently. "Still glad you married me?"

A dazzling smile spread over Fiona "Dutch" Lavenhook's face. She was nearly ten years younger than her husband, and the physical contrast between them was notable. She might have been described as dangerously attractive, particularly when her emerald green eyes lit up as they did at that moment. Long dark hair cascaded about her shoulders, which were bare above a silvery evening dress that accentuated a slender, well-toned figure. "I wouldn't have it any other way."

They were celebrating eleven years together as husband and wife. Brad's official title was "Director of Special Projects" at XUSA. While not schooled directly in the fields of biology and medicine, he claimed to know enough about them to be dangerous but not useful. That was his justification for convincing Larry Claypool to hire Marcus Black years earlier, while privately claiming to prefer hiring those who were smarter than he. How else, he asked, could he move up in the organization if there were no one to replace him?

Dutch had given up the world of practical science five years earlier for a career helping a San Francisco non-profit organization tackle Third World diseases. Her earlier career path had taken her through the world of genomics, but that ended abruptly as the result of one visionary tired of the drug industry's bias towards so-called Western diseases. For the last several months she had been working with a malaria researcher based at San Francisco General Hospital, and was loving every minute of it.

An intrusive chirping sound disturbed their romantic reverie. Brad frowned, pulled out the mobile phone from his jacket pocket, and grimaced when he saw the words "Incoming Call" on the color screen. "Damn. Sorry about that," he said, pressing buttons frantically to silence the machine. Never one to adjust to mobile technology, Brad had only reluctantly agreed to carry a cell phone at all, and then only for emergencies. Fumbling through the menus, he found a screen that indicated the ringing could be silenced. At last the machine stopped beeping and he returned the device to his pocket. "I hate these things. I'd have turned the ringer off if I could only figure out how. I reckon you have to get a whole new degree to operate these crazy doo-hickeys."

"You're such an old goat," his wife remarked. "A cranky, Luddite goat at that."

"Yeah, well, it was a lot easier in the days when we didn't have to spend half our lives communicating about this and that," Brad said. "In a language that bears precious little resemblance to English. All this SMS stuff, or whatever it's called. Why not just pick up the phone and call someone rather than spend three times as long fiddling your way through a ten key number pad just to send a message that you're going to be late because you're stuck in traffic? And the reason you're going to be late is because you ARE the traffic, *as in* a traffic accident, and you caused it because you were distracted by having to mess around with your cell phone."

"Have you finished?"

"Yeah."

She had to admit he had a point, of sorts. "Well, at least you had the good sense to learn how to use the voice activated Bluetooth doo-hickey built into your car." At that moment, another ring tone sounded, this time a crescendo of the first few bars of Mozart's 40th. This time, it came from *her* handbag.

Brad grinned and pointed at her like a cheeky schoolboy. "Your turn."

She fished out the offending phone and looked at it briefly, then frowned. "It's coming from the hospital."

"Why would the hospital be ringing you? Does it have anything to do with the clinical trial?"

"Shouldn't," Dutch replied. "Patient recruitment in Zimbabwe hasn't even started yet." She hesitated, and then pressed the red end call key. It took her only a few button presses to switch the phone to silent mode, a much faster process for her than for her husband. "Let's just enjoy our dinner. It's our time, not work time right now."

"Amen to that."

A moment later, Jacques returned with the wine list. Brad selected a ten year old Coonawarra Shiraz, prompting a mildly disapproving look. "Monsieur? Surely not!"

"Okay, Jacques, you win. The Chateau Margaux it is."

His expression softening, Jacques nodded. "Merci, Monsieur. In a few years I expect our *bons amis* from Down Under to have reached an acceptable level of quality." He walked off with a fresh spring in his step.

"Acceptable, huh?" Brad said scornfully. "Beats the crap out of most of their—"

She cut him off. "Be nice, sweetheart! He's just doing his job for his homeland."

"Oh, give me a break! He's as French as a plate of McDonald's *pommes frites*. Did you see the pickup truck he drives?"

"What?"

"Yeah. That old Ranger out back. I caught him on his way in a couple of years ago when I was hosting that team from Japan. Baseball cap and all. He got out, looked around, took off his cap, and darted into the back. Betcha his real name is Bobby Joe or something like that."

"Dare you to ask him," she said, winking slyly.

"You got a deal. But if his real name IS a plain old American name then I get —"

He was cut off by a different sound, again coming from his jacket pocket. "I thought I turned that thing off," he said, annoyed. Pulling the phone out, he glanced at the screen, which this time signaled a new text message. "How do I access these things again?"

Dutch sighed. "Give it to me." She held out her hand for it, then frowned as she went through the phone's menu. "That's weird."

"What's that?" Brad took the phone back from her and examined the message. It was from a Dr. Milt Rosenthal, asking him to call him at the hospital as soon as possible. "First I get a call, then you get one, and then this text message? I wonder if the first one was also from the hospital? I guess we can check the call logs." They each thumbed through the menus. Dutch read out the most recent incoming call number, and listened as Brad matched each digit exactly. "That's the same one. He's been trying to reach both of us."

"Or either. Why would he do that? And who is this Dr. Rosenthal anyway? I don't know him."

"That's a good question. Why don't I give him a call anyway, as it seems to be so urgent? Just in case it really is an emergency."

She agreed. "Okay. But please don't take too long. I'd really like for us to enjoy our dinner. And dessert. Darling."

Brad looked at his wife, who looked even more beautiful than she did the day she'd agreed to marry him. *How did I get so lucky*, he asked himself. Hitting the return call button, he waited for a few seconds. On the second ring, the party at the other end picked up.

"Dr. Rosenthal, Emergency." The voice had an unmistakable New York twang.

"Yes, hello, Dr. Rosenthal. My name is Bradford King. You called me and sent me a text message as well. Is there something I can help you with? My wife and I are actually on a dinner date right now."

"Yes, Mr. King. I apologize for disturbing you. I'm calling on behalf of a patient who was recently admitted to the ER. He didn't want me to bother you or anyone else, in fact he specifically said you would probably be busy right now, but I took it upon myself to ring you. You see, this man appeared exhausted, dehydrated, and in considerable stress, but was otherwise in good health. Your business cards – by that I mean yours and your wife's – were in his billfold. You were his only local contacts."

Brad frowned. "What do you mean local? Where is this guy from?"

"He has a California driver's license. Lives in Pacifica."

"What's his name?"

Dr. Rosenthal told Brad, whose face lost color. "Mr. King? Are you there?"

"Yes, I'm still here," Brad said at last. "We'll be there right away. Thank you for calling us, and please tell him not to worry. He's not disturbing us at all. For him, we'll make an exception." He ended the call. Pulling out his wallet, he extracted a fifty and left it on the table.

The waiter was just approaching with the couple's appetizers. "Monsieur, madame?"

"Sorry, Jack. Emergency," Brad said as he whisked his wife out of Le Bleu. "We'll have to come back another night."

How did he guess that one, the waiter wondered.

Chapter 3

THE L-SHAPED PIER JUTTED westward from the small coastal town of Pacifica, a quiet community only a few miles south of San Francisco. The spring surf thrashed the pier's criss-cross wooden struts with white boiling violence. Spray occasionally rose above the pier's surface, sprinkling the numerous fishermen patiently waiting for their lines and pots to lure prey for dinner. Gulls circled above, some huge and black-backed, some their immature grey-brown progeny, pausing occasionally to alight on evenly-spaced lamps towering above the superstructure. Several pigeons also competed with their avian brethren for unwanted scraps of bait or food that the anglers failed to clean up.

Children of varying ages scampered along the two hundred yards or so of the long straight section. They wore everything from fading parkas to T-shirts. The majority of them were dark-skinned, some Hispanic, others Filipino, all of them infectiously happy with the arrival of the first sunny weekend of the year. It had been a long, particularly rainy winter for the youngsters, and they reveled in the crisp blueness of that Sunday afternoon. A couple of kids blatantly ignored the "No Skating" signs painted on the inner walls of the pier, skillfully weaving back and forth on rollerblades. Other boys chose to ignore different rules, including the one prohibiting dogs from frequenting the pier. Ironically, it was an ideal day for a boy and his dog, a chance to soak up the wind, sea, surf, sands, and sunshine as only the young and canine can. They also knew there was little chance that any of them would be asked to leave.

Strolling the length of the pier, dodging its various denizens as they went about their business, was a tall, dark-haired man clad in jeans, denim shirt, an old black leather jacket, and sneakers. A pair of Ray-Bans protected his eyes from the late afternoon glare and the shimmering waves that boiled into the seawall behind him. Glancing north and south, he watched the fishermen cast their lines into the ocean, periodically retrieving their infrequently fish-bitten lures. They all ignored him, which he liked. Anonymity was the thing he enjoyed most about Pacifica and its blue-collar energy. No one could be bothered to question him, even when he stood out from the crowd. No one would likely care what the answers were anyway. In the time he'd lived in the small Pacific coast town, few people outside his family, his colleagues, and his daughter's friends had even bothered to learn his name, Stuart P. Gray, and that was just fine with him.

He stopped at the edge of the pier, facing the coast. He loved to walk along the ocean on weekend afternoons, see the crags and hills, inhale the fresh sea scents, and hear the glorious brutality of Nature as she pounded the coast with her unstoppable tidal forces. He smiled and breathed in deeply as he banished the images of the past from his mind, replacing them with the sounds and sights of present time. *Family. Sally. Megan.* That was what mattered the most, not the echoes of what he'd volunteered for years ago.

"Señor, look out!" an Hispanic boy of about nine cried out moments later as his dog bounded into the man, knocking him out of his reverie.

"What the – why don't you – ah, forget it," he muttered as the brown and white beagle careened back toward the boy. *So much for peaceful forgetfulness,* he thought. Apparently it was not going to be possible to avoid the reminders; there were days when they came at him from practically every direction. One after another they poked him with just enough force to be noticed. Even a dog could do it.

Especially a beagle. They used them after they'd finished with the mice and rats.

Damn.

A lone crow cawed to his left, challenging a gull for a piece of smelt that one of the fishermen had generously given away. He loved to watch the birds indulge in their simple, gluttonous struggles. He grinned as the more skilful flyer banked to its left, swooping past the pier's side rail, and snatched the fishy chunk from the floor. The black corvid flew off to persecute less agile competition, perhaps an encumbered pigeon closer to shore. As it traversed the diagonal between the pier's short and long axes, the bird narrowly missed a tweed jacket-clad man who was striding quickly westward. "Goddammit!" the man yelled, ducking and flailing.

Above the natural sounds, Stuart heard the yell and looked up. The tweedy man was fifty feet from him, his arms waving around. One of his hands held a handgun. Stuart couldn't identify it, but it looked like a silenced Glock 9mm. And the hand belonged to a man he thought had long passed from his radar screen. Most of the fishermen and children ignored Tweed, who quickly tucked the weapon into his jacket and proceeded around the long end of the pier. Stuart knew there was no point in running. He contemplated leaping over the side into the froth below, but knew that his chances were slim even then.

"You remember me, don't you," Tweed said, a statement rather than a question. He stopped six feet away from Stuart and stared. He appeared to be at least fifty years old, about five feet nine, balding, his jacket worn and ill-fitting over his pudgy body. Veins in his nose suggested a serious drinking habit. His complexion was sallow, unhealthy.

"I haven't come here for you," Tweed said, not waiting for an answer. "Out of the whole group, they only let a small number of us live. I, unfortunately, was not one of them." He withdrew the gun from his jacket and engulfed the silencer with bloated lips.

"Stop, wait!" Stuart cried out. He was too late. The bullet emerged from the back of the man's head, arcing in a gruesome parabola into the sea beyond. The body crumpled onto the pier as several fishermen gathered around, yelling in Spanish, Tagalog, English, and Cantonese. A pool of blood began to emerge from Tweed's shattered skull, dripping into the ocean through a crack in the pier. Stuart was stunned, unable to move. Why in God's name had the guy come to Pacifica?

Practicality returned as the babble beside him increased, confusion and shock spreading among the locals. Stuart reached into his jacket and withdrew a cell phone, something he never went anywhere without, and dialed 911.

"I'm sorry, Mrs. MacCallum," Dr. Al Wylie said as he closed the bedroom door behind them. "It's the season for colds and flu. Your husband has a temperature of a hundred and four, that's probably what's causing him to react that way." The young general practitioner had driven over from the Kyle that morning, across the bridge that linked the Isle of Skye with Kyle of Lochalsh in the Scottish Highlands. It was more efficient than the old ferry that used to transport cars between the island and the mainland several times a day, but the charm of the old barge could never be replaced by modern engineering.

Morag MacCallum squeezed the doctor's forearm with anxious hands. "But he's been feeling ill for quite some time now. He's had awful headaches, and he just won't eat or drink!"

Dr. Wylie stopped and faced Morag. The old lady looked at him with a mixture of fear and trust. How could he tell this sweet, kind woman that he didn't have a clue what was wrong with her husband of fifty years? She needed to know that Ian was going to be all right, that they would not be parted. But he couldn't take any chances. "Mrs. MacCallum, can you tell me if you and Mr. MacCallum have been abroad during the last few weeks? To Europe, the United States, Africa perhaps?

Morag's eyes opened wide. "No, Doctor! We've not been east of Portree since August. Ian and I haven't traveled anywhere, not even off the island for months. No reason to go since Ian's retirement. We just want to live quietly and simply."

"Have you been in contact with any animals, by any chance?" Al asked. It was a standard query since "mad cow" or the Creutzfeldt-Jakob disease variant had surfaced.

"Only Tom and Charlie."

"Tom and Charlie?"

Morag led Al to the back door. The MacCallums' house was an old granite farmhouse, sturdy as a mountain, its gray walls insulating them from the frequently harsh climate of the Inner Hebrides. The back door opened onto a sparse lawn. Patches of an unexpected late spring snowfall dotted the dormant grass, which covered a trapezoid-shaped acre of land. A stone wall defined the perimeter, the longest side at the back bisected by a metal gate. Beyond the gate stood an old, open barn, in which several bales of hay lay partly protected from the elements.

Morag pursed her lips together and whistled, a staccato series of eight short peeps followed by a lower note that rose sharply. A black and white border collie poked his head over the far fence, scrambled up and over, and bounded up to Morag. She tickled his ears as he fell in beside her. "Good lad, is our Charlie. We've had him for eight years, now. The finest dog that ever lived."

Alasdair Wylie didn't doubt it. All border collies, at least the ones he'd met, were the finest dog that ever lived, at least in the eyes of their humans, and they were right more often than not. "He's with you all the time, then?"

"Here and about. His da' were Skye champion three years in a row. Still the best herding dog this side of Mallaig, if you ask me. But Charlie takes after his ma. She were a lovely dog, but couldn't box in a flock of one-legged ducks. But he's a real champ to Ian and me."

Charlie wagged his tail and nuzzled his mistress's hand as they arrived at the gate. An enormous old piebald Shire horse stood at the other end of a large paddock. His massive hooves, shaped like inverted funnels, supported his magnificent bulk. "Tom!" Morag called.

The horse looked up and whinnied. Slowly he lumbered across the paddock to the gate, his gentle eyes shining like onyx. He dipped his head to Morag, who scratched his nose affectionately.

Wylie reached up and patted the horse's neck. "Hello, Tom," he said. "He's beautiful," he added, smiling at his patient's wife.

"Aye, that he is. Thirty years old and still as strong as an elephant." Morag reached into her pocket for an apple and held it out on her hand. Tom grabbed the fruit and chomped a few times before swallowing it. "No manners, mind. Takes after Ian that way."

The two of them stood quietly for a few moments, enjoying the crisp early spring air and the company of the gentle, friendly animals. Finally, Morag MacCallum broke the silence. "Doctor, what's wrong with my Ian?"

Al Wylie had seen what he needed to see. Unfortunately, his observations had left more questions than answers. "Mrs. MacCallum, I don't know. What I do know, based on my examination, is that your husband needs more care than you or I can give him at the moment. If you don't mind, I would like to check him into hospital tonight.

She nodded slowly, gritting her teeth. "Aye. Tonight it is then." They walked back to the house in silence, Charlie in step, mirroring Morag's solemn demeanor.

As the back door closed behind them, the bedroom door opened. Ian MacCallum stood in the frame, his eyes wild. He held a short barreled 12-gauge shotgun, its muzzle pointed directly at his own face. "Never forget," he wheezed. "There are only three left."

"Ian!" Morag cried, moving toward him as quickly as she could. Wylie reached for her, restraining her.

Spittle flew from her husband's lips, landing on a tattered hall rug. The old man's breathing was shallow, desperate. "They killed the rest of us," he growled. Then, in a last, desperate conflict within himself, he forced his mouth over the gun barrel, reached for the trigger, and pushed it backwards.

Chapter 4

BRAD DROVE HIS INFINITI into the visitor's parking lot of San Francisco General. He'd been silent throughout the short drive, despite his wife's numerous attempts to elicit detail. It took him several passes to find an open space, leading him to remark that there must be an awful lot of sick people with visitors.

Dutch rolled her eyes. "If it were you, I'm sure you'd want someone to care."

"Oh, I care all right. I just don't want to spend the next twenty minutes driving around looking for a place to park." Always impatient when seeking empty slots, he drove at greater speed than necessary up and down the aisles. Luck yielded him two vacant and adjacent spaces. Straddling the center line, he shifted into park and switched off the engine. "There. And I don't care if I get a ticket. It'll be cheaper than fixing a dent."

She knew not to bother correcting or criticizing him. Given the circumstances, why get bogged down in minutia? She got out of the car and joined him, taking his hand as they walked towards the ER entrance. "What on earth happened? Why are we here?"

He squeezed her hand. "Let me check with Dr. Rosenthal. I don't want to alarm you right now."

Great, she thought. *What a way to generate exactly that response.* "I'm a big girl, Bradford."

"I know, sweetheart. I just want to be sure." He let go of her and approached the reception desk. "I'm here because Dr. Milt Rosenthal called me," he told the duty nurse, a tired-looking, middle-aged Hispanic woman whose badge said "J. Velasquez."

"Your name please?" Ms. Velasquez asked without looking up.

He told her. The nurse's demeanor changed markedly. Now interested, she studied him carefully. "Yes, of course. Do come with me, please." She called out to a younger woman who was scribbling something on a piece of paper nearby. "Lori, can you take care of things for a moment? Dr. Rosenthal needs me."

"No problem," Nurse Lori replied.

Brad and Dutch followed Nurse Velasquez down a passage towards a private room. The nurse instructed them to wait outside before going in. A moment later, a handsome black physician emerged, stethoscope around his neck. "I'm Milt Rosenthal. And you are the Kings?" he asked.

"Yeah. I'm Brad. This is Fiona Lavenhook." They shook hands. "What's happened?"

"Might I speak with you alone, sir?" Rosenthal asked.

"Anything you have to say you can —"

"Say in front of your wife. I know. I've heard it before, and my patient said you'd say exactly that." He looked at Dutch, who appeared understandably annoyed at the patronizing tone. "But I have to respect his wishes. Would you please follow me? Mrs. King, would you mind waiting in the visitor's lobby for a few minutes? There is a coffee machine if you'd like."

"I certainly would NOT like!" Dutch said angrily. "I'm coming in with you, Bradford." She pushed past him into the room and froze.

In the bed lay a pale, unshaven, and exhausted man. Although he was propped up against the pillow, his eyes were closed. He appeared not to have slept in a week.

Brad and Dr. Rosenthal entered. Brad also stopped short of the bed, his jaw dropping open at the sight of the patient. After a long pause, Brad shook his head and spoke. "Marco, what the hell have you done?"

Slowly the man in the bed opened his eyes. "I told him not to bother you. Isn't it your anniversary today?"

Dutch rushed to the bed and sat down beside him, taking his hand in hers. "What happened?"

Marcus did his best to muster a wry smile. "I told the doc to keep you out of it completely. I just — just couldn't handle this shit any more. I'm a stupid goddamned idiot."

Dr. Rosenthal explained to Brad and Dutch. "The cops brought him in last night. They found him passed out in an alley outside Vesuvio. Are you familiar with it?"

They were. It was a famous San Francisco bar on Columbus Avenue, popular with poets and literati. "What were you doing there?" Dutch asked.

"I couldn't stay at home any longer. I couldn't stare at this any more," Marcus said. He held up his free hand, which was shaking slightly. He reached over to the nightstand and lifted up his wallet. He opened it to reveal a

California driver's license, a couple of credit cards, and a folded letter stuffed in one of the pockets. "I got this three days ago. It was postmarked a month after she died."

Dutch took it from him and unfolded it. The handwriting was steady at first, but became progressively more careless as the letter went on.

My darling husband, my own Marcus,

If you are reading this I will no longer be here with you to live our lives as we had hoped and planned. For this I am so sorry. I treasured every moment that we had together and know that you felt the same. You were, I should say are, my love, my life, my very soul. But something inside me is broken, something that happened to me a long time ago, before we ever met. It wasn't supposed to happen this way but there was a mistake. There is nothing you could have done to prevent it from happening. The point is I don't have much time left to tell you this, and I may be putting you in danger by telling you even now.

Several years ago, I took part in an experimental clinical trial. No one could have predicted what the long-term effects might have been, but all the preliminary tests in animals were clear. Remember we were never able to have children together, and had decided not to risk further attempts? The doctors said we both carried a chromosomal defect? That much is true, but there was something else, something they never looked for, which altered my DNA when I took part in the trial.

Gene therapy has been talked about in the media for a couple of decades now, but most believe it has never been successfully implemented, partly because of delivery, partly because the host organism has powerful defenses. The potential application of this technology is so incredible! It will change our world! But in my case, the effects didn't last forever. They only bought me some time, and my time has now come, as you know. I have never believed in assisted suicide until now, but I knew that my pain would not get any better, and there was no cure. And so I turned to someone else to help.

Please have faith that I am doing the right thing. This is one of the hardest things I have ever had to write. If there were an afterlife, I would wait for you, but to a scientist this is just a fanciful dream, so I want you to get on with your life, however long it may last..

My sweet love, my precious husband, I am so sorry our life together was short. But in that time I almost became whole because of you, even if we could not have grown old together. You will be the last thought in my mind when I soon depart. I am so sorry, Marcus, so very sorry. I love you for ever.

Your own Kay.

Dutch stared at the letter, her mouth open, and then dropped it back onto the bed. She too had experienced the loss of friends and family, but never like this. She could not bear contemplating how to deal with the suicide of the one she loved the most. It was one of the most dreadful experiences of her life when she and Brad learned of their friend's death, the horrors of the night Marcus saw the matching wedding ring on her finger at the morgue.

Her husband picked up the letter and read it. Then he ordered, "You're coming home with us tonight. We won't take no for an answer."

Marcus's sunken eyes grew even darker, but now they took on a form of malevolent determination. "I appreciate the offer, and your kindness. I'll take you guys up on it. But if you think for a moment I'm ever going to rest without finding out why this happened, then you're wrong. Whatever the reason, someone is going to pay."

Brad nodded solemnly. This was the start of what promised to be a long, difficult process. Exactly how difficult only time would tell. "We can talk about that tomorrow. Right now, it's time for you to get out of here. As long as the doctor says you can."

Almost on cue, Dr. Rosenthal entered. "How are you feeling?"

"I'm having about as much fun as I would with a good case of Marburg," Marcus replied with a surprising dose of black humor.

"That bad?" The physician's eyebrows popped up for a moment.

"Yeah. But hangovers go away. Am I free to go?"

"If you feel up to it. I'll send someone in with the release forms. Looks like these nice folks are going to give you a place to stay if you need it."

Dutch squeezed his hand. "You bet. We're here for you."

Brad echoed the sentiment, but there was something else he needed to say. "Tomorrow I'll have you meet with an old friend of mine. I'll tell you more later, but for now, let's just get you home, get some food in you, and with any luck, a good night's rest."

The faintest hint of a humorless smile appeared on Marcus Black's face as he picked up Kay's letter again. "Sure. But I'm not going to stop until I find the truth about what happened. Things were – kind of weird lately for Kay and me, stuff I never told you about. I can't explain it, but something just wasn't right with us."

Chapter 5

Matt Gilstrap stared at the high-res screen on his desk. He saw a long sequence of amino acids, arranged three-dimensionally. A kaleidoscopic array of yellow sulfur, blue nitrogen, red oxygen, white hydrogen, and gray carbon atoms slowly spun on the monitor. He was looking at an X-ray crystal structure of a protein. Structural biologists the world over were used to seeing similar snapshots of what proteins looked like when broken down to their atomic level. The protein itself was the result of advanced molecular biology and applied genomics.

Furthermore, the template for this protein didn't come from any human or animal species on Earth. It was an engineered protein with a key feature that promised to open up a whole new sphere of exploration. Excited, he picked up the phone on his desk, thinking that Steve Goudreau would want to see it as soon as possible. He dialed the first three digits of Steve's extension, then hesitated. *Screw it*, he thought. *This is something to take straight to Justin himself.* He hung up and dialed a new set of four digits.

A monotonous female voice answered on the third ring. "Dr. Hernandez's office."

"Hello, Office. It's Dr. Gilstrap's desk."

"Oh, it's you," Hernandez's PA replied. It was an ongoing, albeit silly exchange. "Sorry, but Justin's overseas right now. He'll be back early next week, I believe. Did you want to leave him a message?"

"No thanks, Brenda," Matt said, disappointed. He really wanted to let the head scientist know. "How about Steve? Is he there?"

"Let me take a look." Brenda craned her neck around the side of her cubicle. Goudreau was studying something absorbedly on his monitor. "Yes, he is. Would you like me to transfer you?"

"If you don't mind."

Steve answered immediately. "Got something interesting for me to see?"

"Gotta check this out, but I think the conversion efficiency will go up a notch. It's just a hunch, but based on the structure I think the substrate should have better access. And the protein is even more stable."

Steve had enough experience to curb his enthusiasm until he had a good, critical look. "I'll be over in five minutes. Keep the picture on screen."

Matt waited impatiently, his fingers drumming against the desk. After all his years of school, and the months he'd spent staring at computer screens, after all the molecular constructs, he thought he'd finally achieved his goal. The huge protein was designed to perform vital biological functions on the tiniest of molecules, and it boggled his mind that something so monstrous was needed to perform this kind of molecular surgery. It was like amassing an army of millions to slaughter a fly. Yet the simile was not wholly inaccurate. Most enzyme mechanisms required a degree of molecular precision that only Nature, evolution, and possibly a dash of intelligent design could accomplish. And right before him was the most intelligent design Matthew Gilstrap, Ph.D., had ever achieved.

Steve entered Matt's small office moments later. "What do you have?"

Matt showed him, pointing out the special modifications he'd made to the structure, and how they affected the protein's catalytic efficiency. "This was the kicker, Steve. We took out one methylene group here and reversed the enantiomeric center. Look how it affects the binding site."

His boss frowned. "Not sure what you're getting at."

"Take a look through these. It's a lot easier to see in three dimensions." Matt handed Steve a pair of battery operated 3D glasses. They allowed their wearer a virtual reality view from the inside of the three-dimensional protein structure. Steve donned the glasses and took the mouse from Matt. It took him several minutes to navigate the terrain. When he finished, he took off the glasses. His eyes were wild with excitement. Sweat beads were forming on his forehead.

"My God, I think that's the one! I think you've got it!" he said. "What was the yield of the protein?"

Matt smiled smugly. "You're not going to believe this. The yield in the fermenter was fantastic, based on milligrams per liter. It's almost as if the organism itself is a dominant species!"

Steve thought about it for a while. This was the very same strain Hernandez had wanted to test in the biodomes. Now there was additional proof that all the parts were coming together. Nevertheless, a worry still nagged him. He wasn't sure why, but something wasn't quite kosher. All the same, he couldn't help be excited for his young employee, and for what Matt had achieved in such a short time. Instead of voicing his inward concerns, he gave the young man something more acute to focus on. "This is outstanding, Matt. How does this compare with the natural protein head to head?"

"Take a look." Matt hit Ctrl-Tab on his keyboard. A different picture popped up on the screen. "See how the binding site looks a bit different? The substrate can't get into the pocket as easily. Plus, the protein yield was almost two logs worse."

Two logs, Steve thought. That was a hundredfold less efficient. What the heck had they made? And, more to the point, what could they, *would* they, do with it? "Can you let me run with this? I need to make sure the other guys see this as soon as possible."

"No problem. You're the boss."

"I'll make sure you get the credit."

Matt had heard that sort of thing before, and he didn't like the usual outcome. Something in Steve Goudreau's eyes, however, suggested the Canadian was sincere. "Just as long as you're kind come performance review time," he joked.

"No need to worry. I'll take care of you. I may need the favor repaid one day, but let's just keep it at that for now. Deal?"

"Deal."

Demetek's Senior Vice President of Research gave Matt's shoulder a squeeze. "Thanks," he said before walking out to leave the young man still staring at the picture of the strange, complex protein.

Chapter 6

A SMALL GATHERING OF neighbors and friends convened in the small Portree churchyard to lay the body of Professor MacCallum to rest. The pastor said all the right words, his eulogy somber but comforting.

Al Wylie bowed his head, looking down at the simple pine coffin. The mourners departed one by one, pausing only to pay their respects to Morag. Within minutes, only Al and Morag remained by the gravesite. The pastor waited at a respectful distance.

"You will find out what happened, won't you, Doctor?" Morag asked, her eyes pleading.

"Aye, Mrs. MacCallum, that I will," Wylie replied. He wasn't being dishonest. After all, the cause of death was clear. Speculation served no reasonable purpose at this time. "I'll do whatever I can." Rain began to fall on them as they stood over the burial site. Al recalled a saying his father had mentioned at the funeral of a school friend many years earlier. *Blessed is the grave upon which falls the rain.* It was a comfort to him then and he silently thanked God for helping him remember it now. He placed a consoling hand on Morag's shoulder and then left her alone.

He stopped by his office before going home. There was no one else around. His receptionist had already left for the day. He looked inside the freezer section of a small refrigerator in his surgery, and withdrew a small lock box. He opened it up and checked to see that the contents were still there. There were three layers of sealed baggies. Inside the third was a small piece of gray-pink flesh, fixed in a mixture of formaldehyde and glutaraldehyde. The pellets of dry ice he'd purchased earlier were slowly subliming, but there was still enough to ensure the temperature of the sample would stay low enough for his purpose. He packed a few more pellets around the baggies, locked the box back up again, and returned it to the freezer.

When he arrived home, he picked up the phone and dialed a London number from memory.

"Hello?" a female voice answered at the other end.

"Jenny? It's me, Al. I'm sorry to –"

Click. The phone went dead. He wasn't surprised. Jennifer couldn't be expected to answer cordially, particularly after their unceremonious breakup five years previously. He tried again and again for the next three hours, letting the phone ring at least twenty times before hanging up.

It was late when she finally picked up. "Would you please stop trying to ring me? I have nothing to say and I would prefer to enjoy my evening in peace." She hung up once more.

Al tried one last time. "Jenny, please!"

"WHAT?"

"I would like your professional opinion as a microbiologist," Al said, in as flat a tone as he could manage.

"So this isn't a personal call?"

"I'd like to know if you're doing well, but that wasn't the reason why I rang you."

You'd like to know that I'm doing well, would you? "I'm fine, never been better." *You selfish bastard.* "So why did you spend the last few hours driving me round the bend, not leaving me a moment's peace?"

"Because you're the best in your field, and there's something I need to ask you about a tissue sample. I think I know what it is, but you're the expert and I would very much like to know if I'm at sea on this."

Jennifer Barratt sighed. Her ex-husband could be a royal pain at times, but he always meant well, even if his ideas were occasionally off-base. "Isn't there someone up in Inverness or Edinburgh who can help you?"

"There might be, Jenny, but you're the only one that I know of who has the right kind of experience. I believe this tissue sample may be infected with…"

She cut him off. "Infected tissues? Why haven't you called the right authorities? What do you think you're doing?"

"I don't think it's contagious. Not airborne, at least. The mystery is how my patient was infected."

"Is your patient still alive?"

"No. Unfortunately he passed on last week. He committed suicide, in front of his wife and myself, put a gun to his own head. The tissue sample is from his brain."

"God, that's awful!" Jennifer exclaimed, past grievances taking a back stage for a moment. "But where do I come in?"

Al Wylie inhaled deeply. "His poor widow watched her beloved husband deteriorate rapidly before he shot himself. I didn't ask her too many questions at the time, but I wanted to know about where they had traveled in recent months, whether they were in contact with any wild animals, or tame ones for that matter. She said no, they hadn't left Skye in ages. The only animals Mrs. MacCallum has are a dog and a horse. Both of them were normal. As was she, for that matter."

"Did you say MacCallum? I read about an Ian MacCallum in the obituaries of the Telegraph this morning. It said he lived on the Isle of Skye. Is he the same man?"

"Aye, he was a geneticist. That's the other reason I called you, just in case you might be familiar with his work."

"He stopped publishing over ten years ago, I know that much. I'll go through my files, maybe consult MEDLINE to get a reminder on what exactly he used to do. It's been a while, so I can't recall offhand."

"Thanks. I appreciate it. Listen, about the tissue? I've fixed it, frozen it in dry ice, and will ship it direct, if that's all right with you? I need a genomic scan on it if possible, but if you can't manage that, some histology would help. I can come down to London to get the results."

Jennifer sighed. The last thing she really wanted was to have to get together with him, but scientific curiosity won out. "All right, I suppose so. I'll take the sample to my lab and peer at it under the light."

Good. "Thanks again, Jenny. I'm out of my depth here".

"I'll expect the sample soon, then." She hung up without saying anything else.

Al Wylie closed his eyes. He wondered whether she looked the same or had gotten a complete makeover. Was she still the same petite, auburn-haired beauty that had captured his heart all those years ago, before ambition drove them apart? Did she have a new love in her life? Was there perhaps the ghost of a chance for him?

He put the handset back in its cradle and went upstairs to his bedroom, where he quickly packed three days' worth of clothes before settling into an uneasy sleep. Tomorrow he would make sure Sarah sent the sample by courier. That would be the last thing he'd ask her to do before his regular receptionist, Claire, returned. Maybe then he would at last feel as though some degree of routine were returning to his quiet Western Highlands practice.

Jennifer Barratt sighed and stared at the phone, wondering if it might ring yet again. She did not want to be drawn back into her ex-husband's world, but his call had concerned her a little. As a Lecturer at the London University School of Hygiene and Tropical Medicine, Jenny was no stranger to exotic infections. In a way, she even welcomed them at her professional doorstep, but something Al had said bothered her. Why would a retired professor, who had lived the last several years of his life in benign Western Scotland, suddenly take his own life so brutally?

She took a deep breath and walked over to the stereo system. It was getting late, and she needed some soothing music before calling it a night. She selected a CD of two Mehta-conducted Mozart symphonies and hit the play button. There was little point in speculating. She would simply have to wait for the tissue sample to arrive the following evening.

Chapter 7

WAVES LAPPED AGAINST THE Gulf Coast shoreline as the clear, late evening wore into night. The lights of nearby St. Petersburg Beach hotels blinked from time to time, their reflections rippling across the black sea. A lone jogger bounced along the sand, his feet surprisingly light for one of his build. Over six feet tall, his muscular body bore only a pair of swim trunks. Dark-skinned and handsome, he was in remarkably good shape for a man over sixty. His face was angular, his nose firm and aquiline. Three hours earlier, with the sun still above the horizon, his eyes would have appeared almost black; now, they were ebony. A thick black mustache drooped below the corners of his mouth. His dark hair was cut short. In the light of day, anyone passing to his left might have observed scar tissue in a line from just beneath his armpit to a point a couple of inches under his nipple. Much of the original injury was obscured by hair, but the raised flesh was unmistakable to anyone taking a close enough look.

The scar was from a fight. While not directly involved, he'd been a bystander in the wrong place at the wrong time. The place was Weston Maximum Security State Penitentiary in Illinois. The time was five years earlier. Edmund Solkar was over half way through his sentence, playing basketball in the recreation yard. A lifer, a thuggish giant of a man other inmates called "the Lamb," not because of any pastoral or sheepish nature, but because his name was Lambert, had finally picked on the wrong guy. The wrong guy, a psycho named Vince Hilmy, was doing ten to fifteen for armed robbery. Hilmy was half the Lamb's size, but was wiry and vicious. The bigger con had completely underestimated him. Hilmy had carved himself a sharpened slab of Plexiglass from a picture frame his mother had given him early into his sentence. The Lamb had wanted to show who was in charge – after all, the robber was slender, young, and white. Right away the Lamb discovered the little guy was no pushover, receiving multiple stab wounds in the torso. Ed Solkar witnessed the altercation close-hand, tried to push the Lamb away from the slasher, and in doing so was cut across the chest. Moments later, guards fatally subdued Hilmy.

The Lamb recovered from his wounds within a few weeks, and Ed earned himself a protector, who saved his life more than once. He spent the remainder of his time in relative comfort, and after completing his debt to society, moved from Illinois to the Gulf Coast. He loved the pleasant, warm winters, the solitude in which he could stroll or run along the sand, the clean air, and the slow pace of life. The peace of his surroundings helped him put his wasted years in perspective. He used his nightly jogs to think, to forget, slowly, and even to forgive, one small act at a time.

Edmund Ranjit Solkar, the son of an Indian father and an Irish mother, had been indicted for capital murder fifteen years earlier. Only the intervention of an ambitious but technically sound young public defender had protected him from a lethal injection. She had wheedled the charge down to voluntary manslaughter, after the county prosecutor had chosen to make an example of Solkar. "Domestic violence," District Attorney Daniel Cole III had said, "is abhorrent to society. Ladies and gentlemen of the jury, we cannot tolerate the type of vicious acts perpetrated by the defendant under any circumstance."

. The P.D. did not disagree with Cole on principle, but the D.A. saw it from another viewpoint. To him, Solkar was acting in a jealous, premeditated fashion upon finding his lover with another man. To have burned her body amounted to a vengeful act punishable only by death. The only problem was that in no way could Ed have been linked to the burning of the body. While confessing to slapping her, possibly hard enough to render her unconscious, he claimed to be out of town for his victim's bodily desecration, a fact substantiated by credit card receipts.

Ed's lawyer pointed out that by any stretch of the imagination, the mitigating circumstances alone would justify a case of voluntary manslaughter. Ed offered a guilty plea, which the D.A. accepted. The jury thus never had a chance to deliver a unanimous verdict on the more serious charge. As a result he avoided both death and life sentences.

In the distance, a woman approached Ed as he ran along the beach. As always, she wore an indigo bathing suit beneath a floral wrap. She walked deliberately, her dark brown eyes transfixed on the man. Slender, but with the toned calves and thighs of an athlete, she was about five feet six. A mane of tawny blonde hair cascaded about her shoulders. She had a full mouth, but her lips were not pouty or collagen-overfilled. In her late thirties, she was strikingly beautiful, her facial features delicate, her cheekbones high.

The distance between them dwindled rapidly. In less than a minute they were thirty yards apart. Ed stopped short, his jaw dropping as he recognized her. She continued her steady pace towards him, her eyes never leaving his line of sight. As she drew close, she held out her arms to him. Ed stood, his hands shaking, his heart rate increasing.

"Edmund." Her voice was pleasantly husky.

"I – I...." He was unable to speak.

"It's all right. They're gone now. We can be together again." She smiled seductively at him. There was no madness in her eyes. Ed felt himself weaken as she traced his jawline with long, slim fingers, her body pressed against his chest.

"I – but I..."

"Shhh, my love. There's only a few of us left. I've taken care of the others. We can't be traced."

Ed tried to push her away, but something prevented him. Was it her scent, her touch, the mesmerizing gaze deep within her eyes? He felt his head begin to spin. "You – you can't be real," he protested.

"My darling, I am real. And I've come back."

"Samaya."

"Your Samaya," she whispered.

"It's not possible!" he whispered, tears burning his eyes. "You didn't die?"

"No, Edmund. I'm so sorry I had to do that to you, but I had no choice. There were twelve, remember? And now it's just down to us. I want you to have what you lost, to find your hope once more. I want you to live again!"

She drew herself up to him. He felt as though he was twice her size, but he could feel the strength in her arms as she wrapped them around his neck. She gently kissed him, her tongue darting in and out, nibbling at his lips. The terror returned to him, but he dared not push her away. *Not now.*

Never again, he told himself. *Never again will I do this to anyone.*

Her presence was intoxicating, like a drug he could not live without. He gave in to her, lost, plunging into a realm of darkness that would forever haunt him. She melted into him. He sensed his hands at her waist, moving upwards to the small of her back, then around her neck, *tightening....*

He awoke drenched in sweat, the telephone by his bedside ringing furiously, relentlessly. "Hello," he gasped, panting into the mouthpiece.

No one answered. Only then did he realize the phone hadn't rung at all, for the sound continued uninterrupted. It was simply his alarm clock, telling him to rise for his morning run, to start the day, to return from the disturbing scene that was serene, almost erotic, and yet ominous and terrifying. The nightmare had come and gone yet again, the same one that had begun just a few months ago, but which now periodically ruined his nights as well as draining his waking hours. Sometimes the dream ended there and then, with him strangling her or striking her down. Other times he gave into her, the scene shifting to a passion he could neither avoid nor want.

Why are you back in my thoughts, Samaya? he asked himself.

"I want you to live again," she'd said in the dream.

To live again. How many times had he said those words to himself? Every day he'd spent in jail prior to his sentence, throughout the trial, every day he'd spent in prison, and every day since. *To live again.* "To live again," he said aloud. "To live again. To live again! TO LIVE AGAIN!"

"Hey, would you shut the hell up!" a whisky-laden female voice drawl-yelled through the thin walls. Several sharp thumps followed, no more than two feet away from him. "I'm trying to get some sleep here and you ain't helping!"

Ed ignored the protests as his cries dwindled to a chest-heaving groan. He rolled onto his back, opening his eyes briefly. Dawn was breaking. He glanced at the dime-store clock beside his bed, the one whose alarm he almost never bothered setting because he awoke at six, plus or minus a minute, every day. He swung his legs over the edge of the bed, flexing his toes against the chintzy carpet. He yawned and stretched his arms above his head, feeling his vertebrae click and snap a couple of times. Then he lay back, his feet still on the floor, and breathed deeply a few times. The squawking of gulls brought the sounds of the shore close by. Slowly, the dream faded.

He got to his feet and padded into the bathroom. It contained a commode, a rusty basin, and a shower with a cracked door, all in the space of a four-by-five cubicle. Above the basin was a cheap mirror. Under it was a shelf where he stored his shaving kit, toothbrush and paste, and his comb. He gazed at his reflection for a moment, then turned and stepped into the shower. When he was finished rinsing off all the suds, he stood still for several minutes, letting the water play over his back. It was an old habit, but his best ideas and most productive thoughts always came to him in the shower. He didn't know why, but he enjoyed the way the water freed his mind.

Are you alive, Samaya? Are you really alive? The possibility had disappeared along with his freedom the day of his sentence, but they had never positively ID'ed her body. All they'd had was a charred, unidentifiable corpse, but D.A. Cole had no doubt that the barely human-shaped pile of blackened bones belonged to Samaya Jonas.

No. It was just a dream, a somnolent fantasy. No chance it could reflect reality. "Just as well," he muttered. He turned off the shower, shook the water off his head and body, and stepped out. He grabbed a dingy white towel from the peg on the back of the bathroom door and dried off. He quickly dressed in jeans and a white T-shirt emblazoned with the letters CoCoCo over the left breast. The logo stood for "Cobham Construction Company." CoCoCo had given him a chance to reintegrate into society after his release from Weston. He wasn't the fastest worker on site, but his carpentry was error-free and consistent. His foreman had gradually increased both Ed's workload and the complexity of his tasks. The work wasn't always regular, but at least it gave him a chance to use some of the manual skills he'd learned during his incarceration.

He had another skill, but prison had nothing to do with it. Before his world had crumbled around him, before the darkness had swallowed him up, he'd been an accomplished day trader. The day before his arrest, he had transferred ninety percent of his substantial holdings to a dummy corporation in the British Channel Islands tax haven, and the rest to his parents, now deceased. Their share reverted to him upon their death.

His legal defense had cost nothing – Mickey Durant was a state employee, and a very good lawyer at that. Ed didn't care to squander his entire portfolio on a battery of so-called legal experts who wouldn't have done any better for him than Mickey. After his release, he dissolved the Jersey corporation and transferred the proceeds to a Cayman Islands bank account. There was enough there to cover any emergency, personal or otherwise, but he didn't dream of touching it. Not yet, anyway. There would be a time and a place.

He tied the laces of his heavy boots. Before he left, he reached beneath his bed, shuffling two of the boxes stashed under the springs, and retrieved a laptop computer. The device was the only electronic luxury Ed allowed himself, because he preferred to keep his life materially simple. He liked to avoid complications, questions, and suspicions. A minimalistic lifestyle let him blend in more efficiently. He plugged the modem cable into the wall and switched the computer on. A minute later, the machine dialed his ISP, connecting him automatically with stock quotation engines. When he was satisfied that all his stocks were performing as hoped, he sent a series of instructions to his trading provider, logged off, and powered down. The entire operation took less than ten minutes. He unplugged all the cables and replaced the laptop beneath his bed, hiding it behind the boxes once more.

As he picked up the key to his apartment, getting ready to leave, the telephone rang. Ed normally gave his number to very few individuals and paid extra to keep it unlisted. Only his foreman ever called him at home. "Hello?"

The voice on the other end was female. "Eddie? Is that you?"

"Who wants to know?"

"Eddie, this is Mickey Durant. Do you remember me?"

Ed's heart began to beat faster. Why would his former defense attorney contact him now? They'd become close, but after the trial they'd practically lost touch after the various appeals were rejected. Mickey had moved on to bigger and better things. This was the first time they had spoken since the incident with Vince Hilmy. "Sure I do. I tend to remember those who save me from the gas chamber."

There was a brief pause on the other end. "Eddie, I'm scared. It took a while for me to find you, and I wouldn't have bothered if I wasn't frightened half way out of my mind."

"What do you have to be scared about, Mick? And why would you have to bother me on my way out the door to work? I'm trying to put what's left of my life back together and to live the rest of it in some degree of peace. I don't want to get sucked back into any kind of trouble. I've done my time. I don't know how many years I've got left, but I want to live them in the present, and with all due respect I don't want anything to do with what happened all those years ago if I can possibly avoid it."

"And that includes me, I know." *No matter how I might feel about you.* "A while ago I found a handwritten, anonymous note under my door. It was about you. I didn't think much of it. In my job, I get crazy stuff all the time."

Ed frowned. "What did it say?"

"It was simple. It said: 'If you want to live, find Eddie Solkar.'"

Shit. "Was there anything else?"

"Just a pair of initials. R.S."

Ed suddenly felt weak and helpless, the same way he'd felt during the almost-real dream he'd experienced earlier. After a long pause, he gathered himself. "When did you get this?"

"Oh, I don't know. A week or two ago, maybe three."

"And you didn't try to find me sooner?"

"No. But then I saw the news about your friend Shanahan. He shot himself."

Sweet Jesus. "When?"

"It was on the news. Just a couple of days ago. Right in front of a dozen witnesses." She told him what she remembered from the reports and waited for him to respond.

He took a deep breath. "Mickey, I don't know if you'd even trust me, after all that's happened. Hell, as far as the law's concerned, I was once a vicious killer. But you've got two choices. Either disappear, or wait for me. The former is easy. If that's what you want, then get the heck out of wherever you are. Hide, leave the country, do whatever you have to, just leave. And make sure you aren't followed."

"What do you mean, followed? What's this all about?" she demanded.

"I can't just leave the country on a whim! I have obligations here at the law school!"

You don't understand, Mick. "Then watch your back. Be careful. Sit tight. I'll find you, I promise."

Ed slammed the phone down, his head spinning. This wasn't the way it was supposed to happen, but he had to act fast. He picked up the phone again, dialed his utility companies, and left messages to disconnect all services immediately. He left the telephone company until last, and then packed up only enough personal effects to fill a large backpack. He reached under the bed once more, pulled out his laptop computer, stuffed it into the backpack, and strapped the whole bag over his shoulders. He carried a worn denim jacket with him, knowing he might soon need extra clothing for where he was headed. Lastly, he scribbled a note to his landlady, apologizing for having to break his lease, and left. He left the key on top of the note along with three hundred dollars' cash.

They'd agreed on the signal the last time they'd seen each other, the day before his sentencing. "If there are long-term effects that the study failed to anticipate, I will contact you through your attorney. If by then you are a free man, do whatever is necessary to finish what you started. Remember this message verbatim: If you want to live, find Eddie Solkar. I'll sign with my initials."

The initials belonged to his old friend, Ralph Shanahan.

There would be time enough to reflect on the possible scenarios as he traveled across the country. Bus rides could be long and boring, but they were ideal for blending in. Moreover, no one raised any flags of suspicion when you plunked down cash for your ticket. Ed closed the door behind him for the very last time, made his way to the St. Petersburg bus station, and purchased a one-way ticket to San Jose, California.

Chapter 8

Marcus awoke in the guest room to discover it was still dark. The clock on the nightstand showed red LEDs displaying the digits 5:18, reminding him of how poorly he'd slept. His sheets were soaked with sweat, and his head was throbbing. His throat was dry and his tongue felt swollen. Then he remembered he was still fighting the effects of a drunken stupor, that he'd woken up in SF General, and that his friends had interrupted their anniversary dinner to come and take care of him.

He fumbled around beside the clock and found a switch to the lamp on the nightstand. The sparsely but tastefully furnished room, now bathed in an off-white glow, had two doors, one to the guest bathroom, and one to the hall. He noticed a light under the door to the hallway, and wondered who else was awake.

In the bathroom, he splashed cold water over his face, then stuck his head under the faucet. Gulping copiously, he drank for almost a minute. Finally, he swished some mouthwash from the small bottle perched beside the sink, spat it out, and stared at the man looking back at him. He saw sunken, bloodshot eyes and a wintry pallor. His hair stuck out in every direction, and his salt-and-pepper stubble made him look years older than he was. *What a mess*, he thought. *What a miserable mess.*

He stepped into the shower without waiting for the water to warm up and flinched as the first icy blast rained down on him. Sticking his head beneath the shower head, he held his breath for half a minute, and then stepped back out. The hot was starting to kick in, and the shock was beginning to abate. He found shampoo and soap, and scrubbed his head and body clean. After drying off, he shaved using a disposable razor he found in a multi-pack under the sink. In the mirror he could see the return of some color to his cheeks. He looked more like his usual self, albeit tired and a bit haggard.

He donned a fresh pair of jeans, a denim workshirt, and a pair of sturdy sports socks. The time was almost six o'clock. He opened the guest room door and wandered into the kitchen, where he found Dutch sitting at the breakfast bar, fully dressed, coffee in hand. She smiled at him as he appeared. "Sleep okay?"

"About as well as expected. In other words, not great, but not terrible. How about you? Do you get up this early every day?"

"Couldn't sleep. And Bradford's gone out for a jog."

Marcus's eyes opened wide. "This early? Is he nuts?"

"As the day I met him," she said with a smile. "He has his little addictions but this one ranks with the craziest. He's been hooked ever since he ran his first Bay to Breakers."

"To me there are only two reasons to run," Marcus commented. "Either you're running away from something or chasing something. Nothing else in between."

"Won't get any argument from me. Then again, if it's all part of some mid-life crisis, there are far worse ways to act them out than running 10Ks every day." She sipped some coffee. "Want some?"

He did.

She filled him a large mug. "Still take it army-style like my husband?"

"Only way to go. None of this fru-fru junk in mine. Plain old black is all I need." He took a drink, closed his eyes, and exhaled. "Ah, that's better. Sometimes that first hit solves half the world's problems." He sat down beside Dutch and clinked his mug against hers. "Thanks for last night. Both of you, I mean that. Don't know what I'd have done."

"I just wish you'd have called on us earlier, Marcus," she said. "What are friends for, after all?" She got up and went to the fridge. "Feel like some toast or anything?" He said yes. She fished out some wholegrain bread, toasted it, and dug around for various spreads. After a couple of slices he began to feel more human.

At length he rose and went to the window, where the early light filtered into the Sunset District home through gossamer curtains. Outside, the city was coming to life, greedy, squawking gulls scavenging up and down the beach just two blocks away. He pushed the curtains aside and stared outside. The street was still empty but for a single garbage truck making the rounds.

Dutch followed him to the window and placed an arm around his waist, laying her head against the side of his chest. "I can't even begin to imagine what you're going through."

He looked down at her. Without shoes, she was a foot shorter than he, the same height his wife had been. The two women were not dissimilar in appearance. Some might have thought they were sisters, or at least cousins.

But the eyes ended the resemblance. Kay's had been blue, deep, bewitching. Dutch's eyes were a bright, emerald green that seemed to burst into light whenever she laughed. *Brad's a lucky guy*, he thought as he gave her an affectionate squeeze.

"I supposed there's one tiny positive to all of this," he said at last. "At least we never had kids. I couldn't even imagine how I'd handle that without Kay."

"You never tried?"

"A few times. Found out it wasn't going to happen for sure when we ran a genetic screen after Kay's third miscarriage."

Dutch's mouth opened wide. "Third? Oh, my God. Shit. You must have been devastated."

"Actually, in a strange way, it was a relief. It explained a lot," Marcus said. "I never really talked about it with anyone other than the doctor. It's not the kind of thing one really admits to." He stepped away from the window. She led him into the living room. It was a large, open space decorated with prints of pastoral landscapes. An ornate chandelier hung from the vaulted ceiling. Mounted on one wall above the mantelpiece was a giant flat-screen television.

They made their way to opposite ends of an L-shaped leather seating area. "It started about seven years ago," Marcus began. "We decided to try for a family, but Kay lost the first one at about six weeks. We learned it's not that unusual, but it took a year for her to get over it. I'm not sure it affected me quite as much, but then again, I wasn't carrying our child, so how can I even explain that kind of loss? Anyway, the second time Kay was about five weeks along. That's when we went to the doctor to get things checked out. Turned out Kay carried a genetic abnormality that she had no knowledge of. She told the doctor her parents had been dead for years and that there was no medical history she could obtain to help explain it."

"What was the SNP?"

"That was the strange thing. It was on chromosome 21, which is normally associated with Down's syndrome. But according to the genomics database, this particular SNP was different. There was a weird insertion sequence that no one could explain. The doctor put it down to some analytical anomaly. Maybe it was a sample spillover or PCR amplification that didn't work right, but we didn't follow up on it. We were sure of one thing, it wasn't a Down's SNP. Even so, the specialist made a note of it and suggested we might be at risk for having kids with Down's, but like I said, there wasn't any hereditary evidence for that."

"You said there were three miscarriages."

Marcus nodded. "That was the kicker. It happened about three months later. Maybe we were crazy or selfish for trying again, but in the end it made no difference. Probably just as well."

She looked at him without saying anything, waiting for him to continue.

"Maybe that's callous. People can be judgmental."

"I can promise you we wouldn't ever judge you, for what it's worth."

The click of a key unlocking the front door sounded. Brad was back from his morning constitutional. Dripping with sweat from his early exertion, Brad's body was firm, wiry but muscular. He was in better shape than most men his age. "Hey guys," he panted, slamming the door behind him and striding over to plant a kiss on his wife. "You sleep OK, Marco?"

"Not too bad. I really appreciate you guys giving me a place to crash."

"Not a problem. Did you grab some breakfast?"

"I cooked," Dutch said.

"Really?" Brad's eyes opened wide. "You gave him steak?" To Marcus, he slyly whispered, "She's a marvel with a good slab of beef and nothing else. A strange kind of savant." He failed to dodge the slap on his backside.

"Ew! Sweaty!" Dutch made a face. "Go take your shower and then come back and apologize. Maybe I'll cook you some toast if you're a good boy."

"Now, there's no need for threats," her husband said, this time avoiding the swipe. He ran off to the bathroom, where the staccato of a pulsating shower jet soon resonated through the hall.

Fifteen minutes later, Brad emerged dressed in khakis and a long-sleeved dark blue shirt. He went to Dutch and kissed her before pouring himself a large mug of black coffee. Marcus looked down at his own cup and sipped from it nervously, feeling self-conscious.

"We're going to meet up with an old friend of mine first thing," Brad announced. He'd called Josef the previous night. "Marco, you and I have been friends for a long time, but there's something I never told you about the security division of our little organization." He drank from his mug and put it back down on the counter. "I'm going to introduce you to the main reason why XUSA remains a private company."

"I'd assumed it was so we wouldn't be under the same public and SEC scrutiny as the rest of our competitors," Marcus said. "Hasn't our CEO always said that he considers us, his employees, as XUSA's most valuable asset, and that he would hate to see us be less important than – shareholders?" He made a quote sign gesture.

"True enough. LC means it, and puts his money where his mouth is. We're well funded, because of what we know and what we can do. But there's another factor that makes us vital in our own way, and that's what we can find out. We're detectives, but not in the traditional sense of the word.

Sometimes we have to take a more daring approach, a tad outside the normal channels."

Marcus looked at his friend, unsure what he was driving at.

"I'm not talking about you, personally. Not up until now, but I think the time is right for you to enter the inner circle, if you'll forgive that overused cliché?"

"If the so-called inner circle helps me find out what happened to Kay then I'll forgive even the worst clichés."

Brad took a deep breath. "We can only do so much to pull your ass out of the mire. Sooner or later, you have to grab onto the rope. I may not convince you of that just yet, but if you'll trust me for a while, then maybe you'll find the strength." He clapped Marcus on the shoulder and picked up the phone. "Reckon you can give it a go?"

Marcus gritted his teeth, thinking. He still had so many unanswered questions. He had to admit that in the last month, he had been desperately bogged down in misery, barely able to cope. If he could find out what had triggered this senseless tragedy then perhaps he could find a path, however narrow, towards a space where he might heal. "All right," he said at last. "I'll do it. I'm in."

"You'll like Joe," Brad said. "He has a tendency to pop up when you need him the most."

"This is your old friend?"

"Yeah. We go way back. Way, way back. Him, me, and LC. He's a complete bastard. No redeeming qualities at all. He's a liar, a thief, a cheat, and violence doesn't bother him a bit."

"Charming guy."

"He's our VP of Security."

"Security? Like a rent-a-cop, or something like that?"

"Not even close. He's as far from being a cop as you or me, probably further. Let's just say his title has more to do with securities, as in trading, than with staying in line with the law. And you didn't hear that from me." Brad took his cell phone out of his pocket and started punching numbers. As he waited for the call to connect, he continued. "He's the best corporate spook in the business. Not to mention the best friend a guy in trouble could ever want."

On the other end, a voice answered. "This is Josef."

"Hey Joe. It's me. Marcus is on board."

"That is good. Take him to the city, as we discussed last night. George will pick him up. Come up to Belvedere and bring your lovely wife too. George is finishing up one of his 'fashion shows' as he likes to call them. You would never believe some of the deals that happen in that part of the Tenderloin."

"Got it. I'll see you in a couple of hours." He ended the call and stuffed the phone back in his pocket. "We're on. Let's go into the city and grab some more coffee."

Chapter 9

Detective Sergeant Leo Sampang of the Pacifica Police faced Stuart Gray in the station just off the Coast Highway. Leo's immaculate desk bore only one decoration, a photograph of a pretty woman and two equally pretty pre-teen girls. A telephone, a rack of carefully organized manila folders, and a flat screen monitor were the only other objects on the desktop. "We don't have much violence in Pacifica. I've been a detective here for five years now and this is only the second homicide I've had in all that time."

"Homicide?" Stuart asked. "He killed himself. I mean, in my book, suicide doesn't quite count as a homicide."

"Homicide, according to California law, is the killing of a human being. In this case, it appears that the human being killed himself. Still a homicide."

"What do you mean, 'appears,' Detective? I was right there. I watched him pull the trigger and blow his brains out. A dozen other people saw it!"

"Some things aren't always what they seem, Mr. Gray. There are a few details that don't add up. We thought you could help shed some light on them."

Stuart Gray felt uneasy. He'd done everything he thought was right, calling the police immediately, giving his name, address, number, and a brief statement at the scene to the officer in charge. He'd said that Ralph Shanahan was someone he'd once met in Chicago. That was true enough. The rest of it wasn't important. "What more can I tell you? The guy was clearly unbalanced. Why he chose to do this is beyond me."

The detective leaned forward. He reached into one of the manila folders and pulled out a witness statement. He looked at it and then peered up at Stuart. "I'm not sure I believe you. This witness stated that he heard Mr. Shanahan say that 'out of the whole group, they only let a small number of us live.' That suggests more than a limited acquaintance. Perhaps you can elaborate?"

Stuart stared back. "The man clearly didn't know what he was saying. I'm sure he was just deranged."

"Maybe." Leo sat silently and waited. It was an old but effective method of eliciting further comment. Suspects and innocents alike tended to fill the silence, often volunteering more information than they might have intended.

It worked. "Look, Detective, I met Shanahan a long time ago. He was a psychologist. I can't tell you any more because I haven't seen him since that first time."

"You were a patient of his?"

"No. He wasn't that kind of shrink. He was in research."

"Tell me more. About that first time," Leo prodded, watching Stuart's eyes carefully.

Stuart shrugged. "I don't really remember. Like I said, it was a one time thing. He presented a seminar at the place I was working at in Chicago. I went and said hello after the talk, shook his hand, we chatted briefly, and that was it. Can't be any more help than that, I'm afraid."

"Where was it you were working?"

"Doesn't exist any more."

"Tell me anyway."

"Why?"

"Just humor me."

Okay, if you must. "The Henry and Linda Castleford Institute."

"What kind of institute is that?"

"It was a private biotech research foundation."

"And what sort of research were you involved with then?"

Sigh. "Who cares? It was just molecular biology. Besides, why do you want to know about what I was doing back in the early nineties? Some guy I met one time comes up to me on the pier and shoots himself, in front of everyone, and now you want *my* CV?" Stuart shook his head and looked away.

Leo sat still again.

Stuart again failed to resist the temptation to continue. "Look, you have my written statement. I've told you everything I know. I can't give you any more details."

"Most of the time people remember additional facts when they think about it for a while," the detective commented. "That's why we like to talk to witnesses, rather than just look at their written statements."

"Yeah. Well, I'm done talking," Stuart said curtly.

"You didn't tell me about your job in Chicago."

"It wasn't relevant!" Stuart's patience was wearing thin.

"You'd be surprised. Why don't you want to talk about it?"

"Because there's nothing to tell! Are you going to accuse me of something regardless? Should I call a lawyer?"

"I don't think that will be necessary, Mr. Gray. You're not accused of anything."

"Somehow I have the feeling that I still have the right to remain silent, though. Anything I say can and will be used against me. No matter how *irrelevant* it is."

Leo closed his eyes for a moment and sighed. It had been a long week and he just wanted to go home. "Mr. Gray, you're not under arrest."

"Then why the third degree?"

"Well, for starters, there were six eyewitnesses other than you who'd swear up and down that this Shanahan guy killed himself. Two of those witnesses I know personally. One of them is a close friend I've known since grade school and he's the most honest guy I've ever met. They both said you tried to stop Shanahan from shooting himself, but there wasn't much you could have done. Everyone said you called 911 straight away, that you took charge till Sergeant Cook arrived, and that you made sure no one touched anything."

"So why AM I here? What's the problem?"

"You have to look at it from our side. It's what the guy said before he killed himself. When you can explain that properly, I'll consider letting this matter go. Until that's been cleared up, I strongly suggest you don't leave town."

Stuart's heart was thumping as he left the police station. It wasn't just Shanahan's death, but Kay's too. That was what really scared him. Within a very short period of time, two figures from his distant past were dead. But what bothered him most was that his own life and the lives of his family were now in jeopardy. Ralph's words were etched in his mind. *Out of the whole group, they only let a small number of us live. I, unfortunately, was not one of them.*

Madness.

Only it wasn't madness, because Stuart also belonged to the group. He was a volunteer who, like the others, chose to undergo a tailor-made procedure. It was an unsanctioned human clinical trial, a journey into uncharted medical territory.

His own greed was as much a factor as anything. Like the others, he'd sold his soul for twenty pieces of silver apiece. And to what end? A shot in the arm, literally. Shanahan had implied that Stuart was one of the lucky ones, one they'd allowed to live. What had become of the others? Goldfarb, Li, MacCallum? And that crazy IT guy? In fifteen years he'd barely given them a thought.

Ten minutes later he pulled into the driveway of his modest, three-bedroom Linda Mar home. Inside, furnishings were typical of any middle-class family. At one end of the great room were a couch and two easy chairs, a coffee table with several dings along the edges, and a wall unit containing a plasma TV and home theater equipment. At the other end stood a rustic dining table, surrounded by six untidily arranged chairs. A country-style sideboard and hutch completed the set. The kitchen, whose counter was a sickly 1970's style avocado green color, boasted modern stainless steel appliances, as if it were half way through a remodeling exercise. Down the hall, one of the bedrooms was used as a home office for Stuart and his wife, Sally. Their sixteen-year-old daughter Megan kept her laptop in the privacy of her own bedroom.

Stuart called out for both of them. A few seconds later, the bedroom door opened and a stunningly beautiful, tall, brown-eyed blonde girl appeared. Recently coiffed and made over, her arms dangled at her sides, her head tilted slightly. She wore a fluffy pastel-blue sweater, stonewashed jeans with asymmetric tears in each knee, and incongruously expensive Jimmy Choos. Behind her stood a slightly shorter, older version with hazel eyes and a better pair of trousers.

"Hi Dad," the girl said. "Mom and I just got back from Stonestown. We've been trying on new outfits."

"Spending money on torn clothes again, I see," Stuart commented. "Did you buy a needle and thread at the same time?"

"Whatever," Megan replied with the universal I Don't Care response. She looked up at her mother, who rolled her eyes and shook her head.

Sally Gray turned back to her husband. "Don't worry, darling," she said in a remarkably proper Oxford University accent. "I haven't spent all of our daughter's college fund yet."

"If I go to college," the girl said. "Maybe I'll just hang out on the beach down in Santa Monica and try out for the Olympic Beach Volleyball team instead."

"Over my dead body," her father declared, but not without some humor in his voice. Megan Gray possessed both the necessary height and athleticism, but also many of the skills. She was already a star on her high school team. Stuart knew that in a few years he would have little influence over his daughter's plans, and could only hope that firm guidance and a good example would help keep her on the right path.

"Whatever," Megan repeated. Then, upon seeing her mother's stern expression, she softened. "Dad, I'm just kidding. I still want to go to UCLA's Department of Design at the same time. And if Mom spends any more of my college fund I'll need an athletic scholarship anyway." She bounded up to Stuart and planted a kiss on his cheek.

"Women," Stuart sighed, marveling at both of his.

Megan flashed him a radiant Daddy's Girl smile, but Sally's mouth was open in shock. Stuart turned around just in time for the first *thwack* to land in the center of his forehead. He had no chance to see what, or who, had surprised his family. Nor could he see his wife mouthing a single word, a name, before she too was hit.

Chapter 10

Marcus sat at a small table inside the Starbucks at Third and Market. It was one of the half dozen punctuating one of the city's main thoroughfares. He nursed his second *venti* of the day, drumming his fingers idly against the tabletop.

"How ya doing?" a voice next to him said.

Marcus turned to his left to see an individual of indeterminate sex who was trying to appear more female than male. The voice gave it away, if not the shadow above its upper lip. Traces of heavy makeup lingered on the periphery of its face, a white paste designed to hide the complexion flaws it bore. Dressed in a short evening dress, the bewigged she-male raised a half-empty latte glass in a mock toast.

"Could be better, could be worse."

"Know what you mean," it said. "Name's George, by the way." It stuck out a meaty hand.

"Marcus." He ignored the hand for a second or two, then when its owner didn't retract it, he tentatively grasped it.

"Pleased to meet you, Marcus." A grin spread over the she-male's face, revealing well-kept, whitened teeth. "My card."

The she-male calling itself George offered a small piece of cardboard. On one side was an ad for a drag show at a theater on Post Street. On the other side was the name B'heorge Petrescu, and a 415 area code phone number. Nothing else.

Marcus looked at the name. "Buh-he-orge?"

"On stage I go by 'Vorzh.' Josef Rintlen sent me to pick you up. He said to find you here."

That got Marcus's full attention. "Okay, Vorzh, George, or whatever you call yourself. I'm listening."

"Outside." George hopped off his chair and left the coffee shop. The sidewalk was busy with city workers, shoppers, tourists, and panhandlers. The early morning fog had burned off to reveal a pleasantly warm sun and clear blue skies. Marcus drained the remainder of his coffee, and followed.

George was already on his way towards the Moscone Center. He looked over his shoulder and signaled with a motion of his head. "Walk this way." Marcus followed, half wondering if the drag queen meant him to mimic his high-heeled, surprisingly ladylike gait. "Beside me. Now," George ordered, his voice carrying an authoritarian edge. "I'll explain on the way."

Marcus caught up. "Who are you?"

"I'm with XUSA," George said curtly. "I work with Josef. Call me his right hand man or Girl Friday, I don't care. It's what I do, and right now my job is to bring you to him. We're going to take a ride." He marched them past the Marriott opposite Buena Vista Gardens, towards a huge multistory parking lot. Crowds carrying bags of advertising literature and other goodies from a local exhibition filled the sidewalks, most of them oblivious to the outside world. Marcus remembered similar scenes from scientific conventions, conferees blithely walking down the streets, chatting to one another about the talk they'd just heard, or their own fascinating work. Their badges would be slung around their necks or fastened to lapels, as if to say, "Go ahead and mug me."

They reached the parking garage. More geeks bearing trade show freebies congregated around the bank of elevators. It took ages for one of the doors to open, and when it did, the nerds weren't even polite enough to wait for the lift's occupants to depart before barging their way in. "Screw this," George said. "Let's take the stairs." Marcus didn't argue. They climbed six flights. When they reached the top, George wasn't even breaking a sweat. He pointed them towards a late model Honda Accord, parked trunk-in, hood-out. He punched a fob in his pocket and unlocked the doors. "Get in."

Before he could snap his seat belt closed, Marcus saw that George had ripped off the wig, revealing a completely shaven head. They quickly made their exit, turned left on Fourth, crossed Market, and hung a sharp left onto Ellis. Shortly thereafter they were in the Broadway tunnel, and from there they soon came to Van Ness Avenue. Northbound traffic was moving well. George punched a button on the steering wheel to activate a hands-free call.

"Hello," a slightly Germanic-accented voice answered.

"We'll be there in about half an hour."

"Good. See you then." *Click.*

George began to talk once they were through the Waldo Tunnel, north of the city. "This is just a cover, as you can imagine. There's a merger happening between a Swiss company and a major local biotech. The CEO of the local joint has weird tastes in entertainment. The boss can explain more if you care."

"Too much information."

"It ain't like that. This is intelligence gathering."

"And that's what you do?"

"Uh-huh. You just haven't seen the fun side of it yet," George grinned.

Marcus didn't really know how to respond to that. It was true in a way. His own job was to evaluate new products and licensing opportunities for the company, using his own scientific expertise to cast a critical eye over them and ensure good money was not thrown after bad. Besides, Petrescu's brusque, almost truculent tone, had thrown him. "I'd like to think that what we do is above board."

"Don't kid yourself, Black. Let me give you an example. When you started at XUSA, did Brad King give you any kind of safety training, or OSHA-compliant plan?"

Marcus thought about it. There had been a long Powerpoint show on what he could and couldn't do, legally. Brad had made him sign all kinds of papers illustrating he'd read various documents and understood their meaning. It was a bit like his graduate school days when he had to watch gruesome videos of people having bad accidents in hazardous situations. "Yeah. I remember that."

"Right. So you agreed that you understood the company's safety policy. Now, do you know what that policy is for?"

"To protect employees from doing stupid things."

"Bullshit. Company safety policies are designed to protect the safety of the company. The safety of the employees is secondary."

"Sounds a bit cynical to me," Marcus commented.

"Call it what you want. Companies in the US don't want lawsuits. Imagine if someone at company Y gets hurt on the job. His wife threatens to sue the company for failing to train him in safety practices. The company says they trained him and he signed to that effect. Case closed. The company is protected."

"What does that have to do with being above board?"

"It's called a pretext. There are things we say and do as members of the corporate world, but we're just a bunch of liars. Some of us, at least."

"Count yourself in that category?"

"When I need to. But usually for the right reasons."

He flashed Marcus a grin. There was a brief slowdown at the Richardson Bay Bridge just south of Mill Valley. George looked at his passenger. "So what's your story? Where do you come from?"

"Not much to tell." Marcus was never keen on broadcasting his life story, and present time was hard enough. Nevertheless, Petrescu's straightforward, frank style – in spite of appearances – was refreshing enough to prompt a few more details. "Born and raised in Ohio. Small town about an hour north of Columbus. My mother was a teacher, my dad a cabinet maker. One older brother, Gary, who died in the first Gulf War. My folks were never the same after that. I was about ready to follow Gary into the army but my mom persuaded me not to, and quite honestly, it didn't take much persuading."

"Can't say I blame you. What next?"

"I went to school at Ohio State, then did a Ph.D. at Wisconsin."

"You're all Big Ten, then."

"Yeah. Made life a bit tough in football season. But for me it was always the Buckeyes rather than the Badgers."

"I went to Michigan. We hated you guys."

"Feeling was mutual. But such things pass, right? Anyway, I did a post doc on the East Coast. Harvard. Did a few years lab work at a biotech company in your old stomping grounds, Ann Arbor, but got sick of going nowhere fast, not to mention Michigan winters. So, I looked for a job out in sunny California, and here I am. That pretty much sums up my life up to this point."

George nodded wryly. At the Tiburon exit, he turned east and drove several miles to the Belvedere intersection. The exclusive island was home to multimillion dollar mansions, estates, and spectacular vistas. As they made their way up narrow, winding roads, they could see the tall downtown buildings across the Golden Gate. They reached the crest of a hill and turned left into a driveway flanked by tall juniper hedges.

They got out of the car. Still in his evening gown, George looked more absurd than when he had the wig on. Marcus followed him to the front door. Ten seconds later the solid oak door swung open.

"It is good to meet you, Marcus," Josef Rintlen said, smiling broadly. In his early fifties, Josef was tall, solidly built, and completely gray-haired. Intense steel-gray eyes centered a strong-featured face. He had a square jaw, a large nose, and a mouth full of perfectly white teeth.

"You must be Josef,"

"That is right." He naturally spoke with a very faintly Germanic accent, but when called upon was capable of any number of regional styles. Josef Rintlen was the consummate corporate spy, a man who had made his substantial millions through barely legal, unquestionably deviant means. "The others are here too. Both of you, please come in and sit down."

George and Marcus followed Josef down the hallway. High ceilings and white walls, sparsely decorated with small Chinese lithographs, led to a room whose one-eighty degree view of the Bay was completely unobstructed. Above them, a gibbous moon was easily visible in the daytime sky. A ferry between the City and Marin County churned the surface, causing the sunlight to flicker and break up.

As they entered, George pulled at something near his forehead, slipping it backwards. Marcus realized that the drag queen's baldness was as fake as the wig and makeup had been. Beneath the flesh-colored rubber pate was a full head of dark blond hair, cut short and matted down. Its owner fluffed it up just enough to reveal an unremarkable man in his mid-thirties, whose only incongruous feature was the evening dress. He slipped that over his head to reveal a simple T-shirt and shorts.

An oversize leather sofa faced the large picture window. A man and a woman were sitting on it, engaged in deep conversation. They each held half-full wine glasses. As the others entered, they turned around and smiled.

"Hey, Marco," Brad said. "Come on in."

The day was not getting any less complicated, and Marcus's head was beginning to spin. He took a deep breath and obliged, perching on a matching recliner. George took the loveseat opposite. Josef went to a mirrored wet bar on the far end of the room and fetched two glasses and a decanter filled with a deep burgundy liquid on a silver tray. He poured some liquid into each, offered one glass to George and the other to Marcus. "An underrated Zinfandel from the central valley. I do not believe in spending hundreds of dollars on wine when a twenty dollar bottle with a day's breathing tastes just as good."

Marcus sniffed, sipped, swirled, and swallowed. The spectrum of rich flavors hit him all at once. Dense fruits, chocolaty smoothness, and perfectly balanced tannins caressed every taste bud he knew existed, and some he hadn't yet discovered. "Underrated" may have been the understatement of the year. It was more like an earthquake masquerading as a hiccup.

"Not bad, is it?" the German said modestly.

"Wow," was all Marcus could say. At last he added, "Where did you find this? I wouldn't mind a case of this nectar!"

Josef flashed his brilliant smile. "I am sure I will be able to spare a few bottles, all in good time. I have bought the entire supply direct from the winery." He smiled, not a little smugly, and topped up the other three glasses. "Shall we get started?"

Chapter 11

THWACK.

Thwack.

Precise shots felled the remaining members of the Gray family in rapid succession. Two figures, one male, one female, stood together at the end of the hall. Each held a SIG Sauer P250 semiautomatic handgun, fitted with a sound suppressor. The man also carried a large black duffel bag. Both wore black, tight-fitting clothes, thin surgical gloves, and thick cotton socks. They had removed their shoes before entering the house.

The man spoke first. "We have to move them out of here as soon as possible and dispose of their bodies. There can't be any trace of them." He produced three folded plastic sheets from the carryall, and placed one beside each body. He unfolded one sheet, lifted Megan's body by the shoulders, lifting her long blonde hair with the other hand, and slid the plastic beneath her. He set the girl's head back down on the sheet, then hoisted her feet and torso just enough to slip the rest of the plastic under her. "There should be very little blood from their wounds, but we don't want to leave any forensic traces."

He performed the exercise twice more, first with Sally and then with Stuart. Soon he had all three bodies laid out side by side. He then folded the excess plastic over their heads and feet. His companion rolled them through a complete turn, enclosing them completely. Finally, he used cable ties to seal the bodies within their plastic cocoons. The woman lifted the bottom end of Megan's body while her comrade hoisted the top. They carried her down the hall to the kitchen, being careful not to knock anything over on their way. They then brought the other two bodies and laid them in line.

A car key with a big "H" on it hung from a hook on the door at the back of the kitchen. The door connected the house to the two car garage. Like

51

most California residents, the Grays used their garage as an attic rather than a carport, but they'd kept half of it for Sally's Honda Pilot. The man grabbed the key and opened the kitchen door, being careful to avoid tripping over the step into the garage. He shone a flashlight around, revealing the large SUV. Conveniently, Sally had parked it with its rear facing the back. He opened the Pilot's rear door and pulled a lever on each side of the back seats. They folded flat, expanding the interior cargo space. "Come on. Let's get them inside."

The woman helped him load the bodies. When they had finished, she closed the kitchen door, locked it, and went to the converted spare bedroom. She heard the whirring of the garage door, closely followed by the departure of the Pilot, and then the door closing again. Once the noise had stopped, she took note of the computers in the room. Two CPUs, each with front USB ports, appeared to be in standby mode. She dug around in the carryall and retrieved a small portable hard drive. She plugged the small end of a USB cable into the drive, and the other end directly into the port on one of the office computers. The screen lit up immediately as the host machine recognized the device. A few clicks later, and an image of the entire contents of Stuart Gray's hard drive was on its way to the portable drive.

She repeated the task with the other computer. The entire download took twenty minutes, much of which included a bunch of music and video files of no interest to her or her employer. They could sort that all out later. Once the transfers were finished, she plugged a USB memory stick into each machine. The sticks contained a Department of Defense-level track eraser program, which she used to wipe the hard drives thoroughly. Then she ran it twice more on each machine just to be certain nothing could be retrieved.

As she was leaving the home office, a thought occurred to her. *The daughter.* Turning on her heels, she half ran back down the hall to the bedrooms. The door on the left revealed a king sized bed and an open door to the *en-suite* bathroom. Obviously that was the parents' abode. To the right was another door, just beyond the office. Inside she found a room decorated with posters of female athletes, some playing volleyball, some shooting hoops, and some doing track and field. On the bed was an open red-skinned laptop, unconnected to the wall. She snatched up the device and ran a finger across its trackpad. The screen sprang to life and the speaker chimed, startling her.

"Battery Low" the message on the screen said. She looked around for a power cord, but couldn't see one. She decided to take the laptop with her and worry about its contents later. There would be time to transfer any information, not that a sixteen-year-old girl was likely to store anything remotely close to what her parents might. Still, why take chances? It would be simple enough to find a generic power cord, image the hard drive, and then destroy the device. She powered it down, closed the shell, and put it into the duffel.

She made one final check of the room, looking for a mobile phone. There was a candybar-style pink phone in the pocket of Megan's purse, slung over the back of a chair. She looked at it to see if there were any messages. Four texts and three voicemails were waiting to be retrieved, according to the indicators. She found the power button and held it down. Then she pocketed the phone, making a mental note to toss it into the nearest body of deep water she could find.

If they'd looked, police would have discovered an abandoned Honda Pilot parked along the Pacific Coast Highway just north of Big Sur just eight hours later. There were no signs of damage to the vehicle. Almost fifty miles south, in a secluded area of the forest, the ashes of three bodies drifted downriver. No one would ever know that their plastic shrouds contained a special accelerant to help cremate them rapidly.

Two hundred miles north of the slowly dissipating remains of Stuart, Sally, and Megan Gray, a boy knocked repeatedly on the door of his best friend's home. They were supposed to meet after dinner for a movie and maybe an ice cream on the way home. Seventeen year old Balbino Ruiz frowned as he walked around the side of the darkened house, looking for signs of activity. He saw that Mr. Gray's car was parked outside, but that was pretty normal for the time of day. The '85 Buick sedan had enough miles on the clock and enough bodywork to require zero protection from either climatic or criminal elements. Megan had told him once that her dad wanted someone to steal it so he'd have the excuse to buy a new one, but nobody obliged.

Balbino had texted Megan several times during the day without receiving a reply, but that wasn't unusual. Sometimes she was just too busy, but she nearly always emailed him when she got home after volleyball practice On discount movie night, she was as reliable as the sunrise, and that bothered Balbino the most. Still, the only slightly odd thing he saw, peering through the garage's small window, was the absence of Mrs. Gray's car. He wondered if they'd all gone out to dinner to celebrate something, but on reflection, surely Megan would have told him, or even invited him to come along. After all, he was the closest thing she had to a brother.

He dialed her mobile number several times but could only reach her voice mail. Likewise, no one answered at home, although he could clearly hear ringing inside the house. Eventually, he gave up and called Stuart's mobile number.

The instantly recognizable opening riff of Deep Purple's "Smoke On The Water" sounded, a distant bass and snare crescendo emanating from the front of the garage. He darted around the building, where he saw a flashing light in the front of the old Buick. He thought that was odd. Megan had once told him that her father never went anywhere without his cell phone.

The iPhone screen lay face-up on the Buick's passenger seat, indicating five missed calls. Balbino pulled the passenger door, wanting to pick up the cell phone, but found it locked. Frustrated, he made a note to check on Megan first thing in the morning.

Shoot, why wait? He ended the call to Stuart's phone and started to type another text. *Hi Megs, what happened today? Why no movie? You guys go out without telling me? Beep me ASAP luv B.*

Megan's killer finished copying the girl's hard drive image. She was aboard a 50-foot motor yacht anchored four miles off Monterey, and was about to wipe the entire drive clean and toss the whole thing overboard when a familiar "You've Got Mail" icon popped up in the system tray. She almost ignored it, but she and her partner needed to ensure no last traces remained. And there was a final blip, someone signing with a B. Probably another girl, she thought as she scrolled through the names of Megan's contacts. Betsy, Belinda, Bibi, could be anyone.

The sender's email address was Bruizer6pac@gmail.com. Bruizer? B. Ruizer, or something like that? She looked through Megan's contact list and found three people with the last name of Ruiz. Their first names were Angela, Alejandro, and – there it was! B for Balbino. Further details showed his email matched the recent message.

She scribbled down the information she needed, and then wiped Megan's laptop clean. She switched the machine off, took it up on deck, and tossed it over the side. The reddish slab floated for a few seconds, then slowly sank into the blackness. For now her goal was simple: find out if there was anything about the Chicago trial on any of the Gray family's computers.

And if so, chase it down, clean it up, or destroy it. They were counting on her.

Her cell phone vibrated moments later. The words "Private Caller" appeared on the screen. She let the device ring a couple of times before answering. "Yes?"

"Progress report?"

"We took care of the Grays. There's nothing in Stuart's or Sally's files. It looks like they moved on. Don't know about the daughter yet, but I don't think there's anything to be concerned about." She tried to sound convincing. Bambino Balbino would keep for now. No need to bring his name up unless she had to.

"What about MacCallum?" the caller asked.

"That could be a problem. I thought his doctor was going to let it go, but it's a good thing I kept an eye on things. There's no way I could stop him sending a tissue sample for analysis."

"WHAT?"

"MacCallum's doctor sent a tissue sample."

"I heard that. When did this happen? Where did he send it? What were the results? And why the hell didn't you tell me about this?"

She sighed and held the phone away from her ear until the rant was over. "He sent it to a lab in London. His regular receptionist returned the next day. Right before you told us to handle the Grays."

"Then you'd better get on the next flight back to the UK and deal with that bloody sample. Find out what happened to it. You don't exactly have a lot of time. Oh, and one other thing," Don Strathmore ordered. "Go alone. I need Justin back here as soon as possible."

"He sent it to his ex-wife."

"Who did? What ex-wife?"

"MacCallum's doctor. He sent the sample to his ex in London." She gave Strathmore the woman's name.

"I don't care who she is. I don't give a toss if she's a bloody princess. Make sure that nothing about that sample reaches the light of day. Why the hell did you let that happen anyway?"

She shook her head and took a deep breath, imagining Strathmore's complexion reddening. "Don, there are times when you need to know that you can't control everything. Sometimes we have to do the best we can on the fly."

"Bloody hell! You're telling me you had no choice?"

"Not without drawing undue attention. We have to stay under the radar, right?"

Reluctantly, Demetek's CEO agreed. "All right. But you know what you have to do. The ex-wife and the doctor. Deal with them. Now." He hung up.

Back to London it is, then. Why was this all happening now, she wondered. Years go by without a blip, and then, like cicadas emerging from their seventeen-year larval cycle, the whole lot starts chirping at once. Nevertheless, Strathmore was right on one count. The last thing they wanted was any investigative DNA profiling on Ian MacCallum's tissue sample. It had to go away, whatever the cost.

BOOK 2
WIDOWER'S WALK

Chapter 12

"I IMAGINE YOU ARE wondering why I have asked you here, Marcus," Josef began.

That much was true. His best friends, a drag queen who wasn't, a gray-haired security chief whom he'd never met, and himself. Five people, all connected, but in a way he had yet to understand.

"Marcus," Dutch said softly, "Last night Joe told Bradford to make sure we brought you here as soon as we could. He's found some information that might help you."

Brad continued the story. "Joe's vital to our company's success, but there are a few salient facts I never told you. Let's just say that we've had to resort to different methods of funding in recent years." He looked at Josef. "How would you put it, Joe? Financing from one or two dozen wealthy companies that should remain nameless?"

Josef smiled wryly. "Your way with words has improved over the years, King. There was a time when you would have described what we do in a more vulgar manner."

"Blame my wife for changing me for the better if you must," Brad chuckled.

Josef continued. "First, let me tell you a little bit about George. He has been with me for many years now, as my right hand man. We have a wide variety of mutual interests." He smiled gently at Petrescu. "No, we are not gay partners, if that is what you are thinking. But George does live here with me. How much did he tell you on the way up from the city?"

"Some. I understand that he is your eyes and ears when you need them."

Earlier in the day, Brad had told him a little about Josef's uncanny ability to stay ahead of the technology curve. New medical advances and biotech

59

developments could often cause share price spikes. Knowing when these were imminent allowed Josef to reap amazing profits in a short time. When he was younger, he could blend in well but now he was too memorable a physical being to do so. It made sense that he would have trained someone.

George picked up the thread. "Josef discovered me on stage a few years ago in the city. I do have a talent for acting as well as fashion design, but never dreamed about putting it to use like I do know. We got talking, and things progressed from there."

"How?" Marcus wasn't accustomed to that kind of recruiting practice.

"I told him I was a scientist, that I just did the drag show in my spare time. He asked me what my qualifications were, and I told him."

"And they are what?"

"Master's degree in analytical biochemistry. It's really easy to get hired in this part of the world if you have just a master's. Much easier than if you have a Ph.D. or a B.S. Employers don't expect as much of you, there's less competition, and there's a real need for lab assistants and techies with a bit more practical experience."

"Companies also need cleaning staff," Josef added. "When I was doing research the hard way, I watched how people just carelessly left experimental details on their desks, threw scraps of paper in the trash, wrote on whiteboards in labs, things like that. There is much information one can pick up by wandering through research facilities at seven or eight in the evening, when everyone has gone home or to dinner – even the night owls have to eat some time. George works for XUSA in many capacities, but his greatest value is his janitorial work. He has worked for almost fifty companies in one shape or form over the last five years. He does his day job at one company, doing organic compound purification and analysis, and then he moonlights. He puts on makeup and dungarees, showing up to work with the cleaning crew at three or four different sites a night. He is usually home by midnight, with all sorts of useful information. This practice helps me anticipate fluctuations in share prices. You can imagine the benefits."

Marcus was intrigued, but at the same time shocked at Josef's wanton admission. "Can I ask how you obtain this inside stuff?"

George told him. "It's not hard. Lots of people don't log out of their computers, and it's incredibly easy to trawl through company servers to find confidential presentations. It doesn't take much to know when the results of clinical trials are due – and what kind of readouts they'll yield based on proprietary data. I feed the info to Josef, who buys, sells short, or does whatever he needs to reap the profits. Cha-ching!"

"That sounds corrupt, if not illegal. Certainly immoral. Does XUSA really operate this way all the time?"

"Let me explain something in clear terms, Marcus," Josef said. "Wall Street operates on two principles, greed and panic. Some investors do nothing but hoard their ill-gotten gains. Their methods are probably no more honest than ours. But there is a difference. Every dollar that we earn goes back into genuine research rather than into the bank. Look around you. All you see here – do you think this actually belongs to me personally?"

Marcus had wondered about that. "Don't tell me it's government property."

Josef shook his head. "It is not government property. It belongs to Larry Claypool, and therefore to the company."

Now it all makes a bit more sense. "Son of a gun. I should have guessed."

"LC has spent his life trying to make up for some of his father's evils. I will defer to King to enlighten you if he chooses to do so. XUSA's goals are actually quite simple. You need to become part of our team, even though you are not expert in all our methods."

This was genuinely mind-boggling. "So why am I here now?"

Dutch got up, went over to the recliner, and perched on the arm. She took Marcus's hand and gave it a squeeze. "Marcus, Joe thinks Kay's death may have been part of something much bigger. He needs you to dig deeper, not just for your own sake, but also for the company."

He pulled his hand away and got to his feet. "What are you talking about?"

"There was another strange death, over in Scotland of all places. A man named Ian MacCallum. He was retired, but he was also connected to Kay."

"What?" This was out of the blue.

"Come with me. Perhaps I can show you." Josef led Marcus out of the great room and down the hall. At the other end, his triple-sized home office contained no fewer than four high-powered PC's and Macs, each of which drove thirty-inch flatscreen monitors. In the corner stood a color all-in-one laser printer/fax/copier. There were no visible wires to trip over. The entire network was aesthetically concealed behind the wainscoting. A bank of solid teak filing cabinets was flanked on each side by ceiling-high bookshelves that held color-coded binders and assorted volumes. The top level was too high for a person to reach directly. Instead, a ladder on wheels stood in front of the shelf on the right.

They sat down in front of one of the Mac monitors. Josef called up a web page from a Glasgow newspaper, describing the recent tragedy that had taken the life of the old man. The biographical note read as follows:

"Prior to his retirement and subsequent move to the Western Highlands, where he enjoyed his remaining days in quiet seclusion, Professor Ian MacCallum was a noted geneticist whose career spanned over forty years of research into the

aging process. Former students have lauded his work as pioneering, evolutionary, and at the heart of understanding the life process itself. His experiments with mice helped establish the role of telomeres in the turnover of DNA, leading to one of the most highly cited articles ever to be published in the world-renowned journal Nature."

The obit went on to say he was survived by his wife of fifty years, Morag, and that their daughter, Moira, had predeceased him.

"What's the connection here?" Marcus asked after he had reread the article a couple of times.

"I do not know for certain. But I think it is something you should go and check out. I found something else." He pulled up another web page. "I had to resort to some slightly illicit methods to access this."

The page was from a doctor's death certificate. It had been scanned for future entry into a coroner's report not destined for public dissemination. The signature at the bottom belonged to one Alasdair Wylie. The cause of death was a gunshot wound to the head.

Suicide.

If there were any connection, it could best be described as tenuous. "What are you suggesting?"

"At this point I will not infer anything. Instead, I suggest you look at this list." Josef clicked on a link to a page of scholarly articles and bibliographic references. He scrolled down to one of them and highlighted it with the cursor.

"My God," Marcus said as he read the citation. "Either they knew each other, or they collaborated on this work." He took the mouse from Josef and control-clicked the hyperlink. A new window popped up, showing the citation in full, and an option to download the entire article.

"Go ahead. I have a subscription," Josef said, reading the younger man's mind.

Within seconds, the full article appeared on screen. He only needed to read the author list to confirm his suspicions. Among half a dozen others, the names of Ian MacCallum and Kay Rasmussen both appeared. They'd done their work at the same location a decade and a half earlier.

Marcus looked at the XUSA security chief. "What do you suppose this means, if anything?"

"That is what you need to find out. I know that you are in a lot of pain, and that you want answers. This may help you in some way. At this point I don't know if it will bring you closure."

"I don't see how it's going to help."

"There could be something more significant at stake. We need to find out what it is." Josef paused, not wishing to push too hard.

Marcus reflected on the past months, the increasing distance between him and Kay, her periodically depressive state, and then the unthinkable outcome that had sent him into his own spiral of misery. Now he had hints that her death had a historical significance. Was there a trigger of some kind, a push maybe? He had racked his brain for explanations, for any clue as to why his gentle, loving wife had become so tormented. And now this new information had surfaced. A former colleague, a collaborator, had taken his own life violently.

Were there others too? "I don't understand. Not yet, anyway."

"Nor do any of us. But the article might give you some insights. It is a place to start. Besides, you knew your wife better than anyone."

Did I? "I still don't know what you want me to do."

Josef turned his chair around and faced Marcus. "Bringing you here today was not an idle exercise, Dr. Black. This is your job."

"You mean…?"

"Exactly. The company needs you to take a step up to the next level. Now is the right time for you to join our Special Projects team."

Marcus looked into the German's probing, forceful eyes. This wasn't how he'd planned his career at all. He was a scientist, for heaven's sake, not a spy. Nevertheless, he recalled his own determination not to rest until he discovered what had happened to Kay and why. This was his chance.

"You are in search of answers. We also want them. This is your assignment." Josef handed over an envelope. He waited until Marcus had examined the contents. "I would like you to stay here tonight as my guest, where I will be able to brief you further and supply you with any other information that we can retrieve over the next twelve hours. Tomorrow, George will drive you to your house so you can retrieve your passport and any other items you will need, such as your laptop. You will need some warmer clothes. It is still quite chilly in the northern parts of Scotland."

Scotland. Where Ian MacCallum killed himself.

Josef continued. "You should meet with Professor MacCallum's personal physician. I have done some preliminary searching on Dr. Alasdair Wylie. He is a native of Aberdeen. He moved his medical practice to the west coast, following a divorce from his microbiologist wife. I suspect you will be in good company."

"How do you mean?"

"You have both suffered a personal loss. Of course there is no real comparison between your individual situations, and I would not begin to draw parallels. However, Wylie will no doubt be sympathetic. You will want to speak with Professor MacCallum's widow. Wylie can introduce you."

"I guess you're throwing me in the deep end."

Josef frowned. "I would prefer not to put it that way."

"Don't worry. I'm being facetious. This is something I need to do. I just meant that I didn't expect to begin half way around the world."

"We often find ourselves looking in the unlikeliest places. That is why we are successful." He stood and beckoned Marcus to rejoin the group.

They returned to the great room. George was finishing off the last drops of zinfandel. Brad and Dutch were standing at the window looking at an especially opulent motor yacht cruising out of one of the island's far western properties.

"How would you like to live on that one, sweetheart?" Brad asked.

"Hmm," Dutch said. "What kind of crew would we need?"

"That vessel would cost your next twenty years' salary and bonus, King," Josef laughed. "Assuming you could afford a place to keep it."

"LC managed it," Brad commented. "Some bastards get all the luck."

"You will just have to be content with a steady, risk-free job," XUSA's Vice President of Security said pithily.

Dutch gave him a sideways, almost threatening glare. George cocked an eyebrow. Marcus felt sweat beginning to run down the back of his neck.

Josef added, "Remember, we are here for a reason. I will not use that old cliché about a higher purpose, for that would sound hollow and insincere. We are here to ensure that the proceeds from unpublicized developments in biotechnology and medicine are – dare I say – appropriately and safely distributed?"

With that, he marched to the wet bar, uncorked a fresh bottle of wine, and walked around, topping off everyone's glass. "George, if you were dressed in the same way as you had been a few hours ago, I would have proposed that the ladies and gentlemen in the room raise their glasses in a toast. For now, it will have to be 'Madam, Gentlemen, please join me in welcoming Dr. Marcus Black to XUSA's security division.'"

Chapter 13

MATT GILSTRAP'S DAY WAS getting worse. Despite his earlier breakthrough, the new protein on his screen just didn't fit the expected pattern. Every time he tried to arrange the picture into a recognizable series of shapes, something would flip or bend in a way that rendered the entire structure meaningless. He'd had the same problem ever since they introduced Hernandez's newest mutation. The expressed protein had done all that it should, physiologically, but despite Matt's skills and equipment the new batch wouldn't yield a three-dimensional picture that meant anything.

Justin Hernandez had told him that solving the structure was crucial to the project's success. "We need to understand how the redox process works and how to maximize its efficiency. Your job is to understand why, at the molecular level. The expression team will need your information so they can fine-tune the engineered protein. If we don't tweak it in the right direction, the entire project is a write off. Not to mention the billions of dollars that were invested."

Billions of dollars. Not millions. Billions. That was how important Matt's methods were. Who had that kind of money, he wondered? Drug companies were the usual suspects, of course, but this wasn't about developing a drug. At least it didn't appear that way. This was something bigger, something with military implications perhaps. Maybe the government or certain defense contractors could pony up the bucks. Alternatively, perhaps there was a private source of cash. Either way, he could not fathom what any official organization would want with this protein.

He was so immersed in thought that he almost failed to notice the tap on his shoulder. "Come with me," Steve Goudreau ordered. "You need to see this."

"What the…"

"My office. You might want to save your work first."

Matt obliged. He turned off the monitor and followed Steve down a long hallway. He saw laboratories on both sides of the corridor. Inside, gene sequencers, high performance liquid chromatography-based protein purification columns, and mass spectrometers hummed. Robotic arms nudged back and forth, lifting ninety-six well plates from one station to another. Tiny pipets dipped into the wells rhythmically, transferring samples into more plates. In turn, these traveled on conveyors to analysis stations and more robots. The sheer number of machines doing all this work never failed to stagger the imagination. Surprisingly, only two technicians manned them. They wore white protective overalls, slip-on shoe covers, and opaque blue latex caps.

"Where does all the juice come from to run this stuff?" Matt asked as they approached the secure door at the end of the hall.

"Most of it is solar. That's one very good reason why the entire facility was built out here. The Outback has abundant sunshine. The Australian government has been pushing solar power for years, even offering households discounts on private panel construction for their homes. It makes a lot of sense. We might as well take advantage of the drought that many states are suffering. And when a company like ours is trying to prevent the effects of global warming, the least we can do is harness the heat."

They arrived at the end. Steve swiped his security card through the slider and punched in his code. An audible click and hiss followed, permitting them to open up. On the other side, a second identical door appeared. They waited for the first door to close completely before going through the same routine on the second door.

The air lock was essential in maintaining the clean environment between labs, and was present between the corridor and labs as well. However, in the inner work area, the space between doors was large enough to accommodate sanitized personal protective clothing as well. Each Demetek employee, all the way up the ladder to Don Strathmore himself, had to follow strict safety and hygiene protocols.

They passed through the second door into the executive office area. At the far end sat two large corner offices, their faux-mahogany furniture arranged like mirror images of one another. Nameplates on their doors said "J. Hernandez" and "E. Goudreau" respectively. The door to Justin's office was ajar but he was not sitting at his chair. The Canadian's office door remained closed

"Where is everyone, Steve?" Gilstrap inquired.

Goudreau looked at his watch. "Ah, yes. That's about right. One thing we North Americans never get used to is this curious Australian habit of taking a morning tea break around this time every day. Regular as clockwork, they all knock off for a while. Everything stops. Must be a throwback to colonial tradition." He opened his office and motioned for Matt to sit down at a round conference table. At the other end of the office stood a huge L-shaped desk. On it stood two widescreen monitors at right angles to each other. Nothing registered on either screen, but as soon as Steve opened a drawer just to the right of his keyboard, inadvertently nudging the mouse, one sprang to life.

He pulled out a sealed envelope and went back to the small round table, sitting opposite his junior employee. "Matt, we've only got a few minutes during the tea break, but I wanted to thank you for all your efforts over the last few months. I didn't want to do this in public."

Matt immediately felt his heart rate quicken. A bead of sweat formed at the back of his neck. "You're welcome. But – was there something in particular?"

Across the room, the monitor showed a jungle scene, ripe with lush vegetation, fruits hanging off trees, rays of sunshine lighting up the verdant leaves of the undergrowth. With his back to the display, Steve said, "Your contract is finished as of today. I'd like to present you with this as a bonus payment for all your hard work." He handed over an envelope. "Go ahead. Open it."

Matt took the envelope and put it down on the desk. "What about the stuff I was working on? I'm still trying to solve the structure. I thought I at least had another week to figure it out."

Goodreau gave him a rueful smile. "Matt, we're both in the same field. Determining the molecular structure of proteins is as much an art form as a hard science. It's like a Sudoku puzzle. Sometimes what you don't see is just as important."

"That's hardly satisfying! And crystallography isn't exactly Sudoku. I just couldn't figure out why that mutation didn't follow the usual pattern."

"That fact alone is more significant than you could imagine, Matt. Nearly all the others have given us no change in protein activity. But this one – well, let's just say that the 3D structure isn't as vital to know. It does what we want it to do, and that's the point."

Matt's scientific curiosity was getting the better of him, but he let it drop for the moment. "So you don't need me any more, is that what you're saying?"

"This is a tough industry. You knew that coming in. If you wanted job security, you could have gone to work for the government, or academia. This is biotech, where on average, people stay for two or three years at most per company. The days where you worked for one organization your whole life are gone. That's just the way it is. If you don't like roller coaster rides, you shouldn't jump on."

"So I'm fired. Just like that, huh?" Matt looked at the envelope sitting on the table. "What is this? Two week's vacation pay and a month's salary in lieu of notice?" He didn't wait for Goudreau to answer. "Look, I've worked my ass off for you guys, sixteen hour days, weekends, you name it. No vacation at all. Not even a sick day taken. Couldn't you at least have given me some kind of warning? Like 'Hey, Matt, you know that your contract is coming to an end soon, so we wanted you to know that in a month's time you're going to have to look for a new position because we can't renew you. We'll do whatever we can to help in the meantime.' But no, you don't have the decency to give me a heads-up. I can't believe YOU'D want to be treated this way!"

"Are you finished?" Goudreau asked, his eyebrows raised.

"Apparently," Matt replied, sardonically.

"Then open the envelope and look inside. Don't be so judgmental. It's about security. All it takes is one disgruntled ex-employee to go onto company servers and trash or steal files, and the work of dozens of innocent, well-meaning people is totally ruined. You can't blame Demetek."

"So we're all tarred with the same brush, right? You worry about one guy going e-postal and the rest of us are forever stamped with a letter on our foreheads? You hired us in the first place. Haven't you figured out yet that the way you treat your employees reflects on the company as a whole? If you don't trust your people then it shows you can't be trusted yourself. It's called mirroring."

"You dating a pop shrink or something? Or did you just read that on the Internet?"

"No on both counts." *But I did take a course once.* Matt felt deflated. He turned the envelope over a couple of times.

"Go on, open it," Goudreau implored.

The familiar sigh, this time genuine, escaped the young man's lungs. He slid a thumb under the flap and popped the poorly glued thing open. He pulled out a letter and two pieces of paper that were folded in half. One of them had a perforation.

The letter read, *"Dear Matt, Thank you very much for your contributions to Demetek over the past year. Unfortunately, due to legal constraints, we are not able to continue funding your project. We wish you all the best in your future endeavours. Kind regards, Don Strathmore."* The signature was barely discernable.

"That's all, huh?" Matt tossed the letter aside. He picked up one of the other bits of paper and unfolded it. It was an open-dated e-ticket, first class, around the world, in whatever direction he wanted.

"A little parting gift. We don't know where you're going to wind up but at least you'll be able to get there in relative comfort."

Behind Steve, a strange sound came from the monitor. Both men looked up. A howler monkey bellowed sonorously and hurled what appeared to be an apple somewhere off the screen.

"Cute screen saver," Matt commented.

"Sorry about that," Steve said. He quickly rose and went behind the desk. He reached for a dial on the side of the screen, but not before a familiar simian chuckle sounded. An almost imperceptible look of alarm crossed the senior scientist's face as he turned the volume down. He quickly pressed the on/off button on the bottom right hand corner of the monitor. He returned to the round table to find Matt staring at the now blank screen.

"A chimp in the same jungle as a howler monkey? Whoever designed that one mixed up his continents. But it did look incredibly real. Can I get a copy of that somewhere?"

"If you give me your home email address, I'll forward you the link," Steve said. His own heart was now beating rapidly. "Did you check the other item?" he added, pointing to the perforated paper still lying on the table.

The young scientist unfolded it. His eyes opened wide, and his jaw dropped as he looked at the figure on the check. "What on earth – I mean, I only had a few weeks' holiday pay and my salary, well, I – I don't – understand," he stammered.

"Like I said, Matt, we're very grateful for all your efforts. Perhaps now you'll look on me a little more kindly?" Etienne Goudreau wiped a clammy right hand on his trousers, then offered to shake hands. "Can I trust you to do that?"

Matt couldn't even begin to grasp the numbers, but he shook regardless. "Steve, I'm sorry for what I said. And yes. Thank you. This helps. Big time." He looked at the check again. *Half a million dollars.*

"In case you're wondering, this is tax-adjusted. The actual number is closer to eight, so this is all yours to keep. Now, if you'll come with me, I'll escort you from the building. I'll have your personal belongings shipped to you directly. Send me your contact details when you can. You won't need to return to your office."

"Pay me this much, and I'll do anything you ask," Matt said, almost inaudibly.

Demetek's Senior Vice President of Research stopped just before he reached the door. "Matt, I may need your help, but it needs to remain between us. Would you be on board with that? I'm just talking you and me. If we could stay in touch by mobile phone and private email, I'd be really grateful. Just keep anyone else at Demetek out of it."

The young scientist looked at his boss, assessing the grave expression on his face. The check, the ticket, everything Steve had said – was it part of a bribe, a payoff? How much did the other senior managers know about this? He had to know more. "What do you mean?"

"I can't explain right now." Steve Goudreau pulled a card out of his wallet and wrote a series of letters and numbers on it. "Keep this in a safe place or burn it once you've committed it to memory. I'll be in touch if I need to." He handed the card over.

Three hours later, Dr. Matthew Gilstrap was in a private limousine headed for the Alice Springs airport. His bags were packed.

Chapter 14

MARCUS'S FLIGHT TOUCHED DOWN at London's Heathrow airport shortly after six-thirty a.m. It took over an hour to clear customs, in large part due to three other flights arriving from the United States within ten minutes of his own, plus others from Dubai, Delhi, and Johannesburg. Each of them spewed four hundred passengers into the immigration concourses. Like fifteen hundred others, Marcus was unable to take advantage of the EU passport fast track line. The Oxford-accented immigration officer wanted to know how long and where he planned to stay, and whether his visit was business or pleasure. He told a few half-truths, all of which satisfied the busy young official. His reward was a welcome stamp on his passport.

In all honesty, Marcus couldn't predict how long his journey would be. His next move was an internal airport transfer and a flight to Inverness two hours later, and from there, it was anyone's guess. He made the long walk between terminals in relatively short time, obtained his next boarding pass, and once he was through security, he finally felt able to relax. He pulled out his laptop and started to sign up for a wireless hotspot, but half way through the process began feeling drowsy. Despite lying down during the transatlantic flight, sleep had eluded him; a jumble of thoughts, questions, and above all the underlying misery of his personal loss kept him awake. He hadn't fared much better the night before, even in the comfort of Josef's Belvedere mansion. With only two hours of sleep out of thirty-six, plus eight hours of jetlag, exhaustion was overtaking him.

He got up and started to pace around the terminal, forcing himself to stay alert, stopping at a coffee kiosk for a large dose of caffeine. An hour later, he made his way down the long concourse towards the Inverness-bound British Airways 757. His seat assignment was next to a window at the rear of the aircraft, but as soon as he fastened his belt, the line of irritated passengers bashing their way down the aisle faded into oblivion. Miraculously, he didn't wake up until ten minutes before the plane began its descent into Inverness.

The northern Scottish airport was a simple but refreshing change from the teeming hubs of San Francisco and Heathrow. Within five minutes of disembarking, he was on board a rental car shuttle. He had been to the UK a few times before and was used to driving on the other side of the road, but he kept flipping the windshield wipers on and off whenever he tried to signal a turn. Becoming accustomed to a stick shift again took a bit more work, but once he was in the hills of the Western Highlands he stopped worrying about embarrassing himself. He was grateful that the traffic was as sparse as he'd ever seen.

Two hours later, Marcus entered the outskirts of the Kyle of Lochalsh. He pulled over and consulted his notes, discovering Dr. Alasdair Wylie's local surgery was within five minutes of the main road. It was early afternoon, and he imagined the doctor was either finishing lunch or preparing for the day's second shift. When he entered the surgery, however, it was almost empty. Seated in a booth behind an open hatch was a ruddy-cheeked, slim-waisted young woman whose unbuttoned top revealed far more cleavage than her job required. She greeted him with a smile, asking him in a thick Highland accent if she could help him.

"My name is Dr. Black." He felt a bit self-conscious introducing himself that way but this time he sensed it might allow him to get his foot in the door more easily if the receptionist thought he were one of her boss's colleagues.

"Did you have an appointment?" the girl asked, checking a logbook.

"For one forty-five on the 28th. I believe I might have spoken to you about it on the phone a couple of weeks ago?" he bluffed.

The receptionist looked puzzled. "I'm sorry, what was the name again?"

"Black. Dr. Marcus Black."

She shuffled through the pages some more, frowning. "I beg your pardon, but there's no entry in Doctor's appointment book for you today. Are you sure you have the right time and day?"

Time to ramp it up a bit, he thought. "Miss, I've traveled all the way from the States to see Dr. Wylie. I'm not going to make that kind of mistake." He raised his eyebrows in a way he hoped was minimally condescending.

The receptionist stopped thumbing through the diary and looked at the wall clock. "Well, Doctor's not busy right now, so I'll see if he has a few moments to talk to you. Might I tell him what you wish to see him about?"

"I'd prefer to discuss that with Dr. Wylie. It's a confidential matter."

She disappeared out of the back of the booth. Marcus couldn't help notice her bare legs, long and shapely under a short skirt. Odd garb in the cold Western Highlands, but Wylie *was* single. Maybe he was young and good-looking as well.

Seconds later, the physician entered the waiting room from the back door, extending his hand.

Wylie was in his early thirties, maybe five-nine, one-fifty, not handsome, but not unattractive either. He looked tired, his pale complexion not helped by gray skies and the chilly climate. He wore a white coat over ill-fitting clothes. A stethoscope dangled around his neck. "Dr. Black, is it? From America? I don't remember Claire mentioning you were arriving today. What can I do for you?"

"Perhaps we could go inside your office and discuss it, Dr. Wylie. It's a matter of some seriousness." He felt pompous putting it that way,

Al paused for a moment, but then shepherded Marcus into his office. "Why not? I don't have any more patients today."

Marcus sat down behind the cluttered, well-worn oak desk. He didn't see any family pictures, and concluded that receptionist Claire was indeed on the make. "Lovely girl, Claire."

"Aye," Al replied neutrally. "She's only just back today, so if you called before then you probably spoke to Sarah, who was here while Claire was on vacation. Perhaps that's perhaps why she couldn't find your appointment."

"I came here to talk to you about Ian MacCallum," Marcus said, cutting off the small talk.

Al looked up, surprised. Why would this American suddenly appear with questions about his late patient? "I-I-I'm sorry, I'm not allowed to discuss my patients with...."

"I'm here because you know something about MacCallum's death. You signed his death certificate."

Al's expression chilled as he regained some of his professional composure. "That's a matter of public record, but I'm not in any position to elaborate. Professor MacCallum's death is a matter for the family." As he spoke, he looked down at his notes, and began to fidget with other pieces of paper on his desk.

"Is something bothering you, Dr. Wylie?"

Al clenched his teeth and stared at his visitor. He was wondering what results Jenny might deliver on the tissue sample. Now, this guy had shown up out of the blue, wanting to know more details. "Why are you here, Dr. Black?"

How do I put this, he wondered. *How on earth do I even say it out loud?* Marcus stood up and walked around, finding it difficult to face the Scottish physician. At last he spoke softly, and it was the truth, as far as he knew, that helped him decide. "My wife killed herself."

Al stopped fiddling with papers on his desk. "I'm sorry. Very sorry, Doctor. But I don't know how I can help you."

"She was a geneticist. I believe Ian MacCallum was an academic in the same field prior to his retirement."

"With all due respect, I don't see why there should be any…."

"They worked together. A long time ago."

"What?" This time Marcus had Al's attention.

"I can't honestly say if this is more than coincidence," Marcus said. "But if you could tell me anything about MacCallum's health before he died I would appreciate it. Nothing personal, just general stuff, the kind of information that wouldn't violate doctor-patient confidentiality."

Al pondered Marcus's request for a moment. "All right. I can tell you that Ian's health was declining over the last few months. I was treating him for a condition unrelated to his death."

"Are you sure it was unrelated?"

"Oh, quite. But I shouldn't really discuss that further."

Tiredness was causing Marcus to become a little short-tempered, but he chose not to show it. Instead, he appealed to the doctor's conscience. "I understand. But I'm trying to find out what happened to my wife. Do you know what it feels like to lose someone so close to you that you barely care about living yourself?"

Al considered for a moment. While his breakup with Jennifer had been a crushing loss, at least it had no finality. In his case, there remained a flicker of hope that one day she would see the light, understand why he was drawn to the barren, harsh, yet somehow tranquil Highlands rather than the bustle of the city. He'd hoped Jenny would forget her Kentish roots and want to tough it out with him up North, but to no avail. "All right. Look, I'll tell you what I know. But not here, not in my surgery."

"That's fine. Anywhere you choose."

"Come with me. My house is next door." He stood up and opened the office door. He told Claire, "You can take the rest of the day off if you like. Dr. Black and I have a private consultation that will take some time." He led his visitor outside, closed the front door to his surgery and walked briskly down the path.

Marcus followed Al into his house. Two Constable prints adorned the living room. A picture on the mantelpiece showed an attractive redhead standing next to Wylie on a rocky shore. Both wore hiking gear and looked tanned and fit. "Is that your ex?"

"Aye. Jenny and I had different ideas of what we wanted to do with our lives, or at least where we wanted to do it." He stepped into the kitchen and returned moments later with a couple of cans of Younger's. "Care for a beer?" he offered, handing one to his visitor.

"Thanks," Marcus said, popping the top and taking a swig. He then came straight to the point. "Tell me what you can about MacCallum, Al. Please."

Dr. Alasdair Wylie described what he saw on the day the old academic ended his life, and how his widow Morag had begged him to find out what had happened. He mentioned that he'd isolated a small amount of the man's brain tissue and shipped it on dry ice to Jennifer for analysis. He hoped she would be willing to keep the results under wraps for the time being. "I'm planning to travel to London tonight so I can meet up with Jenny tomorrow."

"Mind if I tag along?" Marcus asked.

"You might as well. I take it you weren't planning to stay here for long."

"Actually, I was hoping to meet with Mrs. MacCallum. Any chance of an introduction?"

"I'll drive you there myself." Wylie started to sip his beer, then thought better of it. "Come on."

Chapter 15

Morag MacCallum opened the door to her visitors thirty minutes later. The sun was beginning to poke through an ominous bank of cumulus clouds hovering over the island, sending celestial rays onto the MacCallum property. It was almost four, but the sun was still quite high. At Skye's latitude, it would remain in the sky until almost ten. The old woman looked very tired and beaten, but lit up when she saw Al. She drew him into her arms. "Doctor, it's good to see you. Come in, come in."

He gave her an affectionate peck on the cheek. "Hello, Mrs. Mac. How have you been doing?"

Morag shook her head, her jaw set. "Nae so good, laddie. I've not been able to sleep very well since Ian – well, you know." She led the two men inside. A fire roared in the living room hearth. A mug of steaming tea sat on a rustic coffee table, next to a plate of oatcakes. "I'll get you some piece," she said, shuffling off towards the kitchen.

"Piece?" Marcus mouthed.

"It means the same as afternoon tea or morning tea. Around here, tea means the same as dinner. We call it 'high tea.' Jenny couldn't get used to that either."

Regional definitions of meals and snacks were hard to follow, but when "afternoon piece" returned in the shape of a tray equipped with teapot, more mugs, milk, sugar, and shortbread, Marcus figured he would remember at least one local term.

Marcus gently broached the subject of Kay's death. Morag's hand went to her mouth, stifling a cry. "You poor man, Dr. Black! And so young, too! Was she depressed about anything?"

"I don't know, Mrs. MacCallum. She said she'd had headaches and nightmares twenty, twenty-five years ago. Then, one day, they went away.

She mentioned something about an experimental treatment, but I don't know anything about that, not yet anyway. The reason I came to see you was because Kay must have known Ian. They were co-authors on a publication in the early nineties."

Morag bowed her head. Her hand shook as she placed her cup on the table. "You'd both better come with me," she said, slowly rising.

The two men looked at each other and then went to help the old woman to her feet.

"It's all right, lads, I may not be young but I'm quite hardy," Morag said, declining assistance. "You don't live or work in this part of the world without getting quite fit. Follow me." She led them up a flight of rustic wooden stairs. Marcus had to duck under the low beams. Upstairs, Morag led them past assorted landscape photographs. They were all mounted and aligned precisely. One of the larger ones showed a vast expanse of farmland, rows of corn waving in the breeze. A water tank added perspective to the shot.

"Somewhere in the American heartland?" Marcus pointed at the photo.

"Aye. Is that where you're from?"

"Ohio. I'm guessing that's Nebraska? Eastern Colorado maybe?"

"Very good, Dr. Black!"

"Marcus, please."

"I'm told that not many foreigners appreciate how flat Colorado can be. That shot was just outside Sterling. We took a month off to drive across the country in a Winnebago. Ian was an avid photographer and hated just flying from place to place. To him the journey was as much fun as the destination."

"Did Ian take this photo when you were living in the US?"

"Aye, that's why I brought you up here." She opened a stiff-hinged door, the creak lending a Gothic feel to the atmosphere. They entered to find Ian's archives, shelves filled with journals, albums, and books. The walls bore more nature photographs, taken in monochrome, sepia, and color. Subjects covered every imaginable range of climate and terrain, latitudes from equatorial to polar, and animals at work, rest, and play.

Ian MacCallum's desk was a dusty oaken antique whose edges had seen better days, but its surface still wore a fine sheen. A single drawer on each side was deep enough to hold full-sized manila folders and hanging files. An empty double-layered letter tray, lined with green felt, sat on the desktop. Opposite the door, a small picture window looked out on Portree Harbour, over which the dark clouds were spreading. Framed diplomas of Ian's bachelor's and doctoral degrees, both granted from London's Imperial College, hung on either side of the window. Marcus read them carefully. "He was on the faculty at Imperial, wasn't he?"

Morag opened the left hand drawer. "Aye. He started out as a lecturer and made it all the way through the ranks. Our system here is a bit different to yours in the States." She fished around in the back of the drawer. "Here, this is what I wanted you to see."

Marcus opened the folder to reveal a letter. Dated almost sixteen years earlier, it was from an Illinois address. The writer welcomed Ian to the Henry and Linda Castleford Institute, and hoped he and his family would find the experience rewarding during the next several months. "I'm not sure I understand."

"When Ian was in his late fifties, he took a long service sabbatical," his widow explained. "We had the chance to take six months away from London. Don't most of the larger universities in the States have policies like this?"

"For senior faculty members, that's true."

Morag nodded. "Well, I'd always felt comfortable in Europe, but Ian persuaded me that going to America would be the experience of a lifetime. Ian always traveled there to conferences alone, because I didn't want to go with him." She laughed. "Once we arrived I realized what a silly girl I'd been! It was a wonderful choice and I still kick myself from time to time thinking about all the chances I'd missed. Better late than never, though. We took the journey in March, arrived in a late winter snowstorm, and in two days' time found ourselves in eighty degree sunshine! All in the same city."

"And after Ian's sabbatical you set off in a Winnebago?"

"That's right. We must have driven ten thousand miles in a fortnight. At least it felt that way. But it was the best two weeks' holiday we ever had."

"I've not heard of the Henry and Linda Castleford Institute. Is that a private university?" Al asked, looking at the letter over Marcus's shoulder.

"Technically no, Doctor," Morag said. "It was a research foundation, funded by a couple of philanthropic bankers. They made their money in the savings and loan industry. I don't know if the Castleford Institute exists any more, though. I suspect not."

"What kind of research did they do there?" Marcus asked.

"Chromosomal abnormalities. It's one reason Ian was excited about working there. Did you know that Ian carried a genetic defect himself? Our daughter Moira died young. She was a Downs child."

Marcus felt his heart thumping. *Another parallel.* "Mrs. MacCallum, did the Castleford Institute ever sponsor any clinical trials that you know of?"

"Oh, aye. There were several. Mostly for orphan indications. They were a little easier to conduct. Isn't that right, Doctor?"

"Aye. The regulatory requirements for orphan diseases are still stringent, but drug trials can sometimes be fast-tracked through the approval process."

Experimental drug trials. "Did Ian do any research into these diseases?"

"Not directly. His research was mostly concerned with cellular biology than animal or human work. But he did volunteer for one procedure. They paid him very well for it, he felt he couldn't refuse the money. I didn't have the chance to talk him out of it, much to my regret, because the silly man came home one day having received the first of three shots already."

So that was it. At last, the pattern was beginning to emerge. Was the groundwork laid all these years ago? Or were there other factors? Who else knew about it? "Tell me, did Ian ever mention the names of anyone else who took part in the trial?"

Morag considered the question for several seconds before shaking her head. "No, he never mentioned anyone, not to me. But there's one other place we might be able to look," she added, opening the other desk drawer. She fished behind half a dozen hanging files and pulled a strip of masking tape from the underside of the desk. Attached to it was a key. "Ian kept his valuables in a safe. When he died, I went through it but I didn't find anything that struck a chord. Until now."

She closed the drawer and went to the door. "Are you coming?"

Both men's eyes opened wide. "Where are we going?"

"The barn," Morag told them. She headed downstairs. The office door creaked creepily behind them as it eased shut. She stopped to don a pair of gumboots at the front door. "I'm sorry, I don't have any spares. It'll be a bit messy in there."

The mess wasn't as bad as predicted, but the horsey smell within was pungent enough. Morag led them to an old wooden cupboard at the back of the barn. A padlocked latch held the doors closed. She used the key to open the padlock. Inside the cupboard was a small fireproof box secured with a combination lock. She twiddled the dial a few times, then popped it open to reveal some personal documents, all sealed in a Ziplock freezer baggie. She pulled out a passport, Ian's birth certificate, a signed letter from 1966 World Cup hero Bobby Moore, and a notebook that looked like it belonged in a child's school classroom.

She ignored the letter and ID documents, and flipped through the notebook. Random notes and diagrams gave no hint as to meaning. She stopped ten pages from the back and laid the book flat. The page on the left contained some numbers without any discernable pattern. On the right, a single line divided the page into two columns. In the left column was a series of two and three letter acronyms. On the right were checkmarks and crosses.

No, not acronyms. Initials, Marcus concluded. The letters IM, RS, KR, HL, JDG, SMZ, CJB, VD, JH, SIJ, ERS, and SPG were aligned in the first column. The first six had checkmarks in the right column. The others had crosses. Ian MacCallum. RS, whoever that was. Then Kay's initials. Nine others. *Who were they?*

Marcus dropped the book on the floor. He gently took the old woman by the shoulders. "Who were they, Morag? Who were the others?"

A stern, determined look appeared on Mrs. MacCallum's face, her jaw setting. "I don't know, I really don't. But there's one thing Ian did say before he died that I'll never forget, because he told me not to. He said that there were only three left."

Marcus implored her to tell him more. "Which three? Three of these people? Three others who know? What did he mean? Who are they?"

"I'm sorry, Marcus. I can't say. I would if I could. All I can give you is this." She leaned forward and picked up the notebook. "Perhaps you can make some sense of it. If you do, will you tell me?"

He looked back and forth between Al and Morag. Both of them were looking to him for guidance, a role he was not used to. "Yes. I will. I promise." He took the notebook and walked out of the barn.

Chapter 16

MEGAN GRAY'S KILLER SAW the jogger approaching from the north, running around the uvula-shaped loop of land known as the Isle of Dogs. The boardwalk was popular for those seeking early evening exercise. Blocks of apartments with direct views of the River Thames adorned the perimeter, a quiet neighborhood within a short distance of the Docklands and Canary Wharf. The district was home to the tallest buildings in the city, the instantly recognizable pyramid of One Canada Square visible in the distance. She sensed that could be a problem, so she waited until the jogger approached before breaking into a slow run herself. Twenty seconds later, their paths crossed. The jogger continued on the wide river pathway. The killer maintained a steady rhythm as she kept a distance of ten or so paces.

They went clockwise around the western part of the peninsula, until the jogger reached a park between Westferry Road and the Thames. The jogger then ducked through a railing on the eastern edge of the park. Quickening her pace, the killer ran past a bus stop and saw her prey veer onto a path flanked by a hedge to the right, and an open grassy area to the left. The hedge gave her the cover she needed. She accelerated to catch up, slowing down to match stride as soon as she was alongside.

The jogger's peripheral vision revealed an attractive woman with shoulder-length, dark blonde hair. Her toned torso and legs were sheathed in a spandex one-piece suit. She smiled before uttering a greeting in a lilting brogue. "It's Jenny, isn't it?"

Jennifer Barratt slowed slightly. "Yes."

"My name is Sarah. I work with your husband."

"I'm not married."

"Excuse me, I meant your former husband."

Jennifer Barratt stopped. "Alasdair."

"That's right. From the Kyle. He asked me to send a package to you."

"You know about that?"

"Of course. We have no secrets." Sarah put on the most sincere expression she could. "Did he not tell you I was coming for the results today?"

"I'm sorry, he didn't mention anything about that. Or you," Jennifer said warily.

Sarah reached out and grasped Jennifer's right hand, wrenching it behind her back. "I don't have time to mess around, Dr. Barratt. What did you learn?"

Jennifer grimaced and protested. "Let me go!"

"Just as soon as you tell me about the tissue analysis. Then you can be on your way." Her grip tightened as she forced Jennifer's hand upwards.

"Ouch! Let go of me!"

"The analysis. Now!"

"What analysis?"

"Staining, microscopy. Anything like that."

"There wasn't anything unusual in histo!"

"What about genomics?"

"What do you mean?"

"The DNA scan."

"I didn't run those tests," Jennifer lied.

"Who else handled the sample? Did you send it to any other lab?"

"No! I ran the tests myself. Alasdair asked me to keep it quiet."

As soon as she spoke, she realized her mistake. This strange, violent woman needed nothing else from her. Sarah's hand flashed out. Something shiny extended from her fingers. Jennifer felt the slightest pinch of pain in the small of her back, followed a moment later by a brief giddiness. She yelled out in protest as Sarah sprinted off.

A couple of minutes later Jennifer felt increasingly weak. She wondered whether to sit down or to push on back to her apartment. She chose the latter for the time being, but she found running was impossible. Walking fast caused the dizziness to return, so her pace slowed even more. When she reached the southernmost point of the peninsula, less than a hundred yards from her home, she sensed she might not make it. She felt for the phone in her fanny pack, and fished it out. Perhaps there was some small hope remaining, if she hurried.

Please! Ten more seconds, she begged, fumbling with the keys, trying to type in the numbers. She just finished entering the last letter and tried to press the send key but missed. Her vision was worsening by the second. She pressed hard on one of the buttons, imploring it to be the right one, and put the phone back into her fanny pack.

Thirty more seconds to home. I can make it, she told herself, staggering along the path. The river, the sky, the roads, the trees, the buildings, everything was spinning about her. She crumpled awkwardly onto the path as the quick acting poison won its victory. Moments later, her heart stopped.

Thanks to a call from a Good Samaritan walking his dog along the boardwalk, Metropolitan Police Detective Constable Rajesh Kolluri and his "guv'nor," Detective Inspector Lucy Holcombe, were on the scene within half an hour. The dog's owner had found his pet sniffing at a prone figure, collapsed in a motionless heap. The emergency dispatcher sent uniformed relief and paramedics to the scene, but in this case the plainclothes officers were in the vicinity already.

The paramedics confirmed the victim was deceased. DI Holcombe didn't bother waiting for the CSU tech to arrive to examine the jogger's fanny pack. She found an MP3 player, a mobile phone, and photo ID. The Samaritan couldn't help further as he had not seen Jennifer fall. DC Kolluri canvassed the neighborhood with a couple of uniformed constables. They asked to see CCTV circuits belonging to local merchants and businesses. None apparently had recorded the event. The tapes would be reviewed further, but no additional visual record was likely to surface.

Until Jennifer's family could be informed, all the Met could do was wait. While an ambulance took her body away to the morgue, Kolluri updated Lucy on what he had, or rather hadn't, discovered. "Nobody saw anything, guv. Is it possible she just had a bad heart?"

"Raj, anything's possible at this point but I'd prefer we didn't make any assumptions one way or another. We'll just have to wait for the post-mortem. In the meantime, take Kelly and contact the family."

The jogger's mobile phone listed someone with the name "Mum" in the directory. Raj called the station and obtained the associated address. He drove off with Kelly Shaw, a recently trained family liaison officer, leaving Lucy to wrap things up with the remaining police crew. One of them asked the senior detective casually, "So who was the jogger?"

"She was a doctor, Ray. A Dr. Jennifer Barratt, according to her London School of Hygiene and Tropical Medicine ID."

"Tropical medicine?"

"Yeah."

"Bugger."

"Couldn't have put it more precisely myself." Lucy called her superintendent and recommended sending officers over to the woman's office as soon as possible. There might have been a natural explanation for Jennifer Barratt collapsing and dying as she had but one couldn't be too careful. Besides, if there were nothing else to be concerned about, the superintendent, whose head was known as the coolest in the Met, would ensure minimal panic.

The phone vibrated in Don Strathmore's trouser pocket three hours later. He fished it out, rose, and closed his office door. Glancing at the screen, he recognized the digital signature as secure. He pressed the green talk button and simply said, "Yes?"

"The problem's been taken care of. I think we're just about clear."

"Explain."

"Barratt's dead. After I questioned her, of course. There won't be any traces."

"What about the sample?"

"Nothing unusual. Barratt didn't share any information with anyone else at the facility. That loop is closed. The autopsy will show she died of cardiac arrest – the tox screen won't show why – and the forensics people will just record it as one of those unfortunate events that happens to runners sometimes."

Strathmore thought for a moment. A couple of worries nagged him. "She worked at an infectious disease facility. Won't there be questions? Such as 'was she working on something that killed her' for instance?"

"So what if they do? Wouldn't that make a handy smokescreen."

"Maybe," Strathmore said, not entirely convinced. "There's another problem as well. Why did she get the sample in the first place? Surely that could have been avoided?"

"Unfortunately not. MacCallum's doctor handed the package over to the courier personally. He told Barratt it was on its way. It would have been a little messy if I'd silenced the doctor right there and then. I only had a couple of weeks to get up to speed on everything he was doing, remember?"

"Well, make sure the guy disappears. He'll probably show up at his ex's shop looking for the results. Intercept him and take him out. I don't want him probing this any further. Then get back on the first plane to the States. Do whatever you need to eliminate Solkar."

She remained silent for a moment.

Strathmore barked into the handset. "Did you hear me, Sarah? We can't afford any screw-ups or leaks at this stage of the project."

"I heard you. There won't be," she said, stifling her desire to say something far more vitriolic. She pressed the red end-call button and shook her hair out, wishing she didn't have to deal with this blustering, stereotypical fraud. Only the beliefs she'd held for so long kept her focused; the seeds planted so long ago were at last germinating. Soon, the last witnesses to her sins would vanish.

Chapter 17

IT WAS AFTER FIVE when Marcus and Al left Morag MacCallum's farm, notebook in hand. They stopped by the doctor's office to make a photocopy, but by the time they had completed the exercise, Marcus concluded that the chances of his making the last flight to Heathrow were slim.

"Would you entertain an alternative idea, Marcus?" Al asked.

"I'm all ears."

"There's an overnight sleeper train to Euston. It'll get us where we need to be first thing in the morning. Jenny should have those results for us."

Leaving Claire a note to cancel his appointments for the following day, Al offered to drive the rental car back to Inverness, a favor Marcus gladly accepted. He wasn't sure whether he would stay sufficiently alert to maneuver the hills skillfully, but at least his new comrade was familiar with the area.

At the station, Al booked a shared second-class compartment while Marcus dropped off the rental car. Five minutes later, they climbed aboard. Their cabin was a compact affair, but well appointed and clean. A double bunk bed, made up with crisp white sheets and deep red blankets, occupied one side. Installed beneath the window was a sink. Mounted to its side was a wall cabinet containing bottles of drinking water. A faded sign on the door instructed passengers about emergency procedures. Underneath it, a newer placard advertised access to wireless internet coverage throughout the journey.

The train pulled out of the station ten minutes later. Marcus opened his laptop, accessed the Wi-Fi network, and placed a video call to Josef.

Rintlen answered immediately, raising a cup of coffee in greeting. "Good morning, Marcus. I am surprised to see you so soon. You have clearly been busy! Do you have an update?"

"I do. But first, I'd like you to meet Al Wylie, Professor MacCallum's doctor. Al, this is Josef Rintlen." He twisted the laptop towards the doctor, who was staring at his mobile phone. *Odd*, Marcus thought. He hadn't heard a ringtone or a chirp.

"Good evening, Doctor," Josef said.

No reply.

"Al, what is it?" Marcus said.

Slowly, the other man looked up, his face ashen. He turned his mobile around to show Marcus the screen. At the top, the "From" box highlighted the name Brenda Barratt. The message was simple. "Alasdair, please call as soon as you can. I have to talk to you." The text had been sent an hour ago, while they were still on the road.

"Who's Brenda Barratt?"

"My former mother-in-law. We didn't get along. There's no way she'd contact me unless...." His voice trailed off.

Marcus took the phone and pressed the return call button. It rang three times before a woman tentatively replied, "Hello?" He passed the phone over.

"Hello?" the voice came through again, this time more urgently.

"Brenda?" Al said. "It's me."

The sound of sobbing was all he could hear. For a full minute the woman wept into the phone, before squeezing out the words he dreaded hearing. "It's Jenny, Alasdair. She's gone."

The train rattled around a corner, causing Wylie to drop the phone, but Marcus stopped it from hitting the floor by sticking out a foot. He picked it up and spoke. "Mrs. Barratt? My name is Marcus Black. I'm with your son-in-law. I'm a friend. We're on our way to London right now."

More sobbing. "She was so young." Brenda fought to get the words out. "The police are here. They need to speak with Alasdair."

Momentarily forgotten was the laptop, its webcam pointed askew towards the two cabin occupants. In Belvedere, Josef observed the scene. Of all the live action videos he'd ever seen, this one was not one he'd like to replay. For the time being he kept silent, scribbling notes on a pad next to his mouse.

Marcus handed the device back. "Al, I'm sorry."

"Doctor?" A different female voice spoke. "This is PC Kelly Shaw. I'm the family liaison officer assigned to the case. I'm here with DC Raj Kolluri. He was one of the officers called to the scene."

"Scene?"

"Your former wife was out for a late afternoon jog near her home in Docklands. She was found by a passer-by earlier this evening. I'm very sorry."

"My Jenny," Al said softly. "My beautiful Jenny." He put the phone down.

Marcus picked it up and switched it to speakerphone mode. "Hello? Is anyone there?"

"Doctor?" This time it was Raj on the line. "We found a message in her mobile phone's drafts folder. It appears she was about to send it to a number that is very close to yours."

Al snatched the phone back. "Where is she? Where is her body?"

"Doctor, this is DC Kolluri. Are you able to speak with us?"

"Just tell me where you've taken Jenny!"

"Sir, I need to ask you if you understand this message."

"What message?"

"On Miss Barratt's mobile phone. The first six numbers correspond to your mobile number. The SMS message was a series of numbers. It appears she might have been trying to send you a message, but it doesn't make any sense to us. Perhaps she was pressing random numbers and letters, but then why would she punch in most of your phone number?"

"I don't know! What did it say?"

Raj read the text aloud. "21&15tercmut. I'll forward it to you."

Al shook his head. "I haven't a clue."

"Perhaps you should make a note of it. Let us know if you think of anything." The detective repeated the message and offered his condolences once more.

Al ended the call and stared off into the distance. The clickety-clack of the wheels beneath them slowed as the train approached the first stop on their journey south. Marcus pulled up a new window on his laptop and typed in the cryptic message Detective Kolluri had described. "Did you get that, Josef?"

"I did. I will perform some string searches and see if anything matches. Perhaps you can call me back in an hour?"

"Done."

Marcus severed the connection and put his laptop on standby. Turning towards Al Wylie, he saw only a numb, glazed look of bewilderment. He wondered if that was how Detective Sergeant Sampang had seen him. He'd only known Al for a few hours, and had no idea if the doctor could focus on the original reason for their journey. The connection between Kay and MacCallum was tenuous enough, but what else was at stake?

For instance, could Jennifer Barratt have contracted some pathogen from the tissue sample? That was unlikely, since neither Morag MacCallum nor Al Wylie had displayed any symptoms. It was far more likely that someone else knew about the sample. If so, someone had surely taken elaborate measures to ensure Jennifer's death looked accidental or not totally unnatural. "Al," he asked, shaking the doctor gently.

Wylie slowly looked up. His expression remained blank.

"Al, I'm sorry for your loss, truly I am, but I need you to think for a moment."

No reply. The train began to accelerate again. *Clickety-clack, clickety-clack.*

"Who else knew about the tissue sample?" Marcus waited for a few seconds, hoping to provoke a reaction of any kind. Failing that, he repeated the question. "Who else knew, Al? Who else knew you sent it to London? Did Morag MacCallum know?"

Nothing. And then, a slight shake of the head from side to side. Good, Marcus thought. Wylie was beginning to come back. "You're saying Morag didn't know, right?"

"She didn't know."

Good. That must mean that someone other than Jennifer Barratt herself was tracking the analysis, someone in the London lab, no doubt. But it still didn't sound right. The types of scientist Marcus had worked with over the years ranged from non-geek all the way up to full-blown nerd, but never any genuine lunatics. Naively perhaps, he thought most scientists' thirst for knowledge was nobler than the quest for gold. What, therefore, could be so profound a discovery that its release was worth the sacrifice of human lives? "Do you know if Jenny talked about the sample with anyone else at work?" he asked.

"No. I asked her not to and she said it would be just between us."

"So you shipped the sample to her after you called and asked her to help?"

"Aye."

"Where did you call her from?"

Al frowned, not understanding the issue. "What do you mean?"

"Did you call from your office? Which phone did you use, land line or cell?"

"I don't have a land line at home. I just use my mobile. Why do you ask?"

Marcus explained as best he could, without indulging in too much speculation. He stopped short of insinuating that Al's own curiosity had triggered events down south. That would have been insensitive at best.

It didn't work too well. "Are you saying this might have been my fault?" The anger rose up, Wylie's cheeks reddening.

"No. No one in his right mind would even suggest that. I'm just thinking that someone else might have learned about the sample somewhere along the trail, someone who'd do anything to keep it under wraps. You froze the sample without attaching any kind of official documentation, you told me that earlier. You also told me that Jenny was healthy, in excellent physical shape, so unless she had a hidden cardiac condition, then I'm bound to suspect something else."

"Maybe she really was ill. A heart murmur perhaps." Wylie said dully.

"You'd know, wouldn't you?"

"Aye." The doctor's lips pursed as he tried to recall anything that might point to a relevant medical condition. "No. Nothing at all. She was as healthy as a horse. Ran marathons. Well, half-marathons, anyway."

"Then who else knew about the sample?"

"There's only one possibility," Wylie said. "I gave the box to Sarah, my temporary receptionist, to give to the courier. I watched her hand it over."

"Did she open the package?"

"I don't know. Sometimes couriers like to repackage things and ensure that contents are properly protected, but no way did Sarah open it up herself."

"How long did you say she worked with you?"

The revelation hit Wylie immediately. "Just a couple of weeks. My goodness, that's right. She arrived the day before Claire went on holiday. I thought I was just lucky to have someone fill in. You don't think —"

"I don't know, Al. But if she's the only other person who knew about the sample, then it's worth tracking. Let me call Josef again."

Chapter 18

Josef Rintlen was amazed at how easily one well-planted seed of news could grow, weed-like, no, vine-like, throughout all creation. Media feeds all over the Web were talking about the story of how a young woman in good health had died during her evening jog. Someone at the scene found her workplace ID and rushed to judgment, causing speculation about disease outbreaks and virulent pandemics. But for the actions and well-timed press conference conducted by one Superintendent James Hunnicutt of the Metropolitan Police, calm might have dissolved into calamity.

With no useful purpose other than to keep news-addicted viewers fixed.

Or, he mused, to obscure the facts so skillfully that no one would even imagine looking at other possibilities. Josef had made a small fortune for himself, and a larger one for his employer, by turning dissonant research notes into technological symphonies. By thinking creatively, he could use all his resources, electronic and human, to separate scientific red herrings from genuine breakthroughs. More importantly, he had a good sense of the imminence of dead ends. He trusted his instincts as much as anything, often in spite of countervailing evidence. In this case, his gut told him the whole story was simply too contrived. Whether it was fueled by post-9/11 type rush to judgment, or by a ratings-grabbing pack of media hounds, it didn't matter. He simply wouldn't buy it.

A familiar ring sounded through his computer speakers. It was Marcus, calling from the train, which was just leaving Pitlochry, about 75 miles north of Edinburgh. The light was fading in Scotland, but the video feed revealed heather-covered hills through the train window. "We're back and ready to talk."

"Before you say anything," Josef said, "I would advise Dr. Wylie to go straight to the police tomorrow morning. That would be the sensible course of action."

"Why do you say that?" Al asked.

"I do not wish to sound callous, and I am sorry for your loss, Doctor. Possession or discovery of a scientific threat to governments, companies, or large bank accounts is probably why your former wife died, or why someone killed her. It is an educated guess, perhaps, but if I am correct, you may also be in danger."

"My God! Why?"

"She attempted to send you a message, which I am yet to comprehend fully. There can be no other explanation."

"What does it mean, Josef?" Marcus said.

"I ran a search on the string. The numbers were in a continuous string but my algorithm explores various breaks in the symbols. The four letters 'terc' are used in genetics to stand for 'telomerase RNA component.' The letters 'mut' may well refer to 'mutation.' The numbers 21 and 15 could represent chromosomes."

"That's guesswork," Al said, looking far from convinced.

"Of course it is," Josef admitted. "Unless you look at Professor MacCallum's obituary carefully."

"I'm not following you," said the Scot.

"There is a condition called Zinsser-Cole-Engman syndrome, otherwise called DKC or *dyskeratosis congenita*. It is a mutation of the telomeres on chromosome 15. It is very rare, and results in premature aging. However, its effects are most pronounced among homozygotes, wherein both parents carry this mutation. Did the MacCallums not have a daughter who predeceased them?"

"That's right. Her name was Moira. Morag said she was a Downs child."

"With a mutation on chromosome 21. But that could have also obscured other mutations that Moira suffered. Genetic predispositions her father carried."

"Tell us more about DKC," Marcus said.

"Some milder forms of the disease include premature aging, such as graying, early tooth loss, and predispositions to certain cancers. As I said, DKC is thought by some to result from the failure of telomerase RNA components, or TERCs. However, Professor MacCallum was an old man. He would not have suffered from this condition congenitally."

"We don't know if Moira did either," Al said.

"And we cannot know. Only a DNA test on her mother would help there."

"Wait a minute," Marcus said. "We're taking a leap of faith here based on an incomplete, speculative text message."

"Precisely," Josef agreed.

"But if you're right, and if Ian didn't have DKC despite this mutation showing up in the tissue analysis, how did he acquire it?"

"That, Dr. Black, is the missing piece we are all trying to locate. You will have to explore further, but do not do anything unwise. In the meantime, do you have anything further you wish to share?"

Marcus's jaw set. He nodded grimly, and pulled out the notebook with its list of initials, checks, and crosses. "This is what we discovered at MacCallum's place." He read the information aloud, and then held up the book in front of the webcam.

Josef made some notes. "I will go through Lexis/Nexis first with these. For the ones with checkmarks, I shall look for obituary notices and cross-check with a text search for some common keywords. That should not take long. The ones with crosses – they may be harder to locate because we have no history. Give me another couple of hours. I will email you the results. Call me back when you have read the reports."

"Agreed."

Josef closed the call window, spent fifteen minutes trawling through a carefully structured series of searches, and then called George Petrescu in.

"You rang?" George appeared, barefoot and wearing a T-shirt and jeans.

"I have a little assignment for you."

"Any time."

"I would like you to find a woman called Michelle Durant. She is on the faculty of the law school at UC Davis. She teaches evidence and criminal procedure."

"O-kay," George replied tentatively. This wasn't the kind of research he normally performed. "What's the deal?"

"I need to learn some details about a case she worked on a long time ago, before she turned to teaching. It was a murder trial. Ms. Durant was counsel for the defense. There are parallels between what happened to the victim and to Marcus Black's wife. The cases are connected."

"How?"

"Does the name Edmund Solkar mean anything to you?"

"Should it?"

"It probably would not."

"Then perhaps you'd best join the dots for me."

When Josef finished, George silently rose, left the room for a few minutes, and returned dressed in an Armani suit. "I'll definitely be spelling my name with a G for this."

His boss smiled. "Good man, George."

Chapter 19

Steve Goudreau clicked on the small icon in his system tray, maximizing a window displaying the same screen he'd accidentally shown to Matt Gilstrap. The vegetation was still lush, the rain forest twinkling as rays of sunshine beamed through the plant life. No rain clouds loomed above, despite the water dripping off the giant, succulent green ferns. No howler monkey roared its distinctive call across the upper branches, but only because the volume was turned down.

Two quartets of vertical scales displayed red lines in the upper right hand corner of the monitor. The values on each added up to one hundred, ranging between 0.04 to 78. The left scales were labeled "Coarse" and the ones on the right "Fine." The coarse gauges were almost stationary but the fine gauges bobbed up and down slightly. One of the primates came into view, opened its mouth, and uttered a soft cry. The smallest value on the fine gauges registered a local spike, and then settled down again. The monkey swung away and left the scene in tranquil silence.

Beside him, Justin Hernandez smiled with satisfaction. "Steve, this is working even better than we could have imagined. Two weeks and we see this conversion rate? I'm astonished at how rapidly we've been able to prove the principle."

The chimpanzee appeared on screen. Its round, grinning countenance bared its teeth at the camera. The ape was almost mugging for the camera, making faces before scampering away. Again, the fine gauges spiked and re-equilibrated.

"The system looks stable, Justin. The most recent modification has taken hold. You've done it." Steve offered a high five.

Hernandez ignored the gesture. He smiled thinly. "Your boy figured out the missing piece. No way could we have understood what we needed to engineer without his input. Pity he decided to quit."

"He was homesick."

"Right." Hernandez dragged the word out, giving his colleague a long stare. "Still, if he goes back to Biotech Bay, I'm sure he'll find something useful to do with his life. But I don't think he will, somehow." Hernandez rose and left the room, leaving the Canadian to look once again at the jungle scene. The monkey reappeared briefly, yawned, and then swung out of sight. The ape did not return.

Steve exhaled deeply as Hernandez closed the door behind him. It was time.

Just before midnight, the train pulled into Stirling. Doors began opening, and one last passenger boarded the sleeper car. A few others down the track climbed into the seated cabin area, hauling suitcases behind them. Al Wylie lay in the upper bunk, staring at the ceiling. Marcus was typing notes into his laptop as fast as he could.

"What was your temp's last name?" Marcus asked.

"Innes, if I remember correctly. Claire's surname is Logan."

Marcus added the names to his document. "Okay, thanks. Get some sleep if you can."

A whistle sounded from the platform, and the locomotive's steady diesel, which had been chuntering away at idle speed, came to life. It was a powerfully satisfying sound. As the last doors slammed shut, a second whistle blast resonated through the station. The great convoy of engine and carriages pulled slowly out and accelerated briefly before slowing once more. Falkirk Grahamston, a small two-platform halt, was the train's last stop before the border. At that time of night, the activity in the small Scottish town had all but ceased, and the train only paused for formality. There would only be two more stops planned during the next few hours, Preston North End and Crewe.

Marcus logged into his Outlook account and discovered a single message from Josef. It simply said, "Use the other address." They'd agreed on the protocol the previous day. Josef preferred to convey sensitive information via a secure server that would require the full investigative power of the FBI, NSA, CIA, MI6, the Mossad, and one or two sixteen-year-old geeks to trace. Marcus typed in an ID and password. That got him over the first security hump, and transferred him to a second site requiring a biometric scan. He plugged a small dongle from his keychain into his laptop's USB port. A sliding metallic cover revealed a pad about half an inch wide by an inch in length. He held out his left forefinger and pressed it against the pad. A little icon in his system tray acknowledged that all subsequent operations were secure.

He logged into the account and found Josef's message. It contained a number of links to news reports, and a summary document. The first link was a six-day-old International Herald Tribune piece on a Professor Hong Li, found dead in his Shanghai apartment, the victim of an apparent robbery. Subsequent articles failed to indicate whether the Chinese police had any success locating suspects.

The second link described the recent death of one Julius Daveed Goldfarb of the Weizmann Institute, Israel. Goldfarb had apparently been in ill health for three months battling non-Hodgkin's lymphoma. The report stated that Goldfarb, an avid skydiver, had leaped to his death from a small aircraft, his parachute having failed to open. His family had denounced any speculation that Julius had deliberately packed the chute improperly. Suicide would be a sin in their faith. It would also void life insurance policies, but Goldfarb had not taken one out. That issue was therefore moot. The Weizmann Institute's statement expressed deep regret at the loss of one of their own, a young botanist whose efforts were "exciting," "innovative," and "cutting-edge."

The third report was from several years earlier. It continued the pattern in one way, at least. Stanley Michael Zalewski's bloated, decomposing, forty-year-old body was found in a South Chicago penthouse by a neighbor who had noticed a stench emanating into the hall. Zalewski's life had apparently been devoted to all things computational, with little social purpose. The brief obituary listed one cousin as a survivor. Josef's summary added a few notes from local rags. Zalewski's pad was near a high-crime district known for drug trafficking and prostitution. He'd put his IT talents towards a network of internet-based sites that provided him with a steady and substantial income, little of which was spent on cleaning services or personal hygiene. Investigators confiscated every computer in Zalewski's home, searching for filth, but found nothing they could call illegal or even unseemly. Stan had been clever enough to cover his tracks. Or, as Josef suggested, he may not have been into porn at all, perhaps he was simply an avid online gamer. Zalewski had once worked at the Henry and Linda Castleford Institute as their network guru. He'd been fired for spending too much time playing online shoot-'em-ups.

A pattern was emerging, but where it pointed was anyone's guess. What Marcus now knew, however, was that several of the initials in Ian MacCallum notebook belonged to former Castleford employees. MacCallum's own sabbatical break there gave him a chance to co-author a paper with Kendall Rasmussen. What did it all mean? Five people, five deaths, possibly five suicides? It was almost like a cancer cluster, the kind where unexpectedly high levels of pollutants, radiation, or electromagnetic forces contribute to above average incidences of lymphomas and other neoplasms.

He flashed back to the day he and Kay saw the movie "Erin Brockovich." He'd wanted to see the latest guy movie, replete with violence, car chases, explosions, and babes. She'd wanted to see a chick flick, starring not a single male performer. As a compromise, they'd agreed to see the tale of how a small town became poisoned by high valence chromium. Afterwards, Kay had been silent and withdrawn, clearly affected by the story. On the way home from the movie theater, she stared silently out of the window, her face a mask of sadness. All she had said when they entered their front door was, "There has to be a way to stop this."

"Stop what?" he had asked, gently tilting her face up to look at him.

She'd walked away and locked herself in the upstairs bathroom. He hadn't seen her for another couple of hours. Later in the evening, she'd acted as if nothing had happened, but he remembered treading on eggshells around her for the next couple of days. Without doubt, the effect of pollutants on nature was a hot button, but her reaction to the true-to-life movie seemed just a tad over the top. By the next week, he'd all but forgotten her odd behavior, putting it down simply to a heightened awareness of, and sadness towards the ravages of modern industry.

He recalled their recent years, when Kay attended Earth Day celebrations, joined environmental groups, and ate only organic produce. Without becoming an activist, she'd tried to set an example of healthy living day to day. Marcus was never as vigilant as Kay, but he stayed supportive, even while indulging in the odd processed meal.

The movie made its way into the video stores, pay-per-view, and network TV. Kay never saw it again, but late one night Marcus watched it on HBO, mostly to see if a particular scene might have triggered her behavior. Nothing seemed especially provocative. Later, when he crawled into bed beside Kay, she woke up and asked him why he was so late, and he told her his only lie of their entire marriage. He said he was watching a rerun of a Schwarzenegger flick, the one that took place on Mars. She said she loved that movie and why didn't he tell her it was on, she'd have stayed up with him.

Little fibs like those always stuck. He knew she despised sci-fi action flicks. Now, as the wheels of the train continued their clickety-clack sound, he wondered how he'd ever gotten to this point. The mostly happy life with Kay was gone, taken from him cruelly and irreversibly. But she had not been alone, now there were others like her. *What other lies had been told*, he wondered.

Something new snapped him out of his recollections. Josef's fourth link pointed to a recent San Francisco Chronicle article on the self-shooting of one Ralph Shanahan, aged fifty-nine, a psychologist from Hammond, Indiana.

The reporter described the official statement delivered by Detective Sergeant Leo Sampang of the Pacifica Police. The only other person named in the report was an eyewitness to the incident on the pier. Stuart Gray, a locally employed molecular biologist, claimed that Shanahan sounded deranged and delusional just before he shot himself. The man's initials were consistent with those in Ian MacCallum's notebook, the second pair, right after Ian's own. Ralph Shanahan was the sixth death in the cluster.

Marcus logged off, shut the laptop down, and lay on his back. A million thoughts raced around in his mind, crashing into each other with a rhythm that mimicked that of the wheels beneath. It was another hour before he became drowsy, but he gradually drifted away into a deep, dreamless slumber. He didn't awaken for another five hours.

Chapter 20

A KNOCK CAME ON the cabin door just after seven. A porter carrying a tray of hot tea, two cups, and an assortment of packaged cookies shuffled his way inside. He placed the tray on the sink cover and growled a good morning greeting. Marcus opened one eye to see Al Wylie, standing by the window and peering at his mobile phone. Outside, the Grand Union Canal sparkled in the early morning sunshine.

"Good morning, Marcus. Welcome to North London," Al said. His tone was somber.

"Did you get any sleep?"

"A wee bit. I've been up since Nuneaton."

"Nuneaton?"

"Station."

"Oh." Marcus swung his legs over the side of the bunk bed. "How much longer to London?"

"About thirty, forty minutes. We'll be in Euston soon. I'm going to Jenny's office as soon as I can. I'm going to meet the police there."

"Mind if I tag along?"

"They'd rather I came alone. But I'll keep you in the loop as soon as I've spoken to them. Is that all right with you?" he added, a little peevishly.

It wasn't ideal, but Marcus agreed to hold off. By eight o'clock, everyone aboard the train had alighted and passed into the main terminal area of Euston Station. "Feel like getting some breakfast first?" Marcus suggested as they walked past one of several station cafes.

"Not hungry," Al snapped. "I have to get to Jenny's office."

Marcus clenched his teeth, unable to come up with a response. When Al broke into a run as they approached the doors to Euston Road, he held back as promised, but decided to follow at a respectable distance. The doctor ran into

Euston Square, crossed the road, dodging taxis, buses, and motorists clogging the early morning commute. He headed down Gordon Street, passing an architectural blend of at least three centuries' worth. Marcus loped behind, slowed by the heavy backpack. By the time he reached Gordon Square, a small park to his left, Al was disappearing behind a redbrick and plate glass facade five stories high, straight ahead. Marcus ran to the intersection and turned right, then quickly left. In the distance loomed the enormous British Museum, its unparalleled collections advertised from signs hanging off lampposts along the way. Al continued to run, but Marcus pulled up as he saw a police vehicle in the parking lot just off to the left of the University of London's Founder's Building nearby.

He doubled back towards Gordon Square and turned left around the block onto Gower Street, heading south. Looking west at the Store Street intersection, he could see the front steps of the tropical medicine building. He saw a woman with shoulder-length dark blonde hair, dressed in a blue business suit, reach into her purse and pull out a mobile phone. As Al ran around the corner of the tropical medicine building from the opposite direction, the woman focused on him. Marcus was unable to see her face. She spoke into the phone for a few seconds, and then placed it back in her purse. Marcus wondered whether she might be a reporter, perhaps a plainclothes police detective, or just an interested citizen.

Shouts came from behind the building. Amidst the city noises he had trouble gauging what was going on, but it sounded like Al's voice, demanding to go inside. The cop he'd seen a few minutes earlier was doing his best to maintain calm. The blonde woman, her back still turned, slowly paced west. Marcus wanted to sneak through and observe more closely, but something told him it would be best to maintain a distance. He ducked behind a group of small uniformed schoolchildren waiting to cross, and used their teacher as cover while peering at the scene.

Then he saw Al Wylie run out, arms flailing around as two female constables shouted after him. Al darted across the street and out of sight, running towards the British Museum. The woman in the dark blue suit moved just quickly enough for Marcus to detect her among all the other people in the vicinity. She turned on her heels and strode towards Al. They both disappeared. Marcus ran down Gower Street towards Bedford Square, only stopping at Montague Place long enough to check his bearings. He walked around the edge of the museum just far enough to see the woman engaging Wylie in conversation. The doctor, breathing heavily, looked astonished. The woman reached out to him and touched his arm. Marcus was still unable to see her face in detail, but he felt certain he had never seen her before. She was extremely attractive, if overly coiffed and made up. High cheekbones,

Persephone's Blade

delicate features, full lips, and a body to which he suspected the suit did little justice.

They crossed the street, the blonde looking left to face the traffic. Marcus stayed out of sight as they walked briskly towards Russell Square. She whipped out the mobile phone again, spoke briefly, and then popped it back into her purse. At the corner they turned right, past the vast museum, and then disappeared from view completely. Marcus increased his pace, now that he was a good fifty yards behind them, and then stopped just before he reached the corner of the museum.

He poked his head around to look for them, and then ducked back. The woman was gone. She must have gone inside the museum, Marcus thought. He walked around to the front and looked past the ticket booths to see if she had entered. He was about to dart inside when a museum staff member alerted him that the place wasn't even open yet.

Damn! Where are they? He looked down the street, craning his neck. Then he saw her in the distance, marching towards the park. Al was with her, keeping stride. Was she one of the detectives that had called last night? Was she assigned to meet him as soon as they'd arrived? Was she the reason Al had asked him to stay back? Marcus started jogging after them, but after putting a quarter mile or so behind him, he was forced to give up as they stepped inside a black taxi. It drove away before he could find another in which to pursue her. He slumped, panting, his hands on his thighs, and shook his head.

An hour later, the woman calling herself Sarah Innes told a different cabbie to drive her directly to Paddington Station. In her mind, she added up two weeks' of temporary receptionist wages. The tally was enough to purchase one coach class ticket to San Francisco. *As if the accounting of travel expenses were cause for concern.* Her partners were unlikely to quibble over a double fare upgrade to first. After all, she had successfully tied up one more loose end, pretty as you please. The authorities might have a tough time finding the Barratt woman's ex-husband, but if they did, there would be no longer any reason to pursue the real concern. Ian MacCallum's tissue sample would disappear in a minus-eighty degree freezer somewhere. The important thing was that no one was looking into it any more.

There was only one minor niggle. Who, she wondered, was the guy running after them just before they got into the cab? She made a mental note of his appearance, his build, and his clothing, and considered telling the taxi driver to head back to Russell Square. On further reflection, she thought he would be long gone from the scene.

But why take chances? Instinct told her there was little to be lost and much to be gained by a final check. "Would you turn around, please, driver?"

"As you wish, Miss." The driver executed a perfect U-turn, seemingly oblivious to oncoming traffic, and slid into the reverse flow without missing a beat. When his speed matched the prevailing traffic, he asked for more details.

"I've changed my mind. Euston Station. I think I'll travel north rather than west."

"Right you are, then."

In three minutes' time, the cabbie slowed down. They approached Russell Square and headed towards the large rail terminal. Sarah focused on finding the man she'd seen following her and the doctor. It was like a live game of "Where's Waldo" played with a moving, camouflaged version of the stripy character. The taxi wove between almost stationary cars whose drivers were more intent on checking out the assorted goings-on, blocking her view intermittently.

And then she spotted him, marching out of the station's side door, heading west on Euston Road. Her heart rate quickened. The driver pulled up on the other side of the road and let her out. She gave him a good tip for his trouble, smiled fetchingly, and crossed the road. She felt it shouldn't take long to find an answer to the question starting to percolate in her mind.

What did Wylie tell you? She looked at Wylie's cell phone one more time. The message was the last one in his inbox. *21&15tercmut.*

How could they know?

Chapter 21

MICKEY DURANT, ATTORNEY-AT-LAW AND respected faculty member at U.C. Davis's King Hall School of Law, was busy in her office wrapping things up after the school's spring semester. She had just delivered final exam results for the graduating class, mostly young men and women destined for the California State Bar. Only a few of the third year students had failed to meet their requirements on time, but that was expected. The first year was the hardest, where the pretenders flunked out. Some even packed it in during year two, but most of those who successfully plowed through the basics of "civ pro," torts, contracts, criminal law, and legal research reckoned they had what it took.

There were always a few oddballs. Mickey recalled one student who'd made it through her contracts class and all the others, confidently passing through into 2L. Then one day he stopped by her office, thanked her for all her help, complimented her on her execution of the Socratic teaching method, and said "I quit." It turned out the guy just wasn't into being a lawyer. He preferred manual labor. By contrast, most of the students who finished the course were ambitious young professionals. Many had come through college with history, political science, and liberal arts backgrounds. There were a few scientists. They all wound up studying patent law. Some went on to clerkships for esteemed jurists. Others entered the private sector. King Hall fed the pipeline of environmental lawyers as well as any school in the nation. A few of her students became prosecutors, but more entered public defense. That was no surprise. The school was ultra-liberal, far more than her conservative *alma mater*.

A knock on her closed door startled her as she put some finishing touches on a letter to the University of Michigan Law Review. It was her final task before her planned early summer vacation. Without thinking, she said "Come in."

The door opened to reveal a man in his early thirties, well-groomed, clean-cut, and dressed in formal business attire. He held a thin leather portfolio with a golden clasp. He flashed what looked like an official ID. "Professor Durant?"

Mickey's eyes opened wide. "Yes?" Remaining seated, she looked past the man into the hall. Just about everyone else had left for the day. It was the summer break, and her colleagues had families and lives. She wished she could say the same.

George Petrescu introduced himself. He didn't move to close the door. "May I have five minutes of your time?"

"I'm sorry, I'm just about to leave." she replied. "I don't recall having made an appointment." Mickey realized it was a weak response and somewhat out of character.

"No appointment," George said. "But I don't think you'd have made an appointment if I'd told you what it was about. Of course, if I'd said that I was from the FBI and wanted to know about your recent contact with a former client, you'd have boarded the first flight out of Sacramento. To anywhere but here."

The bluff clearly unsettled her. Mickey's alarmed expression was all he needed to know that he was in. "You'd better sit down," she said.

George closed the door behind him. "Thank you, Ms. Durant. I appreciate the time. I promise this won't take long." He knew the next moments would be crucial. One misstep and he'd lose her. He knew about lawyer-client confidentiality, and he also knew some of the relevant case facts from public records. What he didn't have was the luxury of time to formulate his approach. Josef had given him an hour's worth of background before sending him on his way. The drive from Marin County to Davis, crossing two notoriously congested bridges, and then east towards the I-80 intersection was famous for slow-and-go traffic. It had taken two hours, which was all the time he'd had to rehearse and polish his questions. "In the case of the People of the State of Illinois versus Edmund Ranjit Solkar, you were the attorney of record for the defense."

Simple statement of fact, indisputable. Mickey didn't respond.

He continued. "This was a capital murder case. You saved your client from a possible death penalty. Instead, he served out a sentence for voluntary manslaughter. That was quite the legal victory, no matter how guilty Solkar was." he added editorially.

"What can I help you with, Mr. Petrescu?" Mickey said coldly.

"His alleged victim was a Ms. Samaya Jonas. I believe she may not have been the only one." He looked at the professor squarely, noticing the flecks of brown in her hazel irises.

"What makes you think that?"

George opened the portfolio and withdrew a photograph of Kay Rasmussen's burned body. He pushed it across Mickey's desk. "This young woman was found recently. We believe she may have been murdered."

"Again, what makes you think that?"

"Ms. Durant, if you don't mind, I'll ask the questions." George felt he was beginning to lose the initiative, and to maintain his image he had to play the part a little more convincingly. "Where you were on the night of April 5 this year?"

"What do you mean?" Mickey was indignant. "You can't think…"

George held up a hand. "Of course not. We're just trying to tie up some loose ends regarding your client. Let me ask you again, where were you on April 5 at approximately nine pm?"

She looked at the monitor on her desk, then picked up the mouse and scrolled down her appointment calendar. "As a matter of fact, I was in Sacramento that evening, at the home of Justice Thorndyke. You can check with him if you really must."

"We will follow that up, naturally," George lied. "Have you been in touch with your client, Edmund Solkar, since his release?"

"No." Her answer came a trifle too quickly.

"Why not?"

"What do you mean, why not? Was I supposed to maintain contact? He's a free man. He served his time. There is no need for us to continue our relationship!"

"A bit defensive for a defense attorney," George remarked. "A simple 'No idea where he is' – well, I might have bought that. Then again, maybe not. Either way, I wasn't looking for any particular answer, just your reaction. And you've given it to me." He picked up the photo, stuck it back in the leather portfolio, rose, and turned towards the door. "Appreciate the time, Ms. Durant. We'll be in touch."

Before he grabbed the door handle, he couldn't resist pulling a Columbo-like stunt. "Oh, one last question, if you don't mind. Did Solkar ever mention the name Ralph Shanahan to you?" He enunciated the man's name carefully. "He died recently under tragic circumstances. We know your client could not have been responsible for his death." Theatrically, he turned his back and walked half way through the door.

The little color left in Mickey's face drained out. Her whole body felt like it was about to sink. "Wait," she said. "I'll tell you what you want to know."

George's expression softened. "Thank you." He closed the door and sat back down. "Now, if we're going to be honest, I'm not law enforcement of any kind. I'm a special investigator with XUSA Corporation." He gave her the pre-rehearsed five minute spiel he and Josef had worked out, describing the company's profile. He omitted his own biography.

An hour later, he thanked her, shook her hand, and guaranteed her name would not be mentioned further in connection with the matter, unless she chose to come forward. He left her with Josef's private Belvedere number just in case.

Chapter 22

MARCUS FOUND HIS WAY back to Euston Station, his heart pounding. It had been an hour since he'd seen Al and the woman in the blue suit drive off in the taxi. He'd spent the time trying to regain his bearings, to collect his thoughts, and to come up with some kind of plan. The exercise was futile, but he discovered he'd walked quite the distance among London's busy streets, and he wanted to regroup. Returning to the cafe he'd passed earlier, he took the opportunity to purchase a bagel and some coffee. He spent the next five minutes wolfing the former and gulping the latter, even though it was piping hot. Nerves and frustration were already getting the better of him, but the one thing that tipped him over the edge was his inability to find a trash can. Nowhere could he find a single bin for the coffee cup, into which he'd stuffed the bagel wrapper. He cast about frantically, cursing and grimacing, looking more agitated by the minute.

"Can't find a rubbish bin?" someone said to him over his shoulder. He turned to see a huge black man dressed in the uniform of a security officer.

Right. "Why the hell don't you people have them? Does everybody just toss their garbage onto the ground when they're done? If not, where am I supposed to put it?"

"We don't 'ave 'em," the guard replied, calmly but sternly. He was four or five inches taller than Marcus. That put him in the seriously large, don't-mess-with-me category. "Security. Bomb scares. You Americans always get thrown by that whenever you come here."

"So what do you suggest I do if I want to throw away a paper cup?"

"Most people tend to leave them on the cafe tables," the guard said, pointing to the place where Marcus had bought his breakfast. He pronounced the word "kaff." A few tables remained unoccupied, their surfaces covered with debris.

Marcus closed his eyes and bowed his head slightly. "Look, I'm sorry. I've had some long days and nights, and this was about the last thing I wanted to have to deal with. Really, I apologize for yelling, at you and just, well, yelling."

The security guy decided to take pity. "Listen, mate, we get that sort of thing all the time. But a lot of you Yanks couldn't be bothered to try and do the right thing. At least your heart's in the right place."

Yeah. Even if it's broken. "Well, I'll be on my way, I guess."

"Where are you headed?"

He was thinking the best thing he could do in the short term was find a place to regroup. "Not sure right now. I came down on the sleeper from up north, but I could really use a hotel, a shower, change of clothes et cetera. Know any good ones?"

"Take your pick, mate. Got one right across the street, but it all depends where you're going next. Got friends in London, have you?"

"I know a few people here," Marcus lied. "But I'm not the drop-in unannounced type. I'm actually going back home tomorrow anyway."

"Holiday?"

"Yeah," he fibbed again.

"Not much baggage for a holiday," the guard remarked.

"Lost it. Flight from Heathrow up to Inverness. It could be in Timbuktu for all I know. I had to rush between connections and the bag didn't go as fast as my legs."

"Happens to most people sooner or later. I'm sure it'll turn up one day."

"Thanks. And again, sorry for being a pain."

"No problem." The guard watched Marcus head towards the front door, appearing to walk in the general direction of the hotel he'd suggested. Satisfied, he returned to his patrol.

Marcus popped out for a second, glanced over his shoulder, and then re-entered as soon as the guard disappeared from view. He marched past a newsagent and slipped out the side door. He crossed the street and walked west towards King's Cross. Inside the terminal, he located the Underground sign, and descended the escalator. He found himself in a congested area filled with travelers barging around in every direction. A wall of ticket machines, capable of taking credit cards, notes, coins, and just about everything but an IOU confronted him. His eyes wandered over the various ticket types, unsure which he should buy. The harried Indo-Pakistani at the only manned booth was facing a long line of equally confused customers. The enlightened others madly punched buttons as the machinery spewed forth its assorted passes.

He settled on an all-day, all zone pass just to keep everything simple. He chose Paddington for his next destination because of its high-speed airport connection. Then he negotiated the stiles and escalators, consulting various route maps along the way to ensure he was going in the right direction. Some of the destinations he'd heard of, others were as meaningless as a translation of the works of Shakespeare into Manx.

Upon arrival at Paddington, he found a booth selling hotel deals at local establishments, promising "better rates than any on-line booking sites." Within ten minutes, he was booked into a nearby Marriott.

It was almost noon when he emerged from his shower. Freshly shaven and dressed in a change of clothes, he logged on to the hotel's Wi-Fi connection. Something rolling across the bottom, in ticker tape style, caught his eye. "LATEST HEADLINES – UPDATE ON TROPICAL MEDICINE DOCTOR DEATH."

Clicking on the link, Marcus was redirected to the BBC web site, which was transmitting live video coverage of the outside of the London School of Hygiene and Tropical Medicine. The TV in his room showed the same feed. The place was teeming with reporters jockeying for position and interviews. A senior cop with superintendent insignia on his epaulets occupied center stage. He addressed the mikes thrust underneath his craggy jowls.

"At this time, we are investigating all leads. It appears that the former husband of the deceased attempted to cross a police barrier to the building. He has since disappeared."

"Can you tell us the name of the deceased?" one journalist asked.

"We are withholding that information until family has been notified."

"Superintendent, what can you tell us about his movements prior to his disappearance?"

"It would be inappropriate to speculate at this time."

"Do you know if he was in town alone?"

"Again, we cannot say at this point."

A few more reporters tried to goad the police spokesman into saying something he didn't want to, but the seasoned cop had issued enough statements in his thirty year career to know not to cross that line. He also knew he didn't have long before guesswork would find itself plastered all over the airwaves, and worse, all over the Evening Standard. That newspaper, whose first edition had just hit stands all over the city, would carry relevant headlines all too soon. Later editions would augment the coverage and provide further speculation within. Marcus's fears began to bubble up anew. What if someone canvassing the area, police or journalist, talked to the helpful Euston station guard? Suppose the woman he'd seen with Al Wylie had made similar assumptions? What if either informed the authorities, politely and in the spirit of cooperation, that they'd seen an American male with graying hair, six two, carrying a backpack, acting nervously in the vicinity?

Or, he wondered, was his paranoia simply driven by fatigue? Either way, he didn't want to get stuck somewhere in an interrogation room. He didn't have time to explain exactly what he was doing with Dr. Alasdair Wylie, and why they were on their way to Jennifer Barratt's workplace in search of a series of biological tests. Unable to foretell the questions he would have to face under investigation in a foreign country, he decided the best course of action was to leave, and soon. While innocent of any wrongdoing, he still didn't like the idea of being delayed, or even detained. He wasn't sure where to go, but it had to be somewhere else. Anywhere but London, or the United Kingdom, for that matter. And fast.

The international airports would not be ideal, he thought, nor would the train stations. Buses and taxis were a bit more promising, allowing relative anonymity. What he did not have was the luxury of time. He returned to his laptop, all the while keeping an eye on the TV coverage, and did a quick search for bus services. Faced with a plethora of choices, he then asked himself where he could go on a bus. This was an island with limited exit points. None was especially attractive. The Channel Tunnel was one, but he didn't fancy being dragged into a French or Belgian police station, depending on which train line he selected. Nor did he want to return to St. Pancras, which was perilously close to where everything had unraveled. France, Germany, Holland, and Belgium all seemed less than ideal. There was also the language barrier. He considered returning north, but again felt he'd be in the same boat six hours hence, wondering how to leave the country.

The answer came to him just after one in the afternoon. He Googled the site he wanted and five minutes later was on the phone. It took him another ten minutes to book two round trip flights, the outbound journey to start in three hours' time. There would be enough time to connect, and so what if he didn't come back in two weeks' time? It would be cheaper than a one-way ticket anyhow. Perhaps he could sell the other half on eBay.

Thirty minutes later he left the hotel, without checking out. The credit card he'd used to check in would provide a paper trail if necessary, but no one was likely to look for another twenty-two hours or so. By then he would be long gone. He hailed a taxi outside the lobby and told the driver to go straight to the Victoria Coach Station, figuring he would take the risk. There he boarded a southbound coach. An hour and a half later he was in the small Southampton airport terminal, where he did not have long to wait for the flight to Dublin. The small commuter plane arrived just in time for him to scamper to the Aer Lingus international connection, and within another ten minutes the gate closed.

He fell asleep, again, before the A-330 left the ground, and did not awaken until an hour before the aircraft touched down at Chicago's O'Hare International Airport.

Sarah Innes lost sight of him the moment he disappeared through the security arch at Southampton. She doubted she was dealing with a pro. The last thing Wylie had said to him before she ended his medical career was that he'd shared his cabin on the train with a complete stranger. Random chance booking in second class. It was sheer chance, nothing more. *Probably.* "He's on his way to Dublin."

"Why there?" Strathmore wanted to know.

"How should I know? I just had a gut feeling I should check him out."

"Did you get a shot of him? I can have someone run a search."

"I did. Lighting's not perfect but I'll send it to you regardless." Sarah pulled up a photograph she'd taken from the rear of the bus when the guy was struggling to put his backpack over his shoulder. She emailed it to Strathmore. It took a few minutes to complete the transmission. The return call came through shortly afterwards.

"Never seen him. I'll follow up and get back to you."

"When?"

"It'll take me a couple of days."

"Do we have that long?"

"Relax, Sarah. The deal is set. Shanghai's on board. We're rolling."

As long as I get to Solkar first.

Chapter 23

THE BUS PULLED INTO San Jose at exactly four minutes after noon. Ed Solkar gathered his belongings and stepped into the uncharacteristically chilly drizzle. He paused for long enough at the bus station for a cup of steaming coffee at a nearby stand, and then made his way towards a phone booth. A Hispanic youth stood there yakking. As Ed approached, he turned his back, mumbled a goodbye, and hung up. Instead of moving aside, he fumbled around in his baggy jean pockets, pulled out an Ipod, put the headphones on, fiddled around with the playlists, clicked the play button, adjusted the volume, and eventually shambled off.

Why couldn't you have done that after you'd left, Ed thought. Freaking California. It hadn't changed since the last time he was here. No one gave a rat's ass about anyone but themselves, and everyone chose to ignore the possibility they might be inconveniencing others. Or perhaps it was just teenaged kids, he wondered. Shaking his head, Ed picked up the phone and dialed a number he'd memorized years ago.

"Hello," the familiar voice said after six rings.

"It's me."

There was a long pause. "Thank God. Where are you?"

"San Jose. Are you safe?"

"I'm all right for now. But I'm worried, Eddie. People are asking questions."

"I'll be there by six at the latest. There are a couple of things I need to do first. A promise I made." Ed Solkar hung up and inhaled deeply. It had started.

He slung on his backpack and began to walk down the street. The city had transformed since his last visit, and the downtown district now looked quite attractive. Several blocks on, he popped into a convenience store with a payphone inside. The phone book was intact. He thumbed through the yellow pages and found the address of a nearby used car dealer. He memorized the address and left, pausing only to purchase a large cup of soda.

The dealer wanted five hundred for the late-70's Olds Cutlass Supreme. It was one of the plainest cars on the lot, well hidden from the later models whose asking prices ranged from two to seventeen grand. The car was solid. The salesman said it belonged to a doctor who'd been given the vehicle for his high school graduation. The doctor had kept it pristine until a malpractice suit ruined him. Ed talked the dealer into eating the sales tax, peeled off five C-notes from his roll, and that was that.

He drove north on 101 until he reached the East Palo Alto exit, turned right, and navigated the run-down city streets until he found the neighborhood he was looking for. He parked outside a house whose landscaped garden was in stark contrast to some of its neighbors east of the freeway. The house itself also looked well-cared for, just as it had been described.

The door opened. A large African-American man stood in the doorway. Ed was well-built, but the man at the front door dwarfed him. "May I help you?"

"Good afternoon, sir. May I speak with Lydia Jackson, please?"

"And who might you be?"

Ed introduced himself.

"Don't know anyone by that name."

"This is the address I was given. I don't wish to be any trouble, but does Lydia Jackson live here?"

"Dr. Jackson isn't available right now. She's –"

A female voice called from somewhere inside. "Rondell, honey, is that someone for me? Is it one of my students?"

Rondell looked a little sheepish and opened the door. "Please excuse me. My wife just returned from a conference last week. We wanted to spend a little time together without interruptions."

"I won't keep you long," Ed said, stepping inside. "So you must be Rondell Jackson. Cleve mentioned you by name."

Jackson's expression turned to a scowl. "Please leave. Now," he ordered, blocking Ed's path. Even without raising his voice or issuing a specific threat, he looked capable of delivering precise, decisive violence.

"I came to deliver something to Lydia. I promised her father." Ed stood his ground.

"I'll take care of it," Rondell said, glowering. He held out his hand.

"He asked me to give it to her personally."

They were interrupted by the arrival of a slender woman of about thirty-five. Ed's jaw almost dropped as he turned to face her. She was perhaps the most beautiful woman he had ever seen. Her skin was almost jet-black, her features finely chiseled. She was the teenager in the photograph her father had kept for the last twenty years, only grown up.

"I'm Lydia Jackson," she said. "May I help you?"

Ed unbuttoned his shirt, to the shock of both Jacksons. He showed her the scar on his chest. "Five years ago, your father and I were in prison together. The same man wounded us both. We became friends. He asked me to give you this when I got out."

He reached into his backpack and pulled out a small woodcarving of a rabbit. Crudely etched on the bottom were the words, "To my Lydie. I love you. Daddy." He handed the little rabbit to Cleveland Lambert's only child.

Lydia's face suddenly grew sad. Her lower lip trembled as she clutched the carving. "You're the man who saved his life."

"A waste of time, if you ask me," her husband interrupted.

"Nobody asked you," Lydia said firmly. "Is he all right?"

"He's fine, Lydia."

She invited Ed into the living room, where she offered him a seat. "Tell me, Mr. Solkar. Did he really do all the things they accused him of?"

Ed's jaw set. He'd been rehearsing the speech for days. "Most convicted murderers claim they're innocent. At least the ones in the state penitentiary do. Most are guilty. Not all of us, but most. You know your father admitted killing a man. It doesn't matter that he became a model inmate, that he works with the authorities as an inside counselor. It doesn't matter that he became a born-again Christian, that he finally found peace within himself and brings that peace to others. It doesn't matter that he has saved the lives of a dozen inmates, including mine, and those of a couple of prison guards. And it doesn't matter that he's loved you more than anything in the whole world for the last twenty years. He is a convicted murderer who will probably remain where he is until the day he dies."

Rondell felt like saying that was where he belonged, but Ed's tone caused him to hold his tongue. Lydia sat silently, turning the wooden rabbit over and over in her hands. At last, she said, "My father's sentence was life without the possibility of parole. He will never be released."

"The word 'never' doesn't belong in my vocabulary, for all sorts of reasons. I promised your father I would do whatever I could to make his last days peaceful in some manner, even if all I can do is assure his daughter that he embraced God and is living the right way, as best he can.

Lydia frowned. "What do you mean – his last days?"

"Cleve wanted me to give you a letter as well. He said the best way was to write it all down." Ed reached into the backpack once more and pulled out an envelope, thick with folded paper. He handed it over.

Ten minutes passed in silence. Rondell watched his wife as she read the five-page letter, carefully and legibly drafted. "He's dying of AIDS," she said to no one in particular. Tears welled in her eyes. "How was he when you last saw him?"

"He was in reasonably good health, but we both know the nature of the disease's progression. He may have anywhere between six months and six years. Or more – there's just no way to tell. But he was so proud of you and the work you do. We talked many times about you and your research at Stanford. Cleve didn't care that he'd set such a bad example. He admired you and he feels honored to be your father."

Ed slid his hand into his pocket and withdrew a thin card. He stood up and offered his hand. "I won't keep you any longer. It was a pleasure to meet both of you. Please excuse my interrupting your afternoon."

Lydia shook his hand, taking the small card as she did so. She looked into Solkar's eyes; they were black, intense, and hiding both intelligence and – what? Fear? Pain? Secrets? She couldn't tell. "Thank you for coming."

Ed left without another word. Rondell did not offer to shake hands. As her husband closed the door, Lydia glanced at the card. It had a series of numbers on it, like a telephone number, but with a foreign exchange prefix. Beneath the number was a series of digits that made no immediate sense. She slipped the card into the pocket of her jeans and returned to her husband, who wrapped huge arms around her. In his comforting embrace, Dr. Lydia Lambert Jackson began to weep.

Ed drove back to Highway 101 and headed north. Two days and nights of travel, hunched in the Greyhound's seat, propped up against the window, watching the scenery roll by, had given him plenty of time to think. As he crossed the San Mateo Bridge into Hayward, he reflected on the promises he'd made over the years. There were far too many he'd failed to keep, but at least he had made a start with Lydia.

He had two more on his agenda: the first he could take care of soon; the second would be more difficult. *How can you keep a promise to someone who is no longer alive?* His gut told him he had done the right thing all those years ago, but rational thought told a different tale. The trial had been risky, but he'd taken the chance regardless. Ironically, that was probably why he was still alive, despite the crude technology. A shot in the dark, a bit of guesswork, a couple of site-directed mutations. Only one other person knew why it had worked for him. For the others, with their own customized therapies, the outcomes varied. Now nearly all of them were dead or dying.

Samaya. He still couldn't say her name aloud. Fifteen years had passed, and he struggled to form the syllables of her name on his lips. Then there was

Kay, for whom he'd done everything. Kay, for whom he would do almost anything, but he couldn't undo what she had done to herself. Lightning had struck twice, meting out swift, brutal, and circular justice.

He checked the dashboard. The tank was getting low. He realized that his cash-only deal for the Olds hadn't included a full tank of gas. He pulled into the first Shell station he could find, pumped the cheap stuff in, and paid. Before driving off, he made one more phone call at the payphone. It was time to fulfil another promise.

"Hello?" A male voice answered after two rings.

"It's Ed. I'm going to need your help."

"Any time, old friend. Who's the target?"

"I wish you wouldn't put it like that."

"Let me rephrase. Who are we going to take care of?"

"Professor Michelle Durant."

"After all she did for you?"

After all she did for me. "Here's what we're going to do."

Chapter 24

Marcus checked into an airport hotel that evening. He no longer cared what time zone he was in, and his natural Circadian rhythm was shot anyway. Downstairs, transient sales reps, conferees, and casual travelers were hard at work downing pitchers of beer in the sports bar, watching the Cubbies lose again, or the Black Hawks fighting for their playoff lives, or the Bulls steamrolling through all comers. The White Sox would be on later from the West Coast, as soon as the Oakland rain delay lifted. He had half a mind to join the gathering, blend in for the evening, and enjoy the anonymity of the crowd, one eye on the big screen, downing one beer after another.

Screw it, he thought. *I'm tired of running around.* He put on his shoes and picked up his wallet and phone, then realized he hadn't turned it back on after landing. The familiar welcome jingle finished. Assorted icons signaled a number of missed calls and texts. The first was from Josef Rintlen, asking him to dial in as soon as he could. The second carried a more urgent tone. "Call me NOW."

The voice message was no less persuasive. He looked at the time log and realized the call had come in several hours earlier. Probably while he was en route from Dublin. Quickly, he made the call.

Rintlen picked up on the first ring. "Where have you been?"

"Sorry, Josef. I've been in the air. No phones allowed."

"That rule never stopped me."

"Right now I don't think it would be a good idea if I broke any of the rules," Marcus said. He relayed the events of the previous twenty-four hours, culminating with his convoluted departure. He included the description of the woman he'd seen speaking with Al Wylie just before they disappeared in the taxi.

"Shit," Josef breathed. "Did you get a photo of her?"

"No time." He described her as best he could.

"Well, you were probably correct to leave London. Where next?"

"The Castleford Institute. I was hoping you might have some details on the place. Like who owns or leases it now, whether Henry and Linda are still around, or whether they took their money and ran off to the sunshine."

Josef filled him in. "The University of Chicago bought the building in its entirety to expand its business school. They rebuilt the entire facility internally, but without gutting it. As for the Castlefords, both Henry and Linda passed away three years ago."

"Please don't tell me it was a suicide pact," Marcus said.

"No. Henry died from lung cancer. Linda suffered from Alzheimer's disease. Henry looked after her for years, but the strain took him first. Linda's friends said she probably died of a broken heart rather than complications from her own struggle. Who are we to argue?"

I wouldn't dream of it. "And their estate?"

"An undisclosed amount. It all went to a biotech company based in Alice Springs, Australia, of all places. The company is called Demetek Corporation."

"Never heard of them. What do they do?"

"Their web page suggests botanicals. I would imagine that genetically modified crops form the basis of their intellectual property."

Marcus thought that was odd. Why would a biomedical research foundation change focus so radically? "How big is this outfit?"

"It is hard to know. It is not a public corporation. There is a very limited amount of information available. They are quite secretive about their advisory board and management team. I suspect they do not respond to general inquiries."

"Perhaps we should look further into what they do, huh?"

"I recommend we keep it on our radar screen. The reason I asked you to call as soon as possible concerns the initials on the notebook page you showed me yesterday. George has been investigating."

"He found something else?"

"We both did. Do you recall the report on Shanahan?"

"The shrink who shot himself, right?"

"There was a witness. His name was Stuart Gray. Does that name mean anything to you?"

"Should it?"

"He was the Director of Protein Biochemistry at Lycogen. He lived in Pacifica. His initials also match one of the names in MacCallum's list. Stuart Gray and his family were reported missing last night."

Marcus felt his blood run cold. This was snowballing out of control. Who was behind this? Where were they? How soon would they catch up with him? Family members, innocents, even those only peripherally involved were all disappearing. What in the world were these people trying to hide?

He asked Josef that very question.

"We do not know yet. There is no proof of foul play in the disappearance of the Grays. Their daughter's best friend alerted police when he couldn't find anyone in the family."

"Maybe they just went on vacation?"

"A reasonable theory, and that is why they have not issued an Amber alert yet. They are not treating it as a high priority case. But there is more. I have some further information on one of the others in the list. I looked for any similarities between your wife's death and others over the past twenty years, particularly where the body had been unidentifiable through standard means. I flagged those cases in which family members were asked to identify the victims. My search algorithms turned up over a dozen hits, but I did not have to look far to find a match whose initials were in MacCallum's notebook."

"And?"

"Samaya Isabelle Jonas," Josef continued. "She was the victim in an Illinois case several years ago. Her body was destroyed by fire. There was no way to determine whether she had been disfigured, strangled, raped, or assaulted in any other way. She was in her early twenties, a research assistant employed at the Henry and Linda Castleford Institute."

Marcus felt as though a pair of cold hands were tightening around his neck. He repeated her name slowly. "Samaya Isabelle Jonas." He crosschecked the initials in the notebook. "Okay, so there's a parallel, but is that just a coincidence? She was in the unchecked group. What's the significance?"

"A man named Edmund Ranjit Solkar was convicted for killing her. He claimed he was Jonas's lover. At first, the prosecution wanted the death penalty, but some slick work by his defense lawyer got him a shorter and far less terminal sentence."

The name rang a distant bell, but Marcus attributed it to recollections of old news reports. It hardly mattered now that the man's initials were staring up at him from the notebook.

"That is why I asked George to meet with Solkar's attorney of record," Josef continued. "Michelle Durant, his lawyer, is on the faculty at Davis."

"UC Davis? The law school?"

"The same. A lucky break, one might think, but I do not believe in luck."

Not even bad luck? "Did George learn anything useful?"

"Professor Durant recently contacted her former client. He is apparently in the construction business on the Gulf Coast of Florida. She told George about a message she received. It said, 'If you want to live, find Edmund Solkar' and was signed R.S."

"R.S? Surely that couldn't be Ralph Shanahan again?"

"Uncertain, but a reasonable conclusion."

"And his lawyer did what she was told?"

"So George tells me," Josef said. "He had to present – evidence – to Professor Durant to convince her to talk."

Marcus's heart was already pounding hard enough. "What kind of evidence?"

Josef paused for a moment before answering the question. "I am sorry. It was the only way he could persuade her. The similarities were quite profound."

Marcus closed his eyes and gritted his teeth. "Where is Solkar now? Is there any reason to imagine he's responsible for any of this stuff?"

"We do not know that yet. However, his lawyer is willing to help find him."

"Is she the only person who stays in touch with the guy?"

"The only one we know about. She agreed to let us know the minute she hears from her client. If Solkar had anything to do with Gray's disappearance, he will probably ask her for legal representation."

"And what if he had nothing to do with Gray?" Marcus asked.

"I can almost guarantee they knew each other. Before his arrest and conviction, Edmund Solkar was a professor at the University of Chicago, in the same department as Kay."

Josef's final statement hit Marcus like a mallet to his chest. He wasn't sure if he'd heard right. "Did you say Kay, or Gray?"

"I am sorry, Marcus. You heard me correctly, but I should also have said Gray. All three worked there during the same period. There is no question that your wife and Solkar knew each other. *How* well is an entirely different question."

Chapter 25

DON STRATHMORE PICKED UP the telephone on the second ring. His caller ID said Private Call. "Status report?"

"I think you can relax."

"Not my nature to do that."

"That's why you pay me, right? To help you relax."

"I pay you because I believe in what our company is doing *now*, regardless of its convoluted history. Every great advance in research has its price; we both know that. And if a small number of individuals have to die so we can change the future, with our planet's dwindling resources, isn't that a price worth paying?"

"The alternative, as you saw it, was to for someone to unleash a deadly pathogen, call it superflu, call it anthropox, whatever. A bug capable of pinning back at least fifty percent of the human population. You said that would take care of the problem just fine."

Strathmore recalled their first meeting. Sarah had seduced him four years earlier, her brilliant mind and achingly beautiful body had captivated him, fed his ego, and catered to his every desire. She'd used the oldest trick in the book, but he hadn't cared. They'd spent an entire summer aboard his motor yacht, cruising the Mediterranean, from Gibraltar all the way around the foot of Italy and up the Adriatic, calling on exotic locales along the way. They savored the delights of the French Riviera, the Amalfi Coast, and islands too numerous to count, making love night and day, sharing dreams and visions.

The falsely idyllic relationship, if one could call it that, had lasted until he discovered what she knew. That was when everything changed. No longer did romance play a part in their relationship. Then again, it probably never did; it was surely an acting performance of best-actress-Oscar quality. Yet, to Sarah's surprise, Strathmore was made of the same hard materials. It wasn't easy for him to detach completely, in light of their three month affair, but he had recognized the cooling of the inferno. By the time his yacht docked back at Gibraltar, he knew the flames had dwindled to embers.

No, not embers. They were out completely. But that minor inconvenience didn't stop him. He knew that enough money would overcome just about any obstacle. She delivered what he wanted, everything her mentor had placed on ice before circumstances impeded progress. Strathmore learned that refinement was essential, but eminently possible. The key was to bring Hernandez, Dayne, and Goudreau on board, and without Sarah's help he might never have pulled Justin away from his Texas fiefdom. It also didn't hurt to have rich, dying relatives, and bent attorneys to help them distribute their estates to the right beneficiary.

Money, technology, and the ability to deliver it to the global population. Demetek Corporation had them all, and he, Donald Strathmore was in charge. He had the power to change everything.

Sarah Innes reminded him that she was still there. "Do you have an ID on that photo I sent you?"

"Not yet. For what it's worth, Steve's never seen him, but you're probably chasing shadows. Speaking of which, what's the status on Solkar?"

"Unknown, but as soon as he finds his lawyer he's vulnerable, so I'll make my move then. You okay with that?" She ended the call without waiting for his reply.

Strathmore stood up, his six-foot-four frame athletic and muscular. In his late forties, the well-tanned, dark-haired financier sported a short but immaculately trimmed haircut, a graying goatee, and tinted contacts that enhanced his already blue eyes. He opened his office door and went in search of Justin Hernandez. On the way, he waved a friendly hand at the cube denizens, ignoring their "How ya going?" questions.

His chief scientist was in Steve Goudreau's closed office, which was where he seemed to spend much of his time these days. Both men were staring at the monitor on Steve's desk. "Hey, guys, what's happening?" Strathmore asked.

"Don," Hernandez said coolly. "We've got a problem."

"Yeah? What kind of problem?"

The monitor showed the jungle scene, its bank of little gauges holding steady. Steve was dragging the mouse all over the table, using it as a camera controller, affording viewers a panoramic view. The scroll wheel acted as a zoom device. "See the cursor?" Hernandez asked.

Strathmore peered at the screen. "Okay, I've got it."

"Zoom in, Steve," Hernandez said. Steve's index finger twitched, magnifying a reddish-brown mass beneath a forest of long-leafed ferns. As the camera got closer, the image resolution declined, blurring the red-brown object. Shadows cast by the fern's leaves blended with the image.

"That's as close as I can get," Steve said.

The sienna-colored mass darkened suddenly, and a flash of white and brown flew across the screen. "Whoa!" Strathmore shouted. "What the bloody hell was that?"

Steve zoomed back out far enough to show the swinging howler monkey. Its mouth was agape in the expression he had grown accustomed to seeing. The speakers were muted, so they couldn't hear its cry. "It's just Benicio," he declared flatly.

"You named it?" Strathmore inquired. "It's a bloody monkey. An experiment."

"He's a living creature, Don, not just an experiment. And yes, I did give him a name." The animal clung to a vine and swayed from side to side a few times, before climbing down, hand over hand. When Benicio reached the ground he scampered towards the brown blur, his form shrinking as he went.

All three peered at the blur. Steve swiveled the speaker knob a quarter turn. Now they could hear running water, a light breeze, and the movements of unseen rain forest creatures. The howler stopped at the ferns, looked up to the sky, and screeched.

The sound was a frightening, unearthly shriek that pierced the men's ears. Steve shrank back from the screen, jerking the mouse involuntarily. The motion caused the picture to shift away, leaving only a shot of vegetation and a few patches of blue sky above. Benicio continued his horrifying squall, now off camera.

"Turn the sound down," Hernandez ordered calmly.

Steve fumbled with the speaker knob, rotating it all the way back and reducing the piercing screech to merciful silence.

"Okay. Pull it back slowly. Let's get a bead on what's happening in Bio 1."

Steve took a deep breath and settled anew. He twisted and tweaked the mouse, quickly regaining his bearings. The camera panned over the jungle scene again, its lens directed towards the ground. A slight movement to the left revealed the brown, white, green, and reddish colors occupying a small corner of the screen. He zoomed in to see the silhouette of the howler beginning to take shape. Unfortunately, Benicio was now too far away for anyone to see what he was screaming at.

"Is there a closer camera that you can switch to?" Strathmore suggested.

"Good thought, Don," Hernandez said. "Check under the tools menu."

Steve pressed Ctrl-Tab, popping up a master panel. Under "Tools," he found a "Camera Control" sub-menu. This displayed a list of all the monitors and cameras available, cross-referenced to their respective biodomes. An array of nine separate cameras arranged in a three-by-three grid serviced Bio 1, the jungle area. They had just been using camera 8. "I'll try camera 7. It's the next one to the left." He clicked on a radio button. Moments later, Steve brought the shot of rain forest plants into focus.

Slowly he pushed the mouse forward, using it like a joystick to fly an aircraft. The top of Benicio's head came into view, now in high-def resolution. The monkey's ongoing scream gave only a hint of what was to follow. Steve gripped the desk with his other hand, all his knuckles white. The other men in the room watched, fascinated. Down the camera went, past the howler. The tops of the ferns were crushed, as if something heavy had fallen on them.

And then they saw the brown mass in high-res horror. The chimpanzee lay in a pool of blood, apparently its own. Its head lolled at an angle. The grinning mouth, lips pulled back, gave only a hint of the pain the creature must have felt. Congealing fluids, saliva mixed with more blood, seeped from the corner of the ape's mouth.

"Oh, Jesus!" Steve breathed. "Craig!"

"You named him too?" Strathmore asked. He glanced at Hernandez, who cocked his left eyebrow. The corner of the Texan's mouth turned up ever so slightly.

"Of course I did, you son of a bitch!" the biologist hissed, taking note of his colleague's gesture. "They have feelings, even if you two don't. The monkey's reaction should have been enough to convince you of that." He turned up the speaker. The hideous screaming returned. He deliberately let the cacophony sink in.

Hernandez turned the knob back off. "Steve, I appreciate what you're saying, but we're not here to focus on the emotions of a lab animal. We're here to determine whether the product is ready for launch. So far, all I've seen is evidence that one chimpanzee has died in Bio 1. How it died is something we may never know. Logic would dictate an accidental fall, but it doesn't matter. The real experiment appears sound."

"Accidental fall? An agile primate like Craig?" Steve countered.

"Right, poor dead Craig. I beg his pardon," Hernandez mocked. "Look, the chimp was in an unfamiliar, artificial environment. Not an Old World natural habitat, but one of our making, sharing the space with New World flora and fauna. We have no reason to suspect its death was anything but accidental."

"What about suicide?" Strathmore asked.

"I can't imagine why," Hernandez said, shaking his head. "We worked that bug out years ago. But so what? Where we're planning to deploy, you might argue that a simultaneous population decrease could be quite beneficial."

Goudreau looked at his colleague with revulsion. "You can't be serious."

Justin Hernandez gave the others his widest, most handsome grin. "Don't be ridiculous! I said 'you might argue.' I'm not a goddamned monster!"

Aren't you? Strathmore thought. *Goudreau may see it that way, and if he does, we have to make sure he doesn't interfere.*

Chapter 26

After a couple of hours' fitful sleep, Marcus Black woke to find it was still dark outside. The sound of decelerating jet engines, then a blast of reverse thrust signaling an early arrival at O'Hare, was the only disturbance that could have woken him. The clock on the cheap nightstand told him it was just after six. His head hurt a little, but his acidic stomach was worse. "Stupid, stupid, stupid," he muttered. He remembered going downstairs to the sports bar and staying until well past two in the morning, just trying to forget the past few days. He climbed out of bed and stumbled to the bathroom. He wanted to throttle the guy who'd told him that those who never got hangovers – well, that's the best they'd ever feel. He filled a glass with water, drained it, and then repeated the process three more times. Rehydration (and a day of abstinence) was really the only way to get rid of the cobwebs.

After showering, shaving, and dressing, he ventured downstairs for an early breakfast. Half a pot of coffee and a bowl of cereal later, he began feeling much better. The early edition of the USA Today displayed headlines about the wretched economy, the plight of GIs in danger zones, and a cover story about a woman widowed by *guerillas* in Central America. *Same old, same old*. Very little content concerned non-US-centric world news. Only a short paragraph appeared on the London "scare." Marcus ignored all but the sports pages, where he read about the sad plight of Bay Area sports teams.

Same old, same old.

After breakfast, he called a car agency and organized a rental for ten that morning. In the interim, he logged on to the internet and mapped out a route to what used to be the Henry and Linda Castleford Institute building, now part of the University of Chicago. He hoped someone there would point him towards a records archive. Whether or not he'd gain access was a complete unknown.

The traffic into Naperville, part of the Illinois Technology and Research Corridor, moved well late in the morning, but Marcus imagined it could have been much worse during rush hour. The city was listed as one of the best places to live in the nation. Dozens of major corporations occupied headquarters close to or in the city proper. Oil companies, high-tech research organizations famous for their Nobel prize-winning contributions to society, and financial service leaders all called Naperville home. Major retailers and restaurant chains contributed to one of the country's largest shopping districts, and the population of residents was growing rapidly. Marcus wondered what it looked like a generation ago. He assumed that even then the new office buildings and headquarters signaled a new era of prosperity, with Chicago and Big Ten universities providing the brain trust to feed the machine and make it run the way America should.

The former Castleford Institute building was just off the East-West I-88 tollway. Two blocks from the exit stood a four-story, whitewashed building with a university logo prominent above an arched entry. A "School of Business, Naperville Campus" sign adorned a square concrete bollard beneath the arch. Nearby, a billboard showed directions to the various departments, to the library, and to the lecture theater.

He found a visitor's parking bay and made his way to the reception desk. Inside, a tired looking woman in her early sixties looked up at him. He wondered if she'd been at the job for the last thirty years, a feeling not disabused by her unenthusiastic offer to help.

"Good morning, Ms. Gorelik," Marcus said, observing the name plate on her desk. He'd learned long ago that receptionists appreciated being addressed as individuals. In this case, he sensed she was old enough to prefer title and last name. Perhaps she would warm to him if he avoided her first name until directed.

His instincts were correct, insofar as Janet Gorelik's expression thawed a little. "May I help you?" Her voice was smoky.

Marcus flashed a business card. He asked Ms. Gorelik if she would be so kind as to tell him if she knew anyone who was still on staff dating back fifteen, twenty years. "I'm actually interested in some old records from when this was the Castleford Institute."

"Oh, my!" Janet exclaimed. "You're in luck. I used to work for Mr. Castleford, as his personal assistant. I chose to remain on staff when the University offered me a position here, rather than go with him when he sold up."

"You worked for Henry Castleford yourself?" Marcus couldn't believe his luck. Perhaps she knew some of the people who had worked here. "In this building?"

"Oh, no. Our offices were downtown. I was very lucky to get this job. My daughter and her husband live right here in Naperville. It's much easier for me to spend time with my grandchildren."

"Of course. Less traffic to deal with, no doubt?"

"It's not much fun during the week even now, and on the weekends everyone flocks to the city anyway. But at least the distance is shorter."

"I know what you mean. It's no picnic where I come from."

"Where is that?" Janet asked, before correcting herself. "Oh, of course. It was on your card, somewhere in California."

"That's right. Say, Mrs. Gorelik?"

"Janet, please call me Janet."

"Thank you, I will. And please, call me Marcus. Janet, do you know someone else I could speak with regarding the days of the Institute here? Perhaps someone with access to historical information, maybe the architecture, building plans and stuff? Not personnel records, just public info that you wouldn't easily find on the internet?"

Janet pursed her lips for a moment. "You'd have to talk to Mr. Shea. He's the deputy facilities manager here. Let me get him on the phone." Her fingers worked the switchboard. "Billy?" she asked into a microphone.

"Yeah, Jan?" a voice said through a speaker.

"I've got a Dr. Marcus Black here who's interested in the building from way back when. You're the only other person who used to work here, so I thought you might could answer his questions. Can you spare a few minutes?"

"Sure. No problem. Everything here is running smoothly so I'm just sittin' here twiddlin' my thumbs. I'll be right down."

"Good news?" Marcus said when Janet signed off.

"Maybe so. Mr. Shea will be here in a few moments. If you'd like to take a seat in the lobby?"

While waiting, he wondered why she didn't ask him to sign for a visitor's badge. Perhaps it was a Midwestern trust thing, but maybe it was just because the place was a business school. All manner of students, staff, and traders would be teeming in and out.

Two minutes later an elevator door opened to his left. A wiry, white-haired man with a weathered face emerged. He turned to the receptionist and offered an almost imperceptible wink. Marcus guessed he was about as old as Janet Gorelik, and when the latter's eyes brightened, he wondered if they had something going on. The man's hands were large and callused. "Bill Shea. Pleased to meet you."

Marcus shook hands, noting how firm and powerful Shea's grip was. "Marcus Black. Mrs. Gorelik was kind enough to point me in your direction."

"What can I do for you, Doc?"

"Please, just Marcus. I'm not an M.D." He explained why he was there, and what he was looking for. "Do you know of any old blueprints of the Castleford Institute, as it used to be, anywhere left in the building?"

Shea frowned. "Dunno. There was an old closet up on the top floor where we dumped a bunch of stuff years ago. Can't say that I've been in there in ages, so there's no telling what you might find. You're welcome to have a look, though."

"Thank you. Will you show me the way?"

"Better than that. I'll come with you. I'm a tad curious. It's been a long time." They boarded the elevator, and waited in silence as the cab climbed upwards. At the fourth floor, Shea led the way to the right. "We don't use as much of the space as we used to. 'Til a couple years ago, this entire wing was full, but when the economy started heading south, the faculty shrank. Kind of surprising, if you ask me. In a recession, people who lose their jobs go back to school. Universities thrive, but we weren't so lucky. Everyone blamed the financial sector for what went wrong. If you ask me, we just provided what people wanted. If greedy folks couldn't pay for it, they should have had a bit more self-control."

Old fashioned sanctimony, Marcus thought. But he probably had a point. "So the university lost staff?"

"Guess the initials MBA carry a bit more stigma these days," Shea said. "Me, well, I don't even have a college degree. I learned at the school of life, the one where they tell you to 'do the math.' You add up what you have, and subtract what you owe. If it comes out ahead, you're OK, if it doesn't, you fix it as soon as you can and don't dig yourself any deeper. Call it accountin' one-oh-one if you want, but hell, accountin's just another word for countin' with an 'a' and a 'c' on the front. It ain't hard."

They arrived at a locked door at the end of the hall, next to an exit stairwell, protected by a closed fire door.

Shea rambled on. Marcus wondered how many opportunities he had to chat during the day. "I'm surviving. Never had much, never owed much. The math was always simple for me, and I've spent my life making sure it didn't get any more complicated. Like I said, if I couldn't pay for it, I didn't buy it. And I've got a good job. Don't pay much, but it keeps me busy most of the time."

"Been here a while, Janet mentioned."

Shea turned to him and brightened at the sound of her name. "Jan's a lovely lady. Known her for twenty years. Seen her go through hell and back with that son of a bitch son-in-law of hers. Then Kelly, her daughter, she got the guts to leave the bastard and hook up with a good man. A cop, none the less."

A bit too much information for a first meeting, Marcus thought, but there was no shutting the man up. Perhaps Shea's verbal diarrhea could be useful, especially if he knew where some of the bodies were buried. "Was her second husband the cop?"

"Hell, no. The first one. He was bent as all get-out. Beat the crap out of her too. Nah, the second husband's an engineer. Works for the oil company down the street."

Marcus thought he'd seen the company building Shea was referring to on his drive down I-88. "I know the one. Well, I'm glad she's happy now."

"Ain't that the truth. And her mother's been a lot more inclined to, well, get out and have a good time in these last few years," Shea added.

They arrived at the locked door. "Shall we?" Marcus asked.

"Ah, shucks. Sorry about that, I've been goin' on about stuff." He jangled a keychain on a retractable lanyard tied to his belt loop. He fiddled with three similar-looking keys without luck. The fourth one worked. He pushed open the door to reveal an almost pitch black interior.

Inside, Shea flipped a light switch and revealed a shambolic display of desks, filing cabinets, and bookshelves, all in 1980's office style. The shelves were empty but for a few loose post-it notes still stuck to the dusty surfaces. More little yellow squares lay about the floor. The twelve desks were stacked in twos, top to top, legs up in the air. Behind the desks, eight double width filing cabinets were jammed against the wall, two rows deep. Each cabinet had four drawers.

The closet of retired furniture would not relinquish its skeletons without some muscular exertion. "Looks like you may need a hand shifting this stuff around," Shea offered. "I'm up for it if you are."

"Let's do it," Marcus agreed. They shimmied the half dozen pairs of desks to one side, exposing two of the filing cabinets. "Did you stay in touch with anyone who worked here when this place was the Castleford Institute?"

"Not a one," Shea replied, straining at the first cabinet. "Let me shift these so you can get at the cabinets in back. Judgin' by the weight, I reckon this one doesn't have much in it." He opened one of the drawers and confirmed his prediction. The other three drawers only contained a few empty hanging folders. The second cabinet was as easy to move as the first. It too was virtually empty.

They spent the next ten minutes playing a game of shift-and-search, moving cabinets around like a tile puzzle. Typically, the penultimate cabinet was the only one that still contained papers left inside the hanging folders. These were long forgotten purchase requisitions, filled out by someone named

Vikram de Silva. The items were standard biochemistry assay supplies. Marcus put them on top of the cabinet and dug a little deeper, feeling behind the folders for fallen or misfiled papers.

He was about to give up when his fingers latched onto a plastic box six inches square and four inches deep. Assuming it was an old lunch container, he eased it out, imagining a fifteen-year-old sandwich about to spring forth in live festering horror. Instead, he saw a stack of labeled CD-ROM's inside. The labels had faded, but the disc on top distinctly bore the name "De Silva book 0452 Supplementary Material" inked onto the label with a magic marker.

Lab notebooks, Marcus thought. *What happened to the lab notebooks?* He stared at the box, thinking about how most companies sent archive copies of their bound laboratory records to off-site storage facilities. As valuable as intellectual property was, organizations had to ensure their records were protected. Scientists recorded their experimental data and observations in approved bound books that when signed, witnessed, and indexed, carried weight in the courts.

Data such as printouts from instruments and data recorders contained crucial information to support the scientists' written observations, glued into the master books, signed, and witnessed. In certain cases, so much data might result from a single experiment that it could not all be printed out and glued in. That was where CD-ROMs came in. All supplementary files could be saved and burned to a disk, which itself stayed with the master book.

At off-site archiving facilities, read-only (i.e. non-printable) copies of notebooks were usually available for reference purposes or experimental continuity. Because scientists needed to massage data, perform calculations, draw inferences, and to present conclusions in clear terms, they needed access to raw data and instrument-generated files. Protecting this kind of data was impractical. While most company computers had no CD-burning capabilities, only maximum-security procedures could stop employees from bringing in their own peripherals and generating private archives of scanned notebooks and data tables. Marcus concluded that was what Vikram de Silva had done.

His imagination began to wander. What else was on those disks? Was there something critical lurking deep within some old instrument interface, or some clue to an experiment somewhere? It was all he had, but it was something.

"I have to check those out," he whispered absently.

As soon as I can get them out of here.

BOOK 3
ALICE AFORETHOUGHT

Chapter 27

BILL SHEA WAS THINKING about what he had just found. He was about to point it out, when he thought he heard Marcus speak. The younger man was staring at the transparent plastic box in his hands. "Did you say something?"

Marcus didn't answer immediately. He was too deep in thought. He also didn't want to crack the lid, split the whole box, and send the contents flying into the dust.

"Marcus? You hear me? Did you say something?"

He looked up and shook his head from side to side. "Sorry, Bill. I'm just talking to myself. Say, do you have a good memory for the folks who worked here?"

"For some I did. You remember a murder case from back in the nineties?"

"Around here? I wouldn't know. Was there one in particular?" He sensed what was coming next but didn't want to prompt Shea any more than he had to.

"Guy called Eddie Solkar. There was an unusual fella, if ever there was one. Always pleasant, mind. Never had a bad word to say. Then there was this gal, Sam, we called her. Whoa, Nellie, what a fine piece that one was." He puffed out his cheeks and shook his head. "Sam had Eddie wrapped 'round her little finger. Then one day she was dead, and he 'fessed up. Came clean as a whistle. Never said why, but some hotshot lawyer got his sentence reduced from the big one the state wanted to lay on him. He pleaded guilty to a lesser charge. Myself, I'm not convinced he really did it, and if he did, I reckon she'd provoked him. That one was somethin' else. Anyhow, Eddie went down for the crime, Sam's momma came forward and ID'd the body."

"Her mother? Who was she?"

"She was a prof at the University of Chicago, you know, that fine

135

institution which pays my salary every month. Anyhow, the cops took her to the morgue and showed the poor woman her daughter's body, burned to a freakin' crisp. She pointed out the missing toe on poor Sam's left foot. The piggie that had none. Right next to the one that went wee, wee, wee."

All the way home. Marcus shook his head, bewildered. "Bill, do you happen to remember her mother's name?"

"'Fraid not, right now. It ain't ringin' a bell, but if I think of it I'll let you know. I do remember somethin' about her bein' in the genetics department over at the U. She took a big long leave of absence after the Solkar business, and then packed it in altogether. They replaced her with some French guy. Can't remember his name either but it don't really matter."

"Well, if you do remember hers, I'd be interested." Marcus said, understating his intense desire to know more. "Scientists in scandals – they're not like celebrities so they don't wind up on ET, but that doesn't make their stories any less interesting."

Shea considered the point, and nodded. Then he remembered what he was about to say before he was distracted. "Say, Doc, didn't you say you wanted to see the architecture or building plans?"

"Oh, right," Marcus replied. "I wanted to know where in the building they did different kinds of research. Blueprints would probably be a good clue."

"If so, then how's about you take a look at these?" Shea pulled out a rolled up tube of architectural drawings from one of the other cabinets. He handed them to Marcus, who unraveled them and placed them on one of the upside-down desks.

The top sheet was the building schematic. The others showed more detail of individual floors and sections. Marcus decided to look at the fine drawings later, if Shea let him take them away, but for the time being the overview was plenty. On the top floor, where they were now, chemistry labs occupied both wings of the building, with enough space for 40 workers. On the third floor, large instrument rooms dominated one wing. Chemical and bioanalytical facilities, high-throughput screening robotics, and cell biology labs occupied the other. The biology labs were BSL-2, or biosafety laboratory level 2 facilities. BSL-2 labs permitted the study of microorganisms presenting non-lethal, but potentially hazardous health risks. The entire second floor was devoted to administration and office areas, and a cafeteria. The ground floor contained molecular biology and protein production areas in one wing. These also carried BSL-2 restrictions.

The other ground floor wing, completely self-enclosed, was set up as a BSL-3 level unit. This area handled potentially airborne microorganisms with a high risk of infection. A separate HVAC system, distinct from the rest of the facility, gave the wing multiple and redundant safeguards. Doors with airlocks at each end of the wing presented the only available entry/exit points.

The building's last feature was a basement annex, accessible only through a tunnel that ran about a hundred yards from the rear. The blueprint showed it as BSL-4, the highest standard for containment safety. Pathogens such as Ebola, Marburg, and anthrax could only be handled in such facilities. Also, any newly discovered microorganism with genetic similarities to a known extreme pathogen required BSL-4 safety precautions until someone demonstrated that it would not threaten health or life. BSL-4 regulations demanded far greater security than the Institute's annex afforded, so Marcus concluded it was BSL-4 in design only, and that it did not really house any extreme bugs. "Got any idea what they were doing with this one, Bill?" he asked, pointing at the annex blueprint.

"I never talked about it with anyone. And I didn't go there either. It was off-limits, which was just fine with me. But you meet people in the halls, and they chit-chat by the coffee machine, stuff like that. I overheard a couple of gals talking about the odd virus, and some kind of new vaccine. You ever hear the word 'chimera,' Doc?"

"A mythological creature like a centaur. In microbiology, it's less profound."

"Well, whatever they were workin' on, I didn't think about it a whole lot. Don't reckon they ever used that basement lab for anything deadly, anyhow."

Marcus wondered about the entries in MacCallum's notebook, and Kay's letter. *The trial.* Did the experiment happen right here, in this very building? More importantly, was there anyone left alive who could tell him?

A thought occurred to him. He pointed at the purchase requisitions on top of the last cabinet. "Bill, can you take a look at these? Anything look familiar to you here?"

Shea loped over to the old sheets and stared at them for a moment, before breaking into a grin. "Holy moly, I remember him! Good old Vik de Silva. Everyone called him Gator."

Gator? The odd nickname mystified Marcus. "How come?"

"Hell, when he first got here, one of the other lab guys asked him where he was from. He said he was goin', and the other fella said, 'Okay, see ya later, alligator.' And that kinda stuck."

Marcus had to think about that one. The name was Portuguese, with an Indian first name. Possibly Sri Lankan? Then it clicked. "I get it. He was from Goa. On the west coast of India. Lots of Portuguese settlers there a long time ago. So, when he said he was 'goin',' he was really saying he was Goan." He pronounced it Go-Ann. "Cute."

"Kid could play softball like no one I've ever seen," Bill Shea mused. "He won us championships for three straight years. Never used a glove in the field, and batted about 900. Said he'd never played the game before, but you coulda fooled me. He was our MVP by a long shot." Shea smiled at the distant memory.

"Anything else spring to mind? What did he do here?"

"Oh, heck, he was just the nicest guy, always had a smile for everyone. Did all the bio lab purchasing, 'cos he could talk all the vendors into giving discounts. Must have saved the Institute tens of thousands of dollars every year, maybe more. See this one here? Bought a whole colony of mice. Check out the discount."

Thirty percent, Marcus observed. He had no sense of what the regular cost would be, but the invoice showed the mouse strain as "nude balb-c," each of which would come with a fuzzy "buddy" to help keep the hairless one warm. Nude mice were not cheap on the best of days, and when they were genetically modified and bred accordingly, the cost per animal would rarely, if ever, be discounted. "Must have been a regular shipment."

"Got that right. The shipping and receiving guy was running around all day with all the stuff these labs brought in."

"I can imagine. Say, Bill, I reckon I've got what I came for right here," Marcus said, pointing to the blueprints. "My company's looking at a similar type of design for a new building, and it would be really helpful if I could give the architects a bit of a jump start. Save us a bit of cash if we could borrow the layout concept for a while?"

"No skin off my nose. Take whatever you need." Shea looked at his watch and noted that it was getting dangerously close to lunchtime. "Say, Doc, I don't mean to rush you out of here, but I'm gettin' a bit peckish. Can we finish up some other time?" He wandered over to the door and started to open it.

"Actually, I'm all done," Marcus said, sneaking the small box of CD-ROMs out by folding them up in the blueprints. "I really appreciate your time, Bill. Very useful."

"My pleasure. Nice to have a science jock to talk to again, even if I'm not in that trade myself. All we get here are the folks who want to make a quick buck." Shea held the door open for his visitor, and then locked it behind them. They made their way back down the hall. He whipped out a push-to-talk cell phone and told Janet Gorelik that Dr. Black was on his way down, and that he'd see her a bit later.

At the lobby, Marcus thanked both of them and wished them well. He noticed how Shea looked at Mrs. Gorelik and drifted away himself, thinking of Kay, and how he'd always looked at her that way.

Why? Why did you do that to yourself?

He snapped out of it when he reached his rental car. He got in and placed the blueprints on the passenger seat. He pulled out of the parking lot and drove to a local shopping center, where he stopped in a mostly unoccupied lot. He pulled out the small plastic box. Popping the lid wasn't easy, perhaps due to the length of time it had been sealed. Eventually, he prized it open at the cost of one broken thumbnail.

Beneath the top disk there were a dozen more, mostly labeled the same way, along with a couple of blank-looking CDs without labels or clues as to their content. It appeared that Vikram "Gator" de Silva was either sloppy with his archives or had deliberately stashed additional information.

His laptop was still in the trunk. He retrieved it, powered up, and slid one of the supplementary material disks in. It took a few seconds for the drive to stop whirring, and no "autorun" program started. Perhaps they were simple data disks after all. He opened up the directory to find over a hundred files, all in pdf format. The file names had a pattern suggesting specific notebook pages. He opened a few of them, discovering most were scans of laboratory gels, stained with various visualizing media. Such were the molecular and cellular biologist's tools of the trade.

Page upon page showed similar items: annotated graphs, data tables, and other bits and pieces. Wading through the files probably would not reveal anything useful, yet there might be gems of information. The trick was to find a specific cross-reference to a well-described experiment. That exercise would take a lot more time than his laptop batteries could provide.

He powered down, and stuck the laptop back in his backpack. As an afterthought, he took the unlabeled disks, put them in a couple of empty paper CD sleeves he always carried with him, and placed them in a different pocket inside the backpack. He returned the labeled CDs to the plastic box and stowed everything in the trunk. Next, he walked to the shopping center, found a Mailboxes Etc. franchise, and purchased a large padded mailer. He returned to the car, took the CDs, folded the blueprints carefully around them, and stuffed the assembly inside the mailer. He addressed it to Josef Rintlen, sealed the mailer, and returned to the Mailboxes Etc. store. He paid cash for rush delivery and sent the package on its way.

His next port of call was the local library. Before he could be on his way, he heard his mobile phone chirp, signaling a new text message had arrived. It was short and to the point, and the words chilled him to the bone the moment he saw them.

They know about you.

Chapter 28

DETECTIVE SERGEANT LEO SAMPANG was losing his patience. There was no sign of Megan Gray or her parents. Balbino Ruiz, the kid who'd reported them missing, kept bugging him about what was going on, and because his boss was the kid's uncle, Leo felt obliged to pay a bit more attention than he wanted. By all accounts, there were no signs of foul play; they had just gone away somewhere. If Megan had gone off alone, the priorities might have changed, but when all three were away, the obvious explanation was a family holiday, or perhaps a family emergency. Stuart's wife Sally was from England. Perhaps one of her elderly relatives passed away and they'd all gone to the funeral.

He'd run that idea by the kid. Balbino didn't buy it for a second. Megan would have told him if they'd all had to leave town in a hurry for that kind of reason. Leo then suggested a sudden family illness instead. That didn't wash either. Balbino refused to believe that his friend and her parents would have canceled a dinner occasion just like that, and then disappear. Even if a relative had taken ill, Megan would surely have texted him.

Cars in California tend to occupy driveways rather than their garages, so Leo was unconcerned when Balbino pointed out that Stuart's vehicle was at home, parked outside. They could all have taken an airport shuttle to SFO. Alternatively, the absence of Sally's SUV implied it was probably in one of the long term airport parking lots in San Bruno, but Balbino remained unconvinced. Why would Stuart's cell phone still be in the car? Apparently he never went anywhere without it.

Before he became a detective, Leo often became frustrated when forced to explain mundane irregularities to panicking members of the public. This was no exception. Now he was faced with a young man who would have captured little attention but for one annoying detail.

Balbino Ruiz's mother "knew someone" at the San Francisco Chronicle. Keeping speculation out of the public eye was something every police force had to grapple with every day, except when it aided an investigation. Judicious use of the media was a time-tested tool for law enforcement. In contrast, careless leaks and rumormongering hampered the process. Leo's problem was that Carmen Ruiz's friend had posted photos of the missing Grays on the front page of the local section, along with a short article about the family. The photo was from Balbino's camera phone, one of those fancy gadgets that also played music, games, and did everything but the dishes. The backdrop for the shot was Muir Woods, a popular redwood reserve just north of the Golden Gate Bridge. Judging by the girl's appearance, the photo was quite recent. The piece was on his desk as he faced the young man.

"Do you realize how difficult this makes my job, son?" Leo asked.

Balbino looked at the paper and then at the detective. "I'm worried about them."

"I understand where you're coming from. But you need to let us do our jobs."

"So do you have any leads?"

Leo thought the kid must have watched too many cop shows on TV. "You know I can't tell you about that." He eyed Balbino carefully. Nothing about his demeanor changed. The kid was as determined as the day he'd reported his friend missing.

Initially, Leo had been furious when he'd seen the newspaper. He'd had enough to do in the last few weeks. Pacifica was hardly a homicide hotbed, and when the article suggested obliquely that the Gray family's disappearance might be related to the recent deaths of Kendall Rasmussen and Ralph Shanahan, Leo was ready to rip the reporter, the kid, and his mother to shreds. On further reflection, he realized his reaction might have been premature; after all, the mention of Stuart's occupation was hardly unexpected. The article implied that in light of two scientists' deaths in the last couple of months, the disappearance of a third was a poor advertisement for a research-based career.

There was no obvious connection, but what if the reporter were onto something? It was worth running up the flagpole, and the kid on the other side of his desk was obviously motivated to do what he could. "I understand you're very close to Megan, and that you're worried about her and her parents. Legally, you have to understand, I can't tell you any official details, much as I might like to." Leo paused for a moment, and then continued. "Is there anything you could tell me about the family, any observations about how they've been acting in the last couple of months?"

Balbino shook his head. "They're just really great people. They treat me like I'm one of their own."

"What about Megan? You and she – how close are you, really?" Touchy question, and loaded with heavy ammo.

"It's not like that, Detective. We're like brother and sister."

Leo waited silently, hoping Balbino would continue. It was one of his favorite techniques. When questioned, victims, witnesses, and criminals alike were prone to fill a vacuum, but this kid was different. He pushed some more. "Not romantic at all?"

"No. We really are just best friends."

"You gay, Balbino? Look at her. She's a knockout."

That touched a nerve. Balbino Ruiz bristled. "No."

"You sure? If I was your age and someone like that was in my life I'd move heaven and earth to be with her. Then again, I was a pretty normal teenager once."

"You saying I'm not normal?"

"You tell me."

"Go to hell." He got up and began pacing around the office.

"Sit down, Ruiz," Leo ordered.

Balbino ignored him.

"I said, sit down. You want my help, you answer my questions."

Eventually, Balbino returned to his seat. He slouched, leaning backwards.

"Let me repeat the question, son. Are you gay?"

The kid's eyes blazed. "I'm not gay. I'm not in denial either. And I don't see why that would have anything to do with Megan and her parents disappearing!"

"Perhaps Mr. Gray found something he didn't like about you, and didn't want his daughter to associate with you any more."

"Are you for real? We were all going out for dinner together, and then poof! They leave without saying a word. That's got nothing to do with me."

Leo sighed and showed Balbino the framed photo on his desk. "Look at this for a second, would you? I'm a husband and father too, just like Mr. Gray. I'd do anything I could to protect my family."

"Sergeant, the Grays treated *me* like family. In case you hadn't noticed, I'm trying to help them, and you're wasting time asking me these stupid questions about my sexuality as if that had anything to do with – well, anything."

Leo again just stared back.

This time Balbino did fill the vacuum. "I told you once, and I told you again. I love Megan. I love her parents. I just want them to be okay." His eyes became liquid.

They sat silently for a moment. Eventually Leo spoke. "Okay, I'm convinced."

"Convinced of what?"

"That you're telling the truth."

"I am telling the truth."

"Then I'm going to trust you to help me," Leo said, a new sincerity in his manner. Now was the time to play the reporter's hunch, right or wrong. "I need you to think back over the last couple of months. Did any of the Grays act out of character at any time? Anything you can think of?"

Balbino relaxed a bit. He tilted his head, thinking. "I didn't see or hear anything weird. But they're all pretty cool people. Nothing ever fazed them."

"No texts, emails? Anything at all to make you think something was up?"

Another head tilt, then a shake. "No." Then the kid's eyes brightened somewhat. "Wait a second. Megs said something to me a few weeks ago. It was right after that lady, you know the one, who drove off the cliff at Devil's Slide?"

Leo nodded, waiting.

"It wasn't much, but Megs said her dad might have been going through one of his insomnia periods. She said he hadn't had one for years."

"Insomnia? How bad?"

"Don't know, really. She didn't want to talk about it. She just said – well, he looked like he'd stayed up all night for three straight days. And then he had a good night's sleep, and everything was back to normal again."

That could mean anything. Stuart and Sally might have had a fight, or a problem at work, or some unrelated anxiety. Perhaps he was prone to depression, particularly if he'd had these episodes before. "You say that he hadn't had insomnia for years. Did Megan say anything about the previous occasion?"

"Not really. But she said her mom was really sad when it happened before."

Again, that could mean virtually anything. "When was the previous time?"

"I don't know. Probably before I met any of them, 'cos they always seemed really together, you know what I mean?"

Leo did know. He also knew that outward presentation often masked inward torment. "So – are you saying that something could have been bothering Megan's father a few weeks ago? Something to do with his job perhaps?"

"I don't know. He never talked about work when I was around. But I wouldn't understand, it's all biology and bugs and things. I'm not into that kind of stuff."

The detective stayed quiet again, just to see if anything else would come forth. At last, he concluded that was probably the end of it, but he couldn't let the kid go without a caution of sorts. "I would prefer you don't say anything more to the press," he said, jabbing a finger at the newspaper article. "You've got to see where I'm coming from, and I can't do my job if ..."

A knock on his office door interrupted them. A solidly built, fiftyish Asian-American woman appeared. She wore sergeant's insignia on her blue uniform. The name badge L. Zhu adorned her ample bosom.

"Leo, you may want to come out here for a minute."

He frowned. "Ling, I'm in the middle of something. Can't it wait?"

"No."

Her manner said it could not, and that he shouldn't argue. He rose, apologized to Balbino and said that he would be right back, and followed the sergeant out into the precinct's main lobby. Nothing appeared untoward, but Sergeant Zhu continued through to the door outside.

On the street, a television crew from the local CBS affiliate stood poised, microphones and camera at the ready.

Shit, Leo thought as the reporter barked his first question. Why weren't the police looking into the disappearance of the Gray family?

Across the San Francisco Bay, coverage of a baseball game between the Oakland A's and the Minnesota Twins was interrupted by a special report from the local news station. A young reporter, perched atop the cliffs of Pacifica, mouthed words into a microphone. The sound was inaudible above the noise of thirsty, garrulous Berkeley brewpub customers, but a closed-captioned tickertape provided viewers with a simultaneous transcript. The screen showed a montage of photographs, labeled with the names Kay Rasmussen, Ralph Shanahan, and all three members of the Gray family.

Matt Gilstrap sipped his third pint of pale ale and looked up to check the score. He watched the lettering scroll across the bottom of the screen. "...Until a few short weeks ago, this small town was considered a quiet community where violent crime was rare. In the space of little more than a month, the deaths of Kendall 'Kay' Rasmussen and Ralph Shanahan together might have seemed an unfortunate coincidence, but with the disappearance of Megan Gray and her parents Stuart and Sally, residents of Pacifica and its neighbors, Montara, San Bruno, and Daly City are sensing a possible pattern. Police have not yet issued statements confirming whether we are dealing with a cluster of any kind, but we are monitoring this development closely. Hank?"

The picture returned to the studio, where a bespectacled anchor thanked the on-site reporter, and stated that there would be more on the story during the six o'clock news later that day. "Now, back to your scheduled programming," Anchor Hank said, lowering his gaze towards papers scattered about his desk. The scheduled programming did not return until after the airing of three minutes of local commercials.

Matt ignored the TV ads. He'd stopped caring about the score. Any effects the microbrew had on his lucidity melted away. He turned to the bartender and asked if there was a copy of the Chronicle lying around.

"Might find one over there," the barkeep said, pointing. A wooden bench just inside the entrance served as a storage depot for assorted sections of local papers and specialty trade rags. "Can't promise if it's today's, but someone usually leaves a copy."

Matt thanked the bartender and hunted around for the local section of the San Francisco paper. After a couple of minutes' scouting, he found what he was looking for. The front page had a large section on police corruption within the city's force. About two thirds of the way down the page, he saw the headline: "Pacifica Family Missing." Beneath it was a hard copy of the shots he'd seen on TV, but in black and white. Three faces: an average-looking man, his attractive wife, and their beautiful daughter. At first, he skipped past the adults, but after feasting his eyes on the girl for a few seconds, he returned his attention to them.

"Holy crap," he mouthed. Sally's face showed the character of maturity and age, but he was certain she was the same individual. Her husband certainly was there in the shot. Matt remembered them as much younger, possibly in their early twenties. The tall, prematurely graying woman who stood among them like a proud parent was the same woman who'd recruited him. Dr. Lynne Brady, whose work had inspired him, whose vision of a better planet convinced him to take the long trip to the desert and envision how he could help transform the world. The same Dr. Brady, whose work continued after her retirement, under the direction of Drs. Etienne Goudreau and Justin Hernandez.

"Holy fucking crap," he repeated, his eyes flickering back and forth over the snapshots. An average reasonable person with good photographic recollection would at best feel uneasy, but Matthew Gilstrap, Ph.D., fueled by a few glasses of handcrafted ale, was thrown for a complete loop.

He'd just seen more than two familiar pictures. He'd seen three. Kay Rasmussen was also in Lynne Brady's office photo.

He pulled out his mobile phone and started typing a text message. In spite of the time difference, he didn't have to wait long for the reply. When it came, it told him to wait for further instructions.

His mobile chirped fifteen minutes later with a follow-up directive.

Jeez! What the heck? Matt couldn't believe what he was reading, but he delivered the message regardless. He hoped the recipient wouldn't freak out, at least no worse than he himself had.

Chapter 29

THE NICHOLS LIBRARY ON West Jefferson, one of three branches of the Naperville public library system, was the closest one to Marcus as he drove east on the tollway. Fifteen minutes on side streets took him to the modern glass-and-redbrick building, located close to a small park by the river. Inside, he asked at the help desk to see archival copies of the Chicago Sun-Times. The library assistant, stereotypically bespectacled and bookish, took him to the microfiche table and sat with him for a while, asking specific questions about his search needs.

He was unable to pinpoint exact dates, but he gave her a window he guessed encompassed the Edmund Solkar murder case.

"Is there any particular story you're looking for?" she asked.

"There was a trial here in the early to mid 1990's. I'm looking for a reporter who might have covered the case, so that might be a bit tougher to trawl through."

"If you tell me what the case was about, I can point you in the right direction. The archives of the Sun-Times go back to 1986, so we don't need microfiche. We can do this online." The librarian led him towards a desktop computer whose monitor had seen better days. The keyboard was worse. Grimy from the grease of thousands of fingers, it barely showed the QWERTY symbols.

Marcus's momentary disgust disappeared when the librarian sat at the console and pulled out a small package of disinfectant wipes from her dress pocket. She took one out and swabbed the keyboard down. She then set a second wipe aside. "Even if others aren't prepared to be hygienic, I am."

Marcus, who was convinced he faced an unsavory haul through poorly reproduced or scanned articles, appreciated both the gesture and the offer to help do the searching for him. "Terrific, Ms. – Sorry, I didn't catch your name."

"It's Betsey."

"Betsey, the case in question involved a defendant named Edmund Solkar, who was tried for murder in this county." He spelled the last name and waited while Betsey entered it into the search box.

Several dozen hits popped up. The librarian asked, "Do you want to sort by date? I can do most recent or earliest."

"I'm interested in both, more so than the middle. Let's try the most recent first. I'm looking for a resolution to the case."

She went to the last page of hits. Most of them bore the byline of one Lucinda Wootton. "Is this what you're looking for?"

"The reporter. Can we find out whether she's still at the paper?"

"Not a problem." Betsey searched under her name. The first entry was from 1999. "It doesn't look like she's still writing for the paper. But I can check anyway." She opened up a new tab and Googled her. "She must have retired a few years ago. Nothing listed post 2003. She won't be easy to find, if that's what you want."

"Let's try looking at the early trial case reports. From the police, for instance? I'm sure there's a crime reporter who covered the early stages of the investigation."

A few back-clicks returned them to the original search. The preliminary investigational reports and much of the interim speculation were also written by Lucinda Wootton. It looked like a dead end, unless someone could locate her.

Marcus made a note to have Josef dig a little deeper, when Betsey made a suggestion. "What about the police? Is it worth talking to the investigating officer?" She opened up one of the links. Within the story the name of Detective Sergeant Jason Lubowicz appeared several times.

"Not a bad idea," Marcus said, writing the name down. "Any other cops mentioned in there? Forensics experts or anything?"

She scanned and scrolled through the files, pausing whenever Marcus stopped to write down a name. Within five minutes, he had a manageable list. Betsey asked him if there was anything else she could help him with. "If not, you're welcome to use the terminal for as long as you need."

He thanked her and waited for her to leave. When she was back at the front desk, he Googled the name Vikram de Silva. Thousands of hits popped up, without a common thread. The name, even in quotes, was simply too frequent.

Next he tried "Vikram de Silva" AND "Castleford." This narrowed the hit list down to a few hundred. When he added the word "Illinois" to the search, the total dipped to 75. On the first page, half way down, he found what he was looking for, specifically an abstract pointing to a scholarly article published in the journal *Methods in Cellular Genetics*. Although the article was undoubtedly outdated and/or supplanted by further research, the abstract described a novel method for achieving site directed chromosomal mutations, using the *C. elegans* worm. De Silva was one of the coauthors, along with first author J. M. Brady, J. P. Hernandez and, to Marcus's immediate surprise, I. A. MacCallum.

Noting the names, Marcus searched for Ian A. MacCallum, narrowing the constraints as before. Another hit emerged, again with J. M. Brady as first author, working alongside one Julius D. Goldfarb. This time it was a poster abstract from a viral research conference, but all his attempts to unearth details fell short.

He tried again with J. P. Hernandez, coming up with a paper on chromosomal mutations in zebrafish. Good, he thought, at least they're moving into higher species. The omnipresent J. M. Brady was now the last author, with Hernandez listed first.

A Google search for J. M. Brady exposed her full name: Jaclynne Maude Brady, normally shortened to Lynne. What caused his heart to race, however, was a citation containing the names Brady, Rasmussen, Gray, and Bernasconi. Professor Lynne Brady and three co-workers, two of whom were collaborators from the University of Chicago. Three co-workers, at least two missing or deceased. Gray was AWOL. Was Carlo Bernasconi the CJB in MacCallum's book?

"What in God's name happened?" he whispered. *What did you do, Kay? Or what did they do to you?* His mind was a whirl as he clicked on the citation, trying to access the full paper. The browser went to a subscription-only site that asked him for thirty-one dollars and fifty cents to see the full paper. While money was hardly a concern, there were no printing facilities nearby. Nor did he see a USB port to insert a memory stick and save the document.

Betsey was still busy up front, so he wrote the citation down so he could examine it later. For now, he continued through the hits for additional connections. There were a number of more obscure references, and dead ends everywhere, but at last he found one on page 4 that made his blood run cold.

The paper's title read, "Crossing the blood-brain-barrier: preventive inoculation using site-directed chimeric RNA." The authors, listed alphabetically, were J. M. Brady, S. P. Gray, J. P. Hernandez, K. Rasmussen, R. Shanahan, and E. R. Solkar. The last author bore the star.

Edmund R. Solkar. Murderer, biologist, or key to the whole mystery? Perhaps all three? How did Kay fit in? Did she know what he had done? Why, in all their time together, had she never mentioned Solkar's name? Surely she would have known details, unless their recollection bore a burden too great to bear. What else had his beloved wife hidden from him? What other secrets would he uncover on his journey, his widower's walk? Where was Solkar now? There were so many questions churning in his mind, and he couldn't begin to answer them.

That was when he remembered the message on his mobile. *They know about you.* The text came from a private, untraceable number. Was someone trying to tease, goad, or torture him? Or was it a warning from someone equally scared? Or was this a message from some lunatic? He had to find out more about Solkar. The only lead he could see was the investigating officer in the Chicago area. He deleted his browsing history, cache, and cookies, closed the browser, picked up his notes, and stuffed them inside his backpack.

He was about to leave when he saw the disinfectant wipe Betsey had left behind. He smiled and gave the keys one more swab, then waved thanks, using the wipe as a flag. She smiled back at him and mouthed the words "thank you" to him.

Maybe there was hope for the world, he thought.

He drove directly to the Naperville police precinct, hoping that Detective Lubowicz, probably now a lieutenant or captain, would still be on the job. When he arrived at the police station, the duty officer ordered him to wait in the lobby. Someone, he said, would be with him in a few minutes. A few turned into fifteen, and then into thirty. Periodically, he paced back and forth, prompting the duty officer to demand he sit down. The array of plastic chairs was as uninviting as the ancient coffee machine's contents. After yet another fifteen minutes of discomfort, punctuated by the arrival of several uniformed cops changing shift, a door clicked open to reveal a heavyset African-American woman in her early fifties. She wore her hair short. Small gold earrings dangled from prominent ears. A chartreuse blouse, black midi skirt, and heavy brogues completed the presentation.

"I'm Lieutenant Silvey," the woman announced, her voice crisp, cautiously unfriendly. "I understand you were asking about Detective Sergeant Lubowicz?"

"Yes, I am," he replied brightly. "I'm Dr. Marcus Black." He offered a hand.

She declined to shake. "Doctor? You another of those shrinks?"

"No, ma'am," Marcus said, shaking his head. "I'm a biochemist."

"What would a biochemist want with one of our former detectives?"

"If you'll let me explain, perhaps it'll make a bit more sense. Why would you think I was a shrink, anyway? Is there a problem with Sergeant Lubowicz?"

Silvey sized him up, frowning. It had been ten years or more since Jason retired. Rather, had *been* retired. And now this guy was here asking questions, and that wasn't what the public was supposed to be doing. That was her job. "No problem," she said, arms folded. "You tell me why you're here."

"Can we go somewhere a little less, ah, public? Your office, perhaps?"

"You got something to say?"

This was getting a bit tiring. "Listen, Lieutenant. I'm not here specifically about Sergeant Lubowicz. I just wanted to talk to him about an old case he worked on."

"Which case?" Again, the wariness, the suspicion.

"Could we please talk in private?" Marcus didn't feel like buckling under. Why should he feel any pressure, after all? He'd come to ask a couple of simple questions, and he was being treated unfavorably. He looked at the lieutenant squarely in the eye. The sincere frown on his brow at last persuaded Silvey to melt a little.

"All right. Officer Lang will pat you down. IF," she scowled, "you don't mind." As if on cue, the duty cop came around to open the secure door. He frisked Marcus, stopping at all his pockets, and felt under his jacket for weapons. Lang nodded curtly to his boss, who turned on her heels and barked over her shoulder. "Follow me."

"Why the precautions?" Marcus muttered, half to himself.

"Call it paranoia, Doc, or just call it being safe. I've seen too many crazies."

"In high tech, white collar Naperville?"

"Southside Chicago. Maybe I'm a victim of my own biography, or maybe I just don't want to see any more cops gunned down because they trusted someone with an agenda." She crossed an open area to her office, which was small and simple. A bronze nameplate, Lt. M. Silvey, hung askew on the door. Someone had forgotten to bring a spirit level. A picture of four people sat on the corner of her desk. Two teenagers, one boy and one girl, curly haired and light-skinned, flanked a smiling Silvey. Behind them stood a broad-shouldered, bald white man with a genuine grin as wide as hers.

"Your family?" Marcus asked.

"Which you didn't come here to talk about, but yes," Silvey answered, motioning for her visitor to sit.

"Might I ask what the 'M' stands for, Lieutenant?"

"It stands for Ma'am. But you can still call me Lieutenant if you prefer."

"Message received." The ice hadn't quite melted yet. "I wanted to ask Detective Lubowicz about the Solkar case. It was a long time ago, but the reason I'm asking is because of this." He fished out his wallet and unfolded the clipping he always carried. "My wife recently died in a car crash. I – I couldn't even recognize her."

Silvey read the article. She placed the clipping on her desk and looked up. Her expression softened a little. "I'm very sorry for your loss, Dr. Black. But I don't understand how I can help."

He pulled out one of his notes from the library. "My wife knew Edmund Solkar. They published a paper together shortly before he was arrested. I'm trying to understand the connection, but I do know that Solkar's victim, Samaya Jonas, died in the same manner."

Silvey rose from behind the desk, walked around, and closed the door. "All right, Dr. Black. You've got my attention."

Chapter 30

MARCUS TOOK A DEEP breath. "Thank you. Please, call me Marcus if you like. I'm not big on formality."

Silvey sized him up anew. "Okay. And it's Martha." This time she offered a surprisingly delicate hand. "I get more than my fair share of cranks in this white collar burg. And since 9/11 – well, you know."

"I understand. Can't be easy." He thought it best to come straight to the point. "How good was the evidence against Edmund Solkar?"

"Can't really say. All that happened before I joined the force. But you called correctly on Jase Lubowicz. He handled the investigation, but then he took early retirement. No point in trying to contact him now." Martha opened her desk drawer and pulled out a folder. She pulled out a single sheet of paper, copied from a Miami Herald column five years earlier. "When Jase called it quits, it was either jump or be pushed, if you know what I mean. The Solkar case got to him. He was obsessed with it. He spent every spare minute going over the details, the court reports, and the legal maneuverings. He wouldn't let up, even when Solkar was safely behind bars. The department offered him a choice. He said bye-bye and headed south to Miami to live with his mother." She pushed the newspaper article across the desk.

He read the death notice. "Mother and son die of apparent carbon monoxide poisoning," was the headline. "At ten a.m. on Monday, December 29, neighbors detected a strange odor emanating from the apartment where Tatiana Lubowicz, 89, lived with her son, Jason Lubowicz, 57, a retired police officer. Preliminary examination of the deceased suggested they died from inhalation of lethal concentrations of poisonous gases. Since carbon monoxide is odorless, police assumed the neighbors were alerted by the smell of decomposition. There were no other occupants."

"Poor guy. Did they prove carbon monoxide poisoning?" Marcus asked.

She nodded. "Yeah. A ventilation problem in the apartment block's heating system caused the leak. They fixed it soon after, but that didn't help Jase and his mother. They'd had unseasonably cold weather for southern Florida, which might explain why the maintenance was substandard."

"And right around the holidays, when all the repairmen were on vacation."

Martha was skeptical. "I never bought it. I hate to say this about a fellow cop, but some reckoned Jase did for his mom and then made sure he wouldn't wake up either."

"You have any evidence of that? Like his behavior before he retired, any indication that he wanted to end it all? There's a reason I'm asking."

"Nothing that I know of. But how's about you tell me your reason?"

Marcus paraphrased Kay's letter, leaving out one or two details for the moment. "I have some experience with depression. For a while I was in such bad shape myself that – well, I'd never contemplate doing anything terminal no matter how crappy life was, but then again I'd never say never either. I'm not explaining too well, I'm sorry."

"You're doing fine. For what it's worth, I don't know much about Jason's state of mind, looking at the timeline of the case. But it did affect him, big time."

"Did he think Solkar did it?"

"Couldn't tell you. The evidence was there, the body identified. Jase did his job, testified, and Solkar went down. That's all in the reports, but like I said, all that happened long before I came to Naperville. What I do know is that Jase started writing letters to Solkar's lawyer. Long, drawn out, ramblin' stuff. She must have gotten tired of getting envelopes with Naperville on the postmark. Probably threw them away."

Michelle Durant. "Sounds like I should speak with her."

"If you care, and I sense that you do, that would indeed be the place to start. But remember, she ain't going to break client confidentiality. You'd best tread carefully."

Marcus had to agree it might be difficult to extract much more.

He looked again at the picture of Martha Silvey and her family. When she smiled, her whole persona changed. He wondered if she compartmentalized home and work well. "You guys look happy. Holiday snap?"

"A few years ago. Hawaii's wonderful. Ever been there?"

"Once or twice." He remembered times gone by, holidays he'd spent during the early years of his marriage, and it only caused the sadness to well up inside him anew. Martha sensed this and put out a hand to touch his forearm. "It'll heal, Marcus. In time."

The gesture, so gentle and subtly compassionate from a woman who not long ago he'd sensed would happily have slapped cuffs on him if he so much as said "Boo" almost made him lose it. He closed his eyes and bit down on his lip. "Thanks."

"You need anything else, here's my card. Can't promise I'll be able to help, but if I think of anything I'll let you know. Do you have a contact number?"

Marcus started to hand over a card of his own, then thought twice. He pulled it back and wrote an additional number on the bottom before giving it to the lieutenant. "Here's my cell phone number. I don't give it out very often."

She accepted the card and put it in her desk drawer. "Safe with me." She offered her hand again.

He shook it warmly. "Thanks again, Martha. If it means anything, I get the sense you brought a healthy dose of South Chicago cynicism with you but it hasn't discolored your life."

"Let's hope you're right." She smiled. Just like her picture.

South Chicago. "Wait!" he exclaimed. "You didn't happen to remember a guy called Stanley Zalewski when you were on the force there? Not a cop, a victim."

Martha's eyes sharpened as she reflected on her previous assignment. She rifled through some of the folders in her desk. "I've always kept a few handwritten notes on significant cases as well as putting them on the computer. Call me old fashioned, but I'm a sucker for pen and paper."

Soon she found what she was looking for. The document summed up the Zalewski case. "Yeah, I remember this one. No signs of foul play, but when a body's been decomposing for days it becomes a bit harder on the forensics team, good as they are. We thought Zalewski was a real slimeball, into internet porn. The geek squad went through every hard drive, every floppy, videotape, you name it, but they didn't find a single illicit image or video. And our guys were the best – they could find files on hard drives that had been wiped clean. So, without any trace to internet porn sites, the trail ran as cold as Mr. Stanley Zalewski's corpse."

Marcus speculated out loud. "If he was a geek himself, he would have known how to scrub every last trace. The Department of Defense can do it, so why can't a computer jock?"

"Fair point. We did find a bunch of online gaming sites in his browser cache, dating back months, but they were all legal. If a guy has months-old stuff that innocuous in his cache, maybe he didn't have anything to hide. We figured he just got too deep into gaming. Probably got addicted like those kids in Korea, or wherever, kept himself awake on Red Bull, played Warcraft or something for forty-eight hours straight, and just wound up dyin' of cardiac arrest. He wasn't in good shape, so it wouldn't surprise me if that's what happened. If MY man ever did anything that dumb I'd take the mouse out of his cold dead fingers and shove it down his throat just to teach him a lesson."

"Your husband a gamer?"

"Total gadget freak. Loves shootin' aliens too. Just like the kids."

"I take it you're not into that pastime."

"Hell, no. Sleep's too important to me. Speaking of which, those raccoon eyes show you've had some sleepless nights too."

"Guilty as charged. Mostly jetlag. I've been traveling around a fair bit."

"And your travels have brought you to our fair toddlin' town. So, tell me, how come you know about Stan Zalewski?"

He took a deep breath. "Another tie-in with the other case. Solkar and Zalewski once worked in the same building. The Castleford Institute was right here in Naperville. Zalewski was the on-site IT guy."

Martha tapped a few keys, then raised an eyebrow. "I remember that place. They closed up shop a while back. Guess they ran out of cash. Take a look at this." She swung the monitor around on its swivel stand so Marcus could see the display.

The screen showed a photo of what the institute had looked like before the university took it over. Judging by the cars parked in the front lot, the shot looked over ten years old. He wondered if one of the vehicles belonged to Kay.

As if reading his mind, Martha said, "We checked all the license plates. The late model Subaru second from the left belonged to Zalewski. He kept it after he was fired. Our CSI's ripped it apart, but it was clean. Near as we could tell, the guy didn't do anything illegal."

"Near as you could tell."

"Near as we could tell," she repeated. Her expression suggested she was unsure. She let out a long breath, and then shook her head slowly. "You're trying to put a lot of pieces together, and you don't have a clue what the picture looks like. Am I right?"

Marcus gazed over the detective's shoulder, his mind racing. Here he was, sitting in a suburban Illinois police station, across from an experienced officer whose initial reserve bordered on hostility, but whom he now felt might believe him. All the sleepless nights, punctuated with occasional booze-laden stupors that served only to knock him out for four hours or so at a time, all the searching and unanswered questions had now come down to a single conclusion.

"I think my wife was murdered. I don't know how, or why, or even when. I think it has something to do with her work at the Castleford Institute. You're right about there being a lot of pieces to this puzzle, and also about me not knowing what they'll look like when they all fit into place. But whoever is behind it, I guarantee I will make them pay. You can stick me behind bars the moment after." His unblinking eyes grew cold.

Martha's expression was grave. She'd seen bereft family members react similarly, but most of the time it was a natural response to grief or a knee-jerk desire for revenge. She sensed she was dealing with a different animal here. "You ever killed a human being before, Marcus?"

"No," he replied.

She exhaled deeply. "Are you really a biochemist?"

"Yes. But I'm also a guy who happens to have stumbled across some bad people. And this time they messed with the wrong biochemist." He stood and faced the detective.

She could only warn him. "Be careful."

"I'll stay in touch. It's all I can promise."

"Marcus, I'm serious. Be very careful."

He let her warning sink in, and then excused himself. Without another word, he turned on his heels and left.

Chapter 31

JUSTIN HERNANDEZ PORED OVER the data at his desk, one eye on his monitor. The incident with the chimpanzee and the howler monkey, as horrifying as it sounded, had been completely predictable, within a day of the original estimate. As disturbed as his colleague had been, Hernandez was satisfied.

That was the key difference between them. Goudreau was not a pure scientist, driven by observation, hypothesis, and provable theory. Steve ran on instinct and speculation rather than the unadulterated scientific method. Hernandez, on the other hand, knew deep within that he was as pure a scientist as there was. Profoundly atheistic, he refused to believe that science alone could not answer the most philosophical of "why" questions. Everything could be explained by observation and rationale.

He recalled the day he first pithed a frog in high school biology class. He'd marveled at how its mouth gaped in shock when he jammed a needle through its fragile skull. That was when he knew he was as dominant a creature in the universe as any so-called Supreme Being. He could change the world. As an undergraduate, he imagined he would discover ways to manipulate nature itself, to create and destroy, if not at his command, then through the genetic blueprints of any living organism he chose.

As long as men with conscience didn't get in his way. Men like the insufferable Dr. Goudreau and his anthropomorphisms. Shit, the guy had named a monkey Benicio, a chimpanzee Craig! Perhaps it was some underlying joke, given that the first fully sequenced human genome came from a guy called Craig. It didn't matter if the chimp was called Prince Albert, it was still just a lab animal, a tool, albeit a pretty complicated one.

Just as a few humans had been, back in Chicago. No matter how intelligent, no matter their own beliefs and dreams, ultimately, they were just experimental subjects. Subjects who yielded clear readouts.

That was why Hernandez always liked lower animals on the food chain. Primates had a purpose, because of their similarities to humans, but they were a royal pain to work with. Chimps were downright dangerous, because of their strength and smarts. Even a two-foot rhesus monkey was more than a match for a strong six-foot man. Dogs were okay because of their forgiving nature. Approach them with food, drugs, or toxins, and they would just wag and wolf whatever was on offer.

Rats were even better. Hernandez liked to state that rats had helped save more lives than any species of animal, owing to their ubiquitous need in drug discovery. Invertebrates, down to the *Caenorhabditis elegans* worm, were even easier to deal with. You could manipulate and engineer them with abandon, and they didn't bite.

If only one could test everything on lawyers, he thought with a chuckle. Drug companies loved to extract billions of dollars from unwitting patients suffering from contemporary syndromes rather than infections. Illnesses such as depression and insomnia, the products of terminal Jonesmanship, fueled countless television ads. *"Ask your doctor if Glumbeat is right for you. Side effects may include drowsiness, loss of appetite, nausea, constipation, diarrhea, seizure, and muscle aches."* The lawyer clause, illustrating the very symptoms likely to have precipitated the original visit to the G.P., was part and parcel of every American drug commercial barrage, delivered every night during invasions of reality dreck masquerading as entertainment.

It didn't matter that patients' own lifestyles could cause their hearts to blow up, if a deep-pocketed pharmaceutical scapegoat arrived on the leash of a clever lawyer with an axe to grind. The drug development industry was collapsing under its own weight, and someone had to do something about it. Hernandez recognized this, having predicted the downfall many years earlier, and knew he had the answer.

No, it wasn't one of those *outside the box* approaches. He hated that hackneyed phrase managers loved to throw around. *Think outside the box.* Every time he heard it, he wanted to jump up and scream, "Have you forgotten to look INSIDE the box?" He was a scientist, the best scientist he had ever known, because he *observed*. He looked inside the box. The box was Planet Earth, and it held all the answers.

The phone rang on his desk. He looked at the caller ID and picked up. "This is Justin."

"You'd better get down here," Goudreau's Quebecois voice sounded urgent.

"What's up this time? Another of your buddies take a dive?"

"Lose the sarcasm, Justin. This is good news."

His eyes opened wide. All results were good news to him because they taught him something he didn't know before. Arrogance led him to believe he could anticipate most results: validation rather than revelation, but he occasionally admitted his imperfections. "Where are you? You're obviously not in your office."

"No, I'm in the control room. It's Bio 2."

"I'll be right there." Hernandez hung up and left his office. He swiped his security card and entered the corridor at the end of the hall. He strode past all the sequencers, not stopping to look at the robotic equipment humming away within. At the other end, past another security door, he came to a bank of elevators. He pressed the down button, and immediately heard "ding" sound. The door opened and he walked in. He was on floor B1. He shoved his pass card into a narrow slot just above the G, and then pressed his right forefinger knuckle on the B4 button.

The elevator did not stop on the way. The gap between levels B3 and B4 was substantially greater than between the other floors. B4 had a high level clearance restriction. Only those possessing the necessary pass card, six-digit access code, and recognizable retinas could enter. At B4, Hernandez made his way down an empty gray corridor, lit by blue lamps deployed at three-meter intervals. He counted thirty-four of them. The last one illuminated a solid steel door at the end. To the right of the door, a numeric keypad and card swipe presented the first two security challenges. He obeyed them and placed his chin on a promontory located at average head height. He kept his eyes open while the scanner inspected both eyeballs, and heard a beep and a click as the steel door opened up, revealing a two square meter chamber with a similar set of gatekeeper measures on the far side. He swung the heavy portal aside and stepped through. An electronic voice greeted him. "Please wait fifteen seconds."

Fifteen felt more like fifty. A hiss from behind signaled the airlock as closed. A disinfectant fine spray spurted into the chamber, followed by a flash of light. At this point, the voice commanded him to don safety glasses and lab coat, both of which were hanging on the wall. He ignored the order. He then typed a second access code into the panel mounted on the internal wall, swiped his card again, and suffered a second retina scan. That got him through to the next room. Another hiss bid him hello.

Hernandez walked into a large square room with a pair of double doors on each of the other three sides. Light emanated through the gap underneath the doors opposite. They appeared less secure than those to his left and right. A couple of shadows passed over the gleam, sending an eerie light pattern through the square anteroom. People were in there.

He went across and opened up. The huge control room within looked like the flight deck of the Starship Enterprise. Jam-packed with monitoring equipment, computers, dials, levers, and buttons, the room was a perfect cylinder, seamless LCD screens forming its circumference. The screens were blank. Three technicians clicked away in the background.

Steve Goudreau, Don Strathmore, and Monty Dayne stood in a small cubicle, designed for in-room conferencing. It had a whiteboard, a Polycom hookup, and a small plasma screen. The three men appeared to be in an intense discussion. As Hernandez approached, Strathmore looked up.

"Justin, glad you're here," he said. "We've made the breakthrough we were looking for. Monty's here to ensure that the inventorship legalities are solid, but this is Steve's show. I'll let him take over."

Steve nodded, without smiling at his boss or at Hernandez. "Let's go to the middle. I've asked Tracy to cue up the biodome monitors so we can see the results in the right order." One of the technicians gave him a thumbs-up and started fiddling with another piece of equipment on a bench a few meters away.

Steve clicked on an icon on a monitor in front of him. Up popped a similar image to the scene they had witnessed in his office a day earlier, complete with gauges, and a small clock in the top right. A few seconds later, the panoramic circorama exploded into view and bathed everyone in green light, a virtual jungle seen from the inside out. The plant life was as varied and rich as anything the Amazon could offer. The uninitiated would have felt shock, wonder, and amazement. These viewers had seen it all before, but this time no primates swung through the vines.

"Benicio had to be sacrificed late last night," Goudreau said. "There was no way to save him. He never stopped screeching, after several hours. If you ask me, it was unmitigated grief brought on by the loss of his friend."

Hernandez fought the temptation to scoff at his colleague's sentiment. "Was the chimp's body removed at the same time?"

"Yes. An autopsy will be conducted on both primates in the next couple of days. The tissues are on their way. We have to ensure the vector wasn't responsible."

As if that will tell you anything new. "When do you expect the results?"

"Complete sequencing will require two or three weeks, but we ought to have the preliminaries in a few days."

"Make sure you look at chromosome fifteen on the chimp first. That's where the pilot study fell through. We don't want the same mistake again."

"Same mistake?" Dayne piped in.

"Mistake's too harsh a word," Hernandez corrected, kicking himself mentally. "I regard it more like a suboptimal outcome. Before you came on board, we ran a short term experiment in another species. That study succeeded, but the duration of onset was substantially delayed. This time we wanted to guarantee a far quicker response."

The lawyer nodded slowly, thinking about the scientist's words, then pursed his lips. "You have a record of that? We need to know for patent purposes."

"We do," Hernandez lied again, this time with Strathmore's tacit approval. Steve was busily wading through menus on the screen and seemed not to hear the exchange.

"Now check this out," Goudreau said. "You've seen Bio 1. Take a look at this incredible sight." He clicked on the Bio 2 icon. The cylindrical display darkened briefly, sending the whole control room into blackness. Then they were surrounded by a vast expanse of fully grown grains, yellow and green under a blue sky. The entire area depicted on the screens was no more than a hectare, but the uninitiated might have imagined standing in the middle of Iowa on a late summer's day. All that was missing was the sun.

"Pretty neat," Don Strathmore said, chuckling. "How long did that take?"

"Much less than the natural strain, but that's not the point," Steve said. "Here's the kicker. There's one other thing." He pulled down a menu and checked several of the boxes that appeared. A familiar array of gauges appeared on the big screen.

"Look at the one on the left. Normally, as in non-controlled environments at sea level, it should read just under twenty-one. In Bio 2 the number is twenty point nine seven. Well within constraints and natural variation, you'd imagine. But the right hand gauge is zero point zero one eight. That's a reduction by two hundredths of a percent. I don't need to emphasize how important this result is!"

"Holy shit," Hernandez said aloud. "You realize what this means? If we can confirm it?"

"It's already been confirmed, Justin," Strathmore assured him. "Tell him, Steve."

"The plastome took. We have a viable, dominant strain."

Chapter 32

THE YOUNG MAN FACING Leo Sampang looked sallow and weary. His garb only reinforced that assessment; torn jeans, an untucked T-shirt with white deodorant stains under the arms, and tattered sneakers completed the picture. Bu as Leo took it all in, he began to understand why insomnia was the least of his concerns.

When Matt Gilstrap entered the Pacifica Police station, he had asked to speak with the officer in charge of the investigation into the disappearance of the Gray family. All he could offer was a memory of a photograph. Nevertheless, he had an impeccable eye for detail, along with the gift of instant recall.

Detective Sergeant Sampang listened to Matt's story, how he'd seen the newspaper report in Berkeley, and how he had recalled seeing the photo on Lynne Brady's desk. "Do you mind me asking you where you were on the dates in question?"

"Not a bit," Matt replied. "I was about nine thousand miles away." He reached into his right front pocket and withdrew a small, slightly creased blue book. "Check my passport if you like. Entry and exit stamps in Sydney."

The detective took the passport and thumbed through it. There were two entry stamps, one dated a year previously, a second one about seven months ago. The exit stamps, one only a week after the first, and the second dating back a fortnight, confirmed Matt's words. "You were in Australia twice."

"First time was for the job interview. I took a few extra days to look around and came home. Then I went over there to work after I finished my degree."

"For six months? That's kind of short term to move so far from home."

"I liked the idea of going overseas. Expanding my horizons," Matt explained. "The job finished up kind of early. I did what they hired me to do, so I came home."

"You have a job here now?"

"Not yet. But I'm in no hurry."

"How come? Any special reason?"

Matt didn't want to mention his half million dollar payout. *Not a word. Not unless I say so*, Steve Goudreau had said. "I'm just figuring out what I want to do next with my life. You know how it is," he said, sounding like he was apologizing for it.

"Not really," Leo replied. "But you didn't come here to talk careers with me. You came here because of something you saw a year ago, an old picture on an old lady's desk. And now you're telling me that these two are the same people?" he said, pointing at the Chronicle photo.

"I'd swear to it. I have a photographic memory."

"Sure you do. Next you're going to tell me that the cute girl in the photo was sitting next to you in first class on the plane back from Sydney."

"What makes you think I was in first class?" Matt was astonished.

Leo started to hand the passport back to the young man. At the last second he pulled it away and spread the pages apart. A small piece of paper fluttered out. "I'm a detective, Matty."

It was a boarding pass stub. Printed on it was the composite name MGilstra, the flight number, the airline, and the seat assignment, row 1A. The date on the stub matched the second of the exit stamps from Sydney's Kingsford-Smith airport.

"Okay, Detective. Good call. But two things, okay? One, I've never met these people, any of them. Two, please don't call me Matty. Only my mom gets to do that."

"First class ain't cheap, Matty," Leo said. "You look more like sardine class."

"It was a parting gift from the company, Lee-Oh." Matt's jaw tightened.

The cop's eyes never left Matt Gilstrap's. He used his favorite stay-silent trick, and as usual, it worked. Matt blinked first.

"Why are you asking me about what I was doing, Detective? I came here to help, and you're giving me the third degree."

Leo ignored the protest. "No company I know of gives its junior employees first class tickets as part of a severance package. You sure you're telling me everything?"

"I'm not lying to you."

"I didn't say you were. I asked if you were telling me everything. There is a difference."

"I've told you everything I know. Which isn't much. I've just seen some weird coincidences with new and old photographs."

Coincidence. No such thing existed in Leo's book. Everything happened for a reason, if you looked hard enough. "Come on, Matt. I've been doing this job for twenty years. You're keeping something back."

Matt didn't want to be thought a kook, or worse, a complete nut-job. The TV reporter had shown Kay Rasmussen's photograph too. He wondered how he could broach that subject. Would Sampang believe that all *three* of them were in Lynne Brady's old photo? Could he even believe it himself?

"Out with it," Leo coaxed.

"Okay, so there was one other person in the old photo that I recognized. You're going to think I'm crazy, but it's true. I mean, not that I'm crazy. That it's true that I saw this other person."

Leo had come across many babblers, and there was only one effective way to deal with them. "Take a deep breath and slow down a bit. Then tell me what you saw."

Matt uttered his familiar sigh. "The other person in the old photo was the same woman who was killed in that crash off Devil's Slide. You know, Kendall Rasmussen."

Silence. Leo blinked, waiting for more.

"Do you think there was something going on with the Grays and that woman?"

"Like what?"

"How should I know? It was just a picture. And now all this stuff has happened."

"What stuff?"

"I don't know. Perhaps Ms. Rasmussen and Stuart Gray were having a secret affair, she died in a car accident, and Gray went off the deep end."

The Ruiz kid had said something about Gray having lost sleep recently. Leo wasn't one to speculate, but who knew? He mentally filed that one away and returned his attention to Matt's story. "Take me back to when you first saw this picture. In the office of this woman in Australia – Grady, was that her name?"

"Brady. Lynne Brady."

"My mistake. Now, what exactly were you doing over there?"

"Like I said, it was a job interview."

"Did you ask her about the picture?"

"No. I was too nervous."

"Nervous? About what?"

"Getting the job. It was a really neat opportunity and I didn't want to blow it."

"But you recall the photo pretty well. Nervous people tend to forget things."

"Maybe most do but I'm not like that. I remember staring at the photo and thinking that there were two damn good looking women in it, and wondering why the hell didn't my department in graduate school have any babes like that."

Leo thought that alone could be a fair indicator of Matt's sincerity. "Do you remember any other people in the picture?"

"Yeah, there was one other. He was Asian, I think. Chinese perhaps but I couldn't be sure."

"And what happened to him?"

"How do you mean?"

"Where did he disappear to?"

Matt sighed. "Who said anything about him disappearing? I'm telling you about the others, the ones I *do* know about!"

"Okay," Leo conceded after a long pause. "Tell me more about what you do. In your professional capacity, shall we say? Perhaps it's best if you start at the beginning."

Michelle Durant awakened to find herself in a windowless shed. She was lying on a bed of straw, crudely covered with an army blanket. A second blanket covered her from the shoulders down. Her hands slowly made their way down her body. She was still fully clothed. Rays of light penetrated the wooden shack, and while it took her several seconds to grasp that she was not in the safety of her own bedroom, she discovered that she was also unhurt. But when she sat upright, she felt the blood drain rapidly from her head, before a pulsating ache began between her temples.

Chloroform. Plain old chloroform, she recalled. A cloth had covered her face she approached the front door of her cookie cutter mini-mansion. She had no idea how long she'd been out, but guessed at least a full night. As she began to regain her bearings, she looked around in the shadows to see what, if anything, was inside her prison. The first thing she noticed was a half-gallon army surplus canteen lying in one corner, its cap still attached. She crawled over and shook it. The contents swished around. It was almost full. Gingerly, she grasped the cap and turned it counterclockwise. She detected a faint orange scent from within.

She dipped her forefinger into the liquid and brought it to her tongue. It had a familiar sweet taste tinged with the saltiness of added electrolytes. Something like Gatorade, she imagined. She dipped and licked one more time. Then her burning thirst took over and she hoisted the canteen to her mouth, gulping copiously, quenching her parched throat. It was the most wonderful drink ever. She drained the entire canteen before setting it down again.

Careful, Mickey, she thought. *Not too fast.* She took a deep breath and looked around some more. Her captor, whoever he was, had left some nutritional bars in another corner of the shed. It was just as well they were still sealed, since a huge cockroach was crawling across the topmost one. Disgusted, she shrank away before realizing the beetle was harmless. She shoved it aside and tore open one of the granola-honey slabs. She finished it plus another two before finding the urge to stop. Only then did she venture to try and speak.

"Help!" she cried, crawling around the perimeter of the shack, unable to find a door or any other means of access. The place had to be at ground level or higher, based on the light coming through the cracks, but she had no idea how it had been sealed, or even trapped. But if it was booby-trapped, she thought, why would her captor have left energy bars and Gatorade? Why had she been taken in the first place?

George Petrescu. Was he involved? Yesterday – or was it the day before – she didn't know how long she'd been unconscious, after all – he'd come to her office asking about the old case. She'd answered his questions, and now this had happened. Had he come back for her? She called out his name, but no one replied.

"Petrescu!" she yelled repeatedly. "I know you're there! What do you want with me?" At first, simple anger drove her. Then, as despair took over, tears began to flow. She started to beg. "Please! Please help me!"

Silence.

She continued calling until she became hoarse, but to no avail. The light coming in from the outside dimmed as the sun set, turning the low visibility within the shack into complete darkness. Her thirst returned, and she cursed her inability to conserve the liquid she'd been given. *Why are you doing this to me? I'm a law professor, dammit!*

She sank down on the makeshift straw bed again. The temperature dropped, so she wrapped the second blanket tight around her body, trying to conserve as much warmth as she could, and lay in a fetal position. Then, for the first time in more years than she could remember, Mickey Durant began to pray.

Chapter 33

MARCUS BLACK SLEPT FAR more soundly during his second night at the O'Hare airport hotel. A set of earplugs purchased at a pharmacy near the Naperville police station had done the trick, blocking out sports bar revelry and late night runway action. Abstinence from alcohol helped, and for the first time in weeks he fell into a deep sleep, waking over nine hours later as the cleaners started their morning rounds.

Someone had slid his bill and the latest USA Today beneath his door. Four hundred bucks, something called "room fees," a late booking surcharge, local and city taxes and state tax set the bill at half a grand. The complexity of it aggravated him. *When did it all have to get so complicated*, he thought as he showered. He dried off and put on his last clean set of clothes, and stuffed yesterday's garb into one of the plastic bags provided by the hotel for take-out dry-cleaning. At those prices, he could get a better deal on new stuff at the local K-mart. He wondered if hotels were losing so much money on people wandering off with their plastic bags for dirty clothes that they had to add all the sundry room charges just to make up for the loss.

The front page of the paper showed little new from the previous day, but one item in the state-by-state snippets caught his eye. Like many loyal readers, he'd developed a habit of looking at these Twitter-sized updates from the half dozen states in which he'd spent substantial time. This one was from California.

Davis. Renowned legal academic disappears. Prof. Michelle Durant, an expert on evidentiary testimony, was reported missing by a colleague after she failed to appear for a final assessment of the academic year.

It was too early to call Josef, but Marcus had a few hours before his flight to San Francisco. He booted his laptop and purchased a one hour pass to the hotel's internet provider. The U.C. Davis web site took a long time to load. Marcus trawled through its pages until he located the faculty and administration directory. Michelle Durant's photograph stared back at him, an attractive portrait of a woman about his age. Her brief biography summarized her specialty. The Supreme Court had cited her treatise on scientific evidence in a landmark decision in the late 1990's.

"No wonder your absence drew attention," Marcus said to the screen. Next, he pulled out his notes from the previous day's library searches and retrieved the corresponding references, paying by credit card so he could download the full pdf-tagged documents. He struggled to understand the plethora of acronyms, jargon, and technicalities forming the basis for Lynne Brady's methodology, but what captured his attention most was the second paper, coauthored by Edmund R. Solkar. As he perused the introduction he felt the sense of dread returning.

"Crossing the blood-brain-barrier: preventive inoculation using site-directed chimeric RNA." The title was innocuous enough, but within the text he learned what Solkar had discovered. A chimera was another word for a fused species. In Greek mythology, chimerae bore eagles' heads and lions' bodies. A centaur, the example he'd discussed with Bill Shea, had a man's torso and a horse's body. Griffins and wyverns, creatures of legend, fantasy, and fiction were also chimerae. The paper on his screen, however, was not about any such flights of fancy. What he saw was far more frightening.

The article described how they could fuse a strand of viral RNA onto a mammalian strand, in this case a mouse. The rate of transcription and polymerization that could take place was thus finely tunable. The authors had conducted their initial experiments in a Petri dish, controlling the rate of replication of chromosomal building blocks, and subsequently their conversion into cellular proteins. Following the early stage "in vitro" experiments, the authors demonstrated the principle in mice. They used six groups of animals. They treated the first two groups, one each of wild type (normal) and nude, or immunosuppressed varieties of mouse, with a fused nucleic acid from an active virus. Then they treated two further groups with a fusion RNA from a deactivated virus. Lastly, they treated a fifth and sixth group of animals, wild and nude respectively, with pure mouse RNA, rather than either type of viral fusion protein. The observations, while steeped in biological argot, were alarming, even sensational.

Animals dosed with the *active* viral fusion RNA (groups one and two) all showed a heightened awareness, intelligence, and physiological superiority. Those dosed with the *deactivated* viral fusion RNA (groups three and four) showed equal ability to perform mouse tricks, like going through mazes. They were also physically more robust. The fifth and sixth groups served as controls for comparison.

The kicker was the "awareness" observation. The authors concluded it had to have resulted from the type of viral RNA used. The psychopharmacological opinion provided in the discussion described awareness as the animals' ability to recognize themselves in mirrors. This was a far-reaching conclusion. Previously, only higher species such as great apes and humans were known to be self-aware. The authors of the paper had now shown they could trigger this unprecedented attribute in lower animals using chimeric RNA.

Marcus looked at the author list again. The name R. Shanahan had to have been the psychopharmacologist. The story was starting to come together. All these scientists, or most of them, anyway, were now dead.

Why? Had they discovered something that triggered some latent psychosis? Was there a further experiment, one they didn't publish? There were so many questions, and not nearly enough answers, but one thing was certain. More than ever, he needed to find Edmund Solkar. If there was a single individual on the planet with insights sufficient to cast light on this mystery, then this killer was the one.

Or was there anyone else?

He remembered the unlabeled disks he'd taken from the disused office. He closed the browser and fished out the two CD-ROMs. He inserted one into his laptop's drive bay and waited. It whirred for a few seconds and then stopped. His file explorer showed a single file, named VC2. It had no extension. Marcus right clicked on the file and learned it occupied six hundred forty megabytes. Ten megabytes remained free.

He attempted several methods to run or view the file. All were futile. The only text editor that would open it up at all showed a few lines of unrecognizable characters followed by page upon page of blank space, terminating in a simple ampersand.

Thinking the other CD might contain something more useful, he pressed eject and swapped it in. The whirring repeated itself for ten seconds. Again, there was only one file, this one named VC1. It was a little smaller than VC2, about six hundred megabytes. None of his file finding tricks revealed anything else, but he knew that compact disks that old had a maximum capacity of six hundred fifty megabytes, rather than the newer ones that held seven hundred. The free space left couldn't account for the 50 MB difference, so there had to be additional files on it somewhere.

Was it a different operating system? He knew Windows well, but many academic labs preferred Macintosh systems. Could it be a Mac disk? He then recalled the other disks he'd seen. Vikram "Gator" de Silva's lab notebook supplements had all been readable in his machine. So why not these?

Google the problem, he thought. He typed "find hidden files on CD-ROM" into the search bar, but the hits failed to provide help. He rephrased the problem a few times, and at last discovered a technical forum where an unlikely expert named "Patty Cakes" suggested he change the boot sequence to CD drive first. Be careful, Ms. Cakes suggested, just in case the disk contained a virus, worm, or Trojan. If the disk were bootable, he might find what he needed.

Marcus always carried a backup portable drive in case of catastrophic failure. He plugged it in and ran a full ghost image routine. It took almost half an hour for the complete backup. He then powered down, restarted, and hit the F2 key before the operating system could load. He modified the BIOS setup to change the boot order and put the optical drive at the top of the list, saved, and hit Esc. Then he waited to see if the CD-ROM containing the VC1 file would boot up.

A flashing underscore line at the top left corner of his screen added to the suspense for five full minutes. Expecting an error message any moment, Marcus was about to hit the power switch again and restore the boot order to its previous setting. He wondered if he'd fried the laptop, or if he might have to run a low level reformat and restore exercise, but then the underscore went away. Five seconds later the screen flashed white, then black, and displayed a checkerboard pattern, before an old fashioned C:\ prompt appeared.

Marcus wondered if he could remember anything from his DOS days. Maybe the CD was just that, a portable DOS box. He typed "DIR" on the screen. Some simple file names showed up, less than a page worth. They looked vaguely familiar, but he couldn't remember the syntax to proceed. He tried the command "HELP" and received none. He typed DIR again, and noticed a sub-directory under the root. That led to a new prompt, C:\VDS. One more DIR command gave a single file, named FILM.EXE.

FILM.EXE was an executable file. He hesitated for a moment, and then typed the word "film." The screen went blank, then the checkerboard appeared again. After ten seconds, the disk began whirring so fast Marcus wondered if it might fly out of the drive bay and sever something vital. Then it slowed back down. At the same time, the checkerboard faded. A dialog box appeared on the screen asking him if he wanted sound (Y/N). He typed a Y and waited.

The disk spun again, not so fast this time, and then slowed. Suddenly, the screen burst into view, showing the face of a dark-skinned young man. Dense stubble grew on his cheeks. His huge brown eyes drooped, giving him an achingly sad appearance.

He spoke with an almost pure Midwestern accent, with only a trace of subcontinental lilt. "My name is Vikram de Silva." The portable computer's tinny speakers did little to enhance the sound quality. "You'll need to insert the second disk in exactly ten seconds from my mark. Any other interval will fail."

Ten seconds? Does that mean after ejecting the disk? What if the computer has to reboot? Or if it won't eject the disk at all? Marcus fished for the disk containing the VC2 file, and held it ready. He took off his watch and waited for de Silva to say something else, but nothing happened. The seconds ticked by. Ten passed, twenty, thirty. Nothing. He hit the enter key, the escape, even CTRL-ALT-DEL without success. Five, ten minutes passed. Then, just as he was about to give up, the man known as Gator gave the smallest hint of a smile, winked, and breathed "Mark" silently.

The second hand on his watch read thirty-seven seconds.

Marcus hit the eject button on the side of the drive bay. The disk stopped spinning, the whine dwindled, and the tray popped out. The disk was hot to the touch. Three seconds. Two more to take if off the tray. Another two to get the second disk settled, another to slide the tray almost all the way into the bay.

Forty-six, the second handle on his watch read.

Now. As the second hand rotated to forty-seven, Marcus slammed the disk in, but it didn't catch properly, and bounced back out again. *Forty-eight, forty-nine*, the second hand read. Nothing appeared on the screen. Was it too late?

"Shit!" Marcus swore as the computer locked. Nothing he did would persuade it to show any more pictures of de Silva, or do anything else for that matter. The only course left was to hold down the power switch long enough to trigger a restart.

This time, the disk whirred around but only long enough to generate an error message. The system asked him to press any key to boot. When he did, the hard disk began spinning. A minute later, the familiar Windows desktop reappeared. The CD-ROM hadn't done any damage, apparently, but this was a major disappointment. Marcus realized he'd lost the file.

"Shit, shit, shit," he repeated. He went to the bathroom and stared at the mirror before taking a long drink of water straight from the tap. That was when he realized that the wrong disk was in the bay, and that he'd set the bootable CD aside.

Relieved somewhat, he popped out the VC2 disk and replaced it with its partner. Then he restarted the machine. This time, the little horizontal blip reappeared. He almost went through the whole sequence of de Silva's instructions again, but for some reason he could not focus on the man's silent signal. He completely missed the chance to swap disks, but on the plus side, he figured he could bypass the Windows load sequence and just run a hard reboot just using the power switch.

Ensuring the laptop was plugged into the wall, rather than running off battery juice – he didn't want any more false starts – Marcus gave it one last shot. The second hand on his watch pointed to the fourteen second mark just as Vikram de Silva mouthed his signal. Two seconds to pop out the tray, two more to poke a finger under the disk and remove it, another two to stick the VC2 disk into the tray, and two more to slide the tray almost all the way in.

Twenty-three, twenty – ….

"Four," Marcus said as he firmly but gently shoved the tray back into his laptop. At last it held. The disk spun. The checkerboard appeared again, then faded. This time, de Silva's face was replaced with a new image. It caused his jaw to open wide. The hairs on the back of his neck rose up, and goose flesh covered his arms.

A video showed a dark-haired woman from behind. She wore a white lab coat and held a syringe. She stood over a table. On it were eleven additional syringes, aligned neatly. On each syringe, someone had written a code too blurred to be legible. Lined up before her was a group of six people: two middle-aged men, an Asian man in his mid-to-late twenties, a blond man wearing a yarmulke, and a pallid, bespectacled young man wearing a T-shirt with the Starship Enterprise on the front. A slender young woman wearing a sleeveless blouse stepped forward to receive the first shot, delivered into her bicep. She looked up. Shoulder-length tawny blonde hair fell away from her face.

He felt his pulse quicken. Was she the same attractive woman he saw disappearing with Alasdair Wylie in London? He couldn't be sure. In the video, she must have been in her early twenties. Now, she would be pushing forty.

The others received their shots and left through the back of the room. Five more subjects entered. All but one looked to be in their early or mid twenties, healthy-looking young adults. He recognized one of them, the same guy who had crafted the video, Vikram de Silva. "Gator" received the first shot. Next was a tall, angular young man with lifeless eyes. He got his shot and turned away. Who was that, Marcus wondered? CJB? JH? It had to be one of them, as the next guy had to be Edmund Solkar, judging by his apparent age, ethnic coloring, and authoritative air. The fifth recipient, a dark-haired young man, had intense blue eyes. He mouthed something at the woman with the syringes, and then broke into a laugh. He rolled up his sleeve and grinned at Solkar. The gesture seemed unnatural, as if he were trying to deliver a message.

Solkar's gaze sharpened for an instant. What had he seen? What did Blue Eyes convey? What had he said to the tech, the nurse, doctor, whoever she was? Marcus wanted to burst into the scene and confront him so badly it hurt his already churning guts. Could he rewind the video and read lips? He pressed the small pause button on the laptop, the one he used when playing music CD's, but it didn't work. The video ran on.

The five subjects filed out of the room, leaving the dark-haired nurse alone. One syringe remained on the tray. She slipped off her lab coat, revealing a tight, long-sleeved blouse and skirt. She unbuttoned her blouse and removed it, stripping down to a black lacy bra. The door reopened, and a tall woman in her early forties entered. She wore rimless spectacles, a white shirt, and blue jeans. She reminded Marcus of a reluctant hippie who couldn't quite fit the image. Long, mousy, and frizzy brown hair, parted in the middle and tied back with a rubber band, framed her cheeks and fell down her back almost to her waist. She looked at the semi-naked technician and smiled.

"Your turn," she mouthed.

Marcus almost blanked out a second later. The dark haired woman turned slightly to her left, but even before the video camera revealed her face, he knew. He knew her body, knew it intimately, every curve, every inch. He stared at the face he had loved for years, the mouth slightly upturned at the corners, the perfect nose, her bewitching eyes and flawless skin. Horror overcame him as she held out her arm. He wanted to scream at her to stop, to run, to hide, to turn her back on it all and save herself. The futility of it all was lost on him as he begged, "Don't do it!"

The would-be hippie – possibly the hitherto unseen Lynne Brady – took the last syringe and drove it into his wife's bicep. She depressed the plunger and delivered the contents, the liquid brew whose unknown composition and effects would vanish years later in a fiery death at the bottom of a cliff.

He couldn't bear to watch any more, the horror of his beloved as she willingly accepted her fate. As if somehow sensing this, Vikram de Silva's image appeared abruptly. His dark face stared motionless for several seconds, and then one of his melancholy eyes winked. Moments later, his mouth formed the word "Mark" again.

Chapter 34

SHOCKED INTO ACTION, MARCUS noted his watch's second hand. It had reached the five-second notch. He popped the disk out of the bay, and with less than a second to spare, swapped the VC1 disk back in. At fifteen seconds, he pushed the CD drive in.

The speaker clicked a few times and the familiar checkerboard appeared. It faded to black, but then "Gator" reappeared. He began to speak.

"If you have just watched this video, you will know that an illegal human experiment was performed. The people you saw were all given doses of chimeric RNA, but they were not given the same one. Each was tailored individually. By the time you see this, most of us will have survived long enough to know what the delayed or chronic effects might be. However, we may no longer be alive. There is no way at the time of recording of predicting these outcomes. I have left this video to show you what happened, along with whatever additional materials I was able to hide away.

"The designers of this facility took copies of the original blueprints so they could reproduce the building elsewhere after the University took it over. The Castlefords willed the bulk of their fortune to a trust so that Professor Brady's project could continue. The name of the trust was Demeter Advanced Technologies, later shortened to Demetek."

A date stamp appeared at the end of the video. The grainy film had been made within six months of the publication date of the journal article he was reading earlier. He wondered which experiment had come first: mice, or men – and women.

The disk ejected itself automatically, and the computer began rebooting. Within a minute, the familiar desktop wallpaper appeared. It was as though he was awakening from a bad dream. Marcus's hands shook as he powered the laptop down and stowed it in his backpack. He almost forgot to pull the disk out and put it back in its paper sleeve.

He also forgot how fast his heart was beating. As he stood, he felt dizzy, the blood slamming into his temples. He staggered to the bathroom, bent before the sink, and splashed his face with cold water. Several minutes passed before the throb in his head eased.

He returned to the room and called Josef, not caring how early it was in the morning. The two-hour time difference turned out to be irrelevant. Rintlen answered on the first ring.

"It's me, Josef," Marcus said shakily. "I'm coming back to San Francisco today."

"I will have George pick you up. Did you have something you wanted to tell me before you arrive?"

Marcus considered unloading all of what he had just witnessed, but thought better of it. Best go over that in person. "I Fedexed you a package yesterday. You should receive it before ten this morning, local time."

"I'll keep an eye out. What is it?"

"A few CD-ROMs and some architectural diagrams."

Josef was unable to hide his surprise. "Blueprints? What of?"

"The Castleford Institute building. That's where this all began. I believe the blueprints were used to recreate the facility elsewhere."

"Demetek," Rintlen said. "When Henry and Linda died, that is where their money went. The company is located in central Australia."

"But the company started out with a different name. Demeter Advanced Technologies. Does that mean anything to you? I didn't have time to look them up, but you have better access to online data."

"Wait a moment. I will search." *Click, tap, tap, click.* "I am sorry, Marcus. There is no company registered here in the United States by that name. It might have existed ten or fifteen years ago, but keeping track of changes in corporate ownership, particularly among private companies, is what you might call a crapshoot."

"What about other similar names?"

"I tried a fuzzy logic search. Nothing of interest other than Demetek itself. There are no public or limited private records that I can find beyond the generic web site."

Marcus thought for a minute. "What about the name itself? Any clues there? If I remember correctly, Demeter was something to do with ancient mythology. Some kind of Roman god or goddess?"

More clicking and tapping followed. "Almost. Demeter was not Roman but Greek, specifically the goddess of agriculture. The equivalent in Roman mythology was Ceres – hence the Latin root of the word cereal. Demeter was sister to Zeus, Poseidon, Hades, and one or two others."

"Leader of the Greek gods, the god of the sea, the underworld, et cetera."

"Probably high on the corporate ladder," Josef quipped. "According to Wikipedia, she controlled the seasons and the harvest, and therefore was capable of destroying all life on earth. Her greatest gifts were cereal, which we already knew about, but also the so-called Mysteries, which gave mankind higher hopes in the present and the hereafter." He paused for a moment, reading further, and then continued. "The legend goes something like this. Her brother Hades kidnapped her daughter Persephone, which angered Demeter so much she prevented any new life on the planet. The earth began to die. Zeus could not put up with this any more and so he persuaded his brother, Hades, to release Persephone, for a price. Hades agreed only on condition that she had not eaten any food in the underworld before her release. It turned out that she had consumed a few pomegranate seeds. The deal struck by the principals stated that she should return to the underworld every year for a month per seed she had eaten. During the time she was released, with her mother, the earth would flourish, but when she had to return down under, the world would be ravaged by famine."

Down under. "Funny you should use those words, Josef."

"Which ones?"

Marcus told him. "Just a strange irony. Demetek is in Australia. Not to suggest anything sinister is going on there." He wondered, though, if there was a modern day Persephone somewhere, symbolic if not human.

"There is more, Marcus."

"What are you talking about?"

"Another myth. Demeter is said to have been welcomed by the king of Eleusis, named Celeus. This monarch had a son named Triptolemus. Demeter thanked Celeus for his hospitality by teaching Triptolemus the art of agriculture, and helped him educate the Greeks to sow and reap. Demeter and Persephone both cared for Triptolemus while he was doing this. One day, Triptolemus taught agriculture to the king of the Scythians, Lyncus, but he refused to pass it on to his own people and thus Demeter took revenge on him by turning him into a lynx."

"So Triptolemus was a good guy. An educator, just like his mentor. But he picked the wrong student."

"Indeed. Persephone herself was no angel, her name means "she who brings destruction.""

"Makes you wonder. Who, if anyone, is the modern equivalent of this little drama, and if they exist, are they having a chuckle at our expense?"

"I do not believe there would be anything amusing in that case. There was one other thing that may be of interest, something a little more contemporary."

"Go ahead."

Click. "In Australia the term 'Demeter' is a registered trademark for certified biodynamic products. In short, it pertains to fertilizer free, chemical free farming, based on living soil, it says here. In the process, organic matter in the top soil is increased. The deeper soil is richer in humus as well, increasing the efficiency of new growth."

"That sounds pretty benign, even beneficial, to me."

"It is environmentally friendly and helpful to plants and animals. It is not revolutionary, having been practiced for several decades, but it sets an example to those who would prefer to use more artificial means to increase yield."

"So is that what Demetek does?"

"That is hard to say without knowing the company's roots, as it were."

"Consider the bad pun forgiven. In the meantime, did you learn anything else about Henry and Linda Castleford?"

"There is one fact that may point to an antipodean connection. Linda Castleford was born in Melbourne, Victoria. Henry's money was new. Hers was old."

"So we should follow the money."

"Precisely. We will talk further when you arrive."

After hanging up and collecting his belongings, Marcus left the hotel room. His westbound flight was due to depart in two hours. He was about to board the shuttle when he remembered the text on his mobile. During his eagerness to discover what was on the disks he'd found yesterday, he had forgotten completely about the cryptic, yet disturbingly direct message.

They know about you.

He reopened his inbox, looking for an electronic signature tag, but found none. He tried the reply option, keyed in the word *who*, and hit the send button, not knowing what might come back.

Five minutes later, his cell phone chirped again. One new message.

She saw you in London.

Marcus frowned, but chose to pursue the conversation further. He punched in a new question, one he wished he'd asked originally. *What's your name?*

The bus pulled into the terminal before he received a reply. As he waited in line for a desk agent, the phone beeped again. It said, *Tell me where we can meet.*

When you tell me your name.

The name was unfamiliar. He typed: *meet @ arrivals of sfo, by bgge carousl 5 in ua term. wear kc royls bb cap.*

The *ok* response came as Marcus passed through airport security.

Chapter 35

Mickey Durant woke from a restless sleep at the sound of footsteps crunching on the ground outside. She could tell it was early dawn by the faint light coming through the shack's cracks. How many days was it now? Two? Three? Probably the former, she thought, but hunger and thirst led her to think otherwise. She rolled towards the sound to hear the prowler circumnavigating the shack. Was it an animal, a dog perhaps, maybe a mountain lion, a bear? She listened carefully, trying to determine whether the gait was four-legged or two-legged, but without success.

The sound stopped. She heard something metallic: a click, followed by a wrenching noise. A firing mechanism? Was her captor about to shoot her in cold blood? The sound repeated itself, a click, and another metallic whine. Was it a hinge? If the click were a gun being loaded, why do it twice? It had to be a padlock, maybe two.

"Stay back from the door," a voice commanded. "I'm going to open up."

Mickey did as she was told. A boot kicked the door inwards. Blue-gray light flashed on her face, showing a streaky mixture of dirt and dried tears. Then a high-intensity LED flashlight blinded her, forcing her to turn away.

"Where is he?" the voice demanded.

"Where is who? Who are you?" Mickey begged.

"I asked you a question. You're the only one who can help me find him."

"Who are you talking about?"

"Your client, who else?"

"I have lots of clients. I'm a lawyer."

"Don't play games with me, Michelle. You know who I'm talking about."

"No, I don't. I don't know who or what you're talking about." She couldn't see her captor's face behind the beam.

"Have you ever noticed that phrase is a dead giveaway that someone is lying?" the voice carrying the light said.

Of course I have. I'm a lawyer. "Not in this case. I really don't know. Would you stop shining that light on me?" she pleaded.

"When you tell me what I want to know."

Mickey cowered in the back corner of the shack. "I need water."

A filled plastic bottle flew at her, narrowly missing her face. It hit her in the shoulder, causing her to wince.

"Don't drink it all at once," the visitor said.

Half blind, Mickey scrabbled around in the dirt. She uncapped the bottle, her fingers shaking, and gulped.

"I said DON'T drink it all at once!" The stalker lunged forward and slapped the bottle out of Mickey's hand. The remaining liquid drained onto the dirt. "See what you've done? Now you won't have any more water for a whole day."

Mickey cried out. "Why are you doing this? What do you want with me?"

"Was there something you didn't understand about my original question? I want to know where your client is. I owe him."

"Who are you?" Mickey tried again. She shielded her eyes.

The intruder fiddled with a knob on the flashlight, dimming its beam. Slowly, her silhouette came into focus. "Remember me?" The voice softened.

"Oh, my God. You – you're still…."

"Alive? And well," Sarah Innes said. "You might say I've been having a long holiday. And you're almost the last person in my way." She approached, catlike, a new object suddenly materializing in her right hand. It was a fine-gauged needle. A droplet ominously formed at its end. "This won't take long. But if you fail to tell me where your client is, I can make it last much longer, and I guarantee, much more painfully."

"I still don't know what you're talking about."

Smack! Sarah's left hand crashed into Mickey's face, sending her sideways into the dirt, where she lay sobbing. "Liar!" She wrenched her back onto her rear end and held the needle inches away from her eye.

"They'll find me," Mickey said, blood dripping from an already swelling lower lip. "They'll know what you did, and how."

"I don't think so. It's fast acting and rapidly cleared. I've used it successfully many times. Now, are you going to tell me where he is?"

"I'm right here," a voice said behind her.

Both women looked up in surprise. A broad-shouldered, dark-skinned man, dressed in a black T-shirt and jeans, stood in the crude doorway. The light was improving slightly as dawn began to break.

"Leave her alone," the man said, inching closer towards Sarah.

"I can't. You know that," Sarah said. She raised her right hand. "I can't let anyone stop what we started." She turned towards Mickey, who was crab-walking away as fast as she could, desperately trying to put distance between the two of them.

A sledgehammer kick stunned Sarah as it slammed into the side of her head, knocking her aside. She fell limp, onto the straw mattress.

The man was not finished. He knelt and reached for her right wrist and hand, carefully avoiding the needle. He held the hand in a tight grip, her slender forearm in the other, and twisted, stretching and wrenching. Her joint dislocated with a horrible cracking sound that reverberated through the shack.

She made no sound. The man rose to his feet and placed a boot on the supine woman's throat, ready to crush her larynx.

"You bitch, Samaya!" he spat. "I lost my life because of you!"

"Eddie, stop," Mickey cried. She rose to her feet and went to him, shaking him by the shoulders. "Don't do it! You've paid the price already!"

"So I have nothing to lose, do I, Mick? They can't convict me again, can they? You should know about the double jeopardy clause!"

"It doesn't work that way, Eddie, really, it doesn't!" She pushed him back gently, far enough so he was no longer pressing down on Sarah/Samaya's throat. Then she took his face in her hands and stared deep into his black eyes, gathering the strength she'd almost lost. "It didn't go to the jury, remember? You pleaded to a lesser charge. Look, you have to listen to me, you can't do this. Not now. We'll get the original verdict overturned. We'll get you a pardon from the governor of Illinois. We'll get you compensation. Anything. I'll be there for you, Eddie, I promise." The words spewed out of her uncontrollably.

"You don't know what she did to me, Mick. I've been through hell and back, and now I'm going to die, like the rest of them. She needs to pay."

Like the rest of them? Mickey didn't understand. "I don't know what you mean, but let the police take care of it. It's their job. Samaya kidnapped me to get to you. She was going to kill me. I'll tell them you were just trying to protect me."

"Right. They'll really believe that, a convicted killer who came back to protect his lawyer from being killed by same the woman he'd allegedly murdered all those years ago. As if anyone would believe that." *As if I'd believe that.* He stepped back.

Michelle Durant, attorney-at-law and evidentiary expert, felt the other woman's throat. A gurgling sound came out of Samaya's mouth, then a moan, as she started to come to. "I'd believe it, Eddie. I believed you all those years ago, about what really happened, and I still believe you now. I believe *in* you."

Samaya tried to lift her right hand. Agony coursed up her arm to her shoulder. Unable to move for the pain, she gritted her teeth and hissed.

"This time it's my turn," Mickey said, summoning up what strength she had left. She grabbed Samaya's hand and lifted it, ignoring the tortured scream as she twisted it around. Then she thrust the needle deep into her neck. Mickey squeezed the bulb behind it, delivering the poison. "I think we'll be able to position your body to show that you fell over and broke your arm, and accidentally stuck yourself," she said. "Or perhaps I'll just fess up to the whole thing, that it was simple self-defense. I do have a witness, after all."

The poison acted as rapidly as advertised. Samaya's body jerked once, then stiffened, before falling still. Mickey felt for a pulse, both at her throat and on her good arm, and looked up at her client. "She's unconscious. Her pulse is thready, but I'm no doctor. I don't know if this is going to kill her."

Something inside Ed seemed to break. His shoulders slumped, his eyes closed, and then his chest heaved. Sensing his exhaustion, Mickey staggered over to him, placing her arms around his waist and burying her face against his chest. He smelled of sweat and dust, and she could feel his heart thumping a mile a minute. He wrapped his arms around her gently, drawing her into his body. After a long, silent period, he released her and led her outside to the rising sun.

The shack was in the middle of a forest. She had no way to know how far they were from civilization, or from a road, but sensed that one had to be nearby, given that Ed had followed them. She saw a plastic yellow can, designed for small volumes of gasoline, standing outside the door to the shack.

"Samaya would have incinerated you once she had what she wanted, Mick," Ed said. "That's her M.O. I reckon the stuff in that can isn't gas but something that burns a helluva lot hotter and quicker. She wouldn't want to get caught in a forest fire up here at this time of the year."

She pointed at the incendiary can. "What's stopping us from finishing it?"

"I'd rather leave her to nature's whims. There are enough carnivores in this forest to take care of her. She'll be eaten before anyone ever finds her."

Mickey looked around them, and then up at Solkar. He was more handsome now than she remembered. The attraction had been there ever since she was first assigned to his case, all professional detachment aside. "What did she want, Eddie?"

"She wanted to kill me. Because I can stop them, if I can get to them in time."

"Stop who? Get where, when? You're not making sense." She reached for his arm.

"The trial."

"What trial? Your trial? The murder trial?"

He whirled around, his black eyes fiery. "The human trial. The one we conducted. We needed to see the consequences of the engineered chimera injections."

"You're still not making sense, Eddie. I don't understand."

"It was biotech gone mad, Mick. I trusted them."

Trusted who? "Go on."

"They made unnatural changes, mutations that never should have been attempted, and then delivered them to mice, rats, dogs, and monkeys. They played God with Nature." He strode away, onto a narrow pathway leading them through the trees.

Mickey followed. She walked unsteadily after the long night's ordeal. "How far away are we from the road?" she asked.

"About half a mile," Solkar said. "Can you make it?"

"I think so. If you have anything to drink or eat that would help,"

He whipped out a granola bar, still wrapped. "Will this do?"

It did. "You didn't come prepared to live off the land for a week," she joked.

"I learned how to survive in prison. Not in the wild, of course, but the place did toughen me up some." He began to quicken his pace, but slowed and turned back when he realized that she had stopped.

"Wait! I don't feel so good." She sank to her knees and promptly regurgitated the contents of her stomach, wincing as the heaves hit her hard.

Solkar knelt and held her shoulders. "It's okay, Mick. Take it easy. No rush."

She spat out saliva and bile, tears streaming from her eyes as she reacted to the bitter taste. "Shit," she grumbled. "I hate puking. What was in that granola bar?"

"An energy spike your body couldn't handle, apparently. Look, we need to get you to the car and get some fluids in you as soon as possible. Then we need to have a serious talk. It seems my scientific past has come back to haunt me." He pulled some folded tissues from his back pocket and wiped the debris from her face, gently dabbing her moist cheeks. He tossed the paper aside, apologizing aloud for the act of littering, as if anyone would care, and helped Mickey to her feet.

"I don't think I can walk all the way, Eddie," she said, still feeling weak.

Ed slipped an arm around her shoulder, and then bent slightly. In a swift motion he reached around the back of her knees and lifted her clean off the ground. She threw an arm around his neck in surprise. "Like I said, prison toughened me up. Not to mention working construction." He began the trek through the trees.

They reached the car almost an hour later. He lowered her, pulled open the door, and helped her to the passenger seat. He got in beside her, opened the glove compartment, and pulled out a full bottle of mineral water. He unscrewed the cap and offered it to her.

"You first," she said. "You did all the work."

"You need it more. But take it slowly."

She did. They shared, swapping the bottle until it was empty.

Solkar cranked the ignition. "Okay, time to hit the road. Got any bright ideas about where we go next?"

Mickey no longer had her purse. George Petrescu's card was probably lying in a bin somewhere, along with the rest of her credit cards and license. She vaguely remembered the number had a 415 area code, but what was the rest of it? Even if she could remember, it would not be easy to find him. "I met a man two days ago. He came to my office in Davis. I think he was trying to warn me. I just can't remember his number, where he was based, you know?"

"Who did he work for?"

"Not sure. I think it began with an X. X, then USA. Wait, that's it! XUSA. Sounds like 'Zoosa.'"

"Location?"

She thought for a moment. "Damn, I should have paid more attention. It began with a B, I think. Bel, maybe?"

"Belvedere? That's a nice neighborhood, so they say, but it's hardly a place for high tech."

Her eyes brightened. "That's it! Belvedere. I remember now. That's where we need to go. We have to find George Petrescu. Get me back on the road and I can use my Blackberry to – oh, damn!"

"What?"

"It was in my purse too. Along with my keys. I can't even get into my house or into my office."

"Don't worry," Ed said. "We'll find an internet café. Or a friendly janitor to let you into your office. This is one of the easier problems to solve. Trust me."

Mickey Durant looked at her client, the convicted felon who'd just saved her life, the unlikely hero who'd carried her all the way back to his ancient Oldsmobile, the man who – what? What was he really doing here?

Something else didn't add up. Ed had to have followed her and Samaya at a safe distance, and parked out of sight. Then, after tracking them, he'd come across the cabin. Where was Samaya's vehicle? Surely it was between the cabin and where they sat right now, so why didn't they pass it on the way back? She felt her guts churn anew. Was this all a set-up?

"I don't know who to trust or what to think any more," she said.

He took her hand in his. She expected rough-hewn flesh, but his hands were warm and surprisingly soft, despite their strength. "There's something else I need to tell you before we hit the road. If you can't understand or trust me then, I'll leave you the keys and let you go by yourself. If you do trust me, then we'll go and find this Petrescu guy together and work with him, and whoever he's tied up with. Okay?"

Pressed to choose one way or the other, she took a leap of faith. It was at least worth hearing what else he had left unsaid. "All right. Tell me everything. And don't leave anything out."

Fifteen minutes later, the color was barely returning to her face.

Chapter 36

THE TELEPHONE CONTINUED TO ring, adding to Don Strathmore's frustration. He had tried Sarah's mobile three times in the last hour without success. Where the hell was she? She'd guaranteed she would find and eliminate Solkar, but her failure to check in as planned bothered him. He slammed the handset down, and stormed out of his office. This was not the time for screw-ups, especially with the imminent release of Demetek's groundbreaking new product. There was also the not-so-small matter of a painfully large check, no doubt some kind of capital expenditure authorized without his approval. Who the hell was responsible for that?

Justin Hernandez joined his CEO. They were heading to an all hands company gathering in the main lecture theater one level below ground. It was time to deliver the timetable for product rollout. Hernandez bubbled with enthusiasm as he greeted Strathmore with a slap on the back. "Don! We've confirmed the Bio 2 strain is superior in every aspect, but that's not all."

"What do you mean?" Strathmore demanded. They entered the corridor between the sequencing labs and the elevators.

"We got the autopsy result from Steve's beloved chimp."

"And?"

"Chromosome fifteen was normal. The food-borne prophylactic worked even better than the vaccine. It's untraceable."

"In layman's language, are you saying that the dietary supplement eliminated all the side effects you'd struggled with at the beginning of this project?"

"Except for one minor clinical endpoint. The chimp didn't survive."

"Why?"

"No way of knowing yet. At least the primary side effect went away. It appears the brain tissue wasn't affected. But do we really care? The product can still be deployed where it's needed, and we can control any collateral damage."

"You got the original vaccine, mate. You should be on borrowed time."

Hernandez leered. "No problem. I got a blank. We swapped it in for my little shot of personalized medicine right before everyone got dosed. Good thing, right? Or you wouldn't be making millions off this deal." He high-fived his boss.

They reached the end of the corridor. At the elevator, the door cooperatively pinged and opened, precisely anticipating their arrival. Hernandez pressed the B1 button to take them to the lecture theater.

Strathmore pushed him aside and pressed the emergency stop.

"What are you doing, Don?" Hernandez frowned.

The CEO picked up the emergency handset and spoke into it. "Mike, it's Don here, calling from the lift. I've stopped it for a moment to have a quick word with Justin before the all hands meeting. Should only be a minute or two."

Mike Baltazzi from security said, "No worries. You know the drill, punch in the access code and we all go blind and deaf to you. Give me a shout if you don't get it started up again when you're finished and I'll fix it from here."

"Cheers." Strathmore keyed in a six digit code. "There. We're completely secure now. Bet you didn't know this simple little lift had a cone of silence built in."

"Can Baltazzi see us through the CCTV or hidden microphones?"

"Nope. It's just you and me. Not a soul can see or hear us. So now, it's time for you to tell me the truth."

"What are you talking about, Don? I'm confused." Hernandez's demeanor changed subtly, a nervous half-grin replacing the usual unbridled confidence.

Strathmore reached into his jacket pocket and pulled out a single sheet of paper. "How about explaining this?"

Demetek's CSO looked at the sheet. It was an extract from a recent expense report. "What's the problem?"

"Nearly three quarters of a million dollars is the problem, Justin. You're the only person at this company other than me with that kind of signature authority. I didn't sign for this, obviously, so why did you?"

Hernandez looked back and forth between Strathmore and the invoice, examining the signature carefully. "I didn't sign this, Don. I don't know who did, but that isn't my signature on the req. This is forged. I don't know where this money has gone. And if I did know and failed to tell you, that would be about the dumbest thing since – well, I don't know when. I'm lost for words."

Strathmore glared at Hernandez, then let out a puff of air. "I checked with my personal accountant. This exact amount is unusual but for one simple calculation. If you deduct a specific percentage based on tax withholding rates, the arithmetic works out very nicely at half a million net. Care to hazard a guess as to who walked away from here with a huge cash payoff?"

"No, I don't care to hazard a guess, Don. And I resent any implication that I had anything to do with this."

"Your autograph is on the paperwork. What am I supposed to think?"

Hernandez sighed and looked at his watch. "We're going to be late."

"They can bloody well wait for us, Justin. Now how about telling me what the hell you think you're doing pilfering that kind of cash from the company just to send that Gilstrap twit on an all expenses paid trip around the world with enough spending money to last him a fucking lifetime?" Strathmore fished out a ticketing receipt and brandished it. "Explain this, Justin!" Spittle flew from his lips. He shoved the receipt in Hernandez's face and jabbed at his chest with his free hand.

Although two inches shorter than his boss, Hernandez had ten years' youth and twenty pounds of muscle in his favor. Fire raged inside him as he slapped Strathmore's hand aside. He grabbed the older man by the lapels and hissed, eyes blazing. "If you ever touch me again, or make accusations for which you have no basis in fact, then I will end you. That is a guarantee." He shoved the CEO against the wall of the elevator and sharply drove a fist into the man's belly, causing him to double over in agony. "I had NOTHING to do with this embezzlement, and if you took the time to think about it instead of assaulting me on the day of this company's greatest triumph then you might just figure out that piss-ant Canadian wimp was behind this. Get my MEANING?"

Strathmore gasped for breath. "W-w-wait!" His chest heaved as his lungs desperately tried to recover.

Hernandez yanked his boss's tie to one side contemptuously.

"All right, all right. He took deepening breaths, regaining his strength. "Bloody hell, Justin, you have a nasty temper!"

Nasty enough to make you back off, I hope. "What the hell were you thinking?"

"I don't know. Really, I don't. Look, I'm sorry, I haven't slept properly in weeks. This thing with the new strain, it's getting to me."

The new strain, Hernandez thought. *Soon to be deployed.* Several hundred kilometers away, in remote Western Australia, the prototype in Bio 2 appeared an extraordinary success. Now, the same methods were yielding the creation he had dreamed of his whole professional life, in Bio 3. Screw that goddamned monkey in Bio 1. They'd just made a mistake with the inoculation. The same thing had happened to the little shit-for-brains IT guy in Chicago, that Scottish eccentric, the know-it-all Jew, and what's-his-face. That was the best trick of all, switching the dose so the sanctimonious little shrink wouldn't know what hit him years later. That had been Sam's idea of course. Still, progress was progress, and if anyone wanted to stop Hernandez from playing God, they would have to pay the price. Now, with Strathmore starting to crack, he wondered whether the man could last long enough for him to complete his life's mission.

"It has to be Goudreau. Dayne wouldn't dare screw with you. I don't know if he was taking out some kind of insurance policy by sending his young friend back into the world with a bribe, but right after today's announcement, we'll take Dr. Etienne aside. Find out what he knows, what he's done. Then we'll deal with Gilstrap. Screw that, I'll do it myself." He looked at the clock. It was already five minutes past the hour. They were late.

"There's another problem. I can't find Sarah. She's not responding."

"Not responding? What do you mean?"

"She was supposed to check in this morning. She found Solkar's lawyer, the one who saved his ass. She assured me she could handle them both without stirring up trouble, but I haven't heard from her since yesterday."

"What was she doing last time you talked?"

"She found the Durant woman and took her to an old cabin northeast of Sacramento. The idea was to beat the truth about Solkar's whereabouts out of her and take him by surprise. The guy would brick if he saw his poor dead victim come back to life. We just don't know if she succeeded yet."

Crap. "What if he talks?"

"Relax, Justin! No one will believe an ex-con like him anyway. The man's certifiable, by all accounts, and even if he did start spreading his version of events around the bazaars he'd be lumped in with all the other conspiracy nuts. Besides, there's no proof, anywhere. All the records were destroyed except for the useful ones, and they're in the fireproof safe in your office. Right?"

Strathmore picked up the elevator's handset, punched in the security code and spoke. "Mike, we're on our way back down again. Everything's taken care of."

"No worries. You might want to fix your tie, though. It looks a bit skewed."

The CEO flashed his chief scientist a nasty look and straightened it. "Cheers. Thanks for the heads up." He hung up and said to Hernandez, "We're on."

As they entered the lecture theater, virtually everyone gathered within cheered and clapped. No one noticed that Steve Goudreau, despite his false smile, was not participating in the applause. He and Monty Dayne sat at a table on the stage, Steve closest to the lectern, Dayne at the end. Strathmore strode to the podium and raised both hands, palms down, to quiet the throng. Hernandez sandwiched Goudreau between himself and his CEO, and then sat down.

"G'day, everyone!" Strathmore bellowed. "I'm not going to beat around the bush. You know why you're all here. Today is the most significant day in our company's history, but it's much more than that. Today is the first day for the new Earth, and I'm not bullshitting you. The work you've done in the last year leading to the rollout of our landmark product has been a triumph for science, for creativity, and for innovation. Now those phrases may sound like business-speak, and so I'm going to leave them at that. You won't hear me talk about leveraging our technology, changing paradigms, expanding our strategic opportunities, or any of that other crap. This is short and simple."

He pressed a button on the podium. The screen behind him sprang to life. A familiar company logo, depicting a sheaf of wheat, appeared on screen. The image faded to a Powerpoint slide show that took all of ten minutes. Strathmore delivered the message, congratulated the team again, and then finished up with a bid for questions.

No one said anything. By habit as much as anything, Hernandez opened up the floor with a comment instead of a question. "Our Chinese partners will probably see results in a month should the reproduction cycle be as successful as we expect. If so, our revenue will allow us to enter large scale manufacture and distribution to the United States and Europe in time for next year's season."

"This, of course, is only the beginning," Strathmore commented. "The real beneficiary of our technology will be those Third World countries whose climate is as harsh as our own Outback. But at the danger of sounding like a TV pitchman, that's not all."

He paused for effect. "The kicker will be the outcome on our dwindling rain forests. You've all been part of this effort, and now I can tell you with certainty that the engineered protein works, and it works bloody brilliantly! We can now restore the balance disrupted by our greed, pollution, and extravagance, and make our planet a better place to breathe the air."

Steve Goudreau's teeth gritted together at his boss's words. He wondered if there was still time.

Lord, I hope so.

Chapter 37

MARCUS'S FLIGHT TOUCHED DOWN in San Francisco just after three. The terminal was relatively quiet; peak departures and arrivals would not happen for a couple of hours. He reached the baggage claims within five minutes of disembarking. At carousel five, he cast his eyes around for anyone with a Kansas City Royals baseball cap, but without success. Was he a tad early? Whoever was supposed to meet him could have been parking a car or paying cab fare, but the delay didn't help his frayed nerves at all.

More fellow passengers started to congregate: families with children; businessmen and women; the invariable would-be and ex-hippies; and students. They milled around the conveyor belt, waiting for the red light to come on, signaling the imminent delivery of their cargo. Ten minutes passed before the belt began disgorging their goods from the bowels of the system below. After twenty minutes, the red light went off and the carousel's metal slats halted. A few disgusted passengers began cursing the airline, the system, and the handlers, as they trudged off to the lost baggage office. Royals Cap was nowhere.

He felt a tap on his shoulder. It was George Petrescu. No sign of a dress this time. "I assumed you just brought carry-on. Didn't expect to find you down here. Josef's waiting for us. He has something – and someone – you'll want to see."

"What? Who?"

"Best leave that till we get there. He asked me not to say anything until then."

Marcus took a final look around the area. Not a soul remained near the fifth carousel. The fourth and third carousels were equally quiet.

"You still waiting for a suitcase?" George asked.

"No." He craned his neck to look past carousel four. Still no Royals Cap. He jerked a thumb over his shoulder. "I just have what's on my back."

"Then what else is there? Traffic over the bridge is ugly, even with carpool lanes and all."

"I'm looking for someone. Do you see anyone with a baseball cap?"

"Down here? Not from where I'm looking. Sure you got the location right?"

Carousel five. "I told him to meet me right here."

"How did you tell him?"

"Text. I could call, I guess." He pulled out his cell phone to find the screen blanked out. He cursed, forgetting that he hadn't switched it on when the flight landed. As soon as the familiar wake-up jingle sounded, he discovered a single text waiting for him. He opened it up to see the words *cu there. Ill wait til u find me.*

"That's weird," he said, scrolling through the message. Then he discovered his absurd mistake. He'd screwed up the original instruction. *Damned phone.* Instead of a 5, he had input a 2, right below the 5 on the keypad. "He's down at the other end!"

Taking off at a sprint, George in hot pursuit, Marcus soon covered the distance to find a young man wearing a brand new baseball cap, seated on the hard rubber lip surrounding carousel two. He was busy tapping away at his own mobile.

"Looking for me?" Marcus said, panting.

"If you're Marcus Black, I'm Matt Gilstrap," the young man said, standing up. "Guess I don't need to send this one," he added, hitting cancel.

George caught up with them a few seconds later. Marcus introduced him immediately. Then he said to Matt, "Come with us. You'd best tell me what the hell's going on."

They drove onto I-380 and headed up through the city on 19th Avenue. Much of the city was bathed in bright sunshine, but a thick blanket of low clouds shrouded the inaptly named Sunset District. The fog started at the southern end of Daly City, white wisps drifting over Highway 1 as the Accord headed northbound. "I love this town," George commented. "The weather is guaranteed to be different half an hour away from wherever you happen to be. If you don't like what you have, you can change it almost instantly." He drove parallel to Ocean Beach, dunes to his left, and a waste treatment plant to his right. A few minutes later they rounded a curve, passed the landmark Cliff House restaurant, and headed east on Geary.

They turned onto 30th Avenue towards the ultra-expensive Seacliff district. Unsure where to start, Matt wasted no time on tact. "Your wife worked for Lynne Brady."

Marcus turned around in the passenger seat. "You said 'they know about you.' What does my wife have to do with anything?"

"I'll get to that. But I need to give you some background. I saw the picture of Kay, is that what you called her? In the Chronicle. I recognized her from an old photo."

I know Kay worked for Brady. "Who are you? What do you want?" His tone was harsh.

Matt realized he was being insensitive. "Look, I'm sorry. I just came out with that and I didn't even say – well, you know – I'm sorry for your loss, and – well, I mean, of course there's something else. It's just that I wanted to start on the right foot. Guess that's all gone to hell in a handcart, huh?"

Marcus gave him a stern look, and then softened slightly. "Okay. I'm listening. But do me a favor, huh? Don't hold anything back. I've just spent the last several days flying half way around the world trying to find out why and how my wife was killed. If you know something, you'd better tell me now."

They were now well past Seacliff. Cyclists enjoying the afternoon sunshine wound along the coastal road, past the old Presidio army base. George kept his eyes on the road, but listened closely.

Matt started from the beginning. "I recently obtained my Ph.D. in molecular and structural biology. My dissertation was on a high-throughput protein crystallization technique. A biotech company in Australia called Demetek licensed the technology. You heard of them?"

"Vaguely."

"Okay. So last year they flew me from here to Alice Springs, way out in the middle of nowhere, for an interview. It was kind of a lark, because I always wanted to travel to Australia and this was a good way to get a free trip. Graduate students don't exactly make a lot of money, and with fuel prices these days, well, you can imagine."

"Er, Matt, I don't want to sound too pushy here, but we know where Demetek is. Are you going to say they hired you and then fired you? That you're a disgruntled ex-employee, or something like that?"

"No. I mean yes. Or – wait, I mean yes, I was hired and no longer work for them, but I'm not disgruntled. They paid me really well and gave me a pretty sweet severance package. You wouldn't believe how much! I'm just not supposed to talk about it." Matt breathed a big sigh.

"How much?"

"Half a million."

What? "Did I hear you right? That is one mother of a bonus. What did you do to earn that? And what's the Brady connection?"

"That's the weird thing. She interviewed me last year, but when I got there some other guy was in charge of the biology, a guy from Montreal called Steve

Goudreau. Lynne was gone. They told me she'd retired. It's like they wiped out the whole history of the company, including her and everything she'd done. You can't find anything anywhere about the woman. I just remembered the picture because I have that kind of memory for faces and stuff. Your wife was lovely."

Yes, she was. "Matt, would you get to the point? Exactly what did you do at Demetek?"

"I don't know if I should say. I might get sued for breach of confidentiality and stuff."

Marcus's patience was dwindling rapidly. "Listen, I don't care about IP and agreements and things like that. I want to know why my wife died, and I want to know why you contacted *me*. Do I make myself clear?"

"I didn't have anything to do with your wife, Dr. Black," Matt sounded defensive.

"If you did, I suspect you wouldn't be in the back of this car."

Another sigh. "Look, I've been to the police in Pacifica. I told a detective what I saw. You know, the photo thing. It's been on the news here. Your wife and that psychologist guy, and a family's gone missing too. I thought they should know."

"Sampang."

"Huh?"

"Leo Sampang. The cop in Pacifica."

"Oh right. Yeah, he was the one. That was weird. He started giving me all sorts of grief about flying first class and stuff. Like that's relevant, you know?"

For the love of Pete, quit babbling, will you? "I know Detective Sergeant Sampang. Trust me, he's OK. Who else did you talk to?"

"No one! I'm not dumb. I'm kind of scared myself. Steve Goudreau sent me a message that the shit was about to hit the fan at Demetek, but if I went to the authorities they'd probably say I was a complete whacko. I should have believed him instead of talking to that Sampang guy. Steve was the one who told me to contact you."

Marcus was floored. "I've never heard of any Steve Goudreau. How would he know about me or how to contact me?"

"He wouldn't say specifically, but his boss, a guy called Strathmore, showed him a picture of you. It looked like you were in London. Was that recent?"

The woman. The one in the taxi with Al Wylie. She must have followed me, but how? "Yeah. But how would he have known me? What did you say his name was?"

"Steve Goudreau. Only he wasn't really Steve, he was French Canadian.

His real name was Etienne. That's French for Stephen. So – Etienne, Stephen, Steve."

For the first time, the name sounded remotely familiar. Marcus couldn't quite place it. Had Etienne Goudreau ever attended a scientific advisory council meeting at XUSA? He made a note to ask Josef. Or Brad King, even better. He'd know. "All right, so maybe our paths crossed once, maybe not. Still doesn't answer the question."

"Well, there's one possibility. I saw something on his desk once. A manila folder with Lynne's initials on the tab. JMB. He must have taken it out of her office. Did Lynne and your wife get along?"

"I assume they did. I don't know if they stayed in touch regularly." Marcus flashed to Vikram de Silva's video, the disturbingly intimate shot of his half-dressed wife exposing herself to Brady's needle.

The Honda climbed towards the Waldo Tunnel. Matt continued. "What I do know is, Steve's really spooked by whatever's happening at Demetek. One day I saw something on his monitor. It was a jungle scene of some kind. Steve said it wasn't real, more like a screen saver. But to me it looked too much like a live camera feed. Besides, who uses screen savers these days?"

Marcus shrugged. "What's the deal with the jungle scene you're talking about?"

Matt sighed. "Okay, this is going to sound crazy, but there was a howler monkey, you know, like in Central America. There was a chimpanzee too, swinging through the jungle like Cheetah on that old Tarzan show. The scene didn't repeat like a screen saver would, so I guessed it had to be some fake shot of a zoo or some other artificial set-up, but Steve was really nervous about it. Like he was hiding something."

"Why would you say it was artificial?"

"How else do you get a New World monkey like a howler in the same place as a chimp, which is native to Africa? I think they were looking at a jungle biodome."

Biodome? "Did I hear you right? An artificial biodome? Why a jungle? Are they trying to save the rain forests?"

"That's part of the company's message. Maybe I shouldn't have said that. Confidentiality and all."

Screw that, Marcus thought.

Traffic was bunching up on the Richardson Bay bridge, right before the Tiburon Boulevard exit. George zipped past the convoy of stop-and-go early afternoon commuters bound for San Rafael and points north. He turned eastbound towards Tiburon. "We'll be there in fifteen minutes."

"So what did you do at Demetek, Matt?" Marcus asked.

"I just put the method I'd developed for my doctorate to good use. I used site directed mutations of a wild type protein and obtained 3-D structures of them. One day I made a new protein that I couldn't get a structure of, and that's when Steve said my contract was up. Odd, huh?"

"One failure doesn't seem like grounds for dismissal," George commented. "That sounds a little unfair, even in a competitive environment."

"You'd think," Matt agreed. "But when Steve gave me that half mil check, I didn't exactly object. You can't beat that with a stick for doing six months' work."

"Six months? That was all you did?"

"That's how long they said we had to deliver."

"What were you supposed to be making? It couldn't have been a drug candidate. George here and I could each tell you from personal experience that there's no way a drug can be developed in that short period of time, at least not something that you can legally market."

"Well no, even I know that. It wasn't a drug."

"What, then?"

They crossed the short causeway onto the island. This time Matt Gilstrap spoke with more authority. "It was all about rubisco."

Both front seat occupants frowned. "What did you say? Rubisco?" Marcus asked.

"That's the protein I was mutating and crystallizing."

"Sounds like a cookie," Marcus said. "Should I have heard of it?"

"Depends on what you do for a living. It's not a human or animal protein, but you see it everywhere you look. We can't live without it. It's probably the most abundant protein on Earth, and it's just about perfect the way it is. Our mission was to make it even better. But it's probably easier if I show you."

The Honda pulled into Josef's driveway. George used his own key to unlock the front door. They all walked down the long hall to the open living room. Rintlen sat in one of the easy chairs. On the couch sat a dark haired man and a woman. The man's arm was around the woman's shoulder, gently massaging tense muscles.

"Hi Josef," Marcus greeted XUSA's security chief. "This is Matt Gilstrap. I think we're going to want to hear his story."

Josef welcomed Matt. "There are two people here you and Marcus should meet. George has already made their acquaintance."

The man and woman stood up. She was shorter than he by at least eight inches. Dark circles under her eyes showed fatigue, even exhaustion. She introduced them both. "My name is Michelle Durant. This is Edmund Solkar."

Marcus Black's jaw dropped. He didn't know what to do. Should he shake hands? What should he say? No one had prepared him for this encounter.

Matt's mobile phone chimed. He excused himself and looked at the screen. "Sorry, I need to get this." His eyes flickered as he read the message. The phone slipped from his fingers as he blanched. Around the room, everyone stared, waiting for him to say something.

"What is it?" Marcus asked.

"I don't know. I mean – I think – shit! I think we've got a real problem."

Chapter 38

THE DEMETEK EMPLOYEES FILED out of the lecture theater, buzzing with excitement. The entire company was headed for a celebratory outdoor barbecue party. During the meeting, caterers had prepared a full smorgasbord of grilled bush tucker, several kegs of popular beer, and cases of locally bottled wine. The management team promised taxi vouchers for anyone unable to drive home legally following the shindig.

The party was in honor of the product rollout, scheduled for one week hence. Initial sales estimates of one hundred million American dollars tipped the iceberg; projected sales for the following quarter totaled a billion. Strathmore had deferred questions about IPO's, but he guaranteed all the employees profit sharing over the next fiscal year. Everyone, from janitors to senior execs, could expect a bonus proportional to their salary grade. Even the lowest paid staff could expect to bankroll a big chunk of cash within twelve months.

As if money and big parties weren't enough, all the on-site employees, of which there were over one hundred, were promised a chartered tour of the biodomes the following week. A private 737 was booked to ferry them all from nearby Alice Springs to the Western Australia site. Strathmore promised a gourmet on-board feast, complete with open bar. Good times, he said, had returned to the biotechnology world after years of cost-cutting and belt-tightening. This was the beginning of a new age.

As the last stragglers departed the lecture hall, Monty Dayne excused himself. Shanghai was on the line. Dayne had a few last minute i's to dot and t's to cross prior to delivery. This left Strathmore, Hernandez, and Steve Goudreau alone in the large room.

Hernandez carefully steered the Canadian towards the back of the hall.

Strathmore boxed him in and put an arm about his shoulder. "Steve, there's something we need to talk to you about. It's kind of urgent." he said.

"Sure," Steve said. "But don't you want to mix with the troops? It would be good PR for us to be there with everyone."

Strathmore ignored the suggestion. "They'll wait. Let's go to my office."

The office area was deserted. The admin staff, along with almost everyone else, was guzzling shiraz and nibbling on grilled emu strips. They entered the CEO's office. Hernandez closed the door and waited. Strathmore swiveled the blinds, blocking out all external light.

Finally, he fished out the invoice. "Steve, is there something you'd like to talk about with us? Some concern, perhaps, regarding our product?"

Steve frowned. "What kind of concern?"

"You tell me." Strathmore said nothing else. Hernandez followed suit.

"Guys, I'm just naturally cautious. You knew that, months ago. I just don't believe we can guarantee the safety of the product."

"In spite of our exhaustive testing?" Hernandez said. "We showed you that the Bio 2 product was safe in primates, as well as in lower animal species. The accident with the chimpanzee was just that. An accident. You need to accept this, Steve. Move on."

"It's the viability of the strain that worries me."

"Oh, it's viable, Steve. It's dominant. The world has been crying out for it."

"I understand that. We have to be careful *because* of its dominance. Imagine the consequences if we can't control it!" He began pacing fretfully.

Strathmore took up the reins. "Interesting you should use the word control, a term financial people like us bandy about when our budgets diverge from actual spend." He handed the invoice over.

Steve's eyebrows bobbed inadvertently. "What is this? Justin, this looks like your John Hancock."

"It does, Steve. It's a pretty good likeness."

"Likeness? What do you mean? You didn't sign this?" He was doing the best he could to act surprised, but he didn't know if he was pulling it off.

"No, Steve, I didn't. We both know that."

Steve disliked it when people overused his name in conversation. It sounded patronizing. "As a matter of fact, Justin, we don't both know that. And I resent the implication."

"Steve," Strathmore said, "You've been a vital member of our management team and we both hold you in the highest regard as a scientist, especially as Demetek's seed products will revolutionize farming as we know it."

"Stop, both of you!" Steve snapped. "I'm tired of hearing this obsequious crap about how good an employee I am, and how my work is valuable. It's not my work, any more than it is yours."

"That's not entirely true, now, is it, Steve?" Hernandez again.

Steve threw up his hands in disgust. "Fine. Screw both of you. Yes, I signed this invoice. You'd have discarded the guy who made all this possible the moment you had what you needed. I don't believe in treating people that way, so I made sure he was adequately compensated."

"Five hundred thousand dollars," Strathmore said, pronouncing each syllable slowly. "Take home pay, after tax. Total cost to our company of three quarter of a million. Sure that was enough compensation, Steve? Oh, and let's not forget that little bit of icing on the cake, a free first class round the world ticket. Give me one good reason why I don't have you escorted out of the building right now!"

"Go ahead. Toss me out if you want. But if you do, I'll make sure that the product never reaches the market." He regretted his words instantly. *Timing, Etienne!*

Hernandez glared. "Are you threatening us?" He edged towards the Canadian.

"Call it what you want." He pulled a mobile phone from his pocket, dialed a number, and hit the send button.

"Who are you calling?" Hernandez demanded. He reached for the cell phone.

Steve snatched it away and held it to his ear. At last, Matt picked up. "It's me. They know. Listen, I can't talk. You have to stop them. Somehow."

On Strathmore's desk stood a heavy crystal bull. A New York venture capitalist had given it to him two decades earlier, and he had taken it with him everywhere. It symbolized the optimist's market, and the CEO was glad no one ever presented him with a matching bear when Wall Street went into one of its downslides. Justin Hernandez reached for the leaden bovine and swung it viciously, making solid contact with the side of Goudreau's head. Steve crumpled instantly. The phone skidded across the carpet. Hernandez leaped for it and placed it to his ear.

"Who is this?" he barked.

No one answered at the other end.

"I said, who is this!"

Still no response, and then someone in the background said something that sounded like "what is it?" followed by another voice mumbling about a problem. A real problem.

"Oh, you've got a problem all right, you little fuck!" Hernandez screamed.

"Justin!" Strathmore yelled. "Get off the phone and get over here!" The

CEO picked up the glass bull and put it back on his desk. Its horns wore a crimson smudge.

Hernandez ignored him. He roared into the mobile again. "Where are you, Gilstrap?"

Silence.

The call ended. Hernandez punched keys left and right, trying to find the call log. It was a 415 area code. *San Francisco.*

Strathmore knelt beside Steve's body. "I can't feel his pulse, Justin. I don't feel a heartbeat."

Hernandez brushed Strathmore's hand aside and grabbed Goudreau's neck. "You're right. There is none." An ugly indentation had formed on Steve's temple, where the glass bull had met its mark. Blood, no longer circulating, was beginning to seep from the man's crushed skull. "You'd better clean that thing off, Don," he said, pointing to the bull. "I'm sure it's got your prints on it too."

"Shit," the CEO whispered. He pulled out a handkerchief and wiped the residue off the horns. He spat on its side and polished it with some fresh tissues. "What now?"

"We have to deal with this," Hernandez said, pointing at the body on the floor. "There's an autoclave on B3."

Strathmore gaped at his CSO. "Autoclave?"

"If you think we can smuggle a dead body out of here and bury it somewhere in the outback without one of our employees, e.g. your buddy Mike Baltazzi knowing about it, then you're sadly mistaken."

"Smuggle?"

"We don't have a choice. This is damage control, Don. We have to think and act fast. We can't allow anything or anyone to stop this rollout. There's too much at stake here. It's not just Bio 2. Think about Bio 3 as well!"

Strathmore considered. Hernandez was correct. The grain was the cash cow but the real deal was Bio 3. That could change everything. Nothing could get in the way of its deployment. "What do you suggest?"

"Get Goudreau into my office." Hernandez ordered. Their roles had, in an instant, switched. No longer was the American scientist second in command to the Australian money mogul. The CSO was clearly the man in charge, the one with everything to gain and everything to lose. Strathmore began to realize that he could be as much an inconvenience as Goudreau, unless he chose to conspire along with Hernandez.

The body was a dead weight, despite belonging to a slightly built, active man. Together they carried him to Justin's office. Once inside, Hernandez locked the door. They lowered the body to the floor, ensuring the bloody side of the skull touched nothing along the way.

Hernandez threw a small switch behind his desk and waited. The bookshelf behind him shifted slightly. "One advantage of the original blueprints of the Castleford Institute was knowing how easy it was to install a back passage. It gave me a handy way to access any floor I wanted without CCTV intrusion." He flashed Strathmore a cold, toothless smile. Then he slid the ball bearing-mounted shelf aside.

An emergency-style door stood inset from the shelf. Hernandez pushed the bar and opened up onto a square-shaped stairwell, with up and down flights from their present level. He propped the door open with a small rubber wedge. "We'll have to take him down to the lower basement floor."

They maneuvered Steve's body through the emergency door and hauled him four half-flights down. A narrow passage, inset from an aperture about two feet wide and six feet tall, indicated the only other access point at the bottom. Hernandez crouched, wrestling with the body, and wriggled his way into the passage. Strathmore, breathing heavily and fighting hard to squeeze his tall frame inside, followed. The stench of evacuated bladder and bowels was intense, made fouler by the confined space.

The passage was ten meters long. At the end, a blue light lit another emergency door, this time equipped with a simple old-fashioned lock instead of a swipe card panel. Hernandez lowered Steve's head and shoulders to the ground and fished out a key from his pocket. He opened the door, lifted the head and shoulders again, and eased through. Strathmore shuffled behind, noting the spreading stain on Goudreau's trousers.

"Don't let any part of him drop," Hernandez ordered. They were now in a deserted hallway. "There's no CCTV here either, but I'd just as soon not have to explain how human waste is stinking up the joint. Keep it contained."

Strathmore's nose turned up in disgust. Red-faced and panting, he helped his chief scientist to a door twenty meters away. On it was a black symbol on a red background, the universal trefoil sign for biowaste. A large stainless steel appliance stood inside the room. It resembled an oversized, front loading dishwasher, with a panel of dials and touchpads. A steel plate indicated the manufacturer as "Incinoclave, Inc."

Hernandez balanced Goudreau's shoulders on his knees and slid the machine's front door down. Inside was a ceramic chamber, coated with a cylindrical array of small circular holes. He then hoisted the body inside as gingerly as he could so as not to leave any residues on the outside. With Strathmore's help, he shoved the body's legs inside. He slammed the door back up, and pressed a series of buttons on the keypad.

A gentle humming noise began as the treatment of the chamber's contents commenced. "What's going on?" Strathmore demanded.

"This quarter of a million dollar machine is an incinerating autoclave. It'll heat the contents up to fifteen hundred degrees Celsius using high intensity light waves. Same technology as some of the newest ovens you can buy at your favorite appliance store."

"You're cremating him."

"Right," Hernandez confirmed. "Cremating and then vaporizing the ashes. It'll take no more than fifteen minutes, and then we just go back the way we came. Problem solved."

"You're a bloody psycho, Hernandez."

"I love you too, Don."

Strathmore turned away. In spite of all that he'd done, all he'd asked Sarah and Justin to do on the company's behalf, he didn't have the stomach for wetwork, not like this. At the same time, he knew he was as guilty as his lead scientist. All the efforts, founded in what he once believed to be a noble cause, had now distilled down to this. They were nuking a brilliant biologist, just because he had dared to put a stop to the project. He couldn't blame Hernandez any more than himself, though. They'd both used Sarah. Correction. *Samaya.* That had been a stroke of genius. Between the three of them they'd swept the past clean and controlled the science as well, with only a little help from outsiders.

So this was where Lynne Brady "retired." He shuddered at the thought. While part of him hated Justin, an equal part of self-loathing ran through his veins. Now they stood together, with the power to control the most radical change in global botany since the Ice Age. He hoped it would be for the better, for only that could ease his conscience.

The machine completed its cycle and hissed as the cooling mechanism sprang into action. A gauge on the top left indicated the temperature was dropping by over a hundred degrees every thirty seconds. At that rate, the internal ceramic chamber would return to ambient temperature in less than ten minutes, leaving them enough time to go back upstairs, clean up any residual mess along the way, and put in an appearance at the company barbecue.

The time passed agonizingly slowly, but a final hiss signaled it was safe to open the Incinoclave's front door. Hernandez peered inside. Only a few coins remained. "Reckon these are pretty well sterilized," he remarked, handing them to Strathmore. "Consider this partial repayment of Gilstrap's severance package. I'm sure you financial types can come up with some kind of accounting model and use the rest of Steve Goudreau's salary and profit sharing bonus to pay off the rest."

BOOK 4
PERSEPHONE'S BLADE

Chapter 39

Matt Gilstrap gazed around the room. "He said we have to stop them."

"Stop whom?" Josef asked.

"Demetek. Hernandez. The project. Shit, I don't know!"

Ed Solkar spoke up at last. "Are you talking about Justin Hernandez?"

"Yeah. You know him?" Matt replied.

"He was once a friend. A good friend, so I thought. He is in fact a very dangerous man."

"Why? What do you know? What's the story here?" Matt blurted. His nervous demeanor returned in full force.

Josef took the chance to intervene. "Let us all sit down and look at this calmly. There are a number of people in this room who have background information on this problem, and others with the resources to help solve it."

Matt could not take his eyes off Solkar. "Who are you guys, really?" he asked.

Josef Rintlen waited until everyone was seated, and started from the beginning. He left very little out.

Matt was astonished. "You spent all that time in jail for a crime you never committed? How did you survive?"

Ed pursed his lips and raised his eyebrows. He'd practiced the speech for years, practicing it late at night in his head, never knowing when or where the right audience would appear. The time was now, even though he still couldn't reveal one important detail. "It's not as though I didn't have the *mens rea*, as Mickey would tell you. What I didn't have was the *actus reus*. If you have the intent but don't perform the act, you haven't committed the crime. Samaya and Justin staged everything, all the way down to Jane Doe Minus Toe." He bowed his head, not quite able to continue. In spite of all the rehearsals, he remained unable to pull it off flawlessly.

Mickey Durant slid an arm around his waist. "It's okay, Eddie."

"Thanks to this lovely lady, I'm lucky to have done the time in jail at all. The DA would have had me well fried by now. You could say I paid Justin Hernandez's debt to society. So he owes me. But I can't take care of him myself. I'm a convicted felon who can't get a passport, so I'm going to need you guys to help."

Marcus stood up. "Count me in. I've got nothing more to lose, but I'm going to need some more background. I want to know exactly what we're dealing with."

Matt took a deep breath. "It'll be easier if I can show you. Josef, do you have a large screen monitor that I can do an online demonstration on?"

"That is one of the easiest things for me to do. If nothing else, this rented mansion is equipped very nicely." Josef went to the wet bar and slid a small panel aside to reveal a keypad. He pressed a button. Shutters lowered around them, blanking out the view of the San Francisco Bay. Another button opened up an eight foot wide ceiling slot. A clear white screen lowered almost to the floor. "Another time I would show off this home entertainment system but right now we will be better served by an extension of the office desktop. Matthew, please come over here and walk us through."

Matt got up and joined Josef, who pulled a wireless keyboard and mouse out from underneath the bar. Josef pressed one more button on the keypad. A ceiling projector came on. A bright image immediately lit up the screen, with the Windows taskbar along the bottom. "The floor is yours," Josef said, walking back to his seat.

"Okay," Matt said. "Perhaps I ought to start with a silly question. Can I get a sense of how many of you are familiar with rubisco?" No one said anything. Josef's eyebrows raised as he nodded slowly. Ed Solkar raised his left hand like a kid in school nervous about answering the teacher's question.

Matt opened a Web browser and typed an URL into the search bar. Moments later a curious looking blend of colors and patterns popped onto the screen, a series of red, yellow, green, blue, and gray dots connected with ribbons swirling about each other. "Rubisco is possibly the most abundant protein on the planet, especially in leaves. Some say it's the most important enzyme supporting life itself. The word 'rubsico' stands for ribulose 1,5-bisphosphate carboxylase oxygenase. It is responsible for the catalytic conversion of carbon dioxide into fuel that plants can use. Ultimately, it generates oxygen through the photosynthesis pathway. Scientists have been trying for many years to increase the catalytic efficiency of this enzyme, as it can only convert maybe three carbon dioxide molecules per second. The theory is that increased efficiency could somehow counteract the negative effects of increased carbon emissions into the atmosphere, and reverse the process of global warming. Other applications of rubisco engineering include higher yielding crops and the ability to increase rate of growth in the absence of light. Darkness inhibits rubisco activity, so imagine the benefits if your crops could grow 24/7!

"When Demetek hired me, they'd made several advances in rubisco engineering, including the grafting of certain algae variants onto tobacco plants, which are often used in experimental botany. If you look at this web site here," he said, pausing to type in a new URL, "you'll see that there are over four hundred crystal structures of various modified rubiscos from any number of sources. Obviously it's a hot area of research, and judging by the number of successful structure determinations, competitive and potentially lucrative.

"Lynne Brady hired me because I developed a specific method for protein crystallography. I didn't end up working for her, but some of you know that already. Instead, I reported to this guy called Steve Goudreau. Best boss I've ever had. In all my great experience," he added with a wry smile. "Anyway, I brought my method to Demetek and applied it to a series of over a thousand rubiscos. They tested every single one for its ability to process carbon dioxide, but none showed any significant improvement over the native enzyme, at least in terms of catalytic efficiency. Then one day I saw something kind of funky in one particular rubisco model. That led to the breakthrough."

Matt clicked around on the web site, and for a few seconds appeared to be downloading a file. "This is the protein structure I compared our new variant to." He began looking on the start menu for a particular shortcut, but didn't see what he needed. "Josef, you don't happen to have the Pymol program installed here, do you?"

"Not a problem," Josef replied. "I will set it up." He fiddled around, rerouting network configuration paths and access points. A Pymol shortcut icon appeared on the top right hand corner of the screen.

"Thanks," Matt said. He started the program, one of the industry standard tools for viewing detailed protein structures. He opened the file he had just downloaded. He clicked and scrolled around with the mouse, highlighting the active site of the enzyme, the engine that made rubisco work. "If only a couple of you are familiar with rubisco, this may not mean much to the rest of you."

"Can you put it in simple terms?" Marcus asked.

"I'll do my best." Matt rotated the picture. "Most people have used natural amino acids when mutating rubisco. The same ones our DNA encodes for, twenty or so of them. Now watch this."

He rotated the structure again and pointed to a different part of the protein. "When the protein binds carbon dioxide, it bends slightly at the surface. It's hard to see unless you look at these things all day, every day. Take my word for it, that's what happens. Anyway, to cut a long story short, one day I wondered what would happen if we put an unnatural amino acid in right – here!" He spun the picture back and held the cursor over a strand of atoms, then clicked. The strand lit up in yellow.

"What did that do?" Marcus asked.

"We switched the lysine out and put in a (D)-N-methylornithine instead. That way we still allowed CO2 to bind to the enzyme, but there were a couple of kickers. We couldn't form crystals, which made it hard to look at. But the real *coup de grâce* that started the whirlwind, was the way it became markedly more efficient at catalyzing the conversion of carbon dioxide into oxygen."

"(D)-N-methylornithine?" Mickey Durant asked, looking at Ed Solkar. He was strangely captivated by Matt's presentation.

"Right," Matt answered. "Natural amino acids are all labeled L, based on their three-dimensional configuration. Their unnatural counterparts are all labeled D. They're simply mirror images. Mammalian proteins contain nothing but L-amino acids as their building blocks. There are some bacterial proteins with D-amino acids, but we made a rubisco containing a completely unnatural D-amino acid. It's D to begin with, but it has no naturally occurring L-based counterpart. It's totally artificial. But we found a way to engineer it into a plant protein."

Ed spoke up. "What vector did you use for the protein expression?"

"Huh?" Mickey Durant had no idea what he was asking.

Josef explained. "This is one of the principles of molecular biology. When one engineers a protein one must use some kind of natural system, like a bacterium, a virus, or a cellular medium to permit it to ferment."

She wasn't convinced, but slowly nodded. "I'm sorry. Please continue."

"We used a chimeric RNA that contained some bacterial components, some viral, and some mammalian."

Marcus felt his pulse quicken. He waited for Matt to continue.

"Who thought of the (D)-N-methylornithine idea?" Ed asked.

"That was kind of strange. About two months ago, Steve Goudreau made the suggestion. He said he'd pulled it out of an old file. But like I told these guys," Matt added, pointing at Marcus and George, "I'd seen an old folder sitting on his desk with Lynne Brady's initials on it. So I just assumed it was one of her ideas all along. We just made it work."

Edmund Ranjit Solkar left Mickey's side and went to the wet bar. His physical presence alone was enough for Matt to step aside without being asked. Then he began.

"This all started a long time ago."

Chapter 40

"MATT, THE TECHNOLOGY YOU described was first developed by Lynne Brady and her team in the early part of the 1990's," Ed began. "But maybe I should start with more of my own story." He glanced at Mickey, who gave him a reassuring nod.

Matt returned to his seat, next to Marcus. Josef and George flanked Mickey Durant on the couch.

"You have heard about my sentence for the alleged killing of Samaya Jonas. What you may not know is that she was – is – also Lynne Brady's daughter. Lynne didn't exactly approve of our relationship, and I can't say I blamed her. Samaya captivated me with her intelligence, desire to learn, and unprecedented skills in molecular biology techniques. Unfortunately, I have to admit that her physical attributes threw me. It's an old story but it's the truth. I was in my early forties, the same age as Lynne, and should have known better. It doesn't excuse me, despite the fact that many tenured faculty members sleep with their students. Cynics might say so what, everyone does it anyway, screw university policies or ethics. Regardless, I fell into the trap. No, that's not true. I jumped right in without being pushed."

Marcus was about to say something, but Ed held up a hand to silence him. *The time will come.*

He continued. "I was lost to her. My heart, soul, and all I believed, I willingly gave up, just so I could be with her. I surrendered everything, my beliefs, my ideas, my principles. I was stupid. Samaya was evil incarnate, a monster."

Marcus frowned. He recalled the day he met Kay. Something had darkened inside her for a nanosecond. Was she thinking of Samaya? Or Solkar?

Ed continued. "My research at the University of Chicago was all about ribonucleic acid manipulation. It was a field that was just getting started. Of

211

course, these days, many companies are excited about siRNAs. They offer great potential for the treatment of a whole slew of diseases." He pronounced the acronym "serna."

The others watched Ed's face light up as he reflected on his subject. "SiRNAs, or small interfering ribonucleic acids, interfere with the expression of certain genes. The first published report of siRNAs in plants came out in 1999, when a group of scientists from the University of Norwich, in England, demonstrated post-transcriptional gene silencing. We might have gotten there first if I wasn't learning to survive in the exercise yard in the Illinois State Penitentiary," he added ruefully.

"There are many applications of small RNA's, micro RNA's et cetera, that are twenty to twenty-five nucleotides long. There are as many challenges as there are potential uses. These include short duration of action, especially in rapidly dividing cells, and also off-target, or unintended effects. So we had to go down another pathway using DNA, rather than RNA, before we could turn our technology into a product."

Josef looked around the room. *So far, so good.*

Ed continued. "We solved one problem by incorporating DNA into a vector, such as a plasmid. A plasmid is a DNA molecule that isn't part of an organism's overall chromosome package. It can replicate itself independently. In our early days, we prepared some chimeric plasmids that combined properties of bacterial and viral plasmids, as well as mammalian DNA. We attached a long sequence of telomeres to the end of the DNA to prolong the effect even further. Then we transcribed the artificial DNA sequences into short RNA's and injected them into our test species. They improved the duration of action spectacularly. While crude by today's standards, it was way ahead of its time in experimental biology when we started."

Chimeric plasmids. Playing fast and loose with bacteria, viruses, mammals. What else? Marcus wondered how this would all play out.

"We weren't able to anticipate the unwanted effects on host cells. In mice, you can get away with a much shorter experiment, and therefore obtain a quicker readout. Some of the results we obtained were stunning. Josef said that some of you are already familiar with an early paper from our group."

Marcus nodded. *Awareness.*

"One day a young post-doc in Lynne's group approached me. His name was Justin Hernandez. He was familiar with my work and wondered if he might apply it to rubisco engineering. Justin was one of the smartest young scientists I'd ever met. His drive and ambition matched his brain. Samaya was every bit as brilliant, but I was too blind to notice. The three of us spent many hours brainstorming new research projects and applications, and developed a number of proposals. Justin suggested to Lynne that our research teams get together and collaborate. Lynne welcomed the idea, and approached the Castlefords for funding."

"I take it they liked her proposal," Matt supposed.

"They loved it. Real money started flowing. The Castlefords weren't just rich, or even filthy rich. They were in another league, like Bill and Melinda Gates. Linda was one of those social conscience types, even if Henry wasn't, but he was persuadable. Guys with that much cash often like to hoard it, but Linda wouldn't back down when she got an idea in her head. Henry was the one who blinked first. Linda said 'pony up or I saddle my own horse and ride out of here.' Henry coughed up the cash, and held on to both his marriage and bankroll. Ergo – the Institute was born. It had all the state-of-the-art equipment, security, safety, and all the top people on board."

Josef interrupted. "Before you go any further, Professor Solkar, I recommend you tell us where and how you learned of our present crisis." The German's intense eyes said *tread carefully.*

Ed thought about jumping in with both feet regardless of the effect of collateral damage, but he read Josef's expression correctly. For the moment, it was best to remain cautious. *There will be time.*

"Very well. I was on the West Coast of Florida when I received a message from my lawyer. It was a ticking time bomb. It said, 'If you want to live, find Edmund Solkar.' Ms. Durant is the only person here who knew of this message's significance, although she had no idea what it meant. I'll come to that in due course. I immediately left St. Petersburg to come and find her, unaware that your Mr. Petrescu had already approached her."

"Why were you in St. Petersburg?" Marcus wanted to know.

"That's where the Castlefords retired before they died. When I got out of prison, I thought they might have left a series of records that I could use one day. Unfortunately, Henry and Linda passed away before I could approach them."

"Go on," Josef said.

"When I arrived in Davis, I was hoping to find Mickey. However, a ghost beat me to her."

"A ghost?" Matt looked puzzled.

"One I feared more than any prison guard or inmate I've ever encountered. Samaya Jonas wanted to eliminate me, by kidnapping the only person who knew of my whereabouts."

"Why would she want to kill you?" Marcus asked.

"To protect the people she works for. I was one of the only people who knew Justin's motives, and how he might be acting on them. I was a loose end. Samaya is a master at cleaning them up, a seductress with an IQ off the charts, with the moral fiber of a serpent. She would have killed Mickey if I hadn't followed her."

Marcus thought they shared more than mutual protectiveness. He could see it in Solkar's eyes as they settled on her, transmitting an unspoken message.

As if on cue, Mickey Durant stood up and joined Solkar behind the bar. "Samaya kidnapped me from my own home a couple of nights ago. She overpowered me, probably with chloroform, then spirited me off to a shack somewhere northeast of Sacramento, in the forest. I have no doubt that she would have left me to die once she knew where Eddie was. He risked his own life to ensure that wouldn't happen."

"What happened to her?" Marcus asked.

"Eddie knocked her aside just as she was about to inject me. I'll never know what with. She fell unconscious."

"I snapped her wrist." Ed added. "I wanted to kill her, to crush her neck under my boot like a bug, for all the evil she has done. And for what she tried to do to Mickey. This brave woman saved my life. It was my turn to save hers."

Mickey took his hand and squeezed. "I injected her with the poison meant for me. We left her there, in the shack."

Josef Rintlen said the obvious question. "Are you certain she is dead?"

Ed shook his head. "Animals will find her, probably. But she was still alive when we left. Taking the life of another human being stays with you for the rest of your life. It's not something civilized people do unless it's absolutely necessary."

Josef dipped his head very slightly in silent acknowledgment.

"I need to take us all back to the trial," Ed continued. "The human trial that started everything." He minimized Matt's picture and clicked on another icon.

Marcus felt his gorge rise, recalling the video he'd watched earlier that morning. Was Solkar about to show a duplicate?

His question was answered almost immediately. To his relief, there were no moving pictures. Instead they all saw a simple table.

Subject	Graft 1	Graft 2	Blank
IM	✓		
RS	✓		
KR			✓
HL	✓		

JDG	✓		
SMZ	✓		
CJB		✓	
VD		✓	
JH			✓
SIJ		✓	
ERS		✓	
SPG		✓	

The initials corresponded to those from MacCallum's notebook, but there were inconsistencies. Ian had checked the first six names and crossed the second group. This table suggested there were three groups. Which was correct?

Ed read the names in full. "And the ones with checks in Graft 2 were Carlo Bernasconi, Vikram de Silva, Sally Jepson, myself, and Stuart Gray.

"Samaya Jonas was dosed!" Marcus shouted. "She's right there. SIJ, her initials. She got graft two, whatever that was!"

"No. Sally Jepson had the same initials, first and last name. But Samaya's middle name was Margaret. Sally's is Innes. Originally she volunteered for the first group. She worked in Lynne's lab as a general assistant.

Marcus continued to argue. "I saw a video. Look, we can all see it!" He started to open his backpack.

Josef held up a hand. "Let him continue."

"Lynne would never have allowed Samaya to be dosed. She was her daughter, remember?"

So who was the woman on the video? Was she or was she not the one I saw with Al Wylie? Marcus thought about it. "Sally" was often short for Sarah. If she used her middle name, then there you have it. That was Al's temp. The pieces were all there, surely! But there was still something missing.

"Did Sally Jepson marry Stuart Gray?" Matt wanted to know.

Ed confirmed his suspicions. "She did. A month later. It turned out she was pregnant with their child. You can imagine our concern about congenital complications."

Matt explained how he'd recognized their pictures. There was one person from the photo whom he hadn't yet identified, but he guessed it was Hong Li.

"Wait a minute," Marcus said. He stood up. "What about the blank group? I assume they got placebos. JH must be Justin Hernandez. The other subject was Kay Rasmussen, my wife. Only she didn't receive the placebo, did she, Solkar? I think you got that instead." He slowly approached the bar, his eyes blazing.

"That's not true. Only Justin and Kay received blanks."

"Marcus, be careful," Josef warned.

"Would someone care to tell me what these grafts, blanks, placebos and things have to do with rubisco engineering?" Matt demanded, raising his voice enough to draw attention away from the brewing confrontation.

Ed looked at the young man and nodded. "That's probably a good idea. Marcus, you have to bear with me. I'll explain everything, best as I can. Believe me, I feel your loss."

"You don't know a damn thing about how I feel!" Marcus exploded, leaping for the older man. He jumped clear across the bar, sending an empty decanter onto the floor, where it shattered. He wrapped his hands around Ed's throat as weeks of grief, pain, and rage boiled up and overflowed. "You killed my wife, you son of a bitch!"

Mickey shrieked and dodged out of the way.

Ed calmly reached for Marcus's little fingers and bent them backwards simultaneously, generating so much pain that he could not maintain his grip. He watched Marcus's eyes unblinkingly, maintaining the pressure until he saw the tension in his attacker's face subside. Finally, he let go.

Marcus grimaced in agony as his fingers realigned.

"I didn't switch the doses. I would never have done that, Marcus. I swear to you on my own life."

"Why the hell should I believe you?" Marcus spat.

Ed glanced at Josef, who gave him another subtle nod.

"Because Kay was MY daughter."

Chapter 41

KAY RASMUSSEN WAS EDMUND Solkar's daughter. The words hit Marcus almost as hard as the news of her fiery death. Time seemed to stand still as he backed away from the older man. The only sounds were a faint hum from the AV equipment, and a slight crunching noise as he stepped on the fragments of the shattered decanter. No one else seemed to breathe.

"I saw de Silva's notes this afternoon. The ones you found in Chicago, Marcus," Ed said. "He kept meticulous records of every experiment we did."

"What do his notes say?" Mickey pressed.

"The table you're looking at was the original experimental design. Now you need to look at this one." Ed clicked on another icon. A new table popped onto the screen.

Subject	Dose
IM	✓
RS	✓
KR	✓
HL	✓
JDG	✓
SMZ	✓
CJB	X
VD	X
JH	X
SIJ	X
ERS	X
SPG	X

It mirrored the table in MacCallum's notebook perfectly.

"So there were only two groups?" Matt asked. "That's a pretty significant modification from the original experiment."

"Believe me, I'm as surprised as anyone, but the data is all there in those CD-ROMs. De Silva analyzed the residues from each syringe. My dose was indeed a placebo."

So that was it. That was what his mission had been all about, retrieving the truth about the human experiment. The data was buried in a cabinet in the old Castleford building, and he, Marcus Black, had been charged with unearthing it and delivering it. Now what did they want with him? Would they let him seek revenge for what had been done to his wife? He recalled the secret video, the record of how Kay had delivered the doses to all comers but herself. She had injected her own father with the placebo meant for her. Unwittingly, she may have saved Solkar's life at the cost of her own.

"What was in the grafts?" Josef asked.

Ed took a deep breath. "Lynne Brady engineered a rubisco variant that increased carbon dioxide-oxygen conversion efficiency, but she couldn't reproduce it in a living plant. It was too short-lived. I discovered a method that allowed the variant to survive and reproduce."

"Chimeric RNA?" Marcus wanted confirmation.

Ed nodded. "Genetically engineered crops have been a major worry for governments and environmentalists for many years now. One of the greatest qualms people have is that unnatural genes can work their way into the general population and produce devastating results. I think most of us would share that fear."

No one disagreed outwardly.

"We asked the question: what happens to the rubisco-modifying chimeric RNA after it gets incorporated into the plant genome of transfected species? What happens if mammals, and so on up the food chain, ingest the genetically modified plant? We had to test this hypothesis in animal models. We set up a lab in the basement of the Castleford Institute to answer this question. The results in mice were surprising. The only measurable effect was in their awareness, which my friend and colleague Ralph Shanahan assessed."

"What did you do then?" Josef prompted.

"We ran similar tests in rats. We saw no effect at all. I admit, our ability to examine their genomes was limited, but there were no outward clinical signs pointing to anything unexpected or detrimental. We discovered the same result in dogs and in cynomologous monkeys. No effect at all."

"What components did you use for the vector?" Marcus asked.

"We took a highly infectious strain of viral DNA and grafted it onto a bacterial DNA modified to code for a D-amino acid. Then we attached this to the relevant rubisco-coding plasmid. Next, we attached the fourth component of the vector, which was taken from the subject. Finallly, we transcribed the assembly into an RNA that we used for dosing. That way, each graft was individually tailored."

Marcus thought about the implications. Any chimeric material fully foreign to the receiving organism would likely be rejected. The vector could not be incorporated if, say, Hong Li's and Julius Goldfarb's samples were switched. However, for a family member, one who shared fifty percent of his chromosomal material with his daughter, it could well have taken hold. Therefore, there was a chance that when Solkar's and Kay's samples were switched, his RNA, along with the viral, bacterial, and plant material, became embedded in her own DNA. And for rejection to be avoided, then someone other than Solkar himself would have known that Kay was his daughter.

"Samaya knew, as did Justin. Either or both could have made the switch." Ed could see how Marcus was thinking. *You can't tell him the truth. Not yet.*

George Petrescu, who had remained silent throughout, asked the question on everyone's mind. "Why did everyone volunteer for this trial in the first place?"

"Money," Ed said simply. "Each of them was paid a substantial sum from the Institute's reserve funds for participating. You have to remember that students and post-docs aren't exactly well paid. Some had huge student loans, and they saw this as one easy way out of all of their debts. And as the designer of the trial, if I was willing to be injected with my own witch's brew, the others might not have been as concerned. For the record, I didn't accept any payment. I didn't need to. I'm not a poor man."

No, Marcus wanted to say, you're not a *poor* man. You're an *atrocious abomination* of a man.

"There is only one thing I can do now to make up for what Lynne and I started, and that is to ensure that it ends."

"You think that will excuse you? How can you possibly atone for this disgusting experiment?" Marcus demanded, unwilling to disguise his contempt.

"He has paid his debt to society," Mickey Durant said simply, her voice taking on an authority of its own. The advocate in her came forth as she delivered her ad-hoc closing argument. "Irrespective of any other sins, acts, or deeds, Edmund Solkar has spent many years in prison for a crime he did not commit. He has convinced me, not just as his lawyer, but as his friend, that he never intended to harm anyone. I may never convince you of that, and nor, apparently, will he. Therefore, all he can do is try to prevent these experiments from bearing fruit. Marcus, I assure you that your wife's death is as painful to her father as it is to you, because I know this man. I have known him for a long time. He is *not* a killer. He's not the one we need to be concerned about."

Marcus wanted to respond, but something about Mickey's statement stopped him. He considered Vikram "Gator" de Silva's incriminating video, how Lynne Brady, no one else, had ultimately delivered the fatal inoculation into Kay's system. Lynne had planted a ticking time bomb, the countdown set by someone who knew Solkar was Kay's father. It didn't matter whether it was Samaya Jonas or Justin Hernandez. They were both responsible, and yes, he would rip them limb from limb if he could. "I don't believe you," was all he could say.

No one else in the room spoke for a long time.

"Michelle," Josef said at last. "Please come with me. You too, Matthew. I think we need to allow Marcus and Edmund some time together. There is an additional matter that I would welcome some help with."

Mickey and Matt looked at each other, mystified, and then followed the big German. George Petrescu dutifully closed the door behind them and left.

"What do you want from me?" Marcus spoke bitterly.

"Do you want the short answer or the long one?"

"I'll take any answer as long as it's the truth. It's just hard to imagine that anything you say would qualify."

"Understandable."

"Well? The question is the same. What do you want from me?"

"I want you to destroy everything Demetek has built and make sure this technology can never ruin another life. Is that precise enough for you?" Solkar showed that he was not prepared to back down.

"You honestly think I can do that?"

"With the rest of the XUSA team, I believe you can."

For the first time in what seemed like hours, Marcus felt his anger morphing into something else entirely. "You and Josef have been hatching a plan."

He nodded. "You will all fly to Australia tomorrow night. Josef will lead the team. I expect he will ask Dr. Gilstrap to help you all gain access to the facility."

"What about you?"

"I can't come with you. No passport."

Convicted felon. "Not much chance of fixing that. Don't ask me to help you there."

"You will be helping me. Once you understand." Edmund Solkar turned away and left the room.

A shadow flickered over the wall, and a silhouette entered the doorway. "I'm coming too," Bradford King announced.

Marcus's eyes widened as his best friend came in. "Don't tell me you knew…"

"Nah, not all of it. At least not the bomb Eddie here just dropped. Trust me, Marco, I don't like people mucking around with the planet for their own gain. I also don't like psychos. So, I'm going with you, and together we are going to stop this bunch."

"And this is the last time you do this, Bradford," his wife said as she too appeared out of the darkness. "Come home alive, both of you, but don't come home until you've destroyed this menace."

Chapter 42

THE XUSA TEAM ARRIVED in Sydney three days later. A four-hour layover gave them more than enough time to collect their bags, pass through immigration control and customs, and transfer to the domestic terminal. They'd presented a simple story about wanting to visit Uluru and the Northern Territory during the favorable climate. All had booked return flights to San Francisco two weeks hence.

They boarded their connection without difficulty. They landed in the Northern Territory in pleasant afternoon sunshine. The local temperature of twenty-one degrees was the same as a perfect San Francisco seventy Fahrenheit. A short trip to the Avis counter yielded a rental Holden Commodore with a full tank of fuel. Soon they were on their way from the Alice Springs airport, headed north to the Outback city.

The dried up Todd River provided a backdrop for their temporary accommodation, an apartment suite containing a kitchen, two bedrooms, a bathroom, and an extra cot. Matt, who had drawn the short straw, dumped his bag on the fold-out bed, and sighed. "I trust we're not going in this evening."

Josef agreed. "Given the length of our trip it would not be wise." He took the Castleford Institute blueprints from his backpack and unfolded them on the counter. "We will need to establish how deep security is early on, such as the extent of CCTV surveillance."

The team gathered around the diagrams. Marcus said, "The basement level in the Castleford building couldn't have a parallel here. If it did, it would be above ground."

"There is a level down at the bottom," Matt countered. "They didn't give many people access to it. One of the IT people said it leads to the control room."

"Tell us more," Josef said.

"I don't know a whole lot, as I never got to go down there. You need an extra security clearance to make the elevator go all the way down. If anyone unauthorized makes the attempt, there's a remote override that can stop the lift in its tracks."

"So who has clearance?" Bradford King asked.

"The CEO, Hernandez, and my old boss, Steve. Also the head legal guy, Dayne. They're the management team, but there are a couple of others too. The security chief, Mike Baltazzi, the Director of Animal Health, Jordan Cornell. And a few technicians, like Tracy Hirsch, the IT manager. She keeps the whole system running. It's the nerve center of the operation, where they control all the remote site's cameras."

"Short of physically being there, is there any other way we can monitor the biodomes?" George wanted to know.

Matt paced around the room, trying to come up with the most useful answer he could. "The actual site is about seven hundred kilometers west of here. I've never seen it directly – it wasn't part of my job description – but that's where the biodomes are. If Steve could see the place from his office, then we might be able to see it *via* his login. I have Steve's password. I only hope it still works."

Josef held his hand up. "That's good, Matthew. We will want to examine the directory structure, obtain a full ghost image, and obtain any relevant documents to support a legal case should we need to defend ourselves."

"Last time I looked, hacking into another company's web site didn't exactly tend to support a robust defense," Brad remarked. "Then again, it is what we do sometimes, right George?"

Petrescu dipped his head slightly downwards. "I think I'll go and find us something to eat." He excused himself and left the suite. Soon thereafter, the rumble of the rental Commodore signaled that he had driven off.

Josef was wearing a cat-found-the-canary smile. "Hacking into *another* company's web site, that is true. But what if you log into your own company's web site remotely? That might be deviant, but surely not illegal."

"I'm not following," Marcus said. "No one here is a Demetek employee."

It was Matt's turn to grin. "It turns out I still am, according to Ms. Durant. Legally, I'm still on their books as an employee for another month. Before we left California, I couldn't resist checking the HR records, which have full personnel files on everyone, including me. My severance bonus, which you now know was Steve's insurance policy, well, all that did was get me out of town. I'm still officially an employee for another," he looked at his watch, mentally calculating the numbers, "five days. Make that four days. We lost a day coming over here, didn't we? I need to fix the date on this thing."

Josef explained. "Matthew's access to company files may be considered a little underhand, and likely a violation of his contractual obligations, but logging in under a VPN is not a crime. That another employee provided Matthew with a low level password is not evidence of wrongdoing. Even if it were, I suspect our UC Davis advocate would be able to argue our case favorably." *That is the least of our problems*, he thought.

"So Matt's login will get us everything we need?" Marcus asked.

"That is just the easy part."

"What's the hard part, Joe?" Brad asked.

Josef cocked an eyebrow at his old friend.

"Oh, crap. You don't – oh, shit, you do mean it."

"This product must never see the light of day. But there is a better approach. Some good news, maybe?"

"I'll take any good news I can get if we're going to have to wreck an entire research facility, incur no casualties, make it all the way home to my lovely wife, explain what it is I've spent the last week doing, and have any hope of retaining any dignity, respect, or freedom," Brad said.

"There will not be any need for casualties," Josef said. "Two days ago, we learned that the company has chartered an airliner for all employees to visit the remote site for the product rollout. Virtually no one will remain at the Alice Springs building. But let us not get carried away. I do not believe there is any need for a physically destructive approach. That would be silly."

"I want to take Hernandez out. Permanently."

The room fell silent. While everyone understood the need for impersonal retribution, the threat was a step far beyond, even for those who had been forced through their own circumstances to perform that final act. Each man looked at his companions, grim-faced, until Marcus repeated the statement.

"Someone has to eliminate Hernandez. I want to do it."

The others turned towards him. Brad almost tried to convince his friend to take a step away, that he was too emotionally involved, but held his tongue. Matt suddenly looked like he didn't want to be there at all. Marcus held firm, a new resolve steeling him.

At last, Josef broke the uncomfortable pause. "Before we consider any actions at the remote site, we must confirm exactly what we are dealing with, and take the necessary precautions. We have precisely two days to figure out how to infiltrate the main facility, disable, and destroy what we must. On the third day, we will have only a tight window in which to operate. We have few advantages, but we do have state of the art computer expertise, hand to hand skills if needed, and the crucial factor of privileged access, if Matthew is correct."

"We ought to get started on the computer stuff now, Joe," Brad said. "We've got the login info, and I don't think anyone's ready for sleep."

"The systems normally get backed up between ten p.m. and two a.m.," Matt said. "We might want to use that window for our own purposes. Intercept the backup files."

"Are there remote servers used for off-site storage?" Josef asked.

"That's one thing we don't have to worry about," Matt replied. "Demetek is so isolated that they kept everything on site. One of the IT people told me about it once. There are ten petabyte storage drives, driven by two independent but mutually redundant systems, meaning that there are two copies of every file on the main servers. The files get backed up nightly, but as everything is date-stamped, the backups are all sequential and easy to access for restoration purposes. With the kind of stuff we were working on, you have to keep just about everything. These storage drives aren't in the main building, but we don't really need to worry about physical access, unless we want to take a sledgehammer to them."

"As long as we have a copy of the most recent data, there is no need for that," Josef said. "If the backups are sequential, one copy to our own systems will suffice to ensure any damning evidence is in our hands and no one else's. However, it is essential for us to ensure that Demetek's files are no longer usable."

"How do you intend to pull that off?" Brad asked.

The slightest of smiles worked its way onto the gray-haired German's face, as he pulled a small USB stick out of his pocket. To the average observer, it looked like an everyday flash memory-based MP3 player, complete with play, pause, reverse, forward, and stop buttons, and a narrow LCD screen that could show song titles and other tidbits of information. "We will have to rely on Matthew playing Etienne's role, with full administrative privileges. I am certain that Demetek's systems have powerful safeguards designed to prevent disgruntled former and existing employees from causing cyberdamage. If Matthew can indeed gain access as a so-called superuser, then we have a chance to override the security and let my little friend here go to work."

Something Josef had said sounded odd to Marcus. He'd spoken of Goudreau by his given name, as if they knew each other well. Was that a mistake, or was it something else? Or was it a simple affectation? The German never seemed to shorten names or use contractions when speaking. Perhaps Marcus's imagination was playing tricks on him, but this was the second time he'd wondered if he should pursue the issue.

"What's with the memory stick?" Matt asked.

"Nobody knows," Josef replied, his grin broadening. "If they did, there would be an updated definition database to counter it."

"A virus?"

"More like a plague. This one will surely serve a more noble purpose than most."

The front door opened and George entered, bearing several brown bags full of hot food. Greasy stains were starting to seep through. In his other arm he carried a six-pack of Victoria Bitter. "Hope you like souvlakis and kebabs, guys. I got lamb, doner, chicken, the works."

They did, to a man. When they were done, there was little left beyond a pile of wrappings and a few drops of spilled tzatziki sauce. It had taken them less than half an hour to devour the entire supply, but it was a welcome break.

Afterwards, Josef put his laptop on the small table and accessed the Demetek intranet. He called Matt over to test the login.

"You sure this is going to work?" Gilstrap was worried.

"I am never certain of the outcome of an experiment that has not been performed, only that it cannot work if it has not been attempted," Josef philosophized.

"Okay, here goes." Matt typed in Steve's user ID, followed by the password he'd been given. He hit the enter key and waited.

Nothing happened. Everyone stared at the screen. A minute passed without any further response from the computer. Matt went to hit the return key again but Josef placed a hand in the way. "Wait. The connection may not be as fast as an internal LAN."

Then, as Josef himself was about to give up, the screen blanked out. The whirring sound of the laptop's drive ceased and the yellow light above the keyboard faded.

"What happened? What did you do, fry the World Wide Web?" Brad quipped.

Josef took a deep breath, and then reached behind the laptop. He wiggled a narrow cable, and then pulled it in front for all to see. "I suspect someone tripped over this while helping themselves to an extra beer." He looked at the plug on the end of the cable. "It seems we have temporarily lost power. The battery, unfortunately, has been running down for the last ninety minutes. An innocent mistake but this is the kind of carelessness we can hardly afford."

The sobering comment turned out to be precisely what the team needed. It took a minute for them to plug the laptop back in, reboot, and log back in. This time, the screen only went blank for a few seconds before Matt's secure login was accepted. A customized browser screen indicated they were connected. In the top right hand corner of the screen was the company's logo: a single sheaf of wheat, flanked by two blades of grass twisted into a helix.

Matt immediately punched in an URL at the top of the browser. It redirected him to a directory tree organized by department. "This should take us directly to the more sensitive files," he announced.

"Wait," Josef cautioned. "Do we not need a full VPN setup to link to this system?"

"Usually," Matt admitted. "VPN is required for people to download and upload files. Without it they can only view. However," he added, "My IT friend confessed something to me over a beer one night. Well, actually it was several. With a few tequila shots thrown in as well."

"Your point?" Brad said.

"My point is that you can override the VPN requirement with a sequence of shell commands. The IT guys need that in case of an emergency. You can do it from a mobile phone if you have the patience to punch in the right sequence."

"And you have that sequence?" Josef asked.

This time it was Matt's turn to beam. "Let me show you." He opened up a command shell and pinged the on-site server. Then he fished a business card out of his wallet. It was from a sales rep based in Sydney. On it, he'd written a sequence of twelve letters and numbers. He typed in a new sequence that bore no resemblance to what was on the card. "Just a little trick I learned. Never write a password down, but if you need to remember something, at least remember the mnemonic you used to generate it. Then you can back-translate it. Anyone who tries to use the password directly hasn't a prayer, assuming they know what it's for in the first place."

He waited for a moment. The screen flashed, changing to a different wallpaper.

"Bingo! I am now Steve Goudreau, and this is my office computer. Full access to everything! Now, where shall we start?"

George suggested, "How about the HR files? It would be worth knowing a little more about the personnel we're dealing with."

Matt's fingers whizzed across the keys. "Man, I never knew all of this stuff. There's a bucket load of – whoa!"

"What is it?" Josef asked.

A folder on the screen showed three almost identical icons. "These are the remote cameras for biodomes one through three."

"What are you talking about?" Brad inquired.

Matt answered by clicking on the first icon. Moments later, the jungle appeared. "Jeez! This is what I saw that day in Steve's office. That must be the live camera. They put..." His voice tailed off as he moved the mouse around the screen. A camera somewhere several hundred kilometers west picked up his movements and allowed him to see everything inside. He panned left and right, tilted the viewer up and down, and then something caught his eye. He used the mouse's scroll wheel to zoom in and that was when they all saw the same thing.

The howler monkey lay motionless on its back, its mouth wide open. Around it, vegetation had been torn from the jungle plants. Leaves strewn hither and yon could not cover the spectacularly hideous sight.

The monkey's guts were ripped out, its viscera laid open for all to see.

Chapter 43

"JESUS CHRIST ON A tractor, what the hell happened there?" Brad King exclaimed.

The others were all looking at the live image. Josef took the mouse and gently guided the camera away. "I believe we are looking at the consequences of this animal being fed genetically modified foodstuffs," he said. "Precisely what remains to be seen."

"How do we find out?" George asked.

"There are three biodomes in the desert," Josef explained. "At least we now have full viewing capability." He clicked on the next icon. A field of grain, swaying in a gentle breeze, replaced the carnage of Bio 1. The yellow-gold tranquility contrasted starkly to the green jungle. The azure sky was bright and cloudless. "This is Bio 2. I assume we are looking at an engineered crop. At this time of day, the light is clearly artificial."

"Looks like wheat," Brad observed.

"We shall need Matthew's help to locate the relevant project files," Josef said. He passed the mouse to the young scientist, who started trawling through the complex directory structure.

Josef excused himself and went outside. He pulled out his mobile phone and punched in a British country code, followed by a London exchange.

The recipient picked up on the first ring. "Hello? Larry here."

"It is time."

"Understood. The Gulfstream is fueled and ready to go. It'll take me a couple of days, if you add in the time difference. I can be in Dubai by the end of today, and in Singapore ten hours later. From there it's short enough for a direct flight, but I'll have to get through customs in Darwin first. Hold on for a moment, will you?" The sound of someone tapping away on a keyboard continued for a minute. "Good. The forecast is favorable. How many passengers can I expect?"

"There are five of us here. Matthew and Bradford will disable the Alice Springs facility early in the morning. George will be assigned to the charter aircraft. And that leaves Marcus and myself. That makes four plus yourself. However, we both know that adjustments may be needed on the fly, if you will excuse my poor sense of humor."

Larry Claypool ignored him. "Do you have any concerns about the makeup of the team, Josef? Now would be a good time to make any corrections."

"There will always be a risk. But I am confident."

"To the last man?"

"Yes. Even to him," Josef declared.

He thanked his boss and hung up. *Timing. It all has to be done perfectly.*

Next, he called Mickey Durant in California. "Is everything going to plan at your end?"

"We're secure here. But there's something you might want to know about. I don't know if it's relevant."

"Then you had better tell me. Together we will decide."

"There's been another killing in Pacifica."

Josef wasn't sure if he'd heard correctly. "Has that missing family shown up?"

"No, but the police are all over the case now. The young man who reported them missing, a high school student named Balbino Ruiz? His body was found by a couple of hikers earlier today."

"Any suspects?"

"Hard to know. I've pulled a few strings but they're being quite cagey. You can understand."

"All right, Michelle. Thank you for keeping me up to speed. Please give Edmund my regards." He hung up and went back inside.

Matt found the relevant project directory and clicked through files at breakneck speed, searching for the Bio 2 data. The file names used a consistent internal date-tagged system, simplifying the exercise. Hundreds of gigabytes clogged the drives, all of which would take hours to copy even at the fastest broadband speeds. "We're not going to be able to do this from here," he said.

"Is there a summary sheet anywhere?" Brad wondered.

"Should be fairly easy to find, as long as it's a text-based file." Matt typed in a search, and waited. The algorithm was taking for ever to plough through all the characters. "On the other hand, it may not be quick."

"Perhaps we should not focus on such a search right now," Josef said. "A more useful exercise will be to examine company and executive calendars. We should determine what the principals' movements are in the next few days. Matthew, can you find the master schedule?"

"Should be easy. The company was on Outlook." He started a new search.

"Joe," Brad asked, "I've been wondering about the security system."

"I thought you might. You have been hanging around with me for too long not to be concerned."

"You ain't kidding. Do you have any bright ideas on how we're supposed to bypass all the swipes, codes, and retina scans? Even if there is an override mechanism it's going to be a hard call to figure it out in the next couple of days, let alone avoid a complete internal lockdown."

"Then we shall have to find another way, shall we not?" Josef peered over Matt's shoulder. A few moments later, a calendar appeared on screen, showing upcoming company events.

"The whole of Monday is blocked out for the biodome event," Matt observed. It was Friday evening. The weekend days weren't displayed. "Looks like Tuesday's a write-off as well. They're obviously giving everyone a bonus day for recovery."

"Nice," Brad observed. "Reckon we ought to implement that kind of benefit, Joe? How about bringing that one up to LC next time you talk to him?"

Josef gave him a withering glare. "You will be working this weekend, King. You should look at the next screen."

He did. It was the executives' calendar. In contrast to the company version, this one displayed all seven days of the week. Goudreau was listed as "out of office." Hernandez and Strathmore were returning from Sydney on Sunday evening, following weekend meetings with Asian partners. Only one of the execs' whereabouts were not specifically accounted for.

Brad frowned. "I'm starting to wonder where you're going with this, and I'm not sure I like it."

"Matthew," Josef said. "Mr. Dayne appears to be in town this weekend. How well do you know him?"

"Not too well," was the reply. "He lives alone. He has one passion, supposedly. At least if you go by his office. Personal decorations, that kind of thing. He's got them all over the place. Knick-knacks. I don't get it, myself."

"What are you talking about?" Marcus said.

"Golf. He's a golf addict. Plays every weekend that he's in town. He even bought a house overlooking the course."

Josef Rintlen exchanged a glance with Brad King. "I think you know what you need to do. That will be your assignment this weekend."

"He gets to play golf?" Marcus looked at his friend, astonished. "I don't follow."

"You will. Care to explain, Joe?"

XUSA's security chief looked around. "We will require the highest level of access. There are a handful of people with those privileges. Two will be out of town until late Sunday. Strathmore and Hernandez will clearly not cooperate. The IT manager is not someone we need to trouble at this point, for any number of reasons. Nor could we exert leverage over her. That leaves the chief legal officer."

"What else do we know about him?" Marcus asked.

"Thanks to Michelle's expert input, I can safely say that Mr. Montgomery Dayne will be easily persuaded of the error of his ways. He has not led a blemish-free life."

"Damned lawyers," Brad muttered. "I'm beginning to like this idea, if I'm catching your drift, Joe."

"It will require a little creativity on your part, but I have a feeling you are up to the task. Matthew, please pull up Mr. Dayne's personnel file. I would like to ensure that Bradford has every last piece of information he needs to bring this man over to our side."

Matt did as he was told. Within minutes, Brad had the relevant facts committed to memory. He looked at the younger man and said, "Nice job, by the way. You've done the right thing. Maybe there will be a permanent place for you on our team."

Saturday morning arrived with bright sunshine and chilly temperatures. Marcus thought he was the first one up, but he found George Petrescu in the kitchenette, preparing coffee. He accepted a mug, sipped at it, and turned up his nose in disgust.

"Sorry. Instant's all you get here," George said.

"Guess it'll have to do." He spooned some sugar in, stirred, and tried again. "Marginally better. What time is it?"

"Seven thirty. Brad's already off on his assignment. We get to do a little reconnaissance today, along with Matt, who knows the area fairly well. He'll be back in about ten minutes."

Marcus looked surprised. "I don't understand. You've all been up for a while?"

"We thought it best you get as much sleep as you can. It's been harder on you than the rest of us."

That was thoughtful. "Josef? Where's he?"

"He's gone to the airport to run interference for us. Scoping out the charter."

"The aircraft taking the Demetek team to the biodomes."

"Yeah. I get to play flight attendant. That's assuming Josef can land me the role, but as casting agents go, he's second to none." He wandered over to a pile of notes by the laptop and picked up the top sheet. "We discovered something interesting last night after you turned in."

By the time eleven o'clock had rolled around, Marcus was barely able to keep his eyes open. He'd collapsed onto one of the beds and didn't remember a thing for the next eight and a half hours. "What are you talking about?"

George glanced at the piece of paper. "There's a company policy. It's not uncommon. When three or more company execs or officers travel, they have to fly on different aircraft. We should probably have thought of that before, but the upshot is that Strathmore, Hernandez, and Dayne won't all be traveling together to the biodomes."

"How does that help us?"

"Sometimes it's better to be lucky than good. Strathmore and Hernandez are booked on the charter. Mr. Dayne was planning to travel to the biodomes using the company Gulfstream. They'll be expecting the aircraft, at least. It's the same kind of aircraft the rest of you will be taking."

"Don't tell me Josef's a qualified pilot as well?"

"Nope. That role belongs to someone else. We too have a corporate Gulfstream jet. It's on its way as we speak."

I can't wait.

As if reading Marcus's mind, George encouraged his colleague. "You'll have your chance. Trust me. We're counting on you."

Chapter 44

RED CLAY FLANKED THE fifteenth fairway of the Alice Springs golf course. A wayward drive struck by Monty Dayne landed in it with a muffled *plonk* just after nine-thirty on Saturday. The round was going poorly. He'd already suffered three double bogeys, having failed to reach seven of the greens in regulation. Normally a seven-handicapper, he'd already used up those strokes and ten more. Seventeen over par for fourteen holes, and not even a par to show for it thus far, he thought. *That's a bad day.*

When the ball struck ten meters behind him, just before he took his stance for the second shot on the par 4, his temper got the better of him. He backed away from the ball and cursed loudly. Back towards the tee stood a tall man in a red baseball cap. He waved a club in the air and yelled something about being sorry and not seeing Dayne out on the fairway. "Thought you'd moved off!"

American, Dayne thought. *Two of us out here playing solo. What are the chances of that?* He was about to return to his hooked tee shot when it occurred to him to invite the new guy to join him. Perhaps the presence of an equally sloppy player would dilute his own frustrations a little. He motioned with his hand and waited for the red-capped player to pick up his bag and catch up.

"Hey, buddy! I'm sorry about that. I couldn't see where you were after your tee shot. I've been behind you for the last few holes," Brad King said.

"I was going to ask if you wanted to play through, or keep me company for the last few holes." Dayne offered.

"Very kind of you. I'm likely to screw up the next shot and delay your play if I just rush on by, so how about we finish up together?"

They introduced themselves. Brad feigned surprise at finding a fellow American out on the course. "Are you a tourist?"

"Nah. I live here. I work locally. This is just my weekend fun."

234

"Nice course."

"Just about perfect, not too many people crowding it up and watching my lame short game," Dayne declared. "What's your story?"

"I'm just here on vacation. I came here with a couple of buddies from the States to visit the big red rock."

"Uluru."

"That's the one. You been there?"

"Seen it a couple of times. They say you're not supposed to climb it, but I said what the heck, how many chances are you going to get?"

And they wonder why we Americans get a reputation for ugly tourist behavior. "Well, I reckon we'll have a crack at it ourselves. I agree, there's no sense in wasting opportunities."

They played their shots. Dayne's game improved markedly over the last few holes. He even recovered for a par on the fifteenth, and finished up birdie, par, birdie. "You brought me some good luck there, pal. Can I buy you a cup of coffee?"

"Sounds good. Say, Monty, you mentioned you'd bought some property here. How does that compare with, say, California prices? I guess I didn't ask you where you were from originally, so you may not know, but the market's tanked in the Midwest, where we're from. Sent my mortgage under water. I'm pissed about that."

"Don't blame you. I just got out in time myself. The market here didn't suffer quite as badly, but it's probably a couple of years behind the US. At least I got hold of some nice property on the golf course. House came up for sale a week after I got here. I snapped it up in a New York minute."

"That was fortunate. Any other properties in the same development for sale? I'd be kind of interested in taking a look around myself. This is such a nice, quiet part of the world. Looks like a nifty place to retire to."

"You don't look like you're ready for retirement."

"I'm not. My wife is, though. I reckon she'd love it here." Brad wasn't sure if he was lying or not, which kind of made it OK. "You married, Monty?"

"Not any more."

That was convenient, Brad concluded. "Sorry to hear that, buddy."

"That's what most well-meaning people say. One guy said congratulations. I bought him a beer." He chuckled.

"Then congratulations it is." He raised his coffee cup. "I was serious about looking at nearby property, by the way. The wife and I are looking for a change of scenery. Kansas City just doesn't cut it for me any more."

"Ouch. KC, huh? Don't blame you. Bit windy for my tastes." Dayne gave him a rueful grin. "Tell you what. Why don't you follow me home and I'll give you a tour of the local housing area. You can take a look at the layout of my place, see if that's the kind of joint that might suit you. Do you have kids?"

"Nope. Just the two of us, probably will stay that way. But I never say never."

"Good. My house is pretty typical of the design you're likely to come across." He finished his coffee and got up. "You parked out back?"

"Yeah. Let me drop off these rental clubs first."

"Okay. I'll see you out there. I'll be in the dark green Beamer."

What else, Brad thought. He dropped off the clubs, exchanged pleasantries with the clubhouse attendant, and walked outside.

Monty Dayne loaded up his pull cart and bag of Big Berthas into the trunk of a late model BMW. Brad sneaked behind the car parked to Dayne's right, a tall sport utility model that effectively hid him from view. Dayne got in on the right side. He was about to start the ignition when Brad surprised him by pulling open the right passenger door and sliding in behind him. The feel of a sharp point against the back of his neck caused him to freeze.

"That's good. Nice and easy," Brad ordered. "Mr. Dayne, I suggest you do exactly what I say if you want to avoid prosecution. If you make any sudden movements or attempt to resist, then you can expect the pressure you are feeling right now to increase. I don't believe you wish to die, not just yet. Especially while you're enjoying your new found freedom."

Dayne stammered. "W-what do you want from me?"

"I'll tell you where to drive. Follow my instructions to the letter, and you will be taken care of. And I mean legally." He paused, waiting for a reaction.

Dayne said nothing. He switched on the engine. Brad told him to back out carefully and drive away from the golf course. On the main road, he instructed Dayne to drive directly to the hotel. Once, when Dayne appeared to be reaching for something in his pocket, Brad jabbed the point of the ice pick further into the back of his neck. Dayne withdrew his hand immediately.

At the hotel, Brad told him to park outside the front door of the suite, to get out carefully, and not to run. Dayne almost did as he was told. He eased the car door open, and climbed half way out. Then he made a dash for it. Brad to flung the rear door open, slamming the lawyer in the back. He pitched forward, stumbling towards the building. Brad hurtled out of the back seat, ran after him, and tackled him around the shoulders. The two men crashed to the ground a split second before Dayne could reach the mobile phone in his pocket. The lawyer to howled in pain as he struggled under the other man's weight.

Brad yanked Dayne's hand away, grinding a knee into the man's back and twisting his arm up to his shoulder blade. "I told you to follow my instructions, Monty. You didn't listen. Not smart."

"Go to hell."

"You don't want to screw around with me. Trust me on that." Brad twisted Dayne's arm even more, almost dislocating his shoulder.

Between clenched teeth, Dayne hissed, "Fuck you."

The front door to the suite opened. Brad looked up to see George and Marcus. "Help me with this son of a bitch, would you?" He's being uncooperative."

They each grabbed an arm and dragged Dayne inside. Brad fished the man's cell phone from his pocket. He'd entered five digits. Not enough to reach anyone.

Once they'd closed the door, Brad shoved Dayne into an upright chair, and then introduced him. "Guys, this is Mr. Dayne. He's Demetek's chief legal counsel. We'll be needing his services in due course. Monty, meet a couple of my colleagues. Marcus Black's the one on the left. George Petrescu is the other guy.

A flicker of recognition vanished almost immediately as Dayne took stock of his captors. "What do you people want from me?" he demanded.

"That's easy, Mr. Dayne," Brad King answered. "I want your retina."

George produced a sharp looking kitchen knife. Holding it in his right hand, he approached Dayne. "We can either take it from you or have you help us in person. Which would you prefer?"

Dayne wasn't ready to dispense with any of his anatomy, including his retina. "All right. I'll do what you ask. Just don't hurt me, please!"

"That's better, Monty," Brad said. "You've made the right choice. Now, here's what we're going to do. We're going to provide you with an additional incentive." He produced a couple of plastic cable ties and created a double length loop. He wrapped it around Dayne's wrist, lashing him to the chair. He turned the laptop towards Dayne and pressed a key. A minute later, he placed a Skype video call to Belvedere.

The caller answered on the second ring. It took a few seconds for the video feed to kick in, but when it did, the person on the other end made Dayne's eyes open wide.

"Hello, Monty," Mickey Durant said. "Nice to see you've landed on your feet after you resigned from the Illinois State Bar."

Chapter 45

"MISS DURANT," DAYNE SAID. "What the hell –?"

"That's right, it's me. I've done a little research on your clients, the Castlefords. I also know that Linda Castleford's estate, worth over two billion, went to Donald Strathmore, the CEO of your company. How on earth did you persuade your client to leave so much money to one guy?"

Dayne glared silently.

"Maybe you didn't need to persuade anyone. After all, Strathmore was her nephew, isn't that right? The thing is, though, Linda never wanted to leave a cent to Strathmore, did she? You just forged her will after the fact, didn't you?"

Now Dayne began to look uncomfortable.

"I'm right, aren't I?" Mickey asked.

He closed his eyes and then, ever so slowly, began to nod. "A ten percent commission," he confessed.

Ten percent of two billion? Marcus was shocked when he did the math. That was two hundred million, not a bad day's work. Brad, for his part, assumed he'd hidden the money elsewhere. Not even the best house on the Alice golf course would have fetched a drop in that bucket. George just shook his head at the bent attorney.

"It was a deal I couldn't refuse," Dayne admitted.

"I'll tell you what, Monty," Mickey said. "Forging a will violates any number of statutes and moral conduct standards. But I'll give you a break. You do as my friends say and this goes away. Is that a fair proposal?"

Dayne nodded. "Okay, okay. What do you want with me? I'll do it, just let me keep the money, please!"

"You know, squire, we probably will," Brad ventured. "I'm not interested in your crooked probate practice. I'm only concerned with ensuring your employers don't screw up the planet for good. So here's what you're going to do for us." He stood up and marched back and forth in front of the attorney. "Like I said, we'll be using your retina. Not sure which one, but you'll be delivering it regardless."

"No! Please leave my eyes –!"

"Relax! I'm not going to maim you or blind you. I'm a civilized human being. What you're going to do for me, for us, I should say, is to be our eyes deep within the Demetek facility. We will need you as our retina scanning dummy. You will enable us to enter any door, at any time, day or night. Starting today. Is that clear?"

"What are you going to do?" he asked, his voice trembling.

"We're going to stop you. All of you." Marcus said.

Alice Springs' airport, like almost every single one on the planet, was in the process of expanding and/or renovation. Developers were submitting master plans for growth, complete with environmental and commercial strategy white papers. Opinions on the impact of growth on local businesses and assorted carriers only confused and delayed major construction, but grand visions of increased employment, longer runways, and state-of-the-art facilities and equipment kept the planners and their legal representatives in clover while the process dragged on. For the moment, the airport's commercial aviation facilities remained modest.

The small passenger terminal inadequately showcased the airport's capacity for large aircraft. The 8,000 foot runway was capable of handling equipment as large as the United States Air Force C5A Galaxy transport, a fact not unnoticed by Demetek's senior executives. They envisioned large shipments of their products being distributed to Asian destinations without needing interstate haulage by road train or rail. Furthermore, since the product was both hardy and dominant, there was little need for excessive bulk. The strain would soon take over existing wild-type crops and become a prevailing source of grain, suitable for feeding billions. Simultaneously, the rubisco variant engineered into it would purify and cleanse the air of excess carbon dioxide, and slow the effects of global warming.

Josef observed two transport planes parked at the General Aviation building several hundred meters from the main passenger terminal. One of them he didn't recognize immediately. It was a four turboprop aircraft with wings mounted above the fuselage. It slightly resembled the Russian AN-12 Cub, capable of medium-sized payloads like the venerable American C130 Hercules model. This one was different. It sported a glass cockpit, a more streamlined nose than its Russian counterpart, and a modified tail assembly. As he approached the aircraft, he saw the label "Shaanxi Aircraft Industry

Group Yun-9" on the fuselage, between the front landing gear and loading hatch. He recalled seeing a news item a few years earlier about the Chinese aircraft industry wanting to make inroads into the Airbus/Boeing market share, but hadn't yet viewed any of their technology in action. This one looked pretty good, but what on earth was it doing in Alice Springs?

Putting that question aside, he looked at the other large airplane standing out amongst the private jets and small propeller aircraft. In less than two days, it was to carry the whole roster of Demetek employees to the biodome site, constructed with Castleford cash.

Power for the remote site, logically, was all solar. The climate of central Australia made it perfect for harnessing the sun's energy through hectares of panels, requiring very little in the way of piped-in resources. The cost had been staggering, which meant that the payoff had to be even more monumental. The records hadn't been hard to find now that he had access to internal company archives. Blueprints, accounts, construction project history, all the way down to final punch sheets and signed purchase orders had all been scanned, dated, and committed to hard drives.

His team didn't yet know whether they could stop the delivery before it was too late. XUSA had two aces up their sleeves, but their play had to be perfectly calculated. Now was time for the first. As Josef entered the general aviation admin building, he crossed his fingers, a superstition to which he didn't normally subscribe, but what harm could it do?

He identified himself as Lars Soderquist, speaking in a perfect Wisconsin accent, producing a fake Demetek business card. Small letters spelled out his name and title, specifically "Director, Human Resources." The receptionist glanced at the card, ignoring the small print, and looked up. "Oh, yes! You must want to make some final arrangements for the Monday flight."

Excellent. One less thing to explain. "Exactly. Is there someone here I could speak to on that point?" Josef asked. "I would very much like to meet with the crew members." He contemplated stressing that he'd prefer to meet with them one on one, as part of the company's internal security measures, but thought better of it. The receptionist was lively and willing to help, but was not likely to wield much clout.

"You should speak to Mr. Redpath," the receptionist said. "I'll buzz him."

A minute later, a tall, gaunt man in his early sixties appeared. He wore a gray, thin wool cardigan over a white shirt and conservative dark slacks. Josef thought the man would be more at home in an antique shop than an airport. "G'day, Mr. Soderquist," he said. "Dick Redpath. I'm the general manager here. How can I help you?"

Thirty minutes later, Josef had a complete background analysis of the

737-900 charter aircraft's crew, along with their local address and schedule. Dick Redpath, on the other hand, only knew that the deputy chairman of the company's board of directors, one Lawrence Claypool, would arrive late Sunday evening in his private Gulfstream from Darwin, and would very much appreciate some privacy and discretion. Josef explained the company's policy of separate flights for its senior management, and that Mr. Claypool had generously offered to provide transport for those who would not be traveling with the main charter. Redpath, who prided himself on his discretion, understood completely.

On Saturday evening, Matt Gilstrap drove the team's rental car past the familiar sights of Alice Springs, pointing out landmarks and key intersections to Marcus, Josef, and Brad. George Petrescu stayed in the suite with Monty Dayne, ensuring the lawyer made no attempt to run. Had he done so, he would have discovered his sentinel to be quite adept at hand-to-hand restraint.

To the city's north, the XUSA team rode past the School of the Air, a facility enabling youngsters in the Outback to learn via remote classroom instruction. They bypassed the city center on the Stuart Highway, turning right off Telegraph Terrace onto Larapinta Drive. Now westbound, they passed the Central Australia Aviation Museum and Araluen Arts Center. The road curved north around the Alice Springs Desert Park. As they left Alice's residential zone, both housing and agriculture thinned out, replaced with red clay.

A few kilometers further, they arrived at the main Demetek campus, fenced in and guarded by a strategically positioned security station at the only entrance. The horizontal barrier was down. It looked like it would not easily be smashed or split.

"Finesse, not force," Matt stated the obvious. He stopped the car a couple of hundred meters away from the guardhouse, executing a precise U-turn. "Their cameras will take a picture of our license tag but if anyone at the company cares to follow up, they'll just see a bunch of tourists who went the wrong way and thought better of it."

"On Monday we'll use a more familiar vehicle," Brad reminded them. "Squire Dayne's BMW won't attract any undue attention."

It took them twenty minutes to return to the suite. Monty Dayne remained seated and restrained. He bristled at King, who gave him a thin smile. Only when he saw Matt Gilstrap for the first time did it dawn on him that the whole exercise had been assisted by inside help.

"You!" Dayne growled.

"Hello, Monty," Matt replied, his tone not unfriendly. "Nice to see you again."

"What do you think you're doing?"

"I'm helping undo some of the damage I caused." Whatever he felt about his contributions to the company's technology platform, the last few days had soured his emotions. Identifying a rubisco mutation capable of altering the balance of oxygen and carbon dioxide in the atmosphere was one thing, but producing it in quantity was another. Matt's scientific curiosity and youthful enthusiasm hadn't been tempered by conscience until very recently.

"What are you talking about?" the lawyer said.

"Steve saw it. He must have, otherwise he wouldn't have asked for my help."

"If you mean the accident in Bio 1, yes, that was unfortunate."

"Bio 1. The primate jungle. That was the animal test, wasn't it?"

Dayne feigned concern. "It was an early strain. The subsequent modifications overcame those hurdles."

"Meaning what? The company ran additional animal tests?" Matt pressed.

"He's the legal guy, not the biology guru," Marcus interjected.

A look almost resembling gratitude came over Dayne's face. "That's right. I'm in charge of patents and contracts."

"Understood," Marcus said, using the shift in the man's attention to give himself a moment to take up cudgels. He produced a sheaf of papers bearing the legal seal of Demetek Corporation. Turning the pages one by one, he recited a commentary outlining the terms of the contract. "You're the one who drew this agreement up. You'd have to be completely aware of all the science that went into the draft. The finalized document was signed by yourself and Donald Strathmore, and also by the CEO of a Shanghai agricultural biotech company. Care to explain?"

The others in the room stared at him silently.

"You realize what this will do, don't you?" Marcus asked.

Dayne declined to answer.

"Then let me tell you. We've spent the last few hours examining your Bio 2 product. Correct me if I'm wrong, but this is a genetically engineered grain bearing the dominant rubisco strain. According to this contract, Demetek sold exclusive licensing rights to Shanghai's Wudong Agritech for the grain. Do they know what they're buying?"

"Of course," Dayne said. "They're buying a state of the art crop that will not only feed millions of malnourished citizens, but will also help balance atmospheric gases, reduce pollution, and reduce the greenhouse effect. It's a win-win situation! Why wouldn't they want that?"

"Perhaps because they don't understand the side effects, the ones you knew about. The seeds for this were sown a long time ago."

This time, Dayne looked a little confused. "I'm not sure – I don't understand what you mean."

This was it. Time to lay it all out. If not now, he wasn't sure he could turn the lawyer around. "It happened in the early 1990's. Your colleague, Justin Hernandez, found he could modify RNA to help stabilize certain proteins. He wondered what might happen if this RNA vector entered mammals. The food chain, in other words. He engineered a chimeric RNA to test this theory in small rodents, monkeys, and finally in man. The only observable effect in the lower species was a higher awareness, an increased intelligence if you like. But the latent effect was devastating. You saw what happened in Bio 1, after all."

"Hernandez said it was a glitch."

"A glitch? That's bullshit!"

"Careful, Marco," Brad admonished.

"Screw careful! This technology was tested in people, including my wife!" Marcus poked a finger into Dayne's chest. "It destroyed people's lives! Kay killed herself because she couldn't face the pain any longer. Ian MacCallum blew his own brains out. And when his doctor tried to find out why, he was killed too. Zalewski, Goldfarb, Hong Li. All part of the test group. And what about the others? Stuart and Sally Gray, and their teenaged daughter, all disappeared. No trace of them. Your people mopped up everyone who you wanted to keep quiet. Am I wrong? You tell me."

Something in Montgomery Dayne's psyche sank. He closed his eyes and his jowls drooped. He sat motionless for a long moment, then opened his eyes again. He looked around and finally spoke. "All right. I'll help you, on one condition."

"You're in no shape to dictate terms," Brad reminded him.

"I want legal representation. From Ms. Durant."

Josef Rintlen sidled around the back of Dayne's chair. He produced a pair of wire clippers and snapped the cable tie that held the lawyer to the furniture.

Dayne winced. He eased his arms forwards, grimacing as they cramped up. He flexed his fingers, swiveling his hands to help restore their circulation, and then brought them to his lap. "Thank you," he said. A single tear of relief formed at the corner of his eye.

Chapter 46

MONDAY ARRIVED UNDER BRIGHT sunshine. The forecast was similar across the entire continent, but more importantly, there were no delays for the Demetek excursion into the outback. Shortly after eleven, the last bus left campus on the forty-five minute journey to the General Aviation terminal. Not a single employee bothered looking at the black BMW passing the bus on the other side of the road. Had anyone done so, he or she would have recognized the figure of Montgomery Dayne at the wheel, and possibly the man in the passenger seat, but the guy sitting right behind the driver would not have registered with anyone. Dressed in an uncharacteristically dapper suit and tie, Brad King would have looked right at home in any New York law firm boardroom.

The BMW slowed at the gate. Michael Baltazzi, head of security, had volunteered to hold the fort while his junior staff took the opportunity to view the biodomes. Assured that his duties were likely to be minimal, he suffered a rare lapse of concentration as he waved Dayne's car through, complete with its passengers.

Brad and Matt hadn't anticipated such a simple entry, but neither was about to complain. They arrived at the front of the building and waited for Dayne to swipe his security card and punch in his code. Once cleared. they headed directly for the elevators to take them down to level B2. Dayne picked up the handset and called Mike Baltazzi.

"Yeah, mate," Mike answered immediately.

"It's Monty here. I'll be flying out to the biodomes separately but this shouldn't take me long. I reckon an hour at most." He waited to see if Baltazzi might press him on why. His stock answer if needed, was that he had to make a couple of phone calls with Demetek's Asian customers. They were a couple of hours behind the local time zone.

There was no cause for concern, Mike simply asked, "Give me a shout when you're on your way back."

"Thanks." The lawyer punched in the secure access code, Matt watching very closely as each digit was entered. He was still not a hundred percent sure that Dayne was on board with their plans, but now he knew the number Goudreau had given him was the same as the one Dayne had entered. He also now understood that they were in complete isolation. He flashed Brad a brief wink.

"Right. Take us down to the basement, Mr. Dayne," Brad ordered.

Dayne swiped his security card and punched in another code. When they reached level B4, the door opened onto the deep basement corridor. Eerie blue lighting bathed the thin passage as far as the eye could see, bulbs at ten meter intervals. The lawyer led the way to the very end, stopping at the security panel.

"I believe this is where we need your retina?" Brad asked.

"In a moment," Dayne said. "There's an order to this." He slipped his security card into the slot, punched a code in, and placed his chin on the sconce. He waited, eyes open wide, as the beam registered a positive match. A click sounded as the outer door opened. Matt and Brad followed inside, and waited while Dayne repeated the process. As soon as the outer door sealed, the chamber flashed three times. The inner door opened.

"What was that all about?" Matt wondered.

"You don't know?" Dayne stared at his former colleague.

"Never been here. Why should I?"

"Photographic record of everyone entering the annex. It's automated. There's no way to disable it."

"You're going to need to find those records and wipe them," Brad demanded.

"I understand. Believe me, I have no desire to be implicated in what you're about to do," Dayne declared. He led them across the floor to the control room, which was almost completely dark. A few monitors, servers, and banks of LEDs provided the only internal lighting. Dayne located the master switch on the side wall. Immediately, the nerve center burst into all its futuristic glory. "If I remember, this central panel is the one Tracy always used when accessing the master systems." He led them to a desk in the center of the circular room.

"That's enough, Monty," Matt said. "I'll take it from here."

Dayne frowned. "You don't have access."

"Oh, yes, I do. Dr. Goudreau was good enough to give me everything I need."

"What? He – I mean, how did he – why would he?"

"Pass on the company secrets? Insurance. Some people really do have a conscience." Matt started pounding keys at the console. Brad carefully kept an eye on Dayne, in case he decided to make any sudden movements, but for the moment, the lawyer appeared to be cooperating.

Ten minutes later, Matt plugged Josef's USB stick into a port on the front console. "Time for things to happen," he said, grinning.

"What are you doing?" Dayne wanted to know.

It had taken much of the previous Saturday night and much of Sunday morning to set it up, but they had laid the groundwork well. A full data backup of Demetek's historic and archived data, along with every electronic file from the past year had been transmitted to XUSA's servers during the previous twenty-four hours. The ghost image was invisible to anyone but the most diligent of snoops. As a result, both companies had a copy of every file Demetek had generated in its entire lifetime.

In less than an hour, only XUSA would retain possession.

Matt uploaded the code from Josef's USB stick and installed the file. He called up a command prompt, entered several lines of Unix code, and waited. A green glow on the end of the USB stick flashed on and off several times, and then went out for good. He yanked the stick out and watched the monitor.

"What's happening?" Dayne asked.

"We're leaving. That's what's happening." Brad ordered. He led the lawyer away from the console and back out of the control room. Matt followed, switching off the lights. "It's time for us to catch a plane."

Five minutes later, the three of them were back in Dayne's car. As they approached the guardhouse, Mike Baltazzi stepped in front of the vehicle, waving them to stop.

"Sorry, mate. I need to check something before you go," he said to the man behind the wheel. "You're going to have to come with me."

Brad looked at Matt quizzically. The younger man let the slightest hint of a smile venture from the corner of his mouth. He waited for Dayne to climb out and follow Baltazzi. He glanced at his watch. "Should be just about now," he said.

Baltazzi and Dayne stopped just outside the guardhouse. The barrier was rising all by itself. "Hold on, that's not right," the security chief warned as he darted inside.

They all heard him curse five seconds later. "The whole bloody system's down!" he yelled. "Get in here, now!"

Dayne obediently followed. Matt hoisted himself over the armrest to the driver's seat. The engine was still running. He put the BMW in gear, but kept his foot on the brake. He watched Baltazzi frantically punching keys on his console, trying to get the perimeter security back up and running.

"What did you do?" Brad asked. The young structural biologist continued to impress him with his penchant for computer savagery. He made up his mind to recommend, no, demand that Matt stay on with XUSA as soon as the exercise was over. Josef could certainly use someone with his skills.

"It's all on a timer. We leave – NOW!" Matt lifted his foot off the brake and pressed down on the gas pedal. The car zoomed under the barrier just as it began to fall. "I reckon we can let our friendly lawyer explain to Baltazzi exactly what he was doing sabotaging the whole company's systems. Thanks to Josef's e-plague, everything is wiped. The electronics are fried. The power will go offline in about forty-five minutes. Oh, and those photographs of us inside the airlock chamber – well, two of those were deleted. The other one's been sent to Baltazzi's home e-mail address. Should serve as his own insurance policy just in case Monty Dayne decides he'd rather flip sides again."

"Not bad, Dr. Gilstrap. Not bad at all. I think you've demonstrated the kind of mean streak we could use full time!" Brad complimented. "Now let's get our butts over to the airport. The others will be waiting for us."

When they arrived at the general aviation terminal, Josef and Marcus greeted them in the parking lot. "How did things go?" Josef asked.

"Mission accomplished. We have what they had, thanks to this guy." Brad said. "I'm not even sure he needed me."

"Your job isn't complete yet," said a voice behind him. They all turned to see a tall, imposing figure, gray hair slicked back over his temples. He wore a long sleeved blue shirt, open at the collar, black chinos, and expensive Italian loafers. "Pardon my informal appearance, gentlemen. I'd rather be sailing, but this situation called for a more rapid form of transport." He waved an arm behind him.

They all looked at the aircraft on the tarmac. The 737 was ready to move, lights flashing on the leading edges of its wings. Turned up winglets gave the executive charter added range and fuel efficiency, along with a sleek modern profile. Between them and the Boeing, Larry Claypool's private Gulfstream stood, its steps beckoning them to its cabin.

"Our chariot awaits?" Brad asked.

"Fueled and ready to go," LC said with a smile. "There's just one little mystery about the various aircraft bound for the biodomes that didn't add up, but I suspect that in a couple of hours' time, we shall discover the answer."

"What are you talking about?" Marcus wondered.

Josef explained. "Flight plans have been filed for three airplanes today. The first plane left an hour ago. It is a Chinese built transport, specially modified for conveying bulk goods. It should land at the remote site in an hour and a half. The charter is about to take off, with nearly all the Demetek employees aboard, including Donald Strathmore and Justin Hernandez. George is also aboard, monitoring the situation first hand. I arranged for him to replace one of the original crew, who unfortunately came down with severe food poisoning yesterday afternoon. The details of the swap are not important, save to say that Mr. Douglas Davis will recover fully from his malaise, all in good time."

He will thank you one day, LC wanted to say.

Flight attendants serving Demetek's employees aboard the chartered Boeing 737-900 closed its doors. The mandatory safety check followed while the aircraft taxied the short distance to the end of runway 30 of Alice Springs's airport. The aircraft took off to the northwest, then banked gently to port as it headed out across the Northern Territory desert. Under cloudless skies, the ground below was a mixture of reds, browns, and oranges, with very few patches of green. In the distance, the Gosses Bluff meteor crater formed an enormous monument of red cliffs and canyons, which the captain was pleased to describe at length.

The interior of the jet, configured in two plus two rows of seating, was unquestionably first-class. The catering was no less sophisticated, and the passengers, most of whom had never enjoyed the benefits of superior service, gladly partook of everything offered. Champagne and expensive booze flowed like water. Caviar and other delicacies were served as plentifully as peanuts at a baseball game. The only thing missing, one of the attendants observed, was a live performance by the Rolling Stones. Now *that* would be a party.

Said attendant finished serving the front section of sixteen passengers. Many of them were still talking shop. Don Strathmore had borrowed the cabin's speaker system for a moment to tell everyone to let their collective hair down for a while. The instruction fell on deaf ears for those who insisted on discussing the latest results and plans for upcoming experiments. Some scientists just couldn't resist blathering on about their discoveries. The nerd factor was alive and well aboard the plane.

George Petrescu watched from his vantage point in the aircraft's main galley. He saw Strathmore and Hernandez sitting together at the very front of the 737. Perhaps it was the proximity of the intercom system, so they could get up and slap each other on the back, perhaps they wanted to leave the aircraft first and lead tours of the biodomes. George's primary task on arrival was to alert Josef the moment they disembarked. For now, he had another hour to serve, blend in, and interact with dozens of people whose ultimate fate he couldn't predict.

He waited until every passenger had been served appetizers and another round of drinks, and then stepped into the restroom. Unlike standard issue airline toilets, this one looked more like a full sized residential bathroom, complete with hand towels, colognes, and luxury skin lotions. He locked the door and dialed Josef's number on his satphone.

"Yes?"

"It's me. We're about an hour away from the site."

"We left Alice Springs half an hour ago. What have you heard?"

"A lot of chatter. Most of it's pretty mundane or technical. One guy insists on telling the woman he's sitting next to that he's going to modify his expression system to improve the yields when they roll out the rice strain next year. He's convinced that baculovirus doesn't do nearly as well as E. coli. She's been arguing with him for the whole flight."

Rintlen let out a frustrated sigh. "Anything about today's events?"

"I overheard Strathmore hinting at a ceremony at the site. Something about a first delivery."

"To Wudong, no doubt. All right, when you arrive, sit tight. We will be landing shortly after you. There should not be any concerns about the additional aircraft arriving, at least until they see the livery is not identical to that of the jet on which Mr. Dayne was scheduled to fly."

"I take it the timing will have to be spot on."

"I cannot argue with that point. You can at least be assured that the entire Alice facility has been disabled and locked down. Matthew and Bradford have played their parts very nicely."

"Good to know. All right, boss, I'll see you when you get here." He ended the call and returned to the cabin. The party was going strong. Hernandez and Strathmore were in deep conversation. He noticed neither was drinking anything stronger than club soda, unlike the majority of the employees.

Chapter 47

THE 737 BEGAN ITS approach to the remote site, descending over the desert. Those in the window seats could see several acres of solar panels shimmering under the cloudless sky. Strathmore was on the intercom again, describing how the facility was self-sustaining, powered by the most natural of all energy sources. To the port side of the airliner, an airstrip ran perpendicular to three hemispheric blobs rising from the earth. The middle dome was joined to the others by a long cylindrical structure on each side. From the sky the complex resembled a couple of dumbbells, merged together at the middle. On other days, the biodomes would have been camouflaged by a massive retractable shield. Today it had been pulled back into an underground storage bay running parallel to the array.

Outside the center dome a forklift loader was busy transferring sacks to the rear bay of another aircraft. "What you see in the distance, those of you on the left of our charter, is the first delivery of grain to Wudong Agritech, our Chinese partners. They have sent a long range transport to pick it up directly from our facility. It will be delivered to Shanghai in a matter of hours. Soon thereafter, Demetek will have completed its very first sales contract, the first of many. Every single one of you should be proud of your achievements, and I thank you for all your efforts in making this happen."

He paused while another round of applause erupted. "We shall be landing to the west and will taxi around to join the Wudong aircraft. After we're all off the plane, I'll ask you to gather in front of Bio 2, that's the one in the middle, where I will hand over the technology package to Wudong's CEO, Mr. Li, in exchange for a check for one hundred million dollars. And that, my friends, is just the down payment. You can look forward to your share in royalties for many years to come."

Everyone in the 737 cheered again. The aircraft was in its final descent, and the captain's voice replaced Strathmore's to announce the imminent arrival. "Please take your seats, ladies, gentlemen, and cabin crew. We'll be on the ground in less than five minutes. Thank you all, and I hope you've enjoyed your flight out to the middle of the desert." His voice was drowned out by the whine of landing gear and flaps lowering. Moments later the 737 made a perfect landing.

George, who was sitting in the backward-facing crew seat, stared out of the starboard window. Three Asian workers were loading grain onto the Wudong transport. A fourth man, dressed immaculately in a dark suit and tie, appeared to be coordinating the effort. He spoke into a walkie-talkie, but there was no one else in sight carrying the other half of the two-way radio.

Then he saw a figure emerging from Bio 2, dressed in a white jumpsuit. He craned his neck, trying to determine whether it was someone familiar. As the figure lowered the walkie-talkie, George got a fleeting glimpse of the face. What he saw was more alarming than anything he'd imagined to this point.

How in God's name, he wondered, could he convey what, or rather *whom*, he'd just seen to the rest of the team without jeopardizing the entire assignment?

The XUSA team approached the airstrip twenty minutes later. They circled the site once at a safe distance, observing the two large aircraft parked side by side on the ground. When confronted with the physical scope of the complex, most of the team were stunned. "Where did they get the cash to build this place, LC?" Brad asked. "Not to mention the labor."

"According to our records, the construction contract was one of Demetek's great outsourcing triumphs," the Englishman said. "All Chinese materials and labor. Contract workers brought in from overseas. Surprisingly, the solar panel systems they installed were not manufactured locally, but in the Guangdong province."

"Makes you wonder why there wasn't much publicity around the project."

"Oh, there was. It was said to be abandoned several years ago when the Australian government declined to subsidize further construction in the area. That's when an additional billion of Demetek's money somehow found its way into the effort. There are so many ways that money can get shifted around the world these days. If you have enough of it, you can buy just about anything you want."

"Including that transport plane you saw yesterday, Joe," Brad remarked. "Looks like they're gathering outside for a love-in."

Josef's satphone rang. The caller ID told him it was George at the other end. He put it on speaker mode so they could all hear, and then asked, "What is the status?"

"You need to get Hernandez isolated as soon as you can. I suggest Matt provide the diversion, as planned. We have to make sure that Marcus is in Bio 3 waiting for him.

"Agreed. We will run the scenario as discussed yesterday. What else?"

"There may be a problem. There's someone else here whom we didn't anticipate. At least, I didn't think we did. It sounds like they're going to conduct a ceremony any second. Strathmore's going to hand over the tech package any moment now, to a Mr. Li, the CEO of Wudong Agritech."

"Mr. Li?" Marcus asked, frowning.

"It is a common name," Josef said, but his response felt empty. The previous day had been instructive; when discovering which operators, both private and military, had purchased Shaanxi Yun-9 aircraft, he'd matched Wudong to the aircraft's call sign printed on its fuselage. The CEO of Wudong was one Hong Li, a man whose namesake had died in Shanghai in his apartment following a robbery.

Or was he the same man? There had been no suspects, the trail had gone cold, according to the limited reports available. But this was China, a land where Western habits and practices were not standard operating procedure across the board. There was now every reason to believe that Professor Hong Li and Wudong's CEO could be the same individual.

"Strathmore is about to introduce Li to everyone. There's a lot of clapping and handshaking going on."

"Good. The more organized everyone is, the more they are focused on the ceremonial aspects. We do not want employees milling about if we can avoid it."

The Gulfstream landed moments later, pulling up to the front of Bio 3, about two hundred meters away from the entrance to Bio 2. On the ground, the domes appeared smaller than the internal camera views had suggested. The cylindrical walkways connecting them were almost opaque. Two parallel shadowy vertical lines, about two meters apart and close to the ends of the corridors, indicated airlock control doors at the internal entrances to each. Each biodome sported an igloo-like entrance at its front, double-wide and sufficient to permit loading equipment to enter.

Matt and Josef stepped out into the bright sunshine. The others stayed inside the aircraft, waiting for the signal to proceed. Strathmore, distracted by the Gulfstream's arrival, looked away from Hong Li at the two men in the distance. Even by squinting, he was unable to identify them visually, but he assumed his chief legal officer was one of them. "Over here, Monty," he called. "We're just about to start.

Matt began to run towards the gathering. Behind them, Brad and Marcus stepped off the Gulfstream. They took up positions behind its front landing gear, obscured from view.

Josef inched towards Bio 3, ready with the access codes he'd downloaded the previous day. As soon as he entered the numbers he heard an audible click and whirr as the outer access port opened slightly. He paused for a second, watching until Matt had reached the periphery of the semicircle of well-oiled employees applauding and cheering. Then he slid inside.

"Ladies and gentlemen!" Strathmore boomed. "It's my great pleasure to welcome you to Demetek West. Our Chinese partners from Wudong Agritech have made the journey to Western Australia to take an exclusive license of D19, our first grain product. I would like to congratulate Wudong's CEO on a purchase that benefits both our organizations. Dr. Hong Li, whose early contributions to this effort were crucial to its successful rollout, would like to say a few words to all of you."

As Strathmore passed the microphone over to his Asian counterpart, Matt Gilstrap edged his way through his former colleagues. A few of them recognized him immediately, greeting him with handshakes and slaps on the back. Apparently they didn't know he'd been gone for the best part of a month.

Hong Li began to speak. "Thank you, Don. Thank you Demetek!"

Cheers and more applause erupted.

"Today is the first day of the end of global starvation," Li continued. "Together, our companies have forged an alliance that will feed the world's hungry millions. Starving citizens of our planet will no longer have to suffer the effects of malnutrition." He paused for effect between each sentence, his reward being a series of hoorays, but was drowned out as he said the last word. Matt took the opportunity to break through the crowd. He approached Strathmore from the side, and tapped him on the shoulder.

"What is it?" the CEO hissed. Now, of all times, he did not want any interruptions.

"It wasn't Goudreau who betrayed you. It was Dayne."

Strathmore whirled around to face his former employee. "You!'

"Come with me. I'll prove it."

"Not now, you bloody idiot! Can't you see we're in the middle of the biggest event in the company's history?"

"The sale is tainted. You have to stop the deal." Matt was following his script perfectly. He had to isolate the man from the rest of his staff.

Strathmore grabbed Matt by the upper arm and marched him back through the crowd. "You'd better explain yourself, Gilstrap. There's a shitload of money tied up in this deal, and I'm not going to fuck it up now." He looked back at Li, who was about to start speaking again. Beside Li stood Justin Hernandez. The Texan was grinning. "I need to alert Justin."

"Later. First you need to listen!" Matt yanked his arm free. "Goudreau warned me that Dayne was planning to sell you out. He's pulled this kind of stunt before. That's why he called me last week. It wasn't anything to do with the grain. It was a rider in the Wudong contract."

"What?"

"Come with me. I've got proof. If you don't believe me, then get over to the jet. Dayne's in there with Mike Baltazzi. Mike needs to talk to you now."

Strathmore's skin lost all its color. He looked to his left. Li was waving a glass of some sort of sparkling beverage in the air. He was shaking hands with Hernandez. "Justin!" the CEO yelled. "We've got a problem."

Hernandez couldn't make out where the sound was coming from. The crowd was rumbling, cheering, clapping again. He looked around, waved like a politician who'd just received his party's nomination, and then looked back at his Wudong partner. Strathmore called out his name again, and this time Justin felt the firm tug on his sleeve. "What do you want?" he asked absently, thinking it was some drunken underling wanting to make a scene.

"Come with me!" Matt implored.

"Gilstrap." Hernandez's nostrils flared. His upper lip pulled back from his teeth.

"You and Don need to come with me. You can stop the deal but you have to hear me out. It's Dayne. He's screwed everyone." *Not entirely untrue.*

Strathmore and Hernandez pushed their way through the layers of staff. Brad and Marcus circled around behind them, forming a barrier between the two executives and their employees. Neither exec looked back at the crowd. Both broke into a brisk run towards the Gulfstream.

Strathmore was the first to reach the corporate jet. He bounded up the steps into the cabin and yelled. "Mike! Monty! What's going on!" He momentarily ignored the interior's unfamiliar layout. In his hurry, he was so distracted that he failed to look out for the chop applied to the back of his neck, felling him instantly.

Larry Claypool dragged Strathmore to the back of the cabin, where he stuffed a white handkerchief into the man's mouth before rolling him onto his belly. He tied Strathmore's hands behind his back using his own tie. Good use for the thing, he thought. LC felt that it was getting a little warm to be wearing formal attire without the Gulfstream's air conditioning system on, and he was glad he'd taken his jacket off as well. The tweed garment hung over one of the luxury leather chairs.

Justin Hernandez was almost at the Gulfstream's door when Brad and

Marcus rushed him. Each took an arm and twisted it behind his back. "In there," Marcus ordered, pulling the chief scientist towards Bio 3's airlock. From the inside, Josef pulled the outer door open, waiting for his comrades to frog-march their captive through. As soon as all four of them were inside, Josef closed the airlock fully.

"Who the hell are you people?" Hernandez demanded, looking at the three who had accosted him. "I demand to know what this is about!"

"I think you had better open this up and explain what is inside," Josef said, his voice an authoritative calm. "But before you do, you should know that yesterday we spent a good few hours examining the data from Bio 1 and Bio 2. The video feeds were most instructive, but not as much as the protein and structural data. I'm sure you are well aware of what we're talking about."

"I don't know what you mean. And what the hell do you think you are doing here? This is a private function, on private property. How did you...."

"Get here?" Brad asked. "I think you'll have to ask your lawyer that. If you can get to him before your own head of security has his head on a platter. Oh, do forgive me. My name's Bradford King. Director of Special Projects, XUSA Corporation. The guy on my right is Josef Rintlen. He is *our* VP of Security. Don't mess with him, and don't mess with me. If you cooperate with us, you may just come out of this in one piece. Fail, and I can't guarantee anything at all."

"Screw you." Hernandez sneered at Brad, then at Josef, and then at the third intruder. "And you."

Marcus Black felt like he had been waiting his whole life for just this moment. "Open the door, Hernandez."

"No."

Marcus sprang forward and shoved a forearm under Justin's chin, knocking him backwards. His head made a muffled *thunk* sound against the slightly padded interior, dazing him. Marcus then pulled back and kicked Hernandez as hard as he could, right in the groin, causing the Demetek man to double over in pain.

"Goddamn you!" Hernandez growled. "You're not going to get anything –"

Another punch landed, this time in the kidney. "Get up!" Marcus yelled. "Josef can punch in the codes, but I think we'll be using YOUR retina this time." He yanked Hernandez upright. Placing a hand behind Justin's head, he jammed the man's chin on the sconce above the security panel. Josef obligingly entered the codes and waited. A few seconds passed, and the light flashed green. The release of pressure accompanied the sound of Bio 3's inner door opening. Marcus jerked Hernandez's head away from the sconce and shoved him through the inner door, before following him inside. The others stayed in the airlock, waiting.

The time was almost upon them. Brad gritted his teeth. Josef reached out and placed a heavy hand on his old friend's shoulder. "It must happen this way, Bradford. I am sorry. At least he will finally learn the truth."

The president of Wudong Agritech waved goodbye to his Australian partners. Hong Li entered the interior of the Shanghai-bound transport through the rear access ramp for the trip home. Before he disappeared, Li turned and waved to everyone, eliciting yet another cheer. In his peripheral vision, George could have sworn he saw the shadow of a figure traversing the corridor between Bio 2 and Bio 3, but he was momentarily distracted by the sound of the Yun-9's rear door closing shut. He hadn't realized that the loader and every last sack of grain were already aboard.

The 737's captain picked up the microphone and made an announcement. "Ladies and gentlemen, I need to ask you to board the aircraft now. Safety regulations require that everyone be completely clear of the backdraft of departing aircraft, and as you can see, your friends' transport is about to fire up its props. So, quick as you can, let's get back on board, and we'll have you back to Alice in a couple of hours."

One by one, the Demetek employees obediently climbed the 737's boarding stairs. Even the most lubricated and rowdy staffers complied. Two of the cabin crew members were about to follow but stopped half way up the stairs. One of them signaled George. "Mate, where's the boss?"

"He'll be flying back on the corporate jet," George lied. "Mr. Strathmore asked me to pass that on to the captain. Oh, and I'll be going back with them too."

"What about the other guy?"

"Dr. Hernandez?"

"He the dark haired bloke in the fancy suit?"

"He's the one. I'll go check on him. He's over with Mr. Strathmore. I'm guessing he'll be coming back with us too, so you probably don't need to wait. If you don't see him in five minutes or so, just go." George hoped he'd given them enough time. If it wasn't long enough, there was going to be one doozy of a problem if they couldn't alert the appropriate air traffic control people.

The inner door to Bio 3 stayed ajar long enough for Brad to wedge it open with his foot. He reached into his pocket and withdrew the ice pick, not bothering to unsheathe it, and used it to keep the door from closing completely. Then he allowed himself a glance inside.

Marcus Black was standing in front of him, facing inward. Hernandez was on the ground, breathing hard. He was lying on something matted and green.

Grass, Marcus thought. *Nothing but grass, rich, tall, green, green, grass.*

Bio 3 was the testing ground for the ultimate rubisco variant. They had introduced the mutant into the commonest of all plants. Underneath its architect lay a bed of a supergrass, capable of changing the balance of oxygen and carbon dioxide in the atmosphere. The supergrass would not only help cool the planet, so the theory went, but would thrive under the harshest conditions. It was the ultimate triumph for agricultural biotechnology.

Only it wasn't a triumph, he knew. It was that other great impostor, disaster. That was what they had tested in Bio 1 in primates. They'd modified the DNA of jungle plants using the new rubisco and had fed the animals a diet containing mutated plant food. The chimp had gone berserk, or maybe it was the howler. Either way, it didn't matter. The rubisco was now dominant, and it would spread until every living creature on the planet consumed it. The wheat in Bio 2 was the first staple foodstuff, but it was to be carefully controlled. Not so the wild fescue of the third biodome. It would start somewhere, and cover the entire planet. How soon this would happen, he couldn't imagine, but he knew that unless it was destroyed, here and now, it would enter the food chain and slowly devastate everything it touched.

Just like it had killed his wife from the inside out, thanks to this scumbag beneath him.

On the ground, Justin Hernandez started to struggle to his feet. Marcus shoved a foot in his back and pushed him down again. Then he kicked him hard in the ribs. Hernandez howled in pain, clutching his side. Slowly, he twisted around onto his knees. He looked up at his attacker, and then broke into a sardonic laugh.

"You stupid, stupid idiot, Black!"

What? How do you.... Marcus looked at the Texan, his handsome face twisted into a snarl. "You know my name."

"Hell, yeah! I've known about you for a long time! You poor sucker, I almost feel sorry for you!" He raised himself upright.

"What the hell are you talking about?"

"You don't have a goddamned clue. Not a one!" He started to guffaw.

Marcus pulled back his fist and launched a right hook as hard as he could into the side of Hernandez's jaw.

Chapter 48

HERNANDEZ SAGGED, REELING FROM the blow. Marcus laid into him with heavy punches, pounding mercilessly. Around them, an artificial breeze made the supergrass sway gently in waves of green, the combat lending an incongruous disturbance to the artificial field. Hernandez instinctively raised his hands over his head to protect his face, but in doing so left his groin exposed.

Marcus nailed him again with a kick that would have made an NFL punter proud. The taller man collapsed instantly, his breath and essence taken from him.

"You – killed – every – thing – I – loved!" Marcus screamed, stomping on Hernandez's body with every syllable. At last he stopped, and sank to his knees beside the other man, hoping that Hernandez was still sufficiently lucid to feel the pain he'd just inflicted.

Hernandez was still breathing, albeit in shallow gasps. His eyes were closed in agony, and his face was screwed up in a defiant scowl. Both hands clutched at the area between his legs, where a stain was beginning to develop. Marcus didn't know yet whether it was urine or blood, and he didn't care, just as long as the man was in pain. He dealt Hernandez one final boot in the kidney area. The kick held all the hate, all the grief, all the pain he'd carried for the past months. "That was for Kay, you son of a bitch!" Marcus yelled, panting. Then and only then did he stop.

He turned away and began to wade through the supergrass, blades of green powerful enough to change the world. It wasn't just fields of wheat or other grains. Demetek was planning to seed the world with the supergrass, grass that could eliminate, even reverse, the effects of greenhouse gases on global warming.

At the possible cost of all human life.

He turned back to see its architect, its God-playing designer struggle again to rise. "Marcus!" Hernandez hissed out his name. "You don't know!"

"I know enough!" Marcus spat.

"Solkar didn't kill Samaya. She didn't die."

"You're pathetic. We know all that."

"Do you know who really died that day?"

"They never identified her."

"That's right. They never had to. Her mother saw the missing toe. Pretty clever, wasn't it. Same trick they pulled on you."

Marcus stopped, frozen in his tracks. "What do you mean?"

"Dental records. Not too hard to fake them if you get the right set of X-rays in to the right database. All you need is someone powerful enough to pull it off."

"You're full of it."

"Am I? Samaya's still alive. Maybe she's not the only one."

What? He turned around and faced Hernandez. The man had pissed himself, and he felt a tinge of regret that he perhaps hadn't done enough damage. Yet this fleeting realization was replaced by new questions in his mind. What did he mean? His brain reeled as he tried to put it all together, but he was unable to connect the dots. Hernandez could have known about the doses, the custom preparations that had planted the fateful DNA-altering strands germinating many years hence. But what else did he know?

He approached Hernandez again, and then it dawned on him. *He's bluffing. He wants an insurance policy. Just a little one, but enough to save his life.* "Talk to me," he ordered.

Hernandez shook his head. "You think Samaya and I cooked all of this up, Marcus? You don't know a damn thing!"

"I know what I saw," Marcus countered, but his voice, along with his conviction, was growing weaker. "I also knew my wife."

"Not as well as Eddie Solkar knew his daughter," Hernandez wheezed. "Oh, she was a star! A prodigy, a visionary! Man, was she brilliant!" His tone was almost reverent, yet almost taunting. "It was her idea, Marcus. All this." He waved his hands around at the supergrass. "*She* was Persephone. Demeter's daughter, if not by blood, then by shared belief. Lynne Brady, the mother of Demeter Advanced Technologies, and her brilliant protégé, Kendall 'Kay' Rasmussen. She ventured deep into the underworld, and came back to change the world forever."

Marcus said nothing. His mind was in a tailspin.

"Awareness," Hernandez said.

"What?"

"Heightened awareness. Of everything she saw, everything she felt. As if she now knew all the answers. Like a hundred point jump in IQ along with the ability to put all her knowledge into practice, a superintelligence. But the price she had to pay for her brilliance was so, so dear. She could only control it with medication, and only for so long. Her time finally ran out."

The early animal tests. The rodents, then the higher species. And then, the complete breakdown, the horror of knowing too much. "When? When did she design this, Hernandez?"

"Long before she ever met you, Marcus. If it's any consolation, you're probably the only person on the planet who could lay claim to being a victim, albeit of deception. Perhaps one of two people, on second thought."

Surely not? Who was he talking about? "Solkar?"

"Poor bastard. Goes to jail for a crime his daughter committed. You know, I kind of liked Eddie. You have to admire a guy who'd take the rap for something like that. Maybe that's why Kay went underground, in a different sense. It was tied up oh, so neatly, what with Samaya's so-called death, her old man inside, and a new life with a sucker for a husband out west. Did she ever tell you about that Javier guy?"

A few times, Marcus recalled. The one she supposedly lived with after moving to California. "As if I'd care? You going to tell me he didn't really exist?"

"Sorry, pal. No such guy. She had you hook, line, and sinker."

Say you're not a sociopath, please. You're not a sociopath, please. Why? Why utter something like that unless it was in total fun, which was the only conclusion he'd had at the time. That flash of something distant he'd seen, or imagined, had it been real? "Why me?"

"Why you?" Despite the pain coursing through his body, Hernandez almost laughed. "This was never about you! You're just a poor sap who got caught up in an ambitious experiment careening out of control. You, Doctor Black, are just an unlucky bastard in the wrong place at the wrong time. It almost worked, except for one stupid little detail that no one could have predicted!"

"The genetic test," Marcus said softly. "Chromosomes twenty-one and fifteen."

"You carried an incompatible SNP, which you discovered during all those visits to the doctor when you found you couldn't have kids. Your children were supposed to be the guinea pigs."

Marcus suddenly felt ice run through his veins. *Children?* "Guinea pigs? I don't understand. What are you saying?"

"She set you up. It was supposed to be the Grays, but Sally was already pregnant with Megan. She needed another subject. One whom she could control. Someone she could deliver a compatible chimeric RNA strain into, someone she could breed with."

"Dose? Breed? This is bullshit! What the hell is this crap about?"

Hernandez took as deep a breath as he could. He felt a sharp pain in his side. Possibly a cracked rib, internal injuries? Maybe both, but it no longer mattered. The time had come, his time, *her* time. "She dosed you with your own customized hybrid RNA eight years ago."

"That's pure horseshit, Hernandez. I'd have known about that. It's not easy to give someone a shot without them being totally drunk or unconscious. I'm not exactly a heavy sleeper."

"Transdermal delivery. Remember the massages?" He was tempted to say the word "foreplay" as well but resisted the urge.

Back rubs. Aromatherapy. Something in the essential oils? Could it have been that simple? Marcus's jaw dropped. "No. I don't believe you."

A faint click sounded ten feet away from them, followed by the slow opening of the aperture. Hernandez's eyes flicked towards it, but Marcus was too busy absorbing this latest revelation to notice. A moment later, a figure appeared in the open airlock, holding one hand up in a gesture that said "enough."

"It's true, Marcus," said a female voice.

The figure entered Bio 3. Grass swayed about the diminutive frame as if in homage paid to its creator.

A single word stuck in Marcus Black's throat. Or maybe it was a letter.

Chapter 49

"I'm sorry," Kendall Rasmussen said.

She held out her arms to him. But she wasn't *his* Kay any more. This was someone else, a distant shadow of everything he thought he believed. An insane, swirling aura of darkness seemed to surround her as she moved towards him. "All this is for the good of the earth, for the human race. It's bigger than any of us."

Marcus backed away from the woman he'd loved beyond all compare, and then he understood. He understood everything. He felt complete despair rise within him all over again, magnified tenfold. Only this time, he saw the absolute betrayal by the woman to whom he'd given his heart. He saw how her insanity had driven her to destroy everything and everyone around her. And most of all, he understood the pain Edmund Solkar had felt, and the price he'd paid, because he'd loved his daughter.

"Lightning always strikes twice," Hernandez said, inching his way towards Kay. "Isn't that right, Kay? You and Samaya set up your father after he caught us together. Easy enough to fake the body using a cadaver of similar build to Samaya. Which one of you snapped off the toe? Was it you, or she? It doesn't really matter in the end, does it? Because you used the exact same MO this time around. Burned body, identifiable by a close family member. But this time you made a little mistake, didn't you?" Hernandez looked back at Marcus, who was staring in utter disbelief.

Kay reached behind her. Neither man saw the weapon as she whipped it out and pointed it first at Marcus, then at Hernandez.

"What are you doing?" Hernandez called out. "We built this! All of this!"

"This doesn't matter any more, Justin. The harvest is complete. We have what we needed," Kay announced.

It had all distilled down to this. A few seeds. All the years' work, all the advances in sequencing, molecular biology, protein engineering, all the automation, it came down to a few damned seeds. People had died so they could sprout. Would the supergrains and the supergrass make the world a better place? Would they feed starving millions? What would become of the species, animal or human, that ate this wonder of modern biotechnology? Would they go berserk like the chimp? Would the effects be delayed and unpredictable, causing a latent insanity similar to Kay's symptoms? Would others, like Strathmore and himself had done, sell their souls to see the research commercialized? Would they murder all the obstacles that got in their way?

All for a few seeds.

No, it wasn't all for a few seeds. It was the money, pure and simple. He'd helped kill all those people to protect his profit. A Scottish physician and his innocent ex-wife, who was probably trying to cure genuine diseases through legitimate, well-meaning research. The Grays. Their beautiful, talented daughter, all swiftly eliminated just because they got in the way.

Kay tilted her head to the side. She aimed the weapon back and forth between Hernandez and Marcus. Her finger whitened on the trigger as she took aim.

Marcus leaped. He flew at her, no longer caring about his own safety. As they toppled backwards, the gun flew out of her hand. He pinned her on the ground, the supergrass swishing about her exquisite face. Pure adrenaline drove him as he planted a knee on each shoulder. She bucked and twisted, trying to break free.

In spite of everything he had just heard, how his entire world had been eviscerated and replaced with this dreadful reality, part of him wanted, no, *needed* to calm this storm, to settle Kay, to talk to her, to discover the final truth of what she had done. He wrapped his arms around her in a giant bear hug, and squeezed.

Kay's body slowed at last as the breath was pressed out of her. Her strength slowly ebbed, her flailing limbs became limp, and the fire behind her eyes cooled.

She whispered in his ear. "I'm sorry. It was the only way. I couldn't tell you. You would never have forgiven me for what I did."

He let go of her. She slumped, unconscious. He felt for a pulse. There was a thready, uneven beat to it. He climbed off her and got to his feet.

"Marco," a firm, calm voice said. "We knew about Kay. She told us everything."

Hernandez and Marcus looked up at Brad King. Josef held Kay's gun, pointed at the ground.

"It took several weeks for DNA confirmation, but the forensics laboratory in San Francisco proved that the body recovered from Kay's car was not hers."

"You – you knew? Why didn't you tell me?"

It was the moment Brad had been dreading for months, ever since the day Larry Claypool had informed him and Josef about their assignment. "We only had a few weeks to finish this operation. The timing had to be perfect."

"What are you talking about? What assignment, operation, whatever you want to call it? What timing?"

"Marco, you're dying. You have a few months left at most. No more."

Marcus Black's mouth gaped. "I – I – what do you mean?"

"You're the last cohort in the human trial, Marcus," Hernandez said. "You poor, stupid, ignorant prick! You were the key to everything."

Josef drew closer. "It is true, Marcus. You and Kay were genetically modified to give these people an indication of the potential mutagenicity of their agricultural products in higher species, but you were unable to produce children. We needed De Silva's proof of her intent. The data was embedded in the disks you found last week."

Kay wheezed on the ground. Her shallow breathing grew labored. Marcus looked at the woman he'd loved, the wife whom he'd lost not only once, but now twice. The woman who had signed his own death sentence lay at his feet, her life force ebbing away. Who, what was she? A freak of nature? A murderer? And what about himself? What had he evolved into over the course of this desperate atrocity?

"The side effects of this technology are dangerous beyond compare. We had to stop it from being released, but we also had to know exactly what we were dealing with."

Marcus thought about what his XUSA colleague was saying. *We are corporate spies.* "You wanted it for yourself."

"Not for the same reasons," Brad clarified. "We don't want to make money from it. We don't want it released. But yes, we want to know what it is so we can deal with it and ensure it never reaches the general population."

"There's an aircraft flying to Shanghai with a belly full of supergrain," Hernandez bragged. "Try stopping that!"

"The Australian Air Force has been alerted," Josef said. "The Yun-9 will never be allowed to enter international air space. It will be forced to land in a remote area where the contents of its cargo hold can be destroyed."

"No!" Hernandez winced as he began to run at Josef Rintlen. "You can't do that!"

Crack! A single shot exploded out of the gun, hitting Hernandez in the thigh. He collapsed to the ground, clutching his bleeding leg. His face was twisted into rage as he spat out his words. "You'll never stop her!"

Brad looked at Josef. "What did he say?"

"I think he was referring to Samaya. I believe that issue has been taken care of, thanks to Professor Solkar." He spoke slowly and loudly enough for Hernandez to hear.

"Solkar?" Hernandez hissed.

"Yes." The German nodded solemnly. "Your old friend has been very helpful to us, in spite of your attempts to ensure his silence. That you would go so far as to frame him for murder and convince him his own daughter was responsible for killing his lover is only the prologue of your litany of sins. You knew that no one would believe him, that he would be labeled insane himself. Very clever, but you failed to account for one small detail." He raised the weapon and pointed it at Hernandez's heart.

Marcus jumped at Josef. He took the older man by surprise, grabbing the weapon from his fingers. "No! This is my battle." He shoved Josef aside and aimed. His finger whitened as it tightened on the trigger.

"Stop it, Marco," Brad coaxed. "Give Josef the gun. Or me. Just don't do this to yourself. Not now. You have so little time. You need to go home, take Kay home. Enjoy your last days together. Give her the chance to make peace with her father. She owes him that."

"She's as bad as that bastard there on the ground," Marcus yelled. "They all used me! YOU all used me!"

"But you can still end this. You can forgive," Brad begged. "Do you want to lose your soul like Hernandez?" He took a deep breath. "You can still walk away."

King's words churned in Marcus's head. Before him lay the architects of his own shattered life, and so much more. He, Dr. Marcus Black, had the means to end it all right there and then, and yet his friend was imploring him to walk away, to avoid further hatred.

"How can I walk away? This is my body, my life!" He steadied the weapon.

"Talk to me, Marco. We can work through it."

"No, Brad. This is something I have to do. It ends here and now." He pointed the weapon at his friend. "Get out. Go. Go home to Dutch."

"Marco, please!"

"No." He turned away and squeezed the trigger.

A red hole opened up in Justin Hernandez's forehead. The back of his head exploded, the crimson and gray spray polluting the rich green of Bio 3's supergrass.

Brad looked at the unconscious woman on the ground. Kay had been his friend too, and he felt no small pang of remorse as he abandoned her to her fate. He turned away and left, closing the door behind him.

Marcus knelt by his wife and took her hand. He said her name, over and over. She did not respond to his touch or the sound of his voice. He yelled, shaking her, begging her to register some kind of response, but without success. At last, he fell beside her, exhausted.

Above them the artificial azure sky remained cloudless and bright. The sward swished about them, a strange peace beginning to take hold. After all the heartache, after all the uncertainty of the past months, Marcus felt as though he finally knew. He began to breathe, in and out, inhaling the oxygen-enriched air provided by the supergrass.

Time passed. He wasn't sure how much, but it couldn't have been more than a few minutes. He felt a hand slip into his and squeeze, ever so gently. *Kay?*

Slowly, he turned his head to the side. Her breathing had become steady, her chest rising and falling peacefully.

He said her name again. This time she turned towards him and whispered something, barely audible. He inched towards her, trying to hear. "Talk to me!"

"With my life," she repeated. "I trust him with my life, as I trust you with my death."

What? "Who are you talking to?"

She exhaled. "I never meant to hurt you, my love."

It was too late for that, but Marcus felt he had little to lose. "Is it true? Am I dying?"

"Like me. It will start soon."

Oh, Jesus, he thought. *Not that way. Not the nightmares, the depression, the slow descent into hell.* "Can I stop it?"

"No." Kay's voice sounded a little stronger. "It's what will happen if the supergrass ever finds its way into the natural environment."

"And it's in me now?"

"It's in your DNA. It's in mine too."

"What can we do?"

"You have to stop Samaya." Kay closed her eyes, her breathing shallow again.

Marcus sat up. He hoisted his wife to a sitting position, tilting her face up to him. "She's dead, my love. Your father killed her."

Tears began to flow from Kendall Rasmussen's closed eyes. "With my life," she repeated. "With all our lives. I trust him with my life, as I trust you with my death."

He held her close as she wept for the last time.

Outside the biodome, Bradford King heard a single, muffled shot. A few seconds later, he heard another.

Chapter 50

"WE STILL HAVE WORK to do," Josef declared. "We cannot leave until we have destroyed the contents of the biodomes." To their right stood the three hemispherical monuments to Demetek's journey into uncharted science. "There is a jet fuel reservoir to our right. We are fully refueled to leave, but there is plenty left that we can use to set this evil place alight. If anyone would like to help me, I would greatly appreciate it."

It took them the best part of an hour, but the smoldering embers of the contents of biodome number three signaled their job was done. Josef Rintlen took on the grim task of torching Bio 3, ensuring that not a single seed could be allowed to survive. When he had finished, he methodically moved onto the others. Only then did anyone else volunteer to pitch in.

The sun was beginning to set to the west, bathing the desert in a glorious red glow. Brad looked at Josef, wondering how the man he'd known for a quarter of a century managed to live with himself. It was hard enough for Brad sometimes.

Larry "LC" Claypool, CEO of XUSA, laid a hand on King's shoulder as if to read his thoughts. "Sorry, pal."

"Yeah."

"Far greater men than he would never overcome a shock like that."

"We used them."

"It's what we do. It's how we keep technology in the right hands, not the wrong ones."

"A dozen people died for all of this."

"Better than billions."

Too right. "You know, LC, I've worked with you much of my adult life, one way or another, but I've always respected you. I just didn't think that you had any of *your* father in you."

"We all have a bit of our fathers in us, Bradford. Good and bad. It's up to us to make sure that we don't overdo it with the bad bits, and that we make the best of the good traits we inherit."

Brad shook his head. "I don't suppose I should tell Fiona about your little meeting with Kay, should I?"

"Best not, old chap." LC gave his friend another pat on the shoulder.

Josef, George, and Matt wandered over to join them. "What on earth happened in there, guys?" Matt wanted to know.

"I think we're going to have a long conversation on the way home," George surmised.

"Just tell me one thing, Mr. Claypool. Please."

"Fire away, Matthew."

"Was Steve Goudreau part of this? Whose side was he on?"

"His blood is on my hands. He was my responsibility. Etienne was on our advisory board a few years back. He contacted me a little over a year ago after discovering a file buried deep in Lynne Brady's archives. In that file were the names of Professor Brady's coworkers from Chicago and some notes on a project code-named 'Persephone.' He didn't know what the project represented but there was something in the file that alarmed him. A note from Lynne to Kay, scribbled on a Post-it of all things."

Everyone waited for the punch line.

"It said this: 'The host must be fit and young. When you find him, do whatever you must to ensure you can continue the experiment.'"

"Did he know? Marcus, I mean?" Matt asked.

"I believe he did. At the end." LC fixed his eyes on Bio 3. "We arranged for Kay to disappear. We spirited her to Shanghai so she could keep an eye on Wudong Agritech and report back to us. In the end she wanted to atone for everything she had done, including letting her innocent father suffer. Marcus's role was more complicated. We knew he would only cooperate if he believed he was uncovering the reasons for Kay's so-called suicide."

"Seems a bit much to swallow."

"You have to remember what we do. Sometimes we have to make difficult choices, Matthew. Choices that affect the way others would see us, but choices that are ultimately the lesser of two or more evils." Lawrence Claypool headed up the Gulfstream's stairs.

Don Strathmore was propped against a bulkhead. He had regained consciousness but not his composure. Enraged, he struggled against the gag in his mouth and the ties that bound him.

LC ripped the gag from his face. "Mr. Strathmore. How are you today?"

"Go to hell, Claypool."

"As you wish. He reattached the gag. "I think we'll be turning you over to the police."

Matt turned to Josef and Brad. "Is this the way you guys always operate?"

"If we have to. We do what we must," XUSA's security chief confessed. "As our leader suggests, we must make some difficult choices on occasion."

"If it's of any comfort to you, there was no other path we could go down," Brad added. "Solkar was the key. Only he could tell us what happened in Chicago. They were onto him, methodically wiping out all the witnesses, one by one."

"Did they find everyone? Everyone else, I mean?"

"We'll never know. But it doesn't matter any more. They can't unleash this on anyone." Brad pointed to the smoke billowing out of Bio 3.

George recalled the figure he had seen wearing the white jumpsuit, talking to the Asian operative. He remembered having seen the picture Solkar had shown him of the younger version of Samaya Jonas. While he'd only briefly seen the face, the bulge in her forearm stood out. Possibly a bandage or a cast? Solkar said he'd snapped her wrist. Still, in all the confusion, he didn't recollect if the woman with the shoulder length, darkish blonde hair had climbed aboard the Yun-9.

She must have, he concluded. They had swept the biodomes for any remaining persons. George allowed himself a nod of satisfaction, assured the authorities would certainly be able to take care of her the moment the Chinese aircraft landed.

"Come on," he said to Matt. "I think you and I are going to be the future of this company once these other old geezers retire." The two younger men climbed the aircraft's steps without looking back.

"You know," Josef Rintlen remarked with a rare chuckle. "Even a defense lawyer as good as Michelle Durant would not be able to obtain a verdict of justifiable homicide with a body count that high."

Brad allowed himself a rueful smile. "They'll never find their bodies out here, even if anyone finds out what happened."

"What happens in Vegas stays in Vegas," Josef's uncharacteristically dark humor continued.

"Sure. Vegas. A city in the middle of the desert."

"What do you call this?"

"Right now, gentlemen," Brad said, "it's just another friggin' desert. And I don't think I'll be coming back."

"No," LC echoed. "It's time to go home."

Epilogue

Morag MacCallum opened the door after the doorbell rang for a third time. While it was still late summer, the long days, with more than average sunshine for the year, had not drawn her outside as much as in previous seasons. Ian's death, the absence of fresh Scottish air, and the lack of sleep had aged her more in the last few months than the previous three years had done. Her skin, once glowingly ruddy, was now ashen.

The figure standing in the doorway, clad in blue jeans and a sweatshirt with the words "Minnesota Golden Gophers" on the front, greeted her without a smile. Ice-blue eyes stared unblinkingly. "Hello, Morag. I don't know if you remember me. I'm from Dr. Wylie's office." She spoke with a Scottish accent.

Morag frowned. The kind young physician hadn't contacted her in months. She'd been told about some kind of leave of absence. His temporary replacement, a Dr. Adil Mahmood, a thirtyish son of Pakistani immigrants, spoke with a thick Yorkshire accent, and was finding it difficult to settle in. Dr. Mahmood was as good a doctor as Dr. Wylie, and while he tried hard to become part of the community, he was forced to face a xenophobia he had never anticipated while growing up in Leeds. "Don't you mean Dr. Mahmood?"

"No, I mean Dr. Wylie." Morag's visitor squeezed past the old woman and entered the old farmhouse. Her right forearm sported a bandage from hand to elbow. She held a small sealed plastic baggie in her left hand. From what Morag could tell, it contained about a quarter of a pound of seeds. They looked a bit like grass.

"Excuse me, I didn't invite you in," Morag protested. Then it all hit home. "You! I remember you!"

Samaya Jonas smiled thinly. She pulled a small handgun from the back of her jeans and pointed it directly at Morag's face. "Really?"

For the first time in months, Morag felt a new energy coursing through her. "It was you, wasn't it? You're the one who killed my husband. You and that evil, evil man!"

"I came to finish what we started, Mrs. MacCallum," Samaya said, all traces of her Scottish accent gone. "You see these?" She held up the baggie.

"What do you have there?"

"Oh, I think you know what they are, dear Morag."

"Seeds."

"That's right. Seeds. Demeter made the earth barren, until Persephone returned from Hades' domain with seeds."

"There's nothing barren about the earth. You're out of your mind."

"There's nothing wrong with my mind, old woman. Now get out of the house and go to the barn!" Samaya waved the handgun towards the front door. "Now!"

Morag stood her ground.

"NOW!" Samaya swung the handgun through the air and clobbered Morag on the shoulder, causing her to stumble towards the kitchen. "WRONG WAY!" she screeched, darting behind Morag and shoving her back through the living room.

The door was still ajar. Morag lurched towards it, clutching her injured collarbone and crying out in pain. She hit the door hard, causing it to slam shut.

"Open it and get out!" Samaya fired a shot into the ceiling. Plaster and splinters of wood tumbled around them. The noise was deafening, drowning out Morag's howls of terror.

Morag scrabbled at the handle. Eventually she was able to yank it back open. She careened out into the yard.

"Now show me where your husband's records are hidden!" Samaya ordered.

"They were in the barn. But they're all – all gone," Morag whimpered. "Dr. Wylie took them."

"Then you'll die with or without them," Samaya declared. "And then I will disappear again. With one final legacy," she said, holding up the baggie.

"What are you going to do with those?"

"I think this would be the perfect part of the world to introduce the new supergrass into the food chain. Unpopulated, well hydrated. Grass grows well in this part of the world, does it not?"

Morag froze. Her shoulder pain was so intense she feared an imminent heart attack. "A man called King warned me about this! You can't let those seeds loose!"

"Can't I? Just watch me! On second thoughts, maybe I'll spare you that much. You don't have to see me sow them." She aimed the gun at Morag's head.

Morag covered her face with her hands. In doing so, she was unable to see the black and white flash exploding from behind Samaya. A shot rang out, but the bullet pinged off the stone farmhouse. A split second later, the gun was airborne. Shocked but unwounded, Morag dropped her hands to see a snarling, shaking mass. Its bared, bloody teeth tore at Samaya's left arm. The woman was shrieking, flailing, and kicking, but Charlie held on.

Samaya dropped the bag of seeds and began punching the border collie's head, trying to loosen his grip. "Get OFF!"

Something snorted behind Morag. She looked behind her to see an enormous figure, breathing heavily. She dodged aside and cowered. Samaya wrapped her left arm under the dog's body and gave one more almighty heave, sending Charlie flying through the air. He landed awkwardly, yelped, and then limped towards the old woman.

"Good boy, Charlie," Morag cried. "Good boy, what a wonderful boy you are." She held him as he fell down by her side, panting. He looked up at Morag, who gently stroked his head.

Samaya ignored the bloody mess that was her left hand and ran for the gun. Just before she reached it, a sledgehammer blow knocked her clean off her feet. The old shire horse, Tom, reared up and planted an enormous hoof squarely in her back. She fell prone, breathless. Tom's other front hoof came down on her with all his weight behind it, crushing her spine and rib cage.

At last, the life was squeezed out of Samaya Jonas, by two loyal animals protecting their guardian.

It took Morag almost a full hour to recover and do what she had to. The fire burned bright, turning the bag of seeds into ashes. Then, as the sun set over the Isle of Skye, she took the cinders and scattered them to the wind.

One month later

In the prison hospital bed lay a tall African-American, hooked up to an intravenous drip on one side, to a heart monitor on the other. His pulse was a steady seventy-six beats per minute, his blood pressure a slightly elevated 160/95. Given the man's physical size, his cardiovascular health should have been substantially worse. During the last six months, however, Cleveland Lambert, otherwise known as the Lamb, had lost almost a hundred pounds, and now only weighed 210. His chart recorded the daily cocktail of drugs he'd been forced to take. Periodic readings of his antibody levels occupied additional columns in the ten-page table of data. Regardless of the doses of protease inhibitors and reverse transcriptase inhibitors doctors had given him, despite all the medication changes he had endured, his titers were increasing. His CD4 cell counts were going down accordingly.

"No more," he'd told them one day, after a newly marketed me-too drug found its way into his system only to cause a particularly unpleasant side reaction. "I'm here for life, however long it lasts, but I don't want it to last like this."

That was three months ago. Since that time, his health had declined rapidly. His immune system was shutting down and his body was wasting away like so many before him had experienced.

A male nurse entered the ward and walked over to the Lamb's sickbed, obscured from its neighbor by a hospital-green curtain. "Cleve, you have a visitor."

The Lamb looked up. "Who'd want to come see me?"

"I would," a woman's voice said. She pushed the curtain aside. "Hello, Pops."

"Lydie!" The prisoner's eyes grew misty. Tears began to flow down his dark, hollow cheeks. It was the first time the Lamb had seen his daughter since the day of his sentence, two decades earlier. How she had changed, how beautiful she had become!

"Can you give us some time, please?" Lydia Jackson asked the nurse, flashing him a set of brilliant white teeth.

"Take all the time you need. He ain't goin' anywhere."

Oh, yes, he is, Lydia thought. She sat at her father's bedside and took his hand. "Eddie sent me," she whispered.

The Lamb's eyes narrowed. "He kept his promise."

"He told me what you did for him. He also told me what you've done for others. He said you accepted Jesus into your life and have been finding redemption ever since."

"I killed that man, Lydie," he replied. "There's no excuse for what I did."

"Maybe not," his daughter said. "There's something you don't know. Something the police never told you." She opened her purse, which had been inspected by the guards twice: first on the way into the maximum security facility itself, and then before she entered the ward. Untroubled by the intrusion, she showed little concern as she presented her father with a letter addressed to the Illinois State parole board. It was written by a Lieutenant Martha Silvey of the Naperville Police. It described how a report delivered by a Detective Sergeant Jason Lubowicz, now deceased, was discovered in a safety deposit box in St. Petersburg. The report pertained to an investigation conducted over twenty years earlier into police corruption in the South

Chicago precinct where Lubowicz was once stationed. Among the items uncovered included falsified forensic evidence implicating Lambert in the death of one Guillermo Sandoval.

The Lamb read the letter twice before handing it back. "I killed Sandoval."

"Maybe not, Pops," his daughter said. "The evidence in question had to do with how Sandoval died. The medical examiner at the time stated that he may have bled to death from a stab wound to his leg, one which severed his femoral artery. The district attorney persuaded the medical examiner to testify that the knife wound *was* the actual cause."

"Tell me something I don't know," the Lamb said, turning away.

"Someone shot him in the chest two hours later. They couldn't rule it out as a cause of death, because it happened two hours after you confessed to stabbing Sandoval."

He faced her again. "Why'd this never come up at my trial? Why now?"

"Ballistics on the bullet found in Sandoval's body connected it with an organized crime syndicate. Sandoval was just a bit player, a runner who picked the wrong guy to skim the takings. The D.A. didn't care about him and they sure didn't care about you. They wanted the guy at the top. For that they needed the cooperation of the man who shot Sandoval. The only way they could flip him was to make sure he was immune from prosecution. So they made sure the ME only testified to the knife wound."

The Lamb looked at Lydia, deep in thought. At last he asked her, "What next?"

She squeezed his hand. "Pops, they're going to reopen the case. This new evidence is going to get you out of here."

And then what, he wondered. "I'm dying, Lydie. I'm going to die here before they ever get me a new trial," the Lamb said, resigned to his fate.

Lydia Lambert Jackson reached into her purse. "There's one other thing." She pulled out a wrapped candy bar and gave it to her father.

He instinctively took it. "My favorite! You remembered!" It was a king-sized Baby Ruth. "They let you in here with food?"

"I'm a doctor, in case you'd forgotten," Lydia reminded him. "Now unwrap it and eat it. Call it patient compliance, if you like."

He did as he was told. As he peeled the wrapper, he noticed that it seemed to come off less easily than he'd recalled, but that could have been a simple change in packaging over the last generation. Biting into the chewy chocolate treat, his face lit up as he savored the sweet taste. It was the most fantastic food he could remember ever eating, and not just because it was his personal favorite. His own daughter, his Lydie, of whom he had grown so proud in spite of not having seen her in so long, had brought it to him.

There was something a little different about the aftertaste, he thought, but not unpleasantly so. "They change the formula of these things? Put cheap ingredients in them?"

"They might have," Lydia said. "Everything's high fructose corn syrup and stuff these days. Palm oil instead of cocoa butter, things like that."

"Still tastes pretty good to me."

She smiled and flashed back to the note her father's prison buddy had left her, the one with the numbers. It had taken her months to figure out what they meant, but when she did, the revelation was even more mindblowing than Lieutenant Silvey's letter. Her husband Rondell had opposed her actions almost all the way, but when he learned what the access code hid, his *volte-face* was a moment she would treasure for the rest of their lives.

The safety deposit box was in the Cayman Islands. Upon landing in the Caribbean tax haven, it took her only an hour to find the George Town bank where the account was held. Upon presenting the access code, the very British manager escorted her through a steel vault into a room stacked floor-to-ceiling with numbered boxes. The manager pulled the relevant deposit box and excused himself, assuring her that its contents were secure. He offered her thirty minutes' time alone, more if she needed, free from any kind of video recording.

Gingerly, she entered the access numbers for the deposit box. The last digit caused the red LED to change to a fluorescent green. A solid click followed. She slid the box open, its mechanical movement virtually frictionless. Lodged within the hollow was a thick, legal sized interoffice mail transfer envelope. She prized it out and unwound the string that held the flap down. Then she reached inside.

Only someone with an advanced medical degree and a thorough understanding of the document's technicalities would have been able to decipher what was displayed. Dr. Lydia Lambert Jackson, M.D., Ph.D. fit the bill. As she read the papers, her heart rate quickened. Her head spun. *Surely this couldn't be?*

Even the manager, who returned just as she was finishing the document, couldn't help notice the beautiful physician's astonishment. "Would you care for some more time, Doctor?" he asked.

She looked up to see the bespectacled, immaculately dressed official standing at the door. "No. Thank you." She was on the verge of tears.

"Is everything all right? Might I fetch you a cup of tea?" he asked.

Very slowly, she declined with a shake of her head. "No." And then the tears began to flow. Discreetly, the manager withdrew a square linen handkerchief from his breast pocket and offered it. She took it and dabbed at her eyes. He saved them both from any potential awkwardness by requesting she keep the moist accessory.

Most Cayman-based bank managers pride themselves on their legendary ability to maintain confidentiality, but curiosity's temptation remains an ongoing burden some can resist better than others. This manager was among the less curious. Nevertheless, the capacity to state: "I don't know, and I don't want to know" diminishes when a client holds a private document in one's face and draws attention to it.

Lydia Jackson pointed to a single paragraph near the bottom of the last page. It read, "Transcription of the custom chimeric RNA ERS-78 was followed by a single oral dose in a liposomal formulation. After three months, all traces of HIV antibodies disappeared in the subject. The subject remains seroconverted to this day."

Under the typeface was a handwritten comment, in the same script Solkar had given her. "In case you're wondering, I got stuck with an infected needle. Use the same construct for your father – but swap out the liposomes for something he likes to eat. It worked for me. Do it as soon as you can but don't try and sell this idea to drug companies or government agencies. An instant cure would be about the worst thing that could happen to them, economically and politically. Keep it under the radar for now It was the best thing that happened to me, and it's the best thing I could do for Cleve. Fifteen years on and no trace of illness. You'll have the chance to cure others as well, but bide your time. Good luck, Edmund Solkar."

All her scientific bias begged her to treat what she had seen with skepticism and disbelief. And yet here it was, *maybe*. A Holy Grail of antiviral medicine? One formula, one cure? Her mind reeled.

The bank manager nodded very slowly. "Might I suggest that cup of tea now?" Lydia looked up at him and saw a glint of conspiratorial amusement in his eye, but it disappeared almost instantly. "Don't worry, Doctor. I'm paid to keep my mouth closed."

As her mind returned to the present, where she sat with her bedridden father, she gave a silent prayer of thanks for the man who had given them both hope, though only one of them knew the whole story. There would soon be time for her father to catch up.

She leaned over and kissed him on the forehead. "I'll see you, Pops. You're coming home." With that she turned and left, giving the burly nurse a radiant grin.

One year later

Ed Solkar looked out of the window of the cabin. He could hear the gentle lapping of the Indian Ocean waves against the shore. It was a peaceful scene, the early morning sun casting a beam of light rippling towards the sand. *Fathers and daughters,* he thought. *Another daughter whose father went to jail for a crime he didn't commit. At least they'll have the rest of their lives to heal their wounds.*

"What are you thinking about, Eddie?" Michelle Durant asked, putting an arm around him.

"Let's go for a walk, babe," he said. He grabbed the key, one of those old-fashioned types too big to stick in a bathing suit pocket, even without a plastic hotel tag. Dressed in a batik shirt and board shorts, he felt every bit as home here as he did in St. Petersburg Beach, maybe even more so. The months of periodic insomnia had faded into a distant memory. Then again, perhaps it had less to do with his half-Indian blood and more to do with knowing the tragedies of his life were now behind him.

Mickey wrapped a sari around her waist. She too felt at peace. The previous year had been a complete transition for her, the end of a second career, in ways. She stayed on at the university, but took the chance to indulge in a do-nothing sabbatical. All her colleagues agreed she'd earned it. She'd worked hard to secure a full pardon for her client, and in February that winter, Edmund Ranjit Solkar's record was wiped clean. His vindication gave him back all the privileges of freedom that he'd lost, but he also gained something else: her.

They walked along the beach hand in hand. A couple of kids tossed a large inflatable ball back and forth. Other couples enjoyed a full dip in the warm Goan waters as a prelude to a fruit-laden breakfast at the resort's buffet, but Ed and Mickey chose only to wade up to their ankles.

"There was something you never told me, Eddie," she said. "It doesn't really matter, because of what happened next, but I wanted to ask anyway."

"I never hid anything from you, Mick."

"No, I know that. It wasn't a big deal, just something I didn't quite understand."

Before he could pursue the conversation, he was approached by a man who half ran, half walked towards them from behind. In his early forties, his graying hair was immaculately styled. His brown eyes scanned the horizon. Dressed in all-white official resort garb, he held a cordless phone. "Mr. Solkar!" he called, prompting Ed to turn around. "Professor Solkar?" This time he used the formal title. "For you."

Ed took the phone. Who could it be? He couldn't remember who he'd told about their holiday. "This is Ed."

"It's Lydia. I have someone who wants to say hello." Clicking and shuffling sounds followed.

"Eddie," a rich voice sounded. "It's Cleve."

The Lamb. "Hello, my friend. How are you?"

"I'm very well. I won't keep you, but I wanted to thank you for everything. And I mean, everything."

It had been a long time coming, but finally, Ed Solkar felt the tears form in his eyes. "No, Cleve. Thank you." *The world may never know what part you played in saving it.* "You and your family doing good?"

"Hell, yeah! Even Rondell's comin' around. Nothin' quite like a pardon to change peoples' minds. But I don't need to tell you that, do I?"

"No, you don't."

"You and that lovely lawyer of yours have a great time, ya hear?"

"Oh, we will. Our lives are just beginning, just like yours."

"Take care, Eddie."

"You too, Cleve." He smiled and let the tears course down his cheeks. He hung up and handed the phone back.

The resort staffer moved aside, keeping a respectful distance. Mickey ignored him and placed a hand on her husband's cheek, wiping away the wetness. "You okay?"

"Never been better," he said, smiling broadly. "Just got the second best news of my new life. Now, what was it you wanted to ask me?"

"Never mind. It doesn't matter." She'd thought about pressing him, but reconsidered after seeing his reaction to the call.

"You were going to ask me about what happened to Samaya's car, weren't you?" he said, now wearing a wry grin. "That day I found you at the cabin north of Sacramento. Why didn't we pass her car on the way back out?"

Her eyes opened wide. "You know me so well, my darling. It doesn't matter, but yes, that was what I was thinking. I mean wondering. I mean, what I was thinking about asking you."

"I had a little help." Ed took one deep breath and exhaled slowly. "After I saw Lydia Jackson and gave her the Cayman account info, I made another call. Someone else went underground after the trial. We'd agreed to stay in touch."

"Who?" Mickey's eyes opened wide.

The resort staffer looked at them both and turned to walk back to the hotel's admin annex. He needed to purchase supplies for the upcoming season, but he was certain he'd get them at a pretty good discount. It was a skill he'd nurtured for many, many years. Before he left, he coughed, prompting the honeymooners to look at him.

"On my mark," he said. Then Vikram de Silva winked a sad brown eye at his old, dear friend.

Structural and molecular biology goes hand in hand with genomic analysis as the great staples of so-called "targeted medicine." Yet in the grand scheme of things, there is much to learn. Many counterintuitive, even strange, quirks emerge from the field every day. For instance, humans have about thirty thousand genes. A grain of rice has over fifty thousand. The layman would be forgiven for imagining that the rice genome should be a fraction of that of humankind.

Data from human genome sequencing will enable scientists all over the world to develop better, safer, and individually targeted drugs. For example, many people with rheumatoid arthritis might share a common genetic mutation, a "SNP." A diagnostic test for this SNP would tell doctors that otherwise healthy patients with this SNP might be predisposed to getting arthritis. Drug companies could also use this information to develop an appropriate drug, because the gene containing the "arthritis SNP" might translate to a highly active form of the protein. Drug companies would know that inactivating this rogue protein could prevent arthritis, and develop new drugs accordingly.

More importantly, companies could choose to test their new drugs only in patients with the faulty SNP. Instead of expensive, drawn out clinical trials, companies could target much smaller patient populations. Test patients could be pre-screened for the mutated SNP, and the drug would be tested in that sub-population. Thus, the drug would not necessarily be a so-called magic bullet, but at least it would be a well-directed arrow. The benefit to the company would be lower development cost, along with a greater chance of success. New therapies would arrive on the market sooner. The key is to know which SNP's are meaningful and which aren't.

All twenty natural amino acids are coded for on the DNA ladder by a sequence of nucleobases, represented by the letters T, A, C, and G. Ribonucleic acid, or RNA, operates in concert with DNA to transfer the genetic code to a cell's protein synthesis engine. Its nucleobases are abbreviated as A, C, G, and U. There are sixty-four possible ways these letters can be combined in groups of three. Examples would be AUG, ACG, GCC, CCG, and so forth. Each combination of three nucleobases represents a single amino acid that a cell's protein synthesis engine can make. Thus, a sequence of six hundred RNA nucleobases yields a protein containing two hundred amino acids.

The RNA-protein coding system has a redundancy factor. Because there are only twenty-two naturally occurring amino acids that can be coded for by the nucleobases, and sixty-four ways of stringing three nucleobases together, each amino acid has to have more than one way to code for it. This is why the genetic code can have what is known as silent mutations. For instance, people with Gene X might have a nucleobase sequence of GCC at the appropriate point on the RNA string. A small percentage of the population might have a SNP at that same point with the sequence GCA. This could be due to heredity or some other factor causing the disruption. Either way, the cells of both GCC and GCA people would wind up making the same amino acid, and thus the same protein. Most SNPs are like this. Nature gives complex organisms defense mechanism for survival and propagation.

The less common non-silent or functional mutations can cause measurable outcomes, including certain diseases. For example, the sequence GAG yields the amino acid glutamic acid. The sequence CAG makes glutamine and the sequence GGG gives glycine. Sometimes this mutation ends up as part of a dysfunctional protein, and results in a disease state. Cystic fibrosis is a classic example. Most CF patients don't just have an amino acid switch, but lose one entirely. Elimination of a single phenylalanine out of a nearly fifteen hundred amino acid long protein causes a radical change in the way the protein works. Other CF patients haven't lost that amino acid but instead carry an aspartic acid instead of a glycine somewhere else in the protein. The outward effect is still just as bad.

Proteins are not just simple strings of amino acids folded into a three-dimensional space. They can be coupled with sugar molecules, fat molecules, and even contain metal ions. Metals can help them stay in a particular shape or even make the protein do its job. One zinc-containing protein, for instance, is partly responsible for helping body to heal skin wounds. One doesn't want to inhibit such enzymes lest skin lesions never repair themselves. When scientists develop chemicals designed to inhibit a "bad" or out-of-control enzyme, they must ensure the chemical doesn't mess with one of the good guys at the same time. In principle, the more selective a compound is, the safer it is.

The science described in this story is speculative but grounded in published research. As always, some degree of license is inevitable when creating a mystery tale, but the time may well come when synthetic RNA's are used as therapies for everything ranging from dandruff to cancer.

Thanks are due to many individuals, without whom the inspiration for this tale would not have been possible. For the original idea, I must thank Jill G., whose work in Canberra inspired my own twist on the premise of rubisco engineering. Sergeant Joe Spanheimer of the Pacifica Police provided me with assurance that no such person as Leo Sampang exists, although I reckon he'd be a pretty good cop if he did. Jeremy P., may you always be the right kind of chameleon and when needed, look good in a dress. Ed I., – thanks for the inspiration, long ago. And to the late Eki S – what a fine fielder you were. You wouldn't have needed a glove either.